*The perfect catch
might be
right next door...*

Hot Streak

And there he was. His gorgeous bare flesh on blatant display.

Rowdy Blanton.

He wore a pair of black exercise trunks, a high-tech pedometer strapped to his wrist, red and black sneakers, and nothing else. He moved on an elliptical machine, each step a glide of hard muscles and sculpted sinew. His arms pumped the handles as easily as if he were brushing his teeth.

Breeanne was whispering a hallelujah prayer of gratitude, even as every shy bone in her body—all two hundred and six of them—squeaked, *Get out of here*. But her feet froze to the bamboo flooring.

Not to sound like a gushy teenager or anything, but OMG, stripped of his clothing the guy was hotter than an active lava flow. Her fantasies went wild.

By Lori Wilde

BACK IN THE GAME

A STARDUST, TEXAS NOVEL

LORI WILDE

AVON

An Imprint of HarperCollinsPublishers

AVON BOOKS
An Imprint of HarperCollins*Publishers*
195 Broadway
New York, New York 10007

Copyright © 2015 by Laurie Vanzura
ISBN 978-0-06-231126-9
www.avonromance.com

First Avon Books mass market printing: March 2015

Avon Trademark Reg. U.S. Pat. Off. and in Other Countries, Marca Registrada, Hecho en U.S.A.
HarperCollins® is a registered trademark of HarperCollins Publishers.

Printed in the U.S.A.

10 9 8 7 6 5 4 3 2 1

This book is dedicated to the town of Terrell, Texas, and to Maddie, the Hurricane Katrina Survivor.

SPECIAL ACKNOWLEDGMENT

Although the town of Stardust, and the characters in it, are fictional, the warm, loving, supportive community and Timeless Treasure were inspired by the fellowship I found in Terrell and at Books and Crannies bookstore, owned by Ron and Gayle Harris and frequented by an amazing group of readers and friends. The only fictional character with a real-life counterpart is Callie, the Hurricane Sandy-surviving calico cat.

Lori

BACK IN THE
GAME

CHAPTER 1

Baseball breaks your heart. It is designed to break your heart. The game begins in spring, when everything else begins again, and it blossoms in the summer, filling the afternoons and evenings, and then as soon as the chill rains come, it stops and leaves you to face the fall alone.

—A. BARTLETT GIAMATTI

A crack of the bat.

The sound punctuated Rowdy Blanton's life. Permeated everything. Seeped into his dreams.

From sandlot ball in knee-high Johnson grass in his hometown of Stardust, Texas, to luxurious major league diamonds, a crack of the bat spelled freedom. Freedom from boring classrooms where he struggled to read, from the empty belly that kept him awake nights, from watching his father wither and die.

Freedom from pain.

The crack of a bat carried him from poverty to the pinnacle of success, and all the nice things that money could buy. He had arrived, believing his lofty perch would finally ease his suffering.

His head throbbed. Tequila hangover. He squeezed his eyelids shut.

His belly ached. Kobe beef hangover. He clenched his teeth.

His left shoulder burned . . .

Oh God, his pitching arm. He winced, groaned. For one sweet fuzzy moment, he had forgotten about his ruined pitching arm.

A wet tongue licked his cheek. He put his elbow over his face, blocking the amorous kiss.

Undaunted, the persistent tongue laved his chin.

Was it the blonde from last night's Cinco de Mayo party? Or the redhead? Might even be the brunette. She'd pawed him like a kitty at catnip.

No. Couldn't be. He'd sent them all home.

Ever since that devastating night he always sent them home. He should be alone. But obviously, someone had lingered, taking advantage of his tequila-soaked brain.

Ugh.

The hot, wet tongue slurped across his mouth. Sloppy kisser. Which one shared his bed? Blonde? Redhead? Brunette? Someone else entirely?

Sun warmed his face. The smell of chlorine burned his nose. A plush cushion covered the thin metal frame beneath his body. No. Not his bed.

Patio lounger.

Poolside.

Who was he going to have to face, cook breakfast for, walk to her car, kiss good-bye, and never see again?

Terrific.

He might as well get it over with. As much as he hated pain, he wasn't a coward. Dreading what he would find, Rowdy held his breath, opened one eye, and saw . . .

Nolan Ryan.

Thank God.

The old boy sat on his haunches, tail wagging, staring at Rowdy with love and concern shining in his big brown eyes.

At the sight of his bloodhound, the throbbing ebbed, his stomach settled, and a helpless smile overtook his face. He scooted onto his side, and patted a spot beside him.

It took the bloodhound a minute to position his aging legs, but he managed the short hop onto the lounger. Rowdy wrapped his arms around his dog, hugged him tight, buried his nose in Nolan's fur, and for one brief moment felt no pain.

He closed his eyes. Drifted back to sleep.

Found baseball again. Found the lost dream. Touched peace.

The seventh inning stretch. Blue skies. Balmy weather. "Take Me Out to the Ballgame." Hot dogs. Roasted peanuts. Beer. Pretzels. Dot races. The familiar feel of a leather glove against his right palm, the ball weighted in his left hand. Two hundred and sixteen stitches on a major league baseball sewn in red cotton thread.

This was his whole world. His life. The ball. The diamond. The game.

A crack of the bat.

So went the duel between pitcher and batter. The declarative noise he both loved and hated.

Contact.

The batter knocking his left-handed screwball back at him. Line drive? Pop-up fly? Foul ball? Home run?

He looked up, following the ball, but the blue skies disappeared, replaced mysteriously by velvet night.

Neon lights spiked the darkness. A woman's perfume scented his collar. Loud music vibrated the ground. Distant laughter. A Dumpster. The fetid stench of garbage seized his nose. He was on the ground. Fetal position. Right arm held defensively over his face. Left arm separated from his shoulder at the socket, hanging useless at his side.

Ambushed.

Pain. Electric. Stunning. Shiny. Blue-white. Razor-toothed. Relentless. So much goddamn pain.

A man stood over him. Fierce. Swarthy. Extravagantly muscled. Thick black hair. Pit-of-hell black eyes. Flaring nostrils. The tattoo of a striking cobra inked on his right forearm. Louisville Slugger cocked over his shoulder. With each swing of the bat the snake undulated in the yellow glow of the alley security lamp.

His attacker yelling with every whack, again, and again, "Stay away from my wife!"

A crack of the bat.

A crush of bone.

And life as he knew it was over.

Breeanne Carlyle disliked estate sales.

The forlorn belongings of the recently departed, cataloged and arranged for easy browsing, gave her chill bumps in the same way as the turkey buzzards that nested in the loblolly pine outside her bedroom window. Each year the vultures raised a new set of voracious young to patrol the two-lane, farm-to-market road extending from Stardust, Texas, north to Jefferson, keen-eyed for the misfortune of others.

It was not what Breeanne wanted to do with her life, this picking through of things left behind.

But here she was, doing it all the same.

How could she tell her parents that she had dreams beyond Timeless Treasures? While she loved the family business that was part antique store, part bookstore, part tearoom, and the undisputed hub of Stardust for the last twenty-five years, she burned for a real writing career.

She'd enjoyed a tiny bit of literary success, just enough to stoke the flickering candle of her hunger to a raging blaze. She'd written a book about her great-aunt Polly, who played center field for women's professional baseball during WWII. She'd gotten an agent, sold to a regional press for a modest advance, and they had contracted her to write a follow-up book about the history of baseball in Texas.

Foolishly, stupidly, she believed she was on her way.

Then her publisher went out of business. No one else wanted the second book. Her agent quit taking her calls. Doggedly determined to make it as a writer, she self-published her second book.

And promptly fell down the well of Internet obscurity.

The book had been available online for six months, and despite extensive promotional efforts that plowed through her savings, she'd sold the grand total of eighty-seven copies, and as far as she could tell, every single one of those to family and friends.

"That means you have eighty-seven people who love you enough to buy your book," her mother said at Breeanne's disappointment. "You are rich beyond words."

"You're working too hard," Dad had said. "Take a break."

Her father's comment splashed over her like gasoline on a campfire. "No," she declared, shocked by the powerful punch of anger pushing out of her. "You're wrong. I haven't been working hard enough!"

Unaccustomed to opinionated outbursts from their most easygoing daughter, her parents had both taken a step back, and exchanged wary glances.

"You're becoming obsessed with this writing thing," her mother said. "It's not healthy. You need to relax. Go swing in the hammock. Get some sunshine."

Dad smiled a gentle smile. "You know, angel, it's next to impossible to make a living as a writer. The Rangers are playing the Cardinals on TV at two, what say you come watch the game with your old man?"

Because she did love her father and baseball, Breeanne backed down, and instead of going to her room to write, she went to watch the game with him. But the entire time, she couldn't stop thinking, *He doesn't believe in me, they don't believe in me, no one believes in me.*

But stubbornly, against all odds, Breeanne believed in herself. She *would* make this happen. If it took twenty years, then so be it. In the meantime, her close-knit family had expectations of her. So here she was, going picking.

Smile.

Smiling put the blues on notice. It was her go-to expression for smoothing over everything. No room for bad moods. Never mind that she wasn't feeling it. Fake it until you make it. She was finally healthy, and had a family who loved her. The writing would eventually take care of itself as long as she kept at it.

On this Sunday morning in May, navy blue night faded into the deep purple of impending dawn. Every expert bargain hunter knew that arriving after first light meant you were already too late for the good stuff.

Breeanne's oldest sister, Jodi, drove the minivan branded with the name of her business on the back window, "Boxcars and Breakfast." Enterprising Jodi bought old boxcars for cheap, and with her mad carpentry skills, converted them into luxurious sleeping accommodations on land that she'd inherited near the state park.

In her role as second oldest, Kasha rode shotgun. Kasha had a PhD and worked at the VA hospital as a physical therapist.

Breeanne sat in the back with Suki, the baby of the family. Suki ran the Internet side of Timeless Treasures, and had her own jewelry-making business on the side.

Normally, their parents would accompany them on their weekly Sunday morning hunt, but their folks were celebrating their thirtieth wedding anniversary on a romantic getaway to San Antonio.

Bumper-to-bumper traffic idled up the sweeping driveway leading to the impressive Tudor-style mansion. An attendant, wearing a reflective vest and waving a light orange signal cone, directed them to an adjacent field.

Marion County's wealthiest doyenne, Irene Henderson, had died at the age of eighty-five after being thrown from the saddle of her Arabian horse. Breeanne couldn't help admiring the elderly woman's fearless spunk. How did anyone get to be that brave?

Jodi parked the van. Armed with tote bags, they all got out.

Kasha paused and, nostrils flaring, tipped her face to the sky still sprinkled with stars. "It's going to rain."

"Not according to the weather forecast," Jodi said, but she unlocked the van and retrieved two umbrellas. Kasha had an uncanny ability to predict the weather.

A swath of headlights kept coming as more cars pulled in.

"Fierce competition," Jodi said. "We should split up. I'll scout antiques. Kasha, you go for the kitsch. Suki, shop for the tearoom, and anything Art Deco. Breeanne, you're assigned to—"

"Books."

"Don't attempt to carry them. Text us if you find any, and we'll cart them back to the van for you."

Breeanne traced two fingers over the top of the scar lurking beneath the neckline of her blue and green Dallas Gunslingers baseball jersey. "Don't baby me. I tote tomes around the bookstore every day."

"Let's not push it. You've been doing so well. The last thing you need is a setback." Jodi tucked a strand of auburn hair behind one ear.

"I'm fine," Breeanne insisted. How long would it take for her sisters to toss the kid gloves?

Jodi raised an admonishing finger. "Text us."

Her sisters took off in different directions, leaving Breeanne to wander the expansive lawn strewn with rows of folding tables, clothing racks, and metal shelving loaded down with the contents of a life well lived. A man in a security guard uniform policed the area, hands clasped behind his back. He stabbed her with suspicious eyes.

She daubed on a smile and raised I-don't-want-any-trouble palms, and backed off.

Somewhere coffee percolated, tingeing the air with the scent of French roast. People rummaged through items, haggled over prices. Someone elbowed her out of the way. Someone else, headed for an overburdened shoe rack, shoved past her. Another person pushed in, and then another, and another, a current of shoppers washing Breeanne to the outer shore of the yard.

Wasn't that just the theme of her life? Marginalized on the outskirts.

She sighed. What she wouldn't give to be at home working on her book with Callie purring in her lap. Suck it up. Smile. They would be here only a few hours. To pass the time, she leaned against the trunk of a pecan tree, and people-watched as dawn crept over the horizon.

A frowning woman shoved a baby carriage stuffed with knickknacks over bumpy terrain. An Ichabod Crane–esque man in an argyle sweater swung a practice stroke with a driving wood that was much too short for his elongated frame. A family of five, every member almost as big around as they were tall, licked fast-food cinnamon roll glaze off their fingers while investigating a used treadmill.

A brash black Cadillac Escalade muscled through the gate. Heads turned, and a wave of murmurs surfed through the crowd. The SUV did not pull obediently into the field with the other vehicles. Instead, it sailed arrogantly to a stop near the front door, sending pedestrians scattering.

The passenger door swung open, and the town's biggest celebrity—the Dallas Gunslingers former star lefty pitcher—got out. The very same pitcher whose number was on Breeanne's jersey.

Rowdy Blanton.

Her inner fan girl drooled.

Instantly a funnel of humanity swirled toward him, surrounded him, went crazy over him. Breeanne longed to join the rush, but her feet grew roots, anchoring her to the earth. People pushed and shoved to get at him, especially the women, as they all shouted at once.

"Rowdy, Rowdy can I have your autograph!"

"We love you Rowdy!"

"I want to bear your children!"

"I wanna get rough and Rowdy with you!"

The driver of the SUV, a big, bald, beefy bodyguard type, moved people aside, lining them up like he'd done this a million times. Once he had everyone somewhat organized, he took a box of baseballs from the vehicle and started passing them out to excited kids.

While Bodyguard Dude handled crowd control, Rowdy stood beneath a security light, signing autographs, shaking hands, and clapping backs. His laughter burst the dawn, warm and friendly. He wore a baseball cap embroidered with the logo of the Stardust Drillers, the local high school baseball team, cocked jauntily on his head. Tight-fitting Levi's jeans hugged muscular thighs, and a simple white T-shirt accentuated his tanned skin. He moved with the impertinent, nimble-limbed strut of a man fully at ease with life.

She couldn't take her eyes off him. What she wouldn't give to be one of those kids again.

Rowdy glanced up, and stared through the crowd.

Heated estrogen cruised Breeanne's veins, settled deep in her pelvis. Her stomach pinched, and her heart gave a funny stutter that had nothing to do with the medication she was on. Soon, she'd be able to go off even that, prescription-free for the first time in her twenty-five years.

For one heartbeat of a second their eyes met. Full-on freight trains on the same track speeding straight toward each other collided. *Bam.*

Oh.

My.

God.

She could almost hear the screech of metal, smell smoke, feel the jolting impact. She ceased breathing. Ceased thinking. Ceased doing anything except staring at him.

Cool blue eyes, the arresting color of a clear mountain stream, gave her a startling shock. Cheekbones like flint rock. Chiseled chin. Knockout jaw dusted with beard stubble. One corner of his mouth lifted, telegraphing her a gorgeous lopsided grin. Slowly, he winked as if they shared an intimate secret.

And for that sweet second, no one else on earth existed.

Rowdy spied the lone woman standing against the pecan tree, and thought, *This one hasn't ever been off the bench*.

Their eyes met, and he felt . . . well . . .

Weird as hell.

Out of the blue, for no earthly reason whatsoever, he winked at her. Quickly, she hot-potatoed his gaze, and stared off into the distance.

He waited for it. One heartbeat. Two. *C'mon, let's have it, sweetheart. Shoot me The Look.*

Nothing.

Hmm. Maybe she was coyer than most.

Normally, when a woman broke direct eye contact with him, it was a coquettish come-hither signal. He expected her to glance back. Interested women *always* glanced back.

But not this one.

Instead, she pulled a paperback from her tote bag and started reading.

Huh? He blinked, surprised. She wasn't interested?

His cockiness shriveled. So what? Big deal. No skin leaving his teeth. In fact, it was sort of a relief to know that not every woman in the world wanted to hop into his bed. But now he had an overwhelming urge to run over there and charm that denim skirt off her.

He stared at the mousy woman, confused by his thoughts and the way his body hardened.

There was nothing special about her appearance, except for what he could see of shapely legs below the knee-length hem of her skirt. In fact, he'd be hard-pressed to find a woman more ordinary.

No one would ever accuse her of being a beauty. She was far too skinny, and her hair was a blah shade half-way between blond and light brown. It had no particular style. Not short. Not long. Not straight. Not quite curly either. Thick, black-frame glasses smothered her petite features. Her clothes looked like she'd raided the closet of a middle-aged 1950s housewife in the dark. Not a single thing about her screamed sexy, although she *was* kind of cute in a girl-next-door way with those big green eyes, and that bunny rabbit nose.

But he wanted her all the same.

Why?

He tilted his head, squinted, imagining her without the glasses, a better haircut, and several helpings of his famous spaghetti carbonara inside her. Nope. Still not seeing the appeal. Except it dawned on him for the first time that she was wearing a Gunslingers baseball jersey with number eleven emblazoned on it.

His number.

C'mon, was his ego that big? He wanted her just because she was wearing his number?

"Rowdy! Rowdy!"

He looked down to see an exuberant gap-toothed eight-year-old tugging on the hem of his T-shirt, and clutching the autographed baseball he'd just signed for the kid.

"My dad says I can throw a screwball better'n you," the boy bragged.

"No kidding?"

"Wanna see? Wanna see?"

"This might not be the best place to throw a ball around what with—" Rowdy didn't get to finish the sentence because, lightning-fast, the kid cocked his left arm, and slung an impressive screwball that sailed over a table burdened with collectible glassware.

Sending people gasping, scattering and ducking out of the way. Except for Plain Jane standing against the tree reading her book.

She never looked up.

The baseball smacked into the tree trunk above her, and then plopped squarely on top of her head. Her eyes rounded, her mouth curled into a startled O, the book fell from her hands . . .

And she keeled right over.

"Jimmy, what have you done?" the boy's horrified mother exclaimed.

The crowd turned to gawk.

Rowdy was already in motion, instinct shooting him toward the woman as fast as he could run.

CHAPTER 2

*The more self-centered and egotistical a guy is,
the better baseball player he's going to be.*

—BILL "SPACEMAN" LEE

Good grief. How embarrassing.

Breeanne lay on the ground, staring at the baseball
with Rowdy Blanton's name scrawled across it in red
Sharpie, and she quickly put two and two together.
One of the kids he'd given a baseball to had done
what kids inevitably do when they had a ball in their
hands.

Unfortunately, she'd stuck her nose in a book, determined not to let Rowdy see that his sly wink and killer
smile had slammed her with such a one-two punch
that she hadn't seen the baseball headed her way.

Briefly, she closed her eyes, assessing the damage.

Her head stung a bit where the ball had landed, but
the impact had been fairly minimal since the tree had
taken the brunt of the ball's momentum. She wasn't
dizzy, and her thoughts were clear. She knew her
name, the day of the week, and who was the current
president of the United States. The unexpectedness of
the blow had caused her to startle. She'd toppled more
from surprise than the actual hit.

Good to go. She was okay, unless her sisters found

out about this. They'd kick up a huge fuss and insist she go to the hospital.

Get to your feet. Now!

Acutely aware that she was sprawled on the ground in a skirt, she tried as gracefully as she could to gather her legs beneath her.

A big masculine palm, wearing a World Series ring, appeared from nowhere, reaching down to help her up.

Rowdy Blanton.

A burning heat scooped a hole in her stomach. Dear Lord, had he seen her cheetah-print panties?

His firm grip enveloped her hand, and he tugged her gently to her feet.

And there she was nose-to-collarbone with the object of so many of her midnight fantasies.

Most preteen girls got their first crush over boyish pop music stars or baby-faced actors. For Breeanne, it had been this sexy major league pitcher. On her twelfth birthday, and not long after her seventh major surgery, she'd been lying on the couch in the living room with Dad, watching their hometown hero take the mound during his television debut as a rookie pitcher for the Seattle Mariners.

Rowdy had been so green he could have passed for a spinach smoothie, and he walked three batters before the manager pulled him. But he'd strutted off that field as cocky as if he'd struck them out. Anyone who could remain that self-confident in the face of total failure was a rock star in her book.

Two days later, something went wrong with her recovery, and she ended up back in the hospital, facing surgery number eight. That next weekend, the Mariners were in town playing the Gunslingers, and Rowdy had swaggered onto the teen ward at the Dallas Children's Hospital, signing autographs, telling stories, handing out jerseys, and baseballs. The moment he'd signed a ball and pressed it into her perspiring palm, she'd become his lifelong fan. She'd had the baseball mounted, and still kept it on a bookcase in her bedroom. But she wasn't about to tell him that, and only partially because her tongue was welded to the roof of her mouth.

"Are you all right?" His deep, husky voice rasped.

She bobbed her head. Could he feel her pulse jumping through her veins like a steeplechase stallion on race day?

"Do you know what your name is?" he asked.

He wanted to know her name. Um . . . um . . . For a freakishly long second she forgot her own name. Not from the bump on the head, but from this alpha male's distracting scent tangling up in her nose.

She nodded again still unable to speak.

"Can you tell me what your name is?"

Breeanne was vaguely aware that a crowd had gathered, but of course, Rowdy drew a crowd wherever he went. She tugged her hand from his, the loss of contact with his skin finally knocking her tongue loose.

"I'm fine. Don't worry about me." She turned to the crowd, which included a hangdog little boy and his worried mother. She assumed this was the child who'd thrown the ball. "I'm good. All is well. Go back to your shopping."

People lingered.

Rowdy tossed the autographed baseball back to the boy. "Could you folks give us some space?"

Immediately the crowd dispersed.

"What's it like having people jump to do your bidding?" she asked, unaware that the question was going to pop from her mouth.

He chuckled. "Kinda nice actually."

"I bet." She inched away from him, but her foot bumped into a tree root, and she wobbled.

His hand shot out to cup her elbow, sincere concern furrowing his brow. "Are you sure you're all right?"

"Fine. Perfect. Great. Dandy. Couldn't be better. This stuff happens to me all the time. I'm a natural-born klutz."

"You've got some dirt . . ." He leaned over and ran a hand across her shoulder blade, dusting her off, his broad hand circling lower and lower to the small of her back, igniting flames everywhere he touched.

Yikes!

Knots formed in her lower abdomen, tugged, tightened. She shook him off and plastered both palms to her butt, vigorously swiping her seat. "I've got it."

He stepped back, piercing blue eyes stabbing into hers, mischief brimming in his gaze. "So cheetah, huh?"

Mortified, she squeezed her eyes shut for a second, gulped. "Could you pretend you didn't see that?"

"You've got nothing to be embarrassed about."

She scrubbed two fingers over her forehead. "Easy for you to say. You weren't the one laid out with your underwear on display."

He pulled out his weapon of mass destruction, that devastating wink. "I've always had a fondness for women in animal print."

"I imagine you have a fondness for women in pretty much anything," she popped off. What was it about him that brought out this sassiness she hadn't even known lurked inside her?

He lowered his eyelids in a look so sultry that she forgot to breathe. She'd seen men give other women looks like that before but no man had ever looked at *her* that way. She didn't know what to do with it.

Suki would say something flirty. Kasha would act cool and sophisticated. Jodi would snort and roll her eyes, and tell him that she wasn't falling for that slick shtick. But Breeanne didn't know how to flirt, she wasn't sophisticated, and well, she *liked* his slick shtick.

"Sweetheart," he murmured, leaning in closer, his minty breath warm against her cheek. "I prefer that my woman wear nothing at all."

Sweetheart. My woman.

He spoke those words while looking at *her.* Plain, ordinary, pasty-skinned Breeanne Carlyle.

Wildfire heat spread under her skin, tongues of flame licking her from head to toe.

She wasn't going to read anything into those words. Most likely he called every woman sweetheart because he had so many women he couldn't remember their names. Her cheeks burned. She backpedaled, hoping he'd get the hint that it was okay for him to go away and leave her to her humiliation.

And she ran smack up against the tree trunk.

He stepped closer, breaching the breathing-room gap she'd created, and pinned her to the spot with a gaze as sturdy as handcuffs.

Trapped.

She couldn't keep looking into those heartbreaker eyes. Her heart had healed up nicely, thank you very much, and she wasn't about to test the strength of her surgeon's stitches. She dropped her gaze, spied her paperback lying on the ground, and bent to pick it up.

"Allow me." Like some chivalrous knight, he scooped it up. Pausing, he examined the cover. One amused eyebrow shot up on his forehead, disappearing beneath the shadow of the bill of his baseball cap. *"Love's Throbbing Fury?"*

She jutted out her chin, bristling at the humor in his eyes, and snapped, "You got a problem with that?"

He looked as if he was about to make some comment about her choice of reading material, but instead he simply handed her the book.

Squaring her shoulders, she stood her ground. She loved romance novels—granted some of the titles were hokey, but that didn't affect the quality of the story inside—and it irritated her when people put them down without ever having read one.

But even so, she heard defensiveness in her voice. "It's a great book."

"I didn't say anything."

Some of the pages had creased. Carefully, Breeanne smoothed them out. She revered books, all books, any books, and took great care with them. It pained her to see people dog-ear corners, or break the spine on paperbacks.

"I feel the same way about baseballs. It gets me here when it's time to throw them out." He pressed his palm to his solar plexus, and she couldn't help staring at the hard six-pack visible beneath his white cotton T-shirt.

Alarmed that he'd so accurately read her mind, she looked around for her tote bag, but he had already retrieved that too, and now the cloth handle dangled from the end of his long, thick index finger.

She reached for the tote.

In the exchange, their fingertips brushed, sending a shocking current of awareness humming through her arm to invade her entire nervous system. Lighting up all the secret parts of her that she'd never had the opportunity to use.

I want.

She bit down on the inside of her cheek, desperate to keep him from seeing how his touch electrified her.

He cocked his head, studied her like she was something he'd not quite seen before, and didn't know what to make of his new discovery.

Honestly, she didn't know what to make of him either. Why was he still blocking her exit? Why was he still here? Didn't he have someplace to be?

Nut bunnies.

He had no idea the amount of hero worship she had built up inside her, nor was she about to let him find out. She needed to get away from him before she did something irretrievably stupid, like throw herself at his feet, and grovel, *I'm not worthy.* She had no business thinking sexy thoughts about him. None whatsoever.

She adjusted her weight, her gaze, and her fantasies.

And for the first time she noticed the long pink scar running underneath his left arm, and her gut twanged. It was such a shame what had happened to him. That savage, career-ending beating in the alley behind a popular Dallas nightclub dished out by a jealous husband.

Empathy punched her in the throat, and she reached up to rub three fingers over her breastbone scars. Pain she understood far too well.

When the news of Rowdy's attack first broke, some people in Stardust had declared he'd brought it on himself by sleeping with another man's wife. But no one deserved to be brutalized like that, and Breeanne ached for him. He'd sworn in interviews that he had not slept with anyone's wife, and she believed him. The police had not caught his attacker, so no one knew the other side of the story. It might well have been a case of mistaken identity as Rowdy had maintained in TV interviews.

But now that he was standing right in front of her,

looking so much larger-than-life, and more delicious than a triple Dairy Queen dipped cone, it seemed unfathomable that anyone could mistake this man for someone else. He was one of a kind, solid, sexy, masculine, and far more man than she could ever handle.

Ha!

As if he would ever want the likes of her when he had the most beautiful women in the world to pick from. He'd dated models and actresses and female athletes. And yes, so sue her, she followed his sexploits in the tabloids, often pretending she was the woman du jour on his arm.

But even so, even though she knew it was silly and futile, she couldn't stop fantasizing about him. She imagined being pressed beneath those powerful hips as they rocked her relentless as ocean waves, his big body inside hers, his calloused palms gliding over her bare flesh . . .

Snap out of it.

While she was scouting him out, he was scrutinizing her with the same intensity. His gaze traveled from her hair, which the breeze was fluttering against her cheek, to her chest, where his number was stamped across the front of her baseball jersey.

Oh heavens, she was wearing his number, and now because of that he had *her* number. It was no secret she was a fan girl. Easy pickings. No doubt he considered her a pop-fly lay.

Breeanne gulped. Ha. The joke was on him. She'd never been anyone's lay.

But why on earth would Rowdy choose her, no matter how easy he might erroneously perceive her to be?

His eye-trip continued as if he was thoroughly enjoying the journey, his gaze lighting for a long moment on her hips. Was he thinking about the cheetah panties underneath her skirt? Goose bumps coated her arms, and it was all she could do not to shiver under the burn from those hypnotic blue eyes. His roving gaze took a long time sliding down her legs before finally stopping at her feet clad in a comfortable but unattractive pair of purple canvas loafers. Not exactly her sexiest outfit.

As if she owned a sexy outfit. And if she did, as if she would wear said sexy outfit to an estate sale. Okay, true confessions. If she'd known he was going to be here, she would have bought the sexiest outfit she could find, and worn it just for him.

A twig snapped, and they both glanced over to see his chauffeur/bodyguard or whoever the big, bald, badass dude was, standing behind them.

Bodyguard Dude cleared his throat, gave Rowdy a look that said, *Why the hell are you hanging out with this nerdy chick?*

Rowdy's gaze stayed married to hers, but he inclined his head toward his companion. "I gotta go."

"Oh yes." She bobbed her head like one of those silly drinking-bird-toy heat engines. "Me too. Busy, busy, that's me."

"Reading *Love's Throbbing Fury*," he teased.

She flushed, realizing she still held the paperback clutched in her hand, had in fact raised it up to the level of her heart. Quickly, she stuffed the book into her tote.

"Are you sure you're all right?" he asked.

She stapled on a cheery smile. "Yep. Fine. Couldn't be better."

How many times had she daydreamed about this man whispering sweet nothings into her ear in the middle of the night? An endless number. Uncountable.

Double nut bunnies.

Why was she getting weak-kneed over some jock? She was an adult, not a simpering teenager, never mind that she was also a virgin.

"For the record," he whispered, "cheetah is my favorite animal print."

"Really?" she quipped, not having a clue where the sauciness was coming from. "I would have pegged you for snakeskin."

This was so unlike her. She was quiet, studious, and minded her own business. Just ask anyone. But something about this man whetted her tongue, and turned her mind to quicksilver.

It was scary. Startling. And kind of awesome.

His laughter exploded loud enough to cause people to turn and stare at the mousy woman who'd tickled the funny bone of such a vibrant peacock. Playfully, he chucked her under the chin. "Love your sense of humor," he said, then turned and walked away with his companion.

Leaving her with her mouth hanging open, a tingly chin, and the terrifying knowledge that she had just been Rowdy Blantonized.

Rowdy walked away smiling. The image of those cheetah panties permanently imprinted in his brain. That was the most fun he'd had in a long time.

Which was sort of pathetic when you thought about it because he'd done nothing special. Just checked on the woman who'd gotten beaned by one of the freebie baseballs he doled out, and he flirted with her a little.

Is that what his life had come down to, mild joy over mild teasing with a mild woman in a mild place?

Oh how the mighty have fallen.

He rubbed his shoulder. Winced. He was losing

his touch. He hadn't even gotten her name, or phone number.

Who cared? It wasn't like he was going to call her. Or ever see her again.

But damn she looked cute in the baseball jersey with his number on it, that denim skirt, and those surprising cheetah panties. He grinned again just thinking about those rocking panties. She'd done what no one had been able to do in over four months. She'd made him forget about his problems for a few minutes.

Why was he feeling like this? And why hadn't he insisted on getting her name and number?

Before he could fully figure out his unexpected urges, Jenna Tomlinson, his former high school biology partner—and one of the few girls in town that he hadn't dated because she'd been madly in love with her boyfriend—hollered his name. Jenna was Irene Henderson's great-granddaughter, in town from San Francisco with her husband and kids. He'd skipped Irene's funeral, not wanting to intrude on the family's private grief, but he wanted to make time to see Jenna and offer his condolences before she returned to California.

Jenna flung herself into his arms, and Rowdy spun her around. Laughing, she kissed his cheek, slipped her arm through his, and chattering a mile a minute, guided him toward the house.

Just as they stepped inside, Rowdy paused to glance over his shoulder for one last puzzling peek at Miss Cheetah Panties, but she'd already disappeared.

Leaving him feeling vaguely, inexplicably disappointed.

CHAPTER 3

*It's no coincidence that female interest in
baseball increased greatly since ballplayers swapped
baggy flannel uniforms for leotards.*

—MIKE ROYKO

Illogically jealous of the beautiful woman who'd
thrown herself into Rowdy's eager arms, Breeanne
slipped around the other side of the tree, striving to
calm her somersaulting heart. She slapped a palm to
her chest, gulped in a deep breath of air.

Big whoop. What's all the fuss about? The man put
his pants on one leg at a time, just like everyone else.
He was not worth a cardiac arrest.

What *was* the fuss?

Heck, just look at him. He was big, bold, and utterly gorgeous, and her body was still tingling from his
touch. What was up with that?

Time to cut herself some slack. Rowdy was one
sweet slice of man. Any red-blooded female would
respond. Everything about him was impressive, from
his brash, cock-of-the-walk strut, to those sharp blue
eyes that didn't miss a thing, to that slow, lazy smile
designed to charm the cheetah panties right off a girl.

Sighing, she shook her head, reoriented herself.
What was it she was supposed to be doing?

Oh yes. Books. She was scouting for books. The bookstore needed supplying. Family expectations needed meeting.

The sun had cleared the horizon and the temperature warmed, but gray clouds snaked across the sky. Kasha's weather predictions were more accurate than the Farmer's Almanac. How long before the rain started?

Vendor-type stalls had been set up on the right side of the house under a sheltering of pines. Breeanne roamed the booths, picking her away around bargain hunters, her pulse tripping over Rowdy Blanton. She couldn't seem to focus on the task at hand, and within ten minutes she'd reached the last stall, nothing purchase-worthy having caught her eye.

The final stall displayed a collection of 1940s memorabilia from when Irene Henderson had been a young woman—movie posters, WWII collectibles, vintage clothing, plaques, postcards. Pretty cool stuff. She edged closer, wondering if Irene had owned any mementos relating to her great-aunt Polly. It was possible. Her great-aunt and Irene were from the same generation, contemporaries, and Polly had been something of a local celebrity.

Breeanne spied a hope chest tucked into a corner underneath a shelf of dolls. It stood as tall as Breeanne's kneecap, and it was almost as long as a GI's footlocker, the perfect size to fit at the end of her bed.

Buy me, the box dared. *I hold the key to what's missing in your life.*

It was a silly idea, foolish and absurd, but a dizzy sensation came over her, as if she were being tugged down a long tunnel to a parallel dimension, even though her feet were firmly planted on the ground. Her attention shrank to one thing, and one thing only.

That trunk.

Bizarrely, she felt as if she was on the precipice of something monumental, and if she were to open the trunk all her hopes and dreams would come true. She sank to her knees and tugged it from underneath the shelf.

It was not a typical hope chest. Instead of a single lock, it contained five. Five locks for five individual compartments inside one wooden box. In that regard, it reminded her of her father's tool chest.

Admiring the handiwork, she ran a hand over the smooth planks. An expert carpenter had hewn this with talented hands. The black hasps were hammered metal, the locks polished and free of rust. Carved on the trunk's lid, in elaborate script, was a cryptic message. She traced an index finger over etched letters, read:

Treasures are housed within, heart's desires granted, but be careful where wishes are cast, for reckless dreams dared dreamed in the heat of passion will surely come to pass.

"What does it mean?" she murmured.

"It means," said a voice so scratchy and ancient that it was difficult to tell whether it belonged to male or female, "be careful what you wish for, because you *will* get it."

Startled, Breeanne jumped up, banging her knee against the shelf and knocking loose the dolls. She grabbed for them, barely managing to right them before they hit the ground.

Jerking her head around, she searched for the

source of the voice and found a wizened woman that she hadn't noticed before sitting in a small black rocking chair. The woman wore a shapeless floral print dress and men's rubber-soled camouflage hunting boots. A thick gray bun, held in place by two green pencils, sat pinned to the top of her head. She studied Breeanne with yellow, unblinking eyes as if she was a fairy-tale crone debating if Breeanne was worth eating.

The wind gusted, sending pine needles swirling through the air, and the temperature dropped at least five degrees. A shiver, cold as a refrigerated knife blade, sliced down her spine. Vigorously, Breeanne pumped the heels of her palms up and down her arms to warm herself. "Is this a hope chest?"

"It's not for sale," the woman said, sounding as if she regularly gargled with gravel.

"Then why is it here?"

"Someone made a mistake."

"I'll give you two hundred dollars," Breeanne said, surprising herself. What was with her today? Saying things she hadn't thought through.

People milled through the small stall, but they might as well have been on Saturn. Only she and the crone and the trunk existed in this strange new world.

For the first time, the woman blinked. "Not for sale."

Breeanne crouched down to caress the chest once more. Her palm warmed against the wood, and her vision blurred softly the way it did with surgical anesthesia. An ethereal fog rolled over the stall, and it was as if she were watching an old timey television set with fuzzy reception.

In the weird vision, she saw a young woman dressed in a gauzy white gown, bluebonnets braided through her hair, put something inside the trunk. The ethereal woman turned, and Breeanne realized, without surprise, that *she* was that woman.

In the vision, a man came to stand beside Dream Breeanne, who raised her head and held out a hand to him. The image wavered, ghostly and unreliable.

She squinted.

Who was the man?

His chestnut brown hair was mussed, his smile wide and lopsided, a devilish grin that promised a world of bedroom delights. He wore distressed, button-fly blue jeans, and nothing else. His crystal blue eyes cut a hole straight into her heart, and it was as if he knew every single thought that passed through her head and approved of them all.

Rowdy Blanton.

Breeanne sucked in a hot puff of air, and a peppery taste popped into her mouth. Was this a hallucination? Some weird aftermath of being hit on the head with a baseball? Did she have a concussion? Breeanne rubbed the crown of her head where the ball had landed, but the spot wasn't even sore to the touch.

The old woman observed her, a knowing look polishing the yellow of her eyes to a high sheen. Her lips did not move, but Breeanne distinctly heard her say, *Trust your feelings, and don't be afraid.*

The mist rolled away. Breeanne's vision cleared and the out-of-body sensation evaporated.

Don't be afraid.

"What did you say?" she asked the old woman.

"The trunk is unique."

"I can tell."

"It's very old."

"How old?"

"Older than time."

"Nothing is older than time."

The crone shrugged.

Breeanne scratched her cheek, more to release tension than because her skin itched. She disliked haggling. Hated the confrontational nature of it. But she wanted this trunk. "Did the hope chest belong to Irene Henderson?"

"For a time."

"Where did it come from?"

"Across the universe."

Breeanne pressed her palms together and rested her thumbs against her sternum in a quasi yoga prayer pose. It was a calming technique she'd learned as a teen in a support group for kids facing potential death, and she glanced back at the trunk. "What's inside?"

"Whatever you want it to be."

"That's impossible."

"Is it?"

"You're being mysterious."

"Am I? You're the one hankering for the trunk."

"Will you sell it to me?"

The woman sat silent for a time before she said, "This trunk requires a special owner. Someone who believes."

"Believes in what?"

The woman drew bony knees to her chest and tucked tiny feet beneath the hem of her long dress. She set the chair rocking, and smiled a toothless smile. "Why, the unstoppable magic of true love."

Breeanne notched up her chin, felt her heart thump harder beneath the pressure of her thumbs against her breastbone. "I believe."

The woman's eyes narrowed to slits. "Do you?"

"More than anything in the world," Breeanne said. "Will you sell me the trunk?"

She'd been reading romantic fairy tales since she was five years old. Of course she believed. But it was her parents' real-life, thirty-year love story, and their devotion to each other and their four adopted daughters, that truly made her believe in the unstoppable power of true, unconditional love.

"I'm not sure you are strong enough to own it."

"It's just a trunk."

The old woman's eyes flickered, searched her face. "You know it's not."

The smell of rain thickened. Clouds darkened. Wind shook the plastic walls of the stall. People scurried for shelter.

Neither of them moved, nor looked away.

Her cell phone dinged. Jodi texting. She ignored it. She needed this transaction completed before her sisters descended and tried to talk her out of it.

Breeanne almost offered the woman three hundred dollars, but managed to bite her tongue in the nick of time. It was all the money she had in her purse, and it belonged to Timeless Treasures. She didn't have three hundred dollars in her savings account to reimburse her parents. And if she got this trunk, she was not putting it up for sale in the store.

Besides, money wasn't the woman's end game, but Breeanne didn't know what was. "I want the trunk."

The crone's eyes deepened to amber beneath the darkening sky and her mouth quirked into a sly curve. "If you make a wish before opening a compartment for the first time, that wish *will* come true."

"Without fail?"

"Without fail. Make certain you *truly* want what you wish for, because you will pay a great sacrifice for it. And once the wish has been cast, it cannot be undone."

"I understand. So five compartments. Does this mean there are five wishes in total?"

The woman gave a curt nod, as if she was growing bored of her. "Yes, yes."

"What happens if I don't make a wish when I open a compartment?"

"Then you will find nothing inside."

Ha. Likely nothing was inside. She didn't care, because she was buying an exquisite trunk, not what was or wasn't in it. If anything *was* inside . . . bonus. "Two hundred and twenty dollars, but that's my final offer."

The woman considered her a moment, the breeze whipping the material of her faded dress around her.

Breeanne's cell phone pinged again, another text from Jodi.

Finally, the woman stuck out a wrinkled hand, palm upturned. "Done."

Warmth spread through Breeanne's body, pumping adrenaline, jittering her nerve endings, dizzying her head. She shuffled her feet in a happy Snoopy dance. She'd won. The trunk was hers.

She counted out the money.

The woman folded her fist around the twenty-dollar bills and stuffed them into her bra. "All sales are final."

"Where's the key?"

That toothless smile again. "I have no idea."

"But how will I open it?"

"That's for you to figure out."

"You could have mentioned that in the beginning."

"You could have asked."

"Fine." She squatted beside the trunk again, and her irritation vanished. It was such a beautiful hope chest and worth the inconvenience of not having a key. No biggie. She would hire a locksmith.

"Breeanne?" Kasha called. "Where are you?"

She raised her voice. "Here. I'm over here."

Her sisters rounded the corner of the stall, their heads bowed beneath the umbrellas Jodi had brought.

It had started raining, and Breeanne hadn't noticed. Her clothes were plastered to her wet skin. All the stalls, except the one she was crouching in, had been covered with plastic tarps, and people stood huddled beneath them, staring at the odd girl who didn't have enough sense to come in out of the rain.

"What are you doing?" Jodi scolded, rushing over to shield her with the umbrella, Kasha and Suki following close behind. "You'll catch your death."

"I just bought this hope chest." She felt her smile start in her heart, spread upward, outward, flooding her face with white, joyous heat. "Isn't it beautiful?"

"Who did you buy it from?" Jodi asked.

Breeanne understood her sister's bewilderment. She had overlooked the tiny old woman at first too. Without glancing up, she waved in the direction of the rocking chair. "Why, from that lady there."

Jodi leaned over to put a hand to Breeanne's forehead.

Breeanne jerked back. "What are you doing?"

"Checking to see if you're running a fever."

"What for?"

Jodi chuffed out a breath. "You're standing in the rain, seeing imaginary people."

"What do you mean?" Breeanne sprang to her feet, spun around to face the old woman.

But the rocker was empty.

CHAPTER 4

*Baseball is the only place in life where
a sacrifice is really appreciated.*

—AUTHOR UNKNOWN

"Wake up."

A towel snapped against Rowdy's bare feet from where he lay poolside on the patio lounger. He slept better here than in his own bed, although he couldn't really say why. Whenever he lay in his room alone at night, it felt as if the walls were collapsing in on him.

His toes stung. He pried open his eyes to stare at the mammoth-sized man towering at the end of the patio lounger, holding a white terry-cloth gym towel rolled up between two beefy hands. Simultaneously, Nolan Ryan, snuggled against Rowdy's chest, raised his head, and sighed.

"Buzz off, Warwick," he drawled. "We're taking a nap."

His bodyguard, and best friend since kindergarten, threw the towel at him. It landed on Rowdy's chin. "Let's be clear. Nolan Ryan was taking a nap. He got up at dawn. You're just lazy."

"Whatever." Rowdy dragged the towel over his eyes, blocking out the sun. Ah, that was much better.

The truth was he'd been having a sexy dream about

Miss Cheetah Panties, and he wanted to get back to it. He was still perplexed over his attraction, but ever since his encounter with her at yesterday's estate sale, she'd haunted his mind.

Why?

Now that was the million-dollar question.

Forgetting her seemed easy enough in theory, follow-through was where the problem sprouted like a field full of dandelions after a drenching summer rain. Every time he closed his eyes all he saw were cheetah panties, silky black and brown and orange cheetah panties.

As if he'd never seen panties in his entire life.

He imagined the feel of them in his hands, soft and feminine, and soaked with her scent. Christ, he didn't want that image in his head, but it had been lodged there since yesterday morning, leaving him dizzy and slightly nauseated since their encounter, but for the life of him, Rowdy couldn't explain why.

Warwick yanked the towel from Rowdy's face. Sank his hands on his hips. Snorted.

"You look like a sour housewife who's sore because hubby didn't make it home after a long night out with the boys," Rowdy drawled.

"It's eleven a.m. Time for your physical therapy."

"Yes, Mommy."

"You pay lip service to getting your career back on track, but you're not acting like a guy burning for a return to the pitcher's mound."

"Are you trying to piss me off?"

"Is it working?"

"Nah, I'm wise to you." Rowdy yawned and scratched his chest.

"Heath Rankin called again," Warwick said.

He groaned.

Last season, Rowdy had walked out of the Dallas Gunslingers locker room over unfair treatment of his good friend, and teammate, Price Richards. After badly mishandling the career of one of the best second basemen in the league, the Gunslingers general manager and all-around douchebag, Dugan Potts, had released Price. To add insult to injury, not only had Potts not even tried to make a trade for Price, he bad-mouthed him all over the league so no other team would touch him.

Cutting his buddy unfairly was the final straw, just one more stunt in a long list of chickenshit maneuvers Potts had pulled.

And Rowdy had had enough.

Even so, his sense of fair play clashed with his loyalty to his friend, and he'd intended his brief absence from the team as nothing more than a token protest, a four-hour mini-strike to prove a point and grab media attention to showcase Potts's major douchedom.

Rowdy had returned to the clubhouse in plenty of time for the game, even though he hadn't been slated to pitch that night. But Potts intercepted him before he got down to the bullpen, and suspended him indefinitely for insubordination.

In retrospect, maybe he shouldn't have called Potts a hamster during his TV interview with Babe Laufenberg, because c'mon, there was no point insulting defenseless animals.

When Rowdy had been hospitalized after his attack, hopped up on morphine, Heath Rankin, the publisher of Jackdaw Press, fellow Texan, and former minor league baseball pitcher, approached him about writing his autobiography. He and Heath had briefly played on the same team before Rowdy's career took the express train to the majors, and Heath dropped out of baseball in favor of publishing.

Assuming it would give him an easy out, Rowdy confessed to Heath that he was dyslexic. Unfazed, Heath assured him that it was a rare ball player who wrote his own autobiography. Jackdaw would hire a ghostwriter.

Um, yeah, because that was so much more pleasant.

The last thing he wanted was to spend half a year of his life regurgitating stories of his glory days to some nerdy writer. But he'd been floating hazily on those happy drugs, and he'd agreed to think about it. Heath had been pestering him ever since.

"Get up. I'll meet you in the gym. You have five minutes." Warwick turned for the house, whistling to Nolan Ryan.

The bloodhound moseyed after Warwick.

"Traitor," Rowdy called, but swung his legs over the side of the lounger and stood up.

He made his way to the custom gym, a separate building outside the house, situated on the opposite side of the pool, and he plunked down on the weight bench. The big-screen TV mounted on the wall was tuned, as it almost always was, to ESPN.

Warwick came through the door, a glass of water in one hand and a mug of steaming coffee in the other, Nolan Ryan heeling beside him.

Rowdy chugged the water. Sipped the coffee.

"You sleep too much," Warwick said. "Are you depressed?"

Rowdy looked up at him. "My arm is busted, my career shot. What do *you* think?"

"I've never known you to be a quitter."

"Yeah, well, you try losing your career—" He bit

off the words as it dawned on him who he was talking to. Warwick had missed *his* shot in MLB because of Rowdy. "Hey man, I didn't mean it like that."

"I know what you meant." Warwick's face was unreadable.

Rowdy strapped on black workout gloves, and lay down on his back on the weight bench. "Let's hit it. Add ten extra pounds to each side."

"Nope." Warwick loomed over him. "We're staying within the guidelines of your physical therapy regimen."

"I won't get better if I don't push."

"Push too hard, too soon, and you'll make things worse, not better."

Warwick had hit the nail on the head when he said Rowdy was only paying lip service to getting back in the game. He'd been self-indulgent since the attack, wrapped up in feeling sorry for himself.

Honestly, he was scared. As long as he didn't really try to recover there was always the flicker of hope that if he just applied himself he *could* reclaim his career. But what if he tried his best to make a comeback and failed?

What then?

Rowdy started to argue about the weights, but something on television caught his eye. A leggy female reporter was interviewing Dugan Potts on the field at Gunslinger Stadium. He jerked upright, grabbed for the remote, and cranked the volume.

The reporter asked Potts why he had unexpectedly cut the pitcher he'd signed to replace Rowdy.

"Because that's what the asshole does," Rowdy hollered at the TV. "He's enjoys plowing over people."

Potts glowered at the reporter. "Zero tolerance.

That's my policy. No more shenanigans like what Blanton pulled last season. Everyone is on notice. My way or the highway."

"Hey." Warwick nudged him in the shoulder with his elbow. "He mentioned your name. I think he still has a crush on you."

"Bite me."

On screen, a man walked up to Potts and whispered something into the general manager's ear.

Rowdy's gaze shifted to the newcomer. The guy was six-one, two hundred pounds, give or take. Swarthy skin. Thick black hair. Demon black eyes, and . . .

A striking cobra tattooed on his right forearm.

His blood froze in his veins. *No way.*

It was the same guy who'd ambushed him outside the Dallas nightclub Push, on New Year's Eve. Rowdy knew it as surely as he knew his date of birth. His heart slammed against his chest, and with each pump of blood his left arm throbbed from his shoulder all the way down to his fingertips.

In a flash, he was back in the alley of his recurring nightmare. He smelled the rotting garbage. Felt beer bottle shards cutting into his back, and the bat hitting his left side again and again. Tasted cold, bitter fear. Saw the cobra strike. Heard the wood crack.

He'd gotten only a fleeting glance of the man's face before the assailant sprinted off into the darkness, but he could identify that awful tattoo anywhere. It would haunt him for the rest of his days.

A sick feeling rolled over him, and for a moment the water and coffee threatened to come back up. The camera cut away from Potts and his henchman, panned back to the reporter, who wrapped up the story as the network went to commercial.

Rowdy grabbed Warwick's arm. "Did you see the guy just now? The one that came up to Potts?"

"Yeah."

"It's him."

"Who?"

"Louisville Slugger. I swear it's him. You saw the guy. Validate me."

"I barely caught a glimpse of your attacker as he was running away. In the dark. I might add that if you hadn't tried to give me the slip to meet up with some groupie—"

"I'm telling you it's him."

Warwick's shrug said, *You're reaching, but I'll indulge you.* "He's the same build, same hair color, same approximate age. I suppose it's possible, but that description fits hundreds of thousands of men."

"It's the same tattoo."

Warwick ran a palm up the nape of his neck, let out a long breath. "A lot of guys have snake tattoos on their forearms."

"It's *the* guy, and I'm certain Potts hired him to attack me."

"That's a quantum leap. Even if he's the guy, and he works for Potts, that still doesn't mean Potts hired him to attack you."

Rowdy stared at his best friend, incredulous. "You think it's just coincidence?"

"Okay, I admit it smells fishy, but why would Potts hire someone to beat you?"

"To get even with me for publicly humiliating him, and to give him a real excuse to cut me from the team. He could only stretch my suspension so far. Potts was hell-bent on getting rid of me."

Warwick's head shifted left to right, and back again in measured increments.

"Potts is a lot of things, but if he hired someone to beat you, he crossed a line that I didn't know he was capable of crossing."

"I did." The sick feeling in his stomach spread throughout his body.

"For the sake of argument, let's say Potts did hire this guy to bust you up. What can you do about it now? You have no solid proof. It's your word against his. If you go around making unsubstantiated accusations he'll sue you for slander. You know he will."

"I might not be able to prove it in a court of law, but I can write a tell-all book."

"Oh great. Then it will be libel."

"Don't care." Rowdy stalked for the door. "Let him sue. The information will be out there in the public. And who knows? It might encourage other players to come forward, and Potts's house of cards will tumble. This time, he screwed with the wrong player."

"Where are you going?"

"To call the detective who handled my attack, and if he blows me off for lack of solid evidence, then I'm going to call Heath and agree to write that autobiography."

"Are you sure that's a smart move?"

Rowdy stopped, but didn't turn around. He knotted his fists at his side. His past mistakes were a mountain, but he had to climb it. Had to make things right. The chickens had finally come home to roost and he was the only one who could pluck them.

"I gotta try, War."

Warwick came after him, his footsteps echoing in the gym. "You do this, and the truth comes rolling out, your career is well and truly over. Might as well surrender any last hope of a comeback."

Rowdy gulped. He could back off. Let Potts get

away with what he'd done. Or he could fight and let the chips fall. "I didn't ask you to weigh in."

Warwick touched his elbow.

Rowdy pivoted, and met his buddy's eyes. The look Warwick gave him was exasperated, confused, and defeated all at once. Seeing his oldest friend's face fall was like watching an icy glacier calve, impressive but sad.

"Why are you picking a fight with a guy who has no qualms about hiring someone to do you bodily harm?" Warwick lowered his voice. "And if you write that book, you'll have to talk about *it*."

Rowdy softened his jaw, and his tone, but kept his gaze flinty. "I know."

Warwick let out a low, broken whistle. "It's a big step. Give yourself a few days to think it over."

"No."

"Haven't you heard the best revenge is a life well lived?" Warwick had never begged for a thing in his life, but he was almost pleading now. "Make that comeback. Show Potts up that way. It's more your style."

"Or I could just sit on my ass, drinking beer, and throwing parties until I'm a pathetic, washed-up has-been. Does that sound good to you?"

"No."

Another beat of a second passed between them, their eyes still locked. Warwick was worried for him. Hell, he was worried for himself.

Rowdy ate the bitter taste of his own fear, swallowed it back, felt it sink to his stomach, and spin there. "I have to do this."

"Why?"

"Because if I let Potts get away with this, we both know it's gonna end up destroying me."

For a week the hope chest sat unopened behind Breeanne's desk at Bound to Please, the bookstore housed on the second floor of the converted Victorian of her family's antique store.

Timeless Treasures was tucked at the end of Apple Street, two blocks south of Main. Back in the early 1900s Apple Street was where the crème de la crème of Stardust built their homes. But times had changed, so had the economy and zoning, and now the majority of the stately old Victorians were businesses. To the left of the antique store was Twice Around, a vintage clothing boutique. On the right was a dental office. The houses across the street had been turned into law offices, a sandwich shop, and a hair salon. The historical feel was just one of the reasons Breeanne loved living here. Because of the lake, tourism produced a quarter of the town's income, and there were plenty of thriving small businesses. The VA hospital and Stardust Independent School District were the town's biggest employers, as well as a plant that made drilling rig equipment.

Breeanne had called both of the locksmiths in Stardust and neither of them had been able to open any of the locks without drilling into them. Nor could they explain why their lock-picking tools wouldn't work on the trunk. Stubbornly, she refused to mar the hope chest by letting the locksmiths drill into the locks. Instead, she and her sisters had gone through every skeleton key they could find in Timeless Treasures on the off chance that one of them might work.

None of them had.

But the keys had given creative Suki an idea to turn skeleton keys into necklaces and sell them in her Etsy store. To that end, Suki had put a sign in the window offering to pay a dollar apiece for skeleton keys. So far, there had been no takers.

That Saturday afternoon just after closing time, Suki bounded up the steps waving a skeleton key over her head. "I got one, I got one."

"Where did it come from?"

"Some little old lady brought it by."

Goose bumps dotted Breeanne's skin. Could it be the same woman who sold her the trunk? "What did she look like?"

"Tiny little thing. Weird yellow eyes. Wearing a *Little House on the Prairie* dress. Looked to be a hundred and ten, but she moved surprisingly spry."

Breeanne put a palm to her mouth. It *had* to be the same woman. "Did she say anything about the trunk? About me?"

"Nope. Just wanted her dollar."

Breeanne stared at the trunk, feeling a bit disoriented, the way she had when she'd found the hope chest.

"Well?" Suki held out the key. "Aren't you going to try it? The suspense is murderlizing me."

Breeanne took the key from her sister and together they knelt in front of the trunk. She reread the enigmatic warning engraved into the lid.

Treasures are housed within, heart's desires granted, but be careful where wishes are cast, for reckless dreams dared dreamed in the heat of passion will surely come to pass.

"Here goes nothing." Moistening her lips, Breeanne inserted the key into the first lock.

Suki lightly touched her shoulder. "Don't forget to make a wish."

She felt a bit silly, but how was this any sillier than wishing on birthday candles, falling stars, wishing wells, or pulley bones?

The old woman's words of warning floated in her head. *Be careful what you wish for, because you will get it. Once the wish has been cast, it cannot be undone.*

Suki snapped her fingers in front of Breeanne's face. "What's the holdup?"

At that moment, Callie the calico cat, a Hurricane Sandy survivor that Suki had rescued when she attended NYU, dropped down from the bookcase overhead, landing solidly on the lid of the trunk with a loud *thunk*.

Suki let out a high-pitched squeak, and Breeanne jumped.

Callie gave them a smug gotcha-again expression, swished her tail, and narrowed green eyes in her Queen of All She Surveys mien. The cat loved pouncing on unsuspecting victims. The left half of Callie's face was solid black, the right half orange. Her chin and chest were fluffy white, while her left forearm was orange and her right forearm was black. The back of her body was a swirly blend of black, orange, and white, giving her an exotic, one-of-a-kind appearance.

Suki picked up Callie, stroked her fur. "Go for it."

Briefly, Breeanne closed her eyes. Made her wish. She twisted her wrist, but the key didn't budge. She let out a shaky laugh. She'd actually thought it was going to work?

Just for the hell of it, she tried the key on the second lock. It did not open. Nor did the third lock.

Or the fourth.

She was so certain that the key was not going to

open the fifth compartment that she almost forgot to make her wish, but just as she turned the key, she silently whispered, *Please let my writing career take off.*

The key turned. The lock clicked. The compartment cracked open.

Suki hooted. "It worked!"

Touching the tip of her tongue to her upper lip, Breeanne eased back the hinges. Inside the compartment lay a second box. This smaller box was square, about three inches all around, and an inch deep. Carved into the lid of this box was another odd saying.

Two pieces split apart, flung separate and broken, but longing for reunion; one soft touch identifies the other, and they are at last made whole.

"What's it mean?" Suki asked.

Breeanne didn't know. She lifted the lid, and the faint smell of cloves drifted out.

Inside the second box lay a cheetah-print scarf folded into accordion pleats, and bound with raffia. The instant she spied the cheetah print, she thought, *Rowdy*, and a defenseless smile spread across her face.

Attached to the raffia was a yellowed piece of paper the size of an envelope label. On the label, written in the faded, flourishing script of quill pen ink, were the words: "Touch Me."

Breeanne stared at it.

"So touch the scarf already." Suki nudged her with an elbow. "Or are you too scared?"

Breeanne untied the raffia and picked up the scarf.

The cloth rippled through her fingers, smooth and rich as warmed butter. "Wow."

"What is it?"

"This is amazing material." Breeanne rubbed the scarf between her finger and thumb. "It's softer than expensive cashmere."

"Could be vicuna yarn, but it looks too silky for that. Pass it over." Suki put out a hand.

Breeanne pulled her arm back, holding the scarf away from her sister. A foreign sensation pushed up through her chest and into her throat.

"Sheesh. I'm not going to hurt it," Suki said.

Breeanne hesitated. Why was she feeling like a jealous lover? Reluctantly, she forced herself to hand over the scarf.

Suki made a face like she'd inhaled a sunflower seed husk, and jerked her head around to stare at her. "Ha ha. Very funny."

"What are you talking about?"

"The softest material you've ever felt? That's rich. When did you turn snarky?"

"It *is* soft," Breeanne said, more sharply than she intended.

"This is the scratchiest thing I've ever touched. I'd rather wear burlap."

Breeanne reclaimed the scarf and rubbed it between her palms. If anything, it felt softer now than when she first took it from the box. With a stubborn tilt of her chin, she tied the jaunty cheetah print around her neck.

"What exactly did you wish for, a soft scarf? Because a delusional self-fulfilling prophecy is the only explanation I can come up with for why you think this thing is soft." Suki's laughter bounced around the bookstore, spiky and too loud.

"For your information, I wished for a successful writing career."

"I can't imagine how a miserably prickly scarf is going to help with your writing."

At that moment, Breeanne's cell phone rang. Lightly touching the scarf at her neck, she pulled her phone from her pocket and checked the caller ID.

Kip Miller. Her agent.

Her entire body went numb, and she broke out in a sweat. It couldn't be. Could it?

The phone rang again.

"Who is it?" Suki asked.

"My agent," Breeanne whispered.

"I just got chills." Suki shivered, and hugged herself. "You wished for something to happen with your writing career, and *boom*, the agent who's snubbed you for over a year calls out of the blue, and on a Saturday afternoon to boot."

"What do I do?"

"Answer the phone! Hurry. Before he hangs up."

Breeanne tilted her head, and managed to answer coolly despite the fact she was trembling all over. "Hello?"

"Breeanne," her agent's cheery voice boomed. "Kip Miller here. I've got a golden opportunity for you."

She transferred the phone to her other hand, wiped her sweaty palm against her thigh. "What is that?"

"Ever heard of the baseball pitcher Rowdy Blanton?"

Her stomach flipped. "Of course I have, he's from my hometown."

"I know. That's why I'm calling. Jackdaw Press signed him to write his autobiography, and he's in the market for a ghostwriter. I pitched your name, but they weren't all that impressed with your credentials.

However, Blanton's contract gives him final approval on the ghost and he's auditioning writers on Monday. If you're smart you'll get over to his place and convince him you're the woman for the job."

CHAPTER 5

Don't let the fear of striking out hold you back.

—BABE RUTH

Dipped cone.

Breeanne sat in her eleven-year-old blue Nissan Sentra that was parked in front of the private locked gate outside Rowdy Blanton's property. Dead center in the middle of her crisp white blouse, just below where her cleavage would be if she had any, was a big blob of melted chocolate. Every day after lunch for the last six weeks, since Breeanne's cardiologist told her that she needed to gain ten pounds, she had pulled up to the drive-through at Dairy Queen and ordered a chocolate dipped cone. In all that time she'd gained only a measly half pound.

But no one had sympathy for a skinny girl who couldn't gain weight. Or, for that matter, a clumsy girl who dropped waxy dipped cone chocolate onto the front of her crisp white blouse when she was on her way to persuade the biggest celebrity in town to hire her as his ghostwriter.

Dammit.

Why couldn't she have gotten a regular soft-serve cone? Or better yet, an M&M's Blizzard in a cup? A cup was much safer than a cone. Then again why had she stopped for ice cream in the first place? Why hadn't she driven up to his house first thing this morning?

Why?

Because she'd heard through the trusty Stardust grapevine that Rowdy Blanton liked to sleep until noon. He might be grumpy if she awakened him too early, and she would blow her chances straight off the bat.

Really? She was spinning fibs for herself?

Frankly, as badly as she wanted this writing gig, after her encounter with Rowdy on Irene Henderson's lawn, he scared the living daylights out of her.

The man was as devastating as a mudslide, breathtaking as a forest fire, daunting as gale-force winds. Major league baseball should have nicknamed him Force of Nature instead of the Screwgie King, although he was arguably the best screwball pitcher ever to take the mound.

Sweat broke on her brow.

How easy it would be to smack the Sentra into reverse and burn rubber all the way down the hill to Stardust. Normally, she was a people pleaser who preferred the path of least resistance, but this was her writing career. The one thing she wanted most in the world was within her grasp. All she had to do was reach for it.

She would not chicken out. Chocolate or no chocolate, she was going in there and ask for the job. This was her big break. No excuses.

Okay. Resolve strengthened. She could . . . no, she *would* do this.

But how to camouflage the chocolate stain, and how to get through the locked gate?

Whenever she faced a health-related challenge, her parents loved to say, *Don't worry about trying to eat the whole enchilada at once. Take it one bite at a time.*

Right. First things first. Deal with the stain.

She leaned over, popped open the glove compartment, and found a couple of napkins. On the floorboard in the backseat she located a plastic water bottle that had a tablespoon or so of water left in it. She wet the napkins, dabbed at the chocolate blob, watched the stain smear, and widen.

Nut bunnies.

It wasn't working.

What now?

She gnawed the corner of a thumbnail. Stopped. Sat on her hands. Remembered the cheetah scarf in her purse. All weekend, she'd taken the scarf around with her, bugging everyone she met to feel the material, anxious to see if anyone else felt the softness she did. But family and friends, neighbors and acquaintances all said exactly the same thing. The scarf was scratchy, rough, abrasive, coarse.

How was it possible that when she touched the scarf it felt like rose petals, Callie's fur, and chenille throw pillows combined?

Hmm. If artfully draped, could the scarf hide the stain? Blowing out a tight breath, she tied the scarf strategically around her neck and checked her reflection in the rearview mirror.

The chocolate stain disappeared.

Whew. Crisis averted.

One problem down. Now for the second. She approached the ornate wrought-iron gate, searching for an intercom box or a doorbell or something that would grant access, but she didn't see anything.

What did she expect? An open gate, a "Welcome Breeanne Carlyle" sign?

She didn't have an appointment because his phone number was unlisted, and her agent hadn't known what his phone number was either, and that was why he'd told her to go up there in the first place. Rowdy Blanton was so famous he needed a fortress to discourage hangers-on, and looky-loos. She curled her fingers around the cool iron bars, and the gate simply swung inward.

Not locked after all.

Surprised but wary, she stepped back. She distrusted things that came too easily. When things came easily it usually meant strings were attached. Then again, in this situation, what was the worst that could happen? Rowdy would call the cops on her for trespassing? His burly bodyguard would toss her out on her ear?

Or Taser her.

Getting Tasered wouldn't be much fun. And with her heart condition, what if it caused an electrical short-circuit and killed her?

Calm down.

No one was going to Taser her. The sky was not falling. Her heart was healed. How long was it going to take for her to adjust?

The two-minute drive to the top of the hill winded through East Texas pines and fields of vibrant wildflowers. A gigantic mansion constructed of Austin limestone sprawled like a lazy frat boy, overblown, overindulgent, and clearly over budget. Breeanne pulled to a stop in a driveway full of cars.

Rowdy had company.

She squeezed the spongy steering wheel cover. The blue veins at her wrist bulged against the pressure. Her mouth dried and tasted chalky, as if she'd eaten a green persimmon.

Steeling her jaw, she marched stiff-legged up the

cobblestone walkway to the front door. She knocked with a confidence she didn't feel, hung out her cheeriest let's-be-friends smile, and mentally practiced what she was going to say. *Hi, Mr. Blanton, remember me? I'm the girl in the cheetah panties.*

Good grief. No.

The door jerked open. The same domineering guy who'd chauffeured Rowdy to the estate sale in the Escalade stared down at her. His bulky shoulders filled the doorway, blocking her view of the foyer. He wore a small gold hoop earring in one ear, an expensive suit, shaved head, and those same Secret Service sunglasses that shielded his eyes.

He didn't crack a smile, and hers evaporated. He slid the sunglasses down on his nose, his gaze slicing over her without a hint of recognition. Okay, she knew she wasn't particularly memorable, but come on, it had been only a week since they last met.

"What do you want?" He grunted.

"Um . . . um . . ." The words that had been on her tongue rolled down her throat. "I'm . . . I'm . . ." *Spit it out, for godsakes.* "Job interview."

He narrowed his eyes as if he didn't believe her. Women were probably coming to the door all the time on one false pretense or another just to get up close and personal with Rowdy.

"The ghostwriter position. My agent, Kip Miller, told me that Rowdy . . . er . . . Mr. Blanton was conducting interviews today."

The big guy stared impassively at her for so long that her muscles started to twitch. Finally, in a flinty voice, he growled, "He's in the gym."

Gym? Did that mean Rowdy was working out and not taking interviews right now? Or did it mean he was interviewing in people in the gym while he worked out?

At the thought of Rowdy's body sweaty from a workout, her nerve endings lit up like city lights. She blinked, pressed a palm to her breastbone, right over the scarf and the blob of Dairy Queen dipped cone chocolate beneath.

"This way."

She hesitated a split second, but he walked like he was headed for a fire, and she didn't know what else to do, so she hurried after him.

The focal point of the cavernous living room was a massive limestone fireplace. Framed photographs of Rowdy in uniform and baseball memorabilia adorned the walls and crowded the shelves of a beefy glass trophy case celebrating an illustrious career cut short way too soon. From the beamed vaulted ceilings, to the overstuffed leather sectional, to a cowhide rug, to the King Kong flat-screen TV mounted above the mantel, everything about the room screamed testosterone.

It smelled like testosterone too.

Her nose juddered, and a lazy shiver shook her spine bone by bone.

What would it be like to date Rowdy Blanton, and come back to his place for a nightcap? Sink down in one of the leather chairs. Feel the heat from a flickering fire. Drink some exotic cocktail like a Screaming Orgasm. Listen to sexy make-out music. Taste the salt of his skin. Hear his seductive voice whisper her name as he tugged her down onto that rug and had his way with her.

She fluttered a hand to fan herself. Oh dear.

Breeanne had no more grown accustomed to the dark, cavelike atmosphere of the living room than

Bodyguard Dude pushed open the Santa Fe–style door that led into a sun-filled courtyard. The mix of honeyed scents intoxicated, and Breeanne shaded her eyes against the bright sun. Indigenous Texas plants filled the courtyard—the bluish green of Ebbinge's Silverberry, the ruffled white crape myrtle blossoms, the scarlet plume of the bottlebrush, the spiky purple flowers of the hummingbird-attracting chaste tree.

Ahead of them lay an infinity pool.

The faint scent of chlorine mixed with the enticing smell of native pines. She longed to linger at the pool, dig in her heels, adapt to this environment, and investigate the zipline that ran from the crest of Rowdy's property to Stardust Lake glimmering at the bottom of the hill. She'd always wanted to try ziplining, but whenever she mentioned trying daring physical activities, her parents freaked out. Afraid it would somehow stir up heart problems.

"Keep up," Bodyguard Dude barked, and it was only then that she realized she'd stopped to stare at the zipline, picturing herself flying down it.

She scurried to catch up to him. "I'm Breeanne Carlyle. What's your name?" she asked, striving to be friendly. It was a long shot, but if she got the job, she would be dealing with this guy every day.

"Warwick."

"Warwick what?"

"Just Warwick."

"Is it a family name or—"

"I was hatched from an alligator egg. Don't try to get chummy. I bite."

She raised both palms. *Ooh-kay*, this guy cracked hard as a macadamia nut. Got it. But she wasn't giving up. "What is it that you do for Mr. Blanton, Warwick? Bodyguard? Butler? Chauffeur? Jack-of-all-trades?"

"This ain't *60 Minutes*, lady." He maneuvered her toward a solid glass enclosure that was bigger than a Gold's Gym and housed top-of-the-line workout equipment. He shoved the glass door of the glass building open, pushed her inside, and left.

Abandoning her in this foreign environment.

Hard-pumping workout music blasted from the surround sound. The primal beat vibrated the floor and flooded her body with strange sensations. The pulse-revving smell of masculinity in peak physical condition steeped the room. Dazzling sunlight glinted off the glass, bathing the shiny metal in a cathedral of rainbows.

And there he was. His gorgeous bare flesh on blatant display.

Rowdy Blanton.

He wore a pair of black exercise trunks, a high-tech pedometer strapped to his wrist, red and black sneakers, and nothing else. He moved on an elliptical machine, each step a glide of hard muscles and sculpted sinew. His arms pumped the handles as easily as if he were brushing his teeth.

Her girly parts whispering a hallelujah prayer of gratitude, even as every shy bone in her body—all two hundred and six of them—squeaked, *Get out of here*, but her feet froze to the bamboo flooring, and she couldn't have moved if gas well fracking had triggered an earthquake underneath her feet.

Not to sound like a gushy teenager or anything, but OMG, stripped of his clothing the guy was hotter than an active lava flow. Her fantasies went wild.

Him. Her. Exotic lotions. Acrobatic sexual position.

Regretfully, he wasn't alone. Three beautiful women flanked him. A brunette, a blonde and a free spirit whose hair was a shocking shade of electric blue, all of them gazing at him as if he was Hercules, and they his willing concubines.

A fourth woman, a redhead, squatted near a sad-faced bloodhound. Breeanne wasn't sure, but she thought the woman said, "Come on, Nolan Ryan, you know you want to sit on my shoes. Here boy, sit on my shoes."

Huh?

It took her a second to realize that the dog was named Nolan Ryan, but obviously, she'd misheard the rest of it, because for the life of her, she couldn't figure out why the redhead would want the bloodhound to sit on what were clearly expensive designer stilettos.

Breeanne glanced down at her own sensible, discount-store ballet flats, and cringed. What had she been thinking? Dressing like a schlump? She thought she looked professional, but apparently sexy was the order of the day.

Nut bunnies. If she had a do-over, she'd raid Suki's closet.

"So." The redhead giggled. "If I don't get the job, can I apply to be your girlfriend instead?"

These gorgeous women were interviewing to be his ghostwriter as well?

Breeanne's hopes grabbed the last train to nowhere as her chances of convincing him to give her the job dropped from slim-to-none to absolute zero. She might as well leave now. Except she wasn't sure she could find her way back to her car without an escort.

"Sorry," he told the redhead, but he didn't appear the least bit apologetic. "That position is already filled."

"You have a girlfriend?" The free spirit's pierced lip poked out in a pout.

Duh, Blue Hair. Look at the man. Of course he has

a girlfriend, probably one in every major city in the country.

"Yes, I do," he said. "And here she is right now."

Breeanne turned to see what extraordinary creature must have come into the room behind her, but instead of finding a Gisele Bündchen look-alike, all she saw was her own reflection in the mirrored wall. Mossy green eyes stared at her from behind black-frame glasses. The waistband of her skirt was slightly twisted, and there was a big fat run in the back of her pantyhose. Because yes, her legs were so pale she wore hose, banking on the fact that pantyhose were so far out of fashion they were now officially retro.

The only thing remotely chic about her was the cheetah scarf, which on second viewing did not quite cover the chocolate smear.

What a train wreck! She didn't have a prayer of getting the job.

She closed her eyes, swallowed her shame. When she opened them, Rowdy was staring directly at her.

Correction. Not staring *at* her.

He was staring *into* her. As if he could see exactly what she looked like naked, and was enjoying what he saw. No man had ever looked at her as if she was the choicest cut of beef in the butcher shop.

And she liked it.

Rowdy climbed down off the elliptical machine, pulled a pristine white towel from the handlebars, and sauntered toward her, languidly mopping sweat from his handsome brow. As if on cue, programmed precisely for this moment, "Sexy and I Know It" pulsed from the speakers.

Breeanne's knees liquefied.

If she were hooked up to an EKG right now she'd bet her last beta-blocker it would show she was throwing premature ventricular contractions like a diner waitress slinging lunchtime hash.

Did the guy keep a defibrillator handy. Because if he was going to strut around like that he damn well should.

Breathe.

Seemed logical. But somehow the advice was easier to give than take. Her lungs barely moved, allowing in only a thin sip of air. It wasn't enough.

Run.

She couldn't heed that advice either. Not between her noodle knees and her ice-block feet and her granite resolve to land the job. If she wanted to work for him she had to accept that he was the hottest thing on two legs, and just get over it.

Yeah, but how?

He bewitched her with a smile as smooth and creamy as Lindt's milk chocolate truffles. His thick brown hair gleamed with virility. Dark eyebrows framed those stunning blue eyes fringed with long, midnight black lashes. She'd been close to him before, but it had been in the softer light of dawn. In the glass gym, sunlight glinting off his body, she could make out every pore, every whisker, line, and angle.

And nothing, absolutely nothing about him was soft.

Involuntarily, she licked her lips.

Closer and closer he strolled, as leisurely as walking a dog, but with more purpose. His stare was so sexual, so primal, that it crashed into her womb as intrusively as a battering ram.

With each step she took, her body grew tighter, and the room grew warmer, and her head grew lighter.

His gaze never relinquished hers.

She clung to it. Cherishing this moment so she could

pull out the memory again and again, finger the spe-cialness of it late at night when she was alone in her bed. Nothing existed but him. This moment. Exhila-rating. Thrilling . . .

. . . and downright terrifying.

He was close enough to sniff so she did, inhaling and holding a long, deep breath.

He smelled like a predator. She smelled like prey.

"Hi, honey buns," he said in an overly loud voice. "Did you enjoy your outing?"

Huh? She would have glanced over her shoulder again, on the lookout for Gisele, but his eyes wouldn't let her go.

He was speaking to *her*.

But what did he mean?

"I missed you." His tone was a caress and she was a sucker for it. "I hate it when we're apart."

Everything clicked. Now she got it. This had to be a dream. One of her crazy sexual fantasies run amok. Or maybe it was a being-naked-in-public anxiety dream. Or it could be a worse-case-scenario prepara-tory dream, as her subconscious dialed up a how-bad-could-it-get-begging-for-a-job-you-aren't-qualified-for bit of role playing for her to work through.

That had to be it.

A dream.

She was sound asleep in her bed. No dipped cone chocolate on her blouse. No devastatingly handsome, bare-chested baseball star striding straight for her. This moment existed only in her imagination.

Relax.

Since this was a dream, she might as well be ballsy and play along. If he needed a fake girlfriend she was game. She would certainly not have the guts to do it in real life, but in a dream? Hell to the yeah.

"Hey there, slugger." She cooed and fluttered her eyelashes.

One side of his mouth crooked higher, dissolving for the first time into an authentic grin. He was within touching distance, and boy howdy did her fingers itch to do just that.

Go ahead. Why not?

Breeanne gulped, spread her fingers, reached out, and ironed her hand against the sleek ridges of his chest. A complex web of nerve receptors in her palm caught fire, sending tactile messages blazing up to her brain in a crazed Braille of details. Smooth. Warm. Hard. Solid. Flawless perfection.

Holy mother of all nut bunnies!

She dropped her burning hand, unable to bear another exquisite moment. This was the most realistic dream she'd ever had.

A mischievous light flamed in his blue eyes. He dipped his head and pursed his lips and . . .

Stole her personal space. His animal magnetism crowding in on her. She couldn't understand how he could leave her both shivering and sweaty as if she had a hundred-and-ten-degree fever in an ice storm.

His mouth hovered, tempting and maddeningly just out of reach.

Where was that defibrillator? Slap the paddles on her chest. Charge to three hundred joules. Yell, *Clear!* And zap away.

He was not going to kiss her. Of course he wasn't. He wouldn't do that. Gorgeous, successful men who could have any woman they wished did not kiss plain girls like her. Facts of Life 101.

But this was her dream, right? Her fantasy. Why couldn't he kiss her?

His head inched lower, and he murmured, "I am

going to kiss you now. Don't ask questions. Just go with it."

What the frig? She blinked in confusion, staring at the sweaty male chest in front of her, and then peeping into those smoldering blue eyes. His intense scent tore through her like a freshly fired bullet. Her senses stumbled, reeled.

This absolutely *had* to be a dream. Soon enough Callie would jump on the covers, wake her up, and she'd be back in her bed like Dorothy home from Oz.

Gently, he lifted her glasses off her face, his fingers brushing against her temples. The world blurred, went fuzzy.

Helplessly overtaken, she parted her lips, let down her drawbridge, ceding to the marauding intruder. *Come on in, handsome. Make yourself comfy. Pillage away. Take whatever you want. It's all yours.*

His arm went around her waist, and he drew her closer to him, right up against his hard-muscled sweaty body, and engulfing her mouth with his.

She cupped his cheek in her palm, felt the scrape of beard stubble. Her heart oozed wet and slippery. Lord have mercy, the man could kiss, just the right amount of pressure, and moisture.

And the taste of him? Heavenly.

Not that she had tons of practice on that score. She had been kissed no more than a handful of times, but he was so skillful, so accomplished. No experience required on her part.

But this man . . . ah, this man . . . he knew exactly what he was doing. She was the baseball, and he was the bat, his lips rocking her so hard she shot clean out of the stadium.

Yearning burned inside her. More than anything in the entire world she ached to blend blood and bone with him, to tangle her body, her brain, and her fate with his forever.

It felt as if he were marking her. Stamping her with intention that could both irrevocably change and wreck her life.

The desperate need to merge was eerie, inescapable, and ultimately terrifying because it felt so limitless.

This single, earth-stopping, soulful, falling-off-the-edge-of-the-world kiss, absolute in its purity, kidnapped her equilibrium. If he hadn't tightened his grip on her, she would have tumbled right over.

He held her steady, his tongue skimming over hers, kissing her as if they'd been made for each other, as if he would never let her go.

And that was scariest of all.

This was not a dream.

This was real. And for some unfathomable reason Rowdy Blanton had kissed *her*, Breeanne Bliss Carlyle, the mousiest wallflower in all of Stardust.

Oh dear God.

No matter how scintillating, how compelling, his kiss was unreliable. He was a well-known playboy who'd elevated womanizing to an art form. He probably kissed strangers on a daily basis.

The kiss meant nothing to him, but it meant the world to her.

Her heart was a wild jackrabbit, running fast and frantic. No more. She couldn't take any more. Breeanne broke away, staggered back, hand to her mouth, shock rippling through her body.

She peered into his face, dug her fingernails into her palm to hide the trembling. His eyes clouded, but he gave nothing away. No hint of emotion or reaction to what had passed between them. Whatever prompted the kiss, it had nothing to do with her.

As the sweet dream morphed into a humiliating, cheek-scalding nightmare, the emotional ground beneath her shifted, and she felt as if she were plunging headlong off a cliff onto jagged rocks below.

CHAPTER 6

I have no trouble with the twelve inches
between my elbow and my palm.
It's the seven inches between my ears that's bent.

—Tug McGraw

Hell's bells. What was this?

Rowdy's pulse raced harder and faster than Giancarlo Stanton's famous line drive scorcher, the impact of their kiss nearly knocking him to his knees. Sweat bathed his brow. It had nothing to do with the workout he just completed, and everything to do with the soft, pliant mouth that had parted so easily, so innocently for him.

A fresh, sweet mouth filled with wonder and excitement.

He shoved a shaky hand through his hair, his temperature steaming like an overheated engine.

Christ.

She reached up, snatched her glasses from his hand, stuck them on her face, sank delicate hands on her hips, and glared at him.

The look landed in his belly, unspooled, spread fresh heat, switching his body into a five a.m. bakery, all ovens turned on high. The weirdest thoughts poured into his head.

Eureka! I've struck gold.

Mr. Watson, come here, I want to see you.

One small step for man, one giant leap for mankind.

Nothing like this had ever happened to him. Instant chemistry? Yeah sure, plenty of times, but this was something else, something indefinable, and mysterious. Something freakin' primal.

He wanted her.

A lot.

In his bed. On the floor. On the weight bench. In the shower. You name it, and he wanted to have sex with her there. His brain had been hijacked, and he was operating on nothing but physical instinct.

But why? That was the mystery of it. Why her of all women? Why now?

Ever since his attack, Rowdy had been unable to work up the slightest interest in the multitudinous beauties determined to occupy his bed. It was a fact he'd started worrying about, fearing that his libido had permanently flown the coop. But now here he was getting hard as diamonds over a scrawny, wide-eyed wallflower.

And not for the first time.

It had to be the scarf. She'd come wearing cheetah, after he'd confessed it was his favorite print, a clear signal that she was ready, willing, and able for a hookup. That had to be why she was here. To explore the mutual attraction that had struck them both on Irene Henderson's lawn.

He certainly wasn't opposed to the idea.

Strategically, he tucked a corner of his gym towel into the waistband of his shorts to camouflage his swiftly growing arousal. He gulped and slapped on his best pitcher's mound blank stare.

Fully committed to his mission of blowing the whistle on Potts, he'd spent the morning interviewing the three male ghostwriters that Jackdaw had sent over. At noon, he had taken a workout break.

When the four gorgeous women had descended on his home gym, all recent grads from a master's degree in journalism program, saying they'd heard he was looking for a ghostwriter, Rowdy had initially been happy for the eye-candy distraction. But in a matter of minutes, they had him feeling like the only pork chop at a feral pit bull convention.

After a group interview, he'd tried giving the women the old don't-call-me-I'll-call-you routine, but they hadn't taken the hint. They'd stayed, talking, staring, flirting. All four of them had that I-wanna-be-Mrs.-Rowdy-Blanton look in their eyes. He'd seen that look, sidestepped it hundreds of times. He willed Warwick to show up to escort them out, but his buddy hadn't picked up on the mental telepathy.

To keep the beauties at bay, he'd jokingly told them that Nolan Ryan had the last word on whatever ghostwriter he selected. When they asked how he would know if his bloodhound gave his stamp of approval, he'd told them, quite honestly, that if Nolan Ryan liked you, he sat on your feet.

That provided him with a few moments of entertainment as the women tried to coax the bloodhound to sit on their posh shoes. Good old Nolan hadn't been persuaded.

And then *she* had walked into the room. Appearing like magic in the doorway just when he needed rescuing, and wearing that come-get-this-big-boy cheetah scarf.

He had not intended on kissing her. It had been the furthest thing from his mind, but with the beauties converging, he got claustrophobic, panicked, and grasped for a way out. He'd kissed her to prove to the beauties that she was his girlfriend so they would buzz off.

Liar.

All right, cards on the table. The girlfriend thing was an excuse. Truthfully, he'd wanted to kiss her at the estate sale, curious to discover why she hadn't glanced back at him. She'd been wearing his number, after all. If you wore a guy's number on your baseball jersey, you had to be interested in him on some level, right? The opportunity to kiss her had presented itself, so he'd taken advantage of it.

C'mon, that was only a half-truth.

Bone honesty here. The real reason he kissed her? Something inexplicable had come over him. Call it instinct. Call it urge. Call it horniness. Whatever. He'd been compelled to go for it.

He wanted to kiss her. He had kissed her. It was as basic as that.

Big mistake.

Because now he felt strange things, things he'd not felt before. And when it came to women, Rowdy thought that he had felt everything there was to feel.

God, he wished like hell he hadn't kissed her, and stirred this . . . this . . . well, he had no idea what the name of it was, but it was as jolting as falling against a fence he didn't know was electrified.

She glowered at him like she was a sleepy bear he'd poked awake in the middle of winter hibernation. Unable to hold up to her sharp-eyed scrutiny, he swung his gaze back to the other women who'd lined up in a row behind him.

"*That's* your girlfriend?" asked the brunette in a

tone that managed to sound both snotty and incredulous.

Miss Cheetah Panties' face reddened, her shoulders slumped, head ducked.

A fierce protectiveness swept through him and he moved to drape an arm around her thin shoulders, and his next move was pure impulse. "She is."

Her muscles went stony beneath his touch, but she didn't contradict him.

The beauties, who, except for their hair color, had the uniform sameness of fashionable cookie-cutter neighborhoods, exchanged surprised glances. The redhead muttered to the brunette, "She must be really good at blow jobs."

"Why yes," Rowdy said. "Yes she is, and we haven't seen each other in a while, so if you ladies will excuse us . . ."

He dropped his arm from Miss Cheetah Panties' shoulders to her waist, and snugged her closer. The smell of her hair, all lemon drops and sweet flowers, boggled him.

Miss Cheetah Panties' shoulders were so stiff she could have passed for a baseball bat. But he could feel her warm breath on his neck, and it felt good. Wholesome. Inhaling her, he thought of homemade bread, cream of wheat, peanut butter, mashed potatoes, and macaroni and cheese.

She inhaled, the air expanding her lungs and causing his hand to rise with her indrawn breath, her solid life force moving beneath his touch. His own lungs picked up her quick tempo, then took over, and led the way to a more leisurely rhythm. She followed willingly, slowing, calming, relaxing into him.

Pretty damn proud of himself, he smiled. *Gotcha, babe.*

"When will you let us know what you decide about the job?" the redhead asked.

"My agent will call you." He kept the smile welded to his face, and his arm clamped around the woman beside him.

"None of us got the job, did we?" the blue-haired woman asked.

"Sorry," he said, not the least bit contrite. "You should have minded your manners, and not insulted my girlfriend."

The beauties, who in retrospect weren't so beautiful after all, collected their things and scurried off. The instant the door clicked closed behind the women, Miss Cheetah Panties jabbed her elbow into his breadbasket.

Hard.

Air shot from his diaphragm in an explosive *ooph*, emptying his lungs and doubling him over.

"What . . ." He gasped, peering up at her. ". . . was that for?"

"Kissing me, you . . . you . . . *bounder*."

Hand pressed to his belly, he halfway straightened and eyed her warily. "Bounder? Who are you? Jane Austen?"

Her hands landed on her hips, and she scowled at him over the top of her glasses the way his first grade teacher had done just before she hauled him off to the principal's office for putting a frog down the back of some little girl's dress. "Do you even have any idea who Jane Austen is?"

"Sure. I've read *Pride and Prejudice and Zombies*."

"Of course you have." She scowled, squared earnest shoulders, and tossed her head as if she was indeed a prissy lass from a Regency-era drawing room. "My name is Breeanne Carlyle."

Breeanne. Nice name. It made him think of spring training when the season was fresh, and exciting.

"And for your information, there is nothing wrong with being well-read, and with having a wide vocabulary. I opted for the word that fit the situation."

"And bounder won out?"

"Indeed."

"What exactly is a bounder?"

"A cad, a blackguard, a parvenu, a heel—"

"Modern-day English, please."

"A jerk, a creep, a louse, or if you prefer cruder vernacular, which I presume you do, a wanker, a douche, an asshat, a butthead, a—"

"Point taken. I apologize for kissing you."

"I suppose I shouldn't criticize," she said. "It's not your fault."

"What isn't my fault?"

"You can't help yourself." If sarcasm were a deep line drive, her tone would have just loaded the bases. "I'm sure you're used to getting everything you want."

She was right. He *was* accustomed to getting whatever he wanted. And right now he wanted her, even if he had no idea why.

He raised an index finger like an objection. "In my defense, I did ask you to go with it before I kissed you. You had time to say no. You could have said no. Why didn't you say no?"

Her hands flew up to a face that was both alarmed and fascinated. "I was overwhelmed. You overwhelmed me. You're an overwhelming person."

"And you pack a mean elbow." He rubbed his stinging solar plexus. "But you're also a good sport. You did wait until the others left before you punched me. I appreciate that."

"I didn't punch you, I jabbed you. Be precise."

"Okay. You *jabbed* me."

"Why did you pretend I was your girlfriend?"

"You saw them. They were hovering like vultures."

"I assumed you were familiar with that brand of female attention. Courted it, in fact." Her voice was soft, but strong, the rich velvet of Southern drawl back-loaded with Texas grit.

God, he could listen to her talk all day. "Yeah, well, I was feeling pretty exposed all alone in here with those piranhas."

"Poor baby. It must be so hard being you."

"And then there you were." He deepened his smile, stepped closer. This time she didn't back up, but she had that I-wanna-bolt look in her eyes, "My salvation."

She sniffed. "Kissing me was the only solution you could come up with?"

"Not the only one, but the most pleasant."

"For the record, I did not enjoy it," she said. Her nose twitched. Bunny rabbit.

He chuckled. "Liar. You loved letting those snooty witches think you were my girlfriend. And you liked kissing me."

She tossed her head, simultaneously fiery and fearful. If she were a weather report it would read sunny with a chance of hurricane. "My enjoyment is neither here nor there."

"But you liked it." Yeah, he was being smug, but he was one-hundred-percent certain she'd been as into the kiss as he had.

"I like French fries drenched in ketchup, that doesn't mean they're good for me."

He lowered his voice, and his eyelids. "Do you always do what's good for you, Breezy?"

"Breezy?" The scowl dug into her forehead creased

into the Panama Canal. "What do you think you are doing?"

"I figured a cool nickname might loosen you up." Yeah, he was baiting her, but what fun.

"I need neither a nickname, nor loosening up, but thank you for being so concerned about my stiffness."

He couldn't resist sidling closer. "Sweetheart, you are tighter than a rusty door hinge. I can fix that right up for you."

"Back off, buddy." She struck a pugilist stance, fear deepening in her eyes, and held up a clenched fist.

He stopped, confused. Talk about mixed messages. This woman was full of them. "Isn't that why you came up here wearing cheetah print?"

She gasped, looked horrified. "No!"

"The scarf isn't an invitation to—"

"Absolutely not!"

Canting his head, he scratched his temple. "Okay. Then why did you come here?"

"To apply for the job as your ghostwriter."

That was the last thing he'd expected her to say. She looked as if she was barely out of high school. "Really?"

"In hindsight this was a terrible idea. Forget you ever saw me."

That would mean forgetting he kissed her, and there was no way he was going to forget that. "No, let's go ahead with an interview."

"I changed my mind." She backpedaled toward the door. "I don't want the job. If you'll excuse me, I'll be on my way."

"Wait." He sprang to grab for her shoulder, feeling crazy desperate to detain her and properly apologize for the gaffe of assuming she'd come here for a hookup. But she was moving so fast that he caught hold of the cheetah scarf fluttering over her shoulder instead.

The scarf was the softest damn material he'd ever touched in his life.

She spun back toward him, panic flaring her green eyes. "Let go!"

But he'd already raised his palms, and stepped off. "It's okay. It's all right. I'm not going to hurt you. I would never hurt you."

She pitched him a look that said, *You dumbass.* "I didn't think you were going to harm me."

"What is it then?"

She glanced down, and they both stared at a fat chocolate stain on her blouse right between her breasts. "I didn't want you to see what a big klutz I am."

"What happened?" He softened his voice, making sure she understood he was not a threat.

She sighed, gazed mournfully at the ceiling. "Dairy Queen dipped cone."

"Hey." He snapped his fingers. "I love those things."

"Really?" A timid smile tipped the corners of her mouth. "Me too. Aren't they the best?"

They grinned at each other, and then she glanced away, crossing her arms over her chest, and shifting from foot to foot.

He searched for something to say to take the awkwardness out of the room. "What's that scarf made out of, by the way?"

She eyed him as if he was a stranger who'd come knocking on her front door at three in the morning with a flat tire and a dead cell battery story, asking to use her phone. "Does it feel soft to you?"

"It doesn't feel soft to you?"

"Yes, it feels soft to me, but everyone else says it's rough and scratchy."

"It's the softest material I've ever touched," he said.

"I know, right?" But her skin took on a greenish hue as if she might throw up, and she whispered something strange. "One soft touch identifies the other."

"What?"

The greenish hue paled into sickly yellow. "Nothing."

"Are you all right?"

Her lips barely parted, and she blew out a thin, reedy breath as the color slowly returned to her face. "I . . . I just can't believe you feel it too, and no one else does."

"In sync." He winked, trying to make her feel more at ease. "Obviously, we're much more kinesthetic than most people."

"No." Rapidly, she batted her head back and forth.

For some bizarro reason her shake of denial sent a knot of dread bouncing around his insides like a pinball careening off frantic flippers before the feeling finally landed, and lodged, behind his kneecaps. "You make it sound like you'd rather poke your eye out with a bamboo skewer than have something in common with me."

"It's not that—"

"What is it?"

"Something ridiculous." She let her head fall back, rolled it from side to side as if to ease knotted neck muscles. "Forget I said anything."

"C'mon." He wanted to lean in closer, but something told him that wasn't a smart move. "You can tell me. What's bothering you?"

She paused a moment, eyeing him up and down, her gaze lingering too long on his six-pack. He sucked his belly button to his spine, wanting to look his best for her.

"You're nicer than I expected," she mused.

"And that's a bad thing?"

"Yes."

"Why?"

"Like I said, you're overwhelming."

"And you have gorgeous eyes," he blurted, realizing as he said it that it sounded like a cheesy come-on. "Why don't you wear contacts?"

Her nose crinkled in that adorable way that made the knot between his kneecaps pulse. "I'm guessing you didn't get the memo."

"What memo?"

"Guys don't make passes at girls who wear glasses."

"You don't want guys making passes at you?"

"I don't want cocky ballplayers who think they rule the world making passes at me."

There was that dry wit again, sharp and clean. He wanted to provoke her some more just to see what sassy thing she'd say next. "I'm not making a pass at you. I just mentioned that you have pretty eyes. You're supposed to say thank you when someone pays you a compliment."

Her face flushed, and she looked sheepish as if she'd said something irretrievably stupid, and mumbled, "Thank you."

To lighten things up, he asked, "Where are you from?"

"Stardust. I run a bookstore, Bound to Please."

"We have a bookstore in Stardust?"

"The bookstore is housed on the second floor of my parents' antique shop, Timeless Treasures."

"I've heard of that. The antique store has a restaurant inside of it. A date took me there once. The food was good, but kinda girly."

"That's because the Honeysuckle Café is a tearoom. Light fare for the ladies who lunch."

"Oh."

"When you went to the tearoom did you notice the big staircase archway made out of old books?"

"What can I say? That was way back in high school, and reading is not my thing." He lowered his voice. "And confession time, I was too busy staring at my date's butt to notice."

She flung him a look that suggested he was about as enlightened as gum stuck to the bottom of her shoe. "Uh-huh."

"Hey," he said, feeling compelled to apologize for not being an avid reader, but reluctant to tell her he was dyslexic. "I don't have time to read. Baseball takes one-hundred-percent commitment."

"So skirt chasing doesn't detract from your dedication to baseball?"

"An athlete has to keep his body in peak physical condition. Food, exercise, sex . . ."

She put her hands over her ears. "Ugh. Sorry I asked."

"What?" he asked. She was so much fun to tease. "You don't like sex?"

"I don't like talking about other peoples' sex lives."

He studied her for a long moment, and got the same impression that hit him when he first laid eyes on her at the estate sale. *This one hasn't been off the bench.*

She squirmed. "What?"

"You haven't had much sex."

She bristled, drawing herself up into that indignant Jane Austen impersonation again. "That is none of your business."

"Contrary to what I just told the redhead who left here, I'm guessing that blow jobs are *not* your specialty."

"I . . . I . . ." Her face blanched. She put her hands on

her hips again, dropped them, and then brought them back up. "I'm not having this conversation with you."

"Except that you *are* having this conversation with me."

"I'm leaving."

"Then why are you still here, Breezy?"

"Stop calling me that."

"You're not really Breezy, are you? In fact, your body language is pretty stiff. Maybe I should call you Stiffy instead."

"Don't you dare!"

"Stiffy." He tapped his chin as if he was seriously considering it. "Hmm. I sorta like it."

"I'm on my way out the door," she said.

"But you're not moving."

"That's because there's a dog sitting on my shoes."

Rowdy glanced down. Sure enough, during their conversation, Nolan Ryan had loped over and plunked down on her feet.

"That's Nolan Ryan," he said. "He only sits on your feet if he likes you."

"Is that right?" Breeanne bent to scratch the bloodhound's head, muddy blond hair falling over her face. Nolan Ryan sighed blissfully and stretched out, fully anchoring her to the floor. "I like him too. I love animals."

"So do I. Wow, more things we have in common."

"Don't act like it's a big deal. Lots of people love animals."

"May I ask you a question?"

"No," she said.

"How much do you know about baseball?"

Her shoulders lifted, and her face brightened like she'd just gotten a rave compliment. "My great-aunt was Polly Whitcomb."

"As in *the* Polly Whitcomb who played professional women's baseball during World War II?"

"You've heard of her?"

"I know everything there is to know about baseball."

"That's cocky, and I imagine inaccurate. No one can know everything there is to know about baseball."

He gave her a lopsided grin that usually stopped women in their tracks. "What can I say? When you've got it, you've got it."

She snorted. "Everything, huh?"

"Pretty much."

"What are Ty Cobb's stats?"

"Seriously? You're gonna pitch me a home run?"

"You're right. That is way too easy." She pressed three fingers against her chin, screwed her mouth to one side in thought. "What was the least amount of people who ever attended an MLB game?"

"Marlins and the Reds, 2011. Three hundred and forty-seven people—give or take since there was some dispute on the actual headcount—in the stands because of Hurricane Irene."

She looked suitably impressed, but damn, he was impressed too. How did *she* know that?

"What's the life span of an MLB baseball?" she asked.

"Woman, you keep tossing me hanging breaking balls I'm gonna keep lobbing them in the stands. I'm a freaking pitcher. That question doesn't deserve an answer."

"Just checking to see if you were awake." She grinned a had-you-going-there-for-a-moment grin, and darn if her eyes didn't sparkle like polished jade in direct sunlight.

"You came here to interview for the job of my

ghostwriter, right? You're the one who should be answering the questions so I can tell if *you're* qualified."

"Bring it." She wriggled three fingers in a come-on
gesture.

"What was Sandy Koufax's nickname?" he asked.

"Left Arm of God."

"How did Jimmy Piersall celebrate his one hun-
dredth home run?"

"Ran all the bases backward."

"Don Baylor played in three straight World Series,
what team was he with?"

"Trick question. He played for three different
teams, the Red Sox, Twins, and Athletics."

"Smart woman."

Her cheeks flushed. "I also know all your stats," she
said, and rattled them off.

Damn, but he was impressed. Where had she come
from? "What's your background?"

"I published a book about great-aunt Polly with a
small regional press and self-published a book on the
history of baseball in Texas after my publisher went
under. Plus a lot of my dad's family on his mother's
side—my dad, uncles, cousins, his older brother—
played minor league ball. I grew up with three sisters,
and I was the only one who would watch baseball with
Dad. We bonded over the sport."

Ah, a daddy's girl. Normally, he avoided relationships with women who were close to their fathers because they were more likely to believe in white picket
fence fantasies and he was not a commitment-oriented
guy, but this was a business relationship, not an intimate one.

"Who is your dad's family?" he said. "I might know
them."

She waved a hand. "They're mostly from Kansas,

and we're talking Class A short season, small potatoes stuff. Great-Aunt Polly was the real star of the Whitcomb clan."

"I gotta read your book."

"You don't read, remember."

"I'll read about baseball." *And anything you write.* That jolted him. He liked her. A lot. More than he'd liked anyone in a long time.

"Good for you."

Rowdy eyed her up and down. He wanted to give her the job. Not just because she knew his stats. Not just because she came from a baseball family. Not just because he liked her. Not just because she was so easy to talk to.

Although those were all valid reasons enough.

No, the main reason he wanted to offer the job to her was because being near her made him feel good. And this was the first time in a very long time that he felt good about himself. She made him feel alive again, like second chances were possible. As if he was a sleepwalking Rip Van Winkle, and she'd awakened him from a twenty-year nap.

And boy did he need that right now.

His agent, and Heath Rankin, would probably disagree with his choice of ghostwriter. They would argue she was too young or didn't have strong enough publishing credentials. But she had something none of the other applicants had.

Passionate innocence.

Once upon a time, he'd been like that, deeply passionate about baseball without the jadedness of experience. He wanted to feel open and optimistic again. She could do that for him.

Yeah? More likely, she would end up tainted from listening to his confessions. All right. Decision made.

He needed someone fearless in the heat of battle, because after all that's what this book was about—an all-out war with Dugan Potts.

He opened his mouth to tell her he needed a writer with more experience, but instead of saying that he said, "The job is yours."

CHAPTER 7

The other sports are just sports. Baseball is a love.

—BRYANT GUMBEL

"What?" Stunned, Breeanne stared at him. She wasn't sure she'd heard Rowdy correctly, and she needed to hear it again before she totally unleashed an internal Snoopy dance.

He looked as surprised to have offered her the position as she was. She was certain she'd blown her chances, and for a second there, she thought he might say, *Not really. Psych!*

But then he cleared his throat, and met her eyes. "You're my ghostwriter if you want the job."

"Ra-ra-really?" *Stop stuttering and tell him yes, thank you.*

"You've written two books. Your great-aunt is Polly Whitcomb. You know baseball. My dog likes you." He shrugged "I like you."

He liked her? Rowdy Blanton liked her? Oh gosh, oh wow, oh holy cow, she felt like Sally Fields when she won an Academy Award for *Places in the Heart*. He liked her. He really liked her.

"What more could I ask for?"

She glanced down a moment to reorient herself,

before raising her eyes to meet his gaze again. "Um
. . . someone with solider writing credentials."

"Are you trying to talk yourself out of a job?" he
asked.

"No."

"Then say yes."

"I would, except . . ."

"Except what?"

"If I work for you there have got to be some rules."
Why couldn't she just say yes? Why was she—the one
who did not rock boats—tipping this particular canoe
when saying yes would give her everything she ever
wanted?

One eyebrow crept up his forehead, and his upper
lip twitched. "Such as?"

She had to be clear. This was a job. This wasn't a
hookup.

Why can't it be a hookup? asked the part of her that
wanted to Snoopy break-dance? *It could be a hookup.
What was wrong with a hookup?*

Because hooking up with him was beyond insane.
She wasn't the kind of woman who did casual hook-
ups. Heck, she'd never had any hookup, casual or otherwise. She was quiet, and circumspect. She didn't step
outside her comfort zone. Well, that is until today.

"I can't have you pulling those tonsil-hockey moves
again," she said firmly. *Nooo*, wailed Snoopy Dancer.

He held up a Boy Scout palm. "I swear to a strict
hands-off policy."

She shook her head. "I don't trust you." Oh what a
lie, she didn't trust herself.

Seriously, whispered Snoopy Dancer, *I really want
to slap you right now. Hard.*

Rowdy upped the wattage on his smile. "Did I mention the salary?" He quoted a sum so impressive her eyes bugged. She could do so much with that. Move from her parents' house, get a new car, start her life in earnest.

Yeah, gloated Snoopy Dancer. *Say no to that.*

"Say yes, Breeanne," he coaxed. "It's that easy. Just one word. Yes." He leaned in, the dizzy scent of him knocking any last scrap of resistance out of her. She wasn't built to resist. She was a go-with-the-flow kind of girl.

If you don't say yes, threatened Snoopy Dancer, *I'm packing my bags and moving out and taking your one scrap of personality with me.*

"You didn't let me finish," she said.

"Fair enough. What else?"

Breeanne hardened her chin, and fortified her resolve. She'd been accepting things her entire life, rolling over, acquiescing, being agreeable, deferring to opinions, giving in, accommodating, avoiding confrontation because it made her sick to her stomach. He had no idea how hard it was for her to set boundaries. She ached for an easy world filled with yesses and smiles and happy people. But if she gave in to him now he would steamroll her and she'd end up flat on her back in his bed. A pleasant idea that was far too tempting, and far too dangerous.

"Let's get something straight. I'm not one of your women," she said, quite calmly, and proud of herself for such a steady, succinct delivery. She could do this. She was a professional writer, a small businesswoman. Her whole career was at stake. No way she was going to allow a teenage crush and runaway lust to ruin her chance at big league publishing.

The higher his grin tipped up, the more his eyes crinkled. "My women, huh?"

"That's right. If I take the job this would be a strictly professional relationship, and I expect professional behavior."

"Hmm." He canted his head, studied her. "Do you have specific parameters for what you consider professional behavior? You know, a little FYI so I don't cross any lines?"

"First off, don't use me again the way you used me with those other women. Telling them I'm your girlfriend just because you didn't want to appear available. I am not your girlfriend. Please don't behave as if I am. If you need a shield against predatory women call Warwick."

"Okay. What else?"

"We have regular working hours. Nine to five."

"What if something unexpected comes up and we need to reschedule?"

"We can renegotiate at that time."

"What else?"

"We don't socialize together."

"That it?"

"It's all I can think of right now, but I reserve the right to add ground rules as the need arises."

"All right," he said. "I agree to your conditions."

Breeanne blinked. Well, that was easier than she expected. What now?

"Is it official?" he asked.

Was it? She wanted this job more than she wanted to breathe, but she was scared.

"If you're still on the fence, think of the money," he went on. "You could buy—"

Snoopy Dancer just damn well took her hostage. "Yes."

He paused, thrown off by the interruption of his spiel. "Huh?"

"You can stop selling. Yes, I accept the job."

"Wow? Okay. Good. Great." He rubbed his palms together like he'd just gotten a great deal on a used car, and then stuck out his left hand. "I'll call my agent and put this puppy in motion. Let's shake on it, Breeanne Carlyle." He said her name slow, deep, and throaty, his tongue caressing those last two words in an erotic I-wanna-have-sex-with-you sound that shocked her spine with a series of hot shivers.

Still in a daze, and wondering if maybe she was in a dream after all, Breeanne sank her hand into his.

Zap!

Zing!

Static electricity crackled the air, jumping from her to him. Or maybe it was the other way around. Either way there was no denying the hot, succinct snap. Even Snoopy Dancer hollered, *Whoa, wait, what was that?*

Grinning, Rowdy pumped her hand, and a proprietary look came into his eyes as if he'd just claimed her as his.

Leaving Breeanne's pulse skittering for shelter. What had she just gotten herself into?

Hours later, Breeanne could still feel the imprint of his lips on hers. She marveled over the softness of his kiss versus the hardness of his body, but both had been hungry.

For *her.*

Dear Lord, how long would it take for her to feel normal again? She was wound tighter than Elizabeth Bennet over Mr. Darcy. She stood in the middle of her parents' kitchen staring blindly at the extravagant spread laid out on the table.

Her family had insisted on cooking a special celebratory dinner to commemorate her landing the position as Rowdy Blanton's ghostwriter. The Carlyle clan loved celebrations, and used any excuse for fanfare. Dad grilled filet mignon. Jodi made her famous garlic mashed potatoes. Kasha bought champagne. Suki prepared caprese salad with a balsamic vinegar reduction. Mom baked a cake, and wrote "Well Done Breeanne" on it in pink icing.

She felt honored and loved and, quite frankly, more than a little worried as reality nibbled away at her self-confidence. First off, she was nervous about writing on a tight deadline. She'd spent three years researching and writing her book about Great-Aunt Polly. There had been no pressure. This was big league publishing, her make-or-break opportunity. What if she didn't have the writing chops to pull it off?

Secondly, there was that world-altering kiss. If she was around him she feared she'd want more of those kisses, and then she would be the one to break her own rules. Also, she was pretty sure Jackdaw Press would frown on a ghostwriter fooling around with her subject.

Thirdly, and the scariest of all, was the cheetah scarf. No matter how many people she polled, she and Rowdy were the only ones who thought the scarf felt soft. What that meant, she did not know, but she was glad she hadn't told her family that Rowdy felt the softness too. They were bound to turn it into a thing.

"Breeanne, honey, are you listening?" her mother asked.

"Huh?" She blinked rapidly as if it could dispel her obsessive thoughts about Rowdy Blanton.

"We were just talking about the day we brought you home from the hospital," her dad said. "How we had to prepare ourselves in case you died."

"But at the same time, we were determined to keep you alive, no matter what it took," Mom added.

"And now look how far you've come." Pride lit up Dad's face.

"To Breeanne," Suki said, and raised her glass of iced tea. "And to dreams coming true."

They all lifted their glasses. "To Breeanne."

She flushed happily.

"Just think," Jodi said. "You'll be working side by side with your teenage crush. How many of us can say that?"

"A crush that just happens to be a superstar." Kasha sent her a knowing wink, as if she was privy to the chaos going on inside Breeanne's head.

"Better watch out." Suki grinned. "Rumor has it Rowdy is the best kisser in Stardust."

She hoped the heat rising to her cheeks did not give her away. She was so glad that she had not told them that Rowdy had already kissed her. They would turn *that* into a thing.

Dad growled. "I should have a talk with Rowdy. Make sure he knows to keep his hands to himself.

Breeanne's face blanched icy. "Dad, no!"

"Rowdy Blanton is a great ballplayer and I admire his pitching skills, but he's got a reputation as a ladies' man, and when it comes to my daughter, I want to set him straight—"

She pressed her palms together. "Please don't humiliate me."

A frown pinched his face, and his eyes narrowed as if he'd just as soon punch Rowdy as not. "I don't want to see you get hurt."

"Come on, Dad," she wheedled. "Think about. Why would someone like Rowdy be interested in someone like me?"

"Why not? You're an amazing young woman." Dad folded his arms over his chest. "All my girls are."

"He's not interested in me in that way," she insisted.

"You sure? Why did he hire such an inexperienced writer if he didn't have ulterior motives?"

Ouch. There it was, the real truth. Her father didn't believe in her writing. He thought it was much more likely that Rowdy wanted to take her to bed, than she'd been hired for her knowledge and talent.

Stung to the quick, she sank her fingernails into her palms to keep her eyes from misting. "He hired me because I know something about baseball."

"And no male ghostwriter fit that bill?"

"Who's up for cake?" Mom interrupted, giving Dad a lay-off look.

Breeanne smiled gratefully at her mother. "I'll take a slice."

When dinner was finished, the family dispersed. Jodi and Kasha headed to their homes. Suki disappeared upstairs to her room to make jewelry. Dad went outside to clean the grill. Breeanne stayed in the kitchen to help her mother with the dishes.

"Dad doesn't think I can do this," she murmured.

"Your father is just worried about you." Without glancing up, Mom rinsed off a plate and handed it to her to load in the dishwasher.

Callie was under foot and in an affection mood, eeling around Breeanne's legs as she stacked the dishes. The cat's proud fluffy tail brushed against her calves.

"I know." Breeanne was acutely aware that she had been the biggest single drain on her parents' marriage, physically, financially, and emotionally. It was one of the reasons she tried so hard not to rock the boat. She couldn't help being born with a defective heart, but she could make sure that she was easy to get along with.

"I don't think your father fully realizes that you're twenty-five years old."

"He doesn't seem to have any trouble letting Suki grow up."

"For one, Suki has a completely different personality. She's much harder to corral. For another thing, you've been your father's little shadow since you could walk, and because you were so sickly, he still sees you as much younger than you are. Besides, you're special."

Special.

She hated that word. Had heard it her whole life. *Don't carry that Breeanne. You're special. Don't try that, Breeanne. You're special. Don't eat that, Breeanne. You're special.* There had always been love behind those words, but to a kid who just wanted to be like everyone else, it felt like a judgment, and she absorbed the message as: *It's not okay to assert yourself.*

Absentmindedly, she rubbed her breastbone and, without intending to, let out a sigh.

Mom's chin shot up. "What's wrong?"

"Nothing."

Callie hopped onto the sill of the kitchen bay window, sat watching them like a tennis match judge.

"Something *is* bothering you. Are you feeling all right?" Her mother turned the water off, dried her hands on a dish towel, and moved as if to test Breeanne's forehead for a fever.

Feeling like an ungrateful daughter, she stepped back, shook her head, and held up her palms to stave off irritation as much as her mother's attention. "I'm fine. Really."

Concern darkened her mother's eyes. "You haven't been yourself since your father and I got back from San Antonio."

She shrugged, not knowing how to broach the topic

that had been on her mind for a while now. How did she begin to tell her mother that she felt constricted by her family's love?

"Are you second-guessing your decision to write this book?" her mother asked.

"No. Yes. Maybe. A little."

"Is it your ability to do the job that's worrying you, or your attraction to Rowdy?"

"Both," she admitted.

"You know you don't have to do this. The bookstore is yours, and you'll always have a place to live right here with your father and me. There's no reason to step outside your comfort zone, or put yourself in a situation you can't handle."

There it was again, her family's mistaken belief that she wasn't strong enough to take care of herself. It might have been true once, but it wasn't any longer.

"You and Dad can't keep carrying me around on a pillow. I'm fine. I'm not on death's doorstep anymore. I've got a long, healthy life ahead of me."

"I know, honey."

She moistened her lips, worked up the courage to say what she needed to say. "It's time I started acting like a healthy twenty-five-year-old woman."

"I see." Her mother's lips pursed. "You mean sex."

Yes, among other things, she meant sex, but she didn't want the conversation with her mother to veer off in that direction. She needed to get a life of her own, and while that included sex, it wasn't her only objective.

"If you're ready for sex, I'll book an appointment with—"

"Mom! I can book my own doctor appointments. I'm not talking about sex." Well, not to her mother. "I'm talking about finding myself. Now that I'll be getting an advance for ghostwriting Rowdy's book, it's time I moved out."

Her mother looked crestfallen. "All on your own?"

"I'll get a roommate. I'm placing an ad in the Stardust flyer looking for someone to share a house with." She'd thought about it, and decided a roommate was the best option just in case the ghostwriting thing fell through. She didn't want to have to come crawling home.

Her mother's hand crept across her throat. "What house?"

"There's no specific house. Not yet."

"Getting a house is a big step, Breeanne."

"You didn't say that when Jodi moved into the boxcar she renovated when she was nineteen."

"Jodi's different. She's always been more mature than other young people her age, and she's got a good head on her shoulders."

Meaning Breeanne didn't? "And what about Kasha? She'd backpacked through Europe after her sophomore year of college."

"Kasha was homeless until she was six years old. She knows how to take care of herself."

"And you don't think I can."

"Honey, it's just that you've been so ill and—"

"You're right. I was a sickly kid who needed a lot of attention. I'm not self-assured like Jodi, or strong like Kasha, or spunky like Suki, but I'm not going to be if you and Dad won't let me stretch my wings. I need to make up for lost time."

"Well." Mom blinked, and rearranged her features, struggling not to show how upset she was. "If that's the way you really feel."

Her mother had no idea how hard this was for her.

The last thing she wanted was to hurt her parents, but she *had* to do this. "Please, Mom, try to understand."

Her mother didn't say anything for a long time. The second hand on the kitchen wall clock clicked so loudly it was all Breeanne could hear.

Tick. Tick. Tick.

"Does this mean you're not coming back to the bookstore once you've finished writing Rowdy's book?"

"No, no. I love working at the bookstore."

"Oh good." Her mother's eyes lightened. "Because we depend on you. If you're worried that you're a financial burden to us, please don't be."

"I'm so very grateful for everything you and Dad have done for me. You've got to know that."

"Of course we do. And we love you." Mom hugged her. "So very much. We're always one hundred percent behind you."

"Thank you."

"Now." Mom reached to tuck a strand of errant hair behind Breeanne's ear, a loving touch. This woman had saved her life. She and Dad had nursed her to health when no one else believed she would live. "When are you supposed to start writing this book?"

"Rowdy and I begin the interview process on Monday, but I'll start doing preliminary research right away. I told Rowdy that I had to train my replacement at the bookstore. Plus my agent has to iron out the contract details with the publisher."

"You don't have to worry about training someone. Suki can take over at the bookstore until you get back."

"She'll hate that."

"She'll gripe but she'll come through. It's only until

you finish this book. Right?" her mother asked, needing reassurance.

"Yes."

Her mother exhaled audibly. "Good. Then you have time to consider if writing this book is what you really want to do. And you have plenty of time to find the right roommate, the right house. There's no need to rush into something you might end up regretting."

But she didn't need time. As much as her family loved her, or maybe precisely because of how much they loved her, they would never take her seriously until she struck out on her own. Accepting Rowdy's job offer was her first step toward independence, and achieving her heartfelt dream of being a writer. She was about the endeavor, she was fully committed to this path.

No matter what.

But up in her room, as she was slipping into her nightgown, getting ready for bed, she stopped and opened the hope chest she'd moved from the bookstore to the foot of her bed. She knelt, took out the cheetah-print scarf, ran her fingers over the silky smooth cloth, read the quote on the box.

> *Two pieces split apart, flung separate and broken, but longing for reunion; one soft touch identifies the other, and they are at last made whole.*

"One soft touch identifies the other," she whispered.

When she and Rowdy touched this scarf, they felt the same thing. Extreme softness. How could that be? And what did it mean?

The sensible part of her scoffed, unable to believe the way she and Rowdy had connected so instantly. How he looked at her as if she were truly something special. How that look in his wild eyes, the amazing blue of an East Texas summer, had twisted her up inside.

She put the scarf back in the box, put the box back in the trunk. Closed the lid. Read the other inscription.

Treasures are housed within, heart's desires granted, but be careful where wishes are cast, for reckless dreams dared dreamed in the heat of passion will surely come to pass.

The impact of those words fully struck her. She had wished on the hope chest and her wish had come true. And, if the old woman who'd sold her the trunk could be believed, the wish could not be undone.

The prophecy was a clear warning. Suggesting bad things could happen with unwise wishes. Her mind hopped to the obvious risk. She could so easily fall in love with him.

And there was only one way that could end, with her nursing a broken heart. Had she indeed been reckless with her wish?

CHAPTER 8

The pitcher has to find out if the hitter is timid.
And if the hitter is timid,
he has to remind the hitter he's timid.

—DON DRYSDALE

On the following Monday Breeanne drove to Rowdy's place, her mind atwitter. She'd barely slept, kept awake by disturbingly hot thoughts of the blue-eyed pitcher who invaded her dreams.

And her body, well, it was behaving quite badly. Warming up in all the wrong, or maybe all the right places, depending on how you looked at it. *Wrong* places, the good girl in her scolded. Getting all hot and melty over Rowdy Blanton was a stupid idea any way you sliced it.

She had to keep this relationship on a professional keel. At least for the six months she needed to write the book and get the final draft turned in.

Feeling like the queen of the manor, she hit the remote control and opened the front gate. Rowdy had given her the remote after she accepted the job. Pressing it into her hand the way he'd pressed the baseball into her palm more than a dozen years ago on the teen ward at the children's hospital.

She shook off the memory, tucked her notebook

computer under her arm, marched to the front door, and rang the bell just before nine a.m.

The door opened.

She expected to see Warwick, and was caught off guard by a sleepy-eyed Rowdy rocking the bed-head look, snug Levi's, a tight black T-shirt, and delectably bare feet.

Air stalled in her lungs at the sight.

Nut bunnies.

She was going to have to get over this breathlessness whenever she was around him. Breathing was definitely a job requirement.

A lazy smile crinkled the corners of his eyes, and his gaze zeroed in on her mouth. A slug of dark, moist desire latched on to that look, and pulled it straight down to her pelvic floor.

It was all she could do not to lick her lips. *Stop it. Stop it right now, Breeanne Bliss Carlyle.*

It didn't matter how handsome he was or how much he fired her engines with those knowing eyes. Ignoring for the moment that she was writing his autobiography, and that she'd set strict ground rules regarding their working relationship, a girl like her could never hold on to a guy like him. Not for any length of time. He could have any woman he wanted. Yes, he might seem interested, but it was his default expression. She couldn't bank on it.

Not by a long shot.

She read the tabloids. Heard the gossip around town. She knew well enough what he was like. If he was interested in her at all, it was only as a novelty. Someone completely removed from the polished, sleek women he usually dated.

He was born to charm. He couldn't help himself. It was in his DNA. His modus operandi. He could make any woman feel like she was the only person in the room. Until he got what he wanted, and then he would be on to the next conquest.

Determinedly, she leashed her libido, and unleashed an energetic can-do smile. "Ready to get down to work?"

"Are you always this chirpy in the morning?"

"Always," she assured him.

"You're a lark."

"What?"

"You're a meadowlark, like Warwick." He yawned. "I'm a night owl."

"Nine o'clock isn't all that early. I've been up since five." She wasn't about to tell him she'd been so excited that she couldn't sleep. Let him feel guilty for being a lazybones.

Yet part of her couldn't help wondering what it would be like to stay up late into the night with him. She once read a study that said men who were night owls had more sexual stamina than men who were early risers. It was probably bunk, but she couldn't help wanting to test the theory.

With Rowdy.

Dammit. She had to stop thinking like this.

Nolan Ryan loped into the foyer. When the bloodhound saw her, his tail started wagging, and even though his hangdog expression didn't change, he trotted over the threshold, settled onto her feet, and gazed up at her with pet-me eyes.

"You have yourself quite an admirer," Rowdy said.

"It's mutual." She bent to scratch the dog behind the ears, and she could have sworn she heard Rowdy mumble, "I'm jealous."

But when she glanced up, he was walking away. Her gaze snapped onto his gravity-defying butt. High, tight, round, hard. Lord, but the man could fill out a pair of jeans.

"I need coffee," he said over his shoulder. "You want some?"

"I don't drink coffee," she called after him.

"You coming?"

Coming. The word had several connotations, including a particularly naughty one. Good grief. She was acting like a silly sixteen-year-old.

"There's a dog on my shoes," she explained.

Rowdy chuckled, whistled. Nolan Ryan got up and moseyed along after him.

Clutching her computer to her chest, Breeanne followed. In the kitchen, Rowdy waved her onto a bar stool. "Have a seat."

She eased down at the bar, taking in the state-of-the-art kitchen with sleek modern cabinetry and stainless steel appliances, so different from the homey Victorian kitchen of her parents' house.

For the first time Breeanne wondered how she might decorate a kitchen of her own. Maybe she'd start a Pinterest page and find out.

Rowdy went over to the K-cup carousel, selected a coffee cartridge, and plugged it into the individual-serving coffeemaker. She couldn't help noticing how his biceps stretched the seams of his T-shirt, and this time, mesmerized by the map of muscles, she did lick her lips.

"We have tea. Do you want hot tea?" he asked.

"Is it herbal?"

He shrugged. "I don't know."

"A glass of water will do fine."

"You don't drink caffeine?"

"It's not really all that good for you."

He lowered his lashes, slanted a naughty look at her

with those bad-boy eyes. "Do you always do what's good for you?"

"Usually, yes. Except for dipped cones. My one weakness."

"That's your only weakness?"

Oh, that and good-looking left-handed pitchers with dark hair and sky blue eyes. "For the most part. What's your one big weakness?"

He laughed. "Sweetheart, I've got a whole lot more than one."

She should tell him not to call her sweetheart. It went against her ground rules for professional behavior, but it sounded so nice and she wasn't feeling nearly as brave today as when she'd accepted the job.

Instead, she propped her elbows on the bar and dropped her chin into her upturned palms. "I'm not going anywhere."

"Are you taking inventory of my sins for the book or is this for your own amusement?" he asked.

"I've read about you in the tabloids. I can guess what your sins are."

"Don't believe everything you read." He laughed, and slid a glass of ice water in front of her. He slouched against the kitchen counter all hot and manly, sipping his coffee, watching her, and looking thoroughly entertained.

By her? He was fascinated by her? How was that possible? Unnerved, she dropped her gaze and took a long sip of water as if it was the most delicious beverage she had ever tasted.

Silence stretched long and wide and deep. Um . . . this was awkward. What should she say? What should she do? She shifted. Cleared her throat. Waited.

He waited too, eyeing her over the rim of his coffee cup.

Unable to bear the silence one second longer, she set down her glass and turned on her computer. "Shall we get started?"

One maverick eyebrow shot up on his forehead. "Shall we?"

She nodded, feeling out of place. "We shall."

"I'm teasing you, Jane Austen."

"Please don't." God, she sounded desperate.

"I'm a teaser, Breezy. It's what I do. I tease. If you're gonna work for me, you're gonna get teased. Accept it."

She starched her back against the twinge of excitement that fluttered through her at the thought of being teased by him. "This isn't supposed to be fun and games. It's work."

"To me work and play are one and the same. I love what I do for a living." He paused, the light dying in his eyes. "Loved."

She studied his left arm, and that livid pink scar. Her stomach churned up mini-tornadoes of empathy, regret, and adoration. Poor guy. "There's absolutely no chance of a comeback?"

"Not if I write this book."

"What do you mean?"

He waved a hand like he was shooing away a fly. "We'll get to that later."

She wanted to press, but the regretful expression on his face stilled her tongue. She was reluctant to stir his pain, although surely he knew they'd have to go there sooner or later.

"First off," she said. "I'd like to start by confirming my preliminary research on you. If that's all right."

He sauntered over, a six-foot bundle of testosterone, pulled out the bar stool next to her, and plunked down. A river of heat shot through her bloodstream like level six whitewater rapids. Even though he sat a foot away, his presence was so overpowering she felt engulfed.

He leaned the stool back on two legs, balancing with the ease and grace of athletic perfection.

Her pulse thundered a stormy jolt, since he was just as incredibly erotic as ever, and she categorically wished her body didn't spontaneously react to him. But how could anyone with a millimeter of estrogen not respond to someone as flagrantly masculine as Rowdy Blanton?

Restlessly, she tapped the keyboard, pulling up her research notes. "You were born right here in Stardust."

"That's right."

"You were the third in birth order of four children, two boys, two girls. Your two sisters, Olivia and Yvette, are older. You have a younger brother, Zach, who is twenty-five." Her age.

"Uh-huh." Leisurely, his gaze strolled over her.

Between her breasts, she broke out in a cold sweat that she purposely ignored. "Your father had progressive multiple sclerosis and when you were fourteen, his health deteriorated to the point your mother could no longer hold down a job, be his nursemaid and be a mother, so she sent everyone but Zach to live with different relatives."

"I stayed with my uncle Mick."

She consulted her notes. "Mick Blanton is a bachelor geologist who lives in Houston and he let you run wild the two years you lived with him. You got into trouble with the law in Houston, but nothing major. You moved back to Stardust to live with your mom again when your dad died. You impressed a baseball scout your senior year in high school and you were on your way."

Breeanne paused, giving him a chance to refute her

information, but he simply nodded that head of thick chestnut hair.

"Your mother remarried. To an electrician she met on a cruise, and she's now living in Portland, Oregon. Olivia is married to a government contractor, has two children, a boy and a girl and lives in D.C. Yvette is a first grade teacher and she lives in Midland with her oilman husband and their three boys."

"Wow, who gave you a shovel."

Bewildered, she wrinkled her forehead. "Excuse me?"

"You've been digging deep."

"Well this *is* Stardust and people love to talk, especially about you."

"Are all those minute details going into the book?"

"It doesn't matter whether these details end up in the book or not, I need the information in order to understand the man."

He took a long pull on his coffee. "Good luck with that."

"Because you're unknowable?"

He set down his mug, angled his shoulders toward her. The feeling of being engulfed constricted her lungs again. "Because you haven't done a lick of living in your . . . How old are you, by the way?"

"Twenty-five, the same age as your brother."

"Hmm. I pegged you for much younger."

"I'm almost twenty-six and how do you know I haven't done a lick of living?"

"It's written all over you."

She stiffened her back. "In what way?"

"Straitlaced, blushes easily, inexperienced. Besides, I tasted it on you when I kissed you."

She reached up to finger her lips. Every word was true and she hated that she was so easy to read.

"Tell me this, Breezy, are you still a virgin?"

Heat bloomed like a rash across her chest and spread up her neck. Unable to believe he'd asked such a personal question, she swallowed the excess moisture in her mouth. "That is none of your business."

He nodded, more to himself than to her. "You answered my question. Just as I suspected, you've not been off the bench."

"What does my sexuality—"

"Or lack thereof."

She ignored that. "—have to do with writing your autobiography?"

"How can you possibly hope to understand me, when you don't even understand you? And how can you understand yourself until you've lived a little?"

"What are you saying? That I'm not capable of writing your life story because I haven't debauched myself?"

"Debauched. Good one." He chortled. "See there. That Miss Prim expression on your face right now is what gives you away. Debauchery isn't the issue."

"Then what is? Why are we getting sidetracked? Everything's planned. I've got my questions all mapped out for today's interview."

He snapped the front legs of the bar stool down so hard and fast that she jumped like a jackrabbit. "What are you so afraid of?"

You.

"I'm not afraid," she lied.

"You can't run the bases if you never step up to the plate."

"My great-aunt Polly used to say that."

"I know. I read *In Her Own League*."

"You read my book?" Snoopy Dancer was back, gleefully bouncing up and down. He'd read her book!

"Cover to cover. I read the other one too."

"You read my books," she said, still unable to believe it. He told her he didn't read, but even so he'd read *her* books.

"You're a good writer."

She pressed both palms to her lips to stop a helpless smile. He'd read her books.

"See there," he said. "I did something that made me uncomfortable in order to improve our working relationship. And in this case instead of it being painful, reading your book turned out to be a pleasant surprise. So now it's your turn."

"My turn to do what?" she asked, wondering if he was going to kiss her again, secretly hoping that he was going to kiss her again despite her ground rules. Good grief, what was wrong with her?

"To do something that makes you uncomfortable."

"Um." She gulped. That sounded ominous. Was he talking about more than kissing? Snoopy Dancer was overjoyed by the idea, but Breeanne wasn't ready for anything like that. Not with him. Nowhere close. "What do you have in mind?"

Mischief turned his eyes wicked. "Have you ever been on a zipline?"

CHAPTER 9

If you're going to play at all, you're out to win.

—DEREK JETER

Rowdy stood on the zipline platform that marked the highest part of the property, Stardust Lake sparkling in the sunlight at the bottom of the hill. The lake lay just beyond his fence line. While the view was a beaut, it was the woman at his side who captivated his attention.

Breeanne teetered on tiptoes trying to see how far down it was without stepping to the edge of the platform. She wore a pink T-shirt that was a size too big, a pair of white cropped pants that hid too much of those gorgeous legs, and her hair was pulled back into a short ponytail.

The white cotton pants fit snugly, molding to her cute little fanny in a way that made him think—

Stop it, he cautioned himself, and reluctantly raised his gaze to her face.

She waffled between bravery and timidity, fearlessness and uncertainty. As if she was on some personal improvement mission she wasn't quite sure she should be on. He wanted to help her tip the scales toward embracing life.

Embracing and squeezing and—

Christ, there you go again. Knock it off!

She sank back to her heels. "I'm scared."

"Feel the fear and do it anyway."

"You sound like a fortune cookie."

"It's still sound advice."

She shook her head, and backed up. "I don't think I can."

"C'mon, what's the worst that could happen?"

"I could plunge to my death."

"Okay, let's say that happens. Which it won't. But for the sake of argument, how many people can say they went out having fun?"

"Good point, but I doubt I'll remember that during the plummet."

"This puppy is as safe as it gets." Rowdy patted the metal post that supported the zipline. "I have it inspected by a licensed professional every year."

"Hmm." She went up on her tiptoes again, stared down at the hill, gulped so forcefully the column of her throat moved visibly. "How do we get back?"

"If you don't feel like walking back, Warwick will come fetch us."

"I'm really nervous."

She shifted her weight from foot to foot, her modest breasts bouncing with the motion.

He couldn't help staring at them. They were so pert and cute. Plump little oranges just ripe for picking. His mouth watered.

"I'm scared too," he admitted. Scared of the way he was feeling about her.

She looked over at him and he couldn't resist cradling her gaze. She looked like she could use some TLC. Why did he feel compelled to be the one to dole it out to her?

"Why are *you* scared?" she asked.

"This will be the first time I've been on the zipline since . . ." He lifted his left shoulder.

"Your attack," she whispered, filling in the blanks.

"Yeah."

"You wanna call it a morning?" Hope lifted her voice. "Let's go back and finish today's interview."

"Nope."

She mumbled under her breath. "Nut bunnies."

"What?"

She waved a hand. "Just something I say when things aren't going my way."

"Nut bunnies, huh? That's different. Where did you pick it up?"

She wrapped her arms around herself, and gazed off as if staring into the past, a slight smile settling over her lips. "When I was a kid my family raised rabbits for extra income. One day my little sister, Suki, fed them some peanuts. The bunnies got really spunky after that, they broke out of their hutch and went running around the backyard like crazed things. It took us forever to catch all those—"

"Nut bunnies."

"Yeah." She laughed.

Infected, he laughed too. He liked her. A whole lot. Was he in trouble here? "I've got a tandem harness if that makes you feel any better."

Her impressive green eyes widened. With interest? Or was it concern? "What's that?"

"I would strap you in with me so we go down together."

"Oh."

He couldn't tell from the look on her face if she thought going down together was a good thing or not. He'd bought the tandem harness for his nieces and nephews when his sisters and their families came back to Stardust for a visit, but mostly, he broke it out at parties for couples to use. This would be the first time he'd ever used it personally.

"Would the tandem harness make riding the zipline easier for you?" he asked.

"Um . . ." She settled one hand on her hip, pressed her lips together, cocked her head as if considering the pros and cons. "Yeah . . . I guess."

He moved to the metal locker that held the zipline equipment, took out the tandem harness, climbed up on the railing, and set about attaching it to the zipline pulleys overhead.

"Are you sure that's going to hold both of us?"

He angled her a glance from underneath his left arm as he reached up to double check the connections. "C'mon. What do you weigh? A hundred pounds tops?"

"A hundred and two," she clarified.

"I'm one-seventy. The zipline is rated for over three hundred pounds. We've got plenty of room for error."

She cringed. "Don't say that."

"What?"

"Error."

He jumped down from the railing, and the platform vibrated beneath his weight.

Breeanne paled.

Ah hell, he'd scared her worse. "You can back out. No dishonor in that."

She looked tempted to take him up on the offer, but smashed her lips into a determined line. "No. You're right. You pushed yourself to do something uncomfortable for me, it's my turn to push outside my comfort zone."

"Only if you're sure."

"We have to be able to trust each other, right? This

is like one of the corporate team-building activities. It'll be good for us and maybe it'll make things easier for you to open up to me."

"Yeah," he said, his voice coming out thick and heavy in the morning air, ready to tell her that she was right, that this was a bad idea. He swallowed the knot in his throat, thought about all the dark secrets he had to tell her. What would she think of him when she learned the truth?

Her chin set solid. She touched him and he almost came undone. "Let's do this."

"Protection first," he said.

"Protect—" Pink stained her cheeks and she cut herself off as he fished two helmets and two pairs of grip gloves from the equipment locker. "Oh. You meant helmets and gloves."

Amused, he straightened, sized her up. "What on earth did you think I was talking about? Condoms?"

"Of course not." She fluttered a hand, grabbed the helmet he extended toward her.

"You're not going to get an STD from sitting in the harness with me," he said. "Just so you know, I get a complete physical every year. I'm not an irresponsible guy."

"Who cares? I couldn't care less about your sex life. You can keep *that* information to yourself," she babbled.

"You said you needed to know all the details of my life—"

"Not details about your sexual health."

Why was he giving her a hard time? He liked her. He . . . hell, he told her that stuff about getting physical because he wanted her to know that he had a clean bill of health, just in case . . .

Just in case what, Blanton?

She'd set up smart ground rules for their working relationship and he promised not to violate them. *Behave yourself.* He was determined to behave himself.

She raised her arms to snap the chinstrap in place, and despite his best intentions to behave he watched her breasts rise up with the movement, spotted the tight bead of her nipples through her shirt, aha. He wasn't the only one feeling the heat.

He bit down on the tip of his tongue to keep from grinning, and he quickly turned away. He reached for the tandem harness, strapped himself in, and walked to the edge of the platform. Leaning back in the harness, he motioned for her to join him.

She stepped closer, bringing her sweet scent with her, her little butt wriggling around in front of him, and causing him to realize just how big of a mistake this tandem idea was.

You started it, bucko.

"Okay." She spread her arms. "Lash me in."

"C'mere," he said.

She sidled closer, purposefully keeping her eyes on the sky, looking neither down nor behind her.

He slipped his hands around her waist, and his fingers almost touched. What a tiny thing she was! He secured her into the smaller harness in front of him, only the leather strap and their clothing came between their bodies.

Rowdy tried to ignore the way his pulse kicked, pretended his body did not harden.

Christ, this was pathetic. When had he lost all self-control? It had been too damn long since he'd had sex and that was all there was to it.

"You ready?" he asked.

"I think so," she squeaked. "I know you won't let any harm come to me." Her body was tense, and she held the straps in a death grip.

Her earnest trust snatched him up by the short hairs. She was terrified, but she believed in him enough to turn her life over to him. That took guts. Her courage turned him on.

It also made him jealous.

Yep. Jealous. He couldn't remember the last time he'd been as excited as she was now. When had he stopped having fun? For sure not since New Year's Eve, but if he was honest with himself, it had been a long time since he'd done something that thrilled him as much as this was clearly thrilling her.

Well, except for kissing her. That had certainly been exhilarating.

Thinking about it made him want to kiss her again. Nope. Nope. Not going there. He promised and he was a man of his word.

Generally.

For the most part.

"Now!" she urged. "Do it now! If we wait any longer, I'm going to chicken out."

"Okay." He took her at her word, and launched them off the platform.

A high-pitched squeal spilled from her mouth as they barreled down the zipline, skimming above the treetops. The zipline made a whizzing sound. The air blasted over their faces. He could feel her body shaking.

He leaned forward, pressed his mouth against her ear. "How we doing?"

"*Awesommme.*"

Her giddy laughter affected him like champagne bubbles, making his head fizzy and his heart light. Her joy was his joy. Seeing her like this made him ache to show her all manner of things. He wanted to get her off that bench and into the game of life.

Yeah, sure. Total honesty? *He* needed to get back in the game himself. Was that the real reason that he was pushing her? It was easier than pushing himself?

With Breeanne's unbridled glee ringing in his ears, and humming through every cell of his body, things changed. Already, he felt transformed. Reformed. A new man.

He'd thought he was giving her the experience of her life, but the joke was on him. All he could think about was how incredible it felt to be plastered against her tender little tush, her happy noises turning him inside out.

Stardust Lake lay dead ahead. Aw. The ride was almost over. Disappointment tugged at him. Finished way too soon.

They landed with a soft thud, safe on the much lower second platform at his fence line, mere yards from the lake.

Breeanne unlatched the harness and spun around to face him. He was still standing on the edge of the platform, struck anew by her overwhelming exuberance. Her green eyes lit with a grateful fire, and a huge grin pulled her lips upward to her ears.

"Omigosh, omigosh that was amazing! Thank you! Thank for that!"

"No biggie." He shrugged because he didn't want her to see exactly how much taking the ride with her decimated him.

"What do you mean? It was huge. This is the most exciting thing I've ever done in my life. I can't begin to tell you how grateful I am." She was dancing around, spinning like a crazed ballerina.

The next thing he knew she flung her arms around his neck and plastered a kiss on his cheek.

He wasn't braced for the sudden impact, or the feel of her lips branding his skin. Caught off guard, and knocked off balance, Rowdy tumbled off the back of the platform.

Taking Breeanne down with him.

Breeanne lay on top of Rowdy, knees straddling his waist. His palms were splayed against her spine, his back pressed flat into the dirt. She'd broken her ground rule, and he'd broken her fall.

This was all so new to her.

Her family had always protected her. Kept her safe in the cocoon of their love. Discouraged her from taking risks for fear that it would harm her health. She understood that they meant well, but playing it safe had impacted her growth.

And she hadn't fully realized to what extent until now.

For the first time in her life, she felt completely alive. Wild. Adventuresome. Fully engaged in the moment of freefall.

She was happy.

The adrenaline rush was addictive and she wanted more. Yes, there had been a moment of terror when Rowdy first launched them off the platform, and her heart leapfrogged into her throat. But then she felt his arms go around her, and every ounce of fear fell away, and she'd simply relaxed, knowing that he had her back.

The experience was a watershed event. From now on, she would forever gauge her life between the pre-zipline Breeanne, and the post-zipline Breeanne. For years to come, she would recall this as the moment when the switch was flipped and she finally stopped being afraid.

And she had Rowdy to thank for it.

She peered down at him. Saw nothing but miles of big strong man. Smelled nothing but manly scent. Heard nothing but the harsh sound of their comingled motley breathing. Tasted nothing but the salt of his skin on her lips. Felt nothing but his body heat between her thighs.

Briefly, he met her stare, closed his eyes, inhaled so sharply his chest pushed her body upward, and then he opened his eyes, he looked dazed and confused. From the fall? Or was it because he had no idea what to do about her?

On that score they were even. She had no idea what to do about him either.

"You okay?" they asked simultaneously.

"I'm good," she said.

"No broken bones?" he asked.

She raised her eyebrow, tucked her bottom lip up over her top lip. "How is your shoulder?"

He rotated his left shoulder, winced.

Concerned, she placed a hand to her throat, felt her pulse spike the same way it had while they were speeding down the zipline. "You've hurt it."

"No more so than usual. It always aches."

"Are you sure?"

"Pretty much."

"Maybe we should take you to a doctor."

"I'm fine."

"It's all my fault." She was the one who'd thrown herself into his arms, and she'd done it without any consideration for the consequences. She hadn't meant to kiss him, not even on the cheek. It just sort of happened. She'd just been overwhelmed and overjoyed and overheated and . . .

"These things happen," he said. "Don't beat yourself up."

"Not to me."

"What? Falling off zipline platforms?"

Ending up on top of a sexy baseball player she'd had a crush on since she was twelve. But she wasn't about to tell him that. "Um, yeah."

"With every wild adventure comes the inevitable fall," he said.

It wouldn't have happened if she hadn't jumped into his arms. What had she been thinking? That was just it, wasn't it? She hadn't been thinking. The thrill of the zipline had stolen every scrap of her common sense. Filled with glee, she'd simply reacted.

For heaven's sakes, why was she still straddling him? She should get up. ASAP.

But his hands remained at her back, holding her in place as if he didn't want her to get up either.

A helpless smile spread over her face, she tried to fight it off, failed.

He shook his head, but an answering smile brought a lazy sheen to his eyes. She grabbed hold of that smile, tucked it in her breast pocket, and held it close to her heart. What a nice memory to pull out by the fire when she was eighty sitting in her rocking chair, telling stories to her teenage great-granddaughters. "Did I ever tell you girls about the time I straddled the best lefty pitcher in baseball?"

With her luck, one of those imaginary great-granddaughters would be unimpressed and say something snarky like, "If you were such a badass, Granny, why didn't you jump his bones?" That is if teenagers even said things like that in fifty-five years.

Why not indeed?

The denim of his jeans scratched her bare shins, his T-shirt, adorned with a Dallas Gunslingers logo of two pistols with their barrels crossed, stretched over the hard planes of his chest.

And his scent!

His natural aroma smashed into her like a steam-roller, tripping her up, making her forget everything smart and rational. Someone ought to bottle the fragrance and name it Womb Wrecker. Oh yeah, she was in so much freaking trouble.

"Breeanne," he said in deep voice heavily laced with testosterone. "I've got something to tell you."

Her pulse gave up any attempts at behaving, and took off like a Triple Crown contender at the Belmont Stakes. What was he going to say?

"Yes?" she whispered.

Peering into her eyes, he stopped breathing. A few minutes ago when he'd strapped her into the zipline, she thought about how incredibly sexy he looked, so cocky and sure of himself.

While he was still incredibly sexy—hey, maybe even more so since he was trapped between her thighs—the self-assurance had disappeared and he looked like a man who'd stumbled into a situation he didn't know how to get out of.

Oh crap, she found his vulnerability even more arresting than his cockiness.

"What is it?" she prodded, almost afraid to ask.

"Um . . . I think you might have ripped the seat out of your pants."

CHAPTER 10

Progress always involves risks.
You can't steal second base and keep your foot on first.

—FREDERICK B. WILCOX

Heart still racing enjoyably from physical contact with Rowdy's hard body, Breeanne went home to change clothes. After that, she headed over to Timeless Treasures to see how Suki was managing with the bookstore.

Her parents were busy helping customers, and they didn't have time for more than a wave and a quick hello. For that, Breeanne was grateful. She fretted that they'd take one look at her and instantly know that she'd been up to something.

Callie lazed on the second story balcony railing, staring down at the floor below, tail swishing, pretending she was a lioness on the Serengeti, and shoppers in the store her unsuspecting prey.

Breeanne found Suki going through a stack of used paperbacks someone had just brought in. Her younger sister looked as fashionable as ever in a super-short purple and black houndstooth designer skirt, a silky silver top, and silver Roman sandals laced up to her knees.

"Hey," Suki said. "It stinks like old paper and ink and stuffy libraries up here."

Breeanne inhaled deeply. "Isn't it the best smell in the world?"

Her sister wrinkled her nose. "I feel like I'm being punished for a crime I didn't commit."

"Don't worry. I'll be back after I finish writing Rowdy's book."

"In six months." Suki pouted.

"Don't forget, you'll be getting my cut of the bookstore's profits. Extra money."

Suki folded her arms over her chest. "Yeah, for extra work that I don't like."

"Money is money."

"What are you doing here? Shouldn't you be off becoming a famous author? Or didja just drop by to gloat?"

"Rowdy and I knocked off early today." She still couldn't believe she could use his name in conjunction with herself. *Rowdy and I.* As if they were a couple.

Suki narrowed her eyes. "Something's different about you."

Her stomach leaped. "Nothing's different."

"Yeah there is. You look . . ." Suki tilted her head, pressed an index finger into the dimple on her right cheek. "Shiny."

Um, that could be because she felt shiny—shiny and new and full of energy. "Nope. Same old me."

Suki stepped closer, sniffed. "You smell like sunshine and pine trees. What have you been up to?"

Thump. Thump. She could hear her heart in her ears. She was dying to tell someone about her zipline experience, someone who wouldn't have a conniption about it like her parents or Jodi.

"Nothing."

"Oh you liar." Suki leaned over and plucked something from Breeanne's hair, and held it out for her to see. A blade of grass.

Breeanne ran a hand through her hair, dislodged two more blades of grass on the floor. She bent, picked up the grass, along with the grass blade squeezed between Suki's fingers, deposited them in the wastebasket, and then dusted her palms together.

"My mind is drawing conclusions," Suki said. "And if it's what I think it is, I approve."

Breeanne lowered her voice "Can you keep a secret?"

"What is it?" Suki held up a stop-sign hand. "Wait. No. Don't tell me. I'm lousy at keeping secrets."

"You're right. I don't know what I was thinking." Breeanne clamped her lips together.

"Now you've gotta tell me." Suki plucked at Breeanne's sleeve. "I'll keep your secret, I swear. What is it? Did you finally have sex? Who is he?"

"I didn't have sex."

"OMG, is it Rowdy? You had sex with Rowdy?"

"I didn't have sex!" she said, louder than she intended, and immediately clamped a palm over her mouth.

"Well pooh. What other big secret could *you* possibly have?" Suki said "you" as if nothing significant could ever happen to a dullard like Breeanne.

"You can be annoying sometimes," Breeanne said. "You do know that."

"I apologize. That was bitchy. I'm just jealous because you were outside and I'm stuck in here." Suki pressed her palms together in mock prayer. "Please tell me your secret, please, please, please."

Breeanne pleated the ends of the scarf she still wore

tied around her neck. Why had she started this? "You can't tell anyone, Suki."

"Pinky swear." Suki stuck out her pinky.

Breeanne latched her little finger with her sister's and stared her in the eyes. "Swear it."

"I vow to keep your secret, no matter what. Even if keeping it means putting someone's life in peril. Even if I'm kidnapped and tortured relentlessly. Even if—"

"Rowdy took me ziplining."

"What!" Suki squealed and grabbed her arm.

"Shh." Breeanne pressed an index finger to Suki's lips. "Mom and Dad will hear you. If they find out, they'll think Rowdy is a bad influence and pressure me to quit the job."

"He *is* a bad influence," Suki whispered. "But in a good way."

"I think so too." Breeanne grinned.

"That's awesome, sis." Suki hugged her. "I'm so happy for you."

Breeanne cast a glance over her shoulder, making sure they were alone. "There's something else."

"This is the most interesting you've ever been," Suki said. "I love it. What's the scoop?"

She almost told her sister that Rowdy kissed her, but in the end, she thought better of it. That secret might be too hard for her sister to keep. "This cheetah scarf feels soft to Rowdy too."

"No kidding?" Suki screwed her face up the way she did when trying to work a Sudoku puzzle. "What do you think it means?"

"I don't know. That's why I'm asking you."

"What was that saying written on the box the scarf came in?"

" 'Two pieces split apart, flung separate and broken, but longing for reunion; one soft touch identifies the other, and they are at last made whole,'" Breeanne quoted.

Suki scratched her head. "Maybe it means that Rowdy is your soul mate?"

"What?" At the notion, goose bumps spread up over Breeanne's body. "No. It's just a silly saying carved into a box."

"The hope chest was just a saying too, but then you wished for a boost in your writing career and *voilà*." Suki did a tap dance shuffle complete with jazz hands. "Your wish was granted."

"Coincidence."

"Is it? Rowdy *could* be your soul mate. Your one and only. The scarf feels soft to the two of you, and no one else." Suki clapped her hands softly. "This is so exciting!"

"He *can't* be my soul mate."

"Why not?"

"Because Rowdy is all wrong for me."

"Not according to the scarf."

"Stop saying that." Breeanne shook her head vigorously to clear it of romantic nonsense. There was no such thing as wish-granting trunks and soul-mate-locating scarves. "I don't even know that I believe in soul mates."

"What about Mom and Dad? You don't think they were destined?"

Floorboards creaked beneath soft footsteps. They weren't alone in the bookstore.

Was it Mom? Alarmed, Breeanne glanced toward the stairs.

On the landing stood the redhead who'd interviewed with Rowdy. The same red-haired woman who had made the wisecrack about Breeanne being good at blow jobs.

Breeanne's cheeks flooded hot. "May I help you?"

"Hi." The redhead wriggled her fingers, managing to look both adorable and contrite with a tentative smile. "Are you the one who posted the ad looking for a roommate?"

"I am."

The redhead's name turned out to be named Stephanie Jensen and she'd just gotten her master's degree in journalism from the University of North Texas. She'd also self-published, under a pseudonym, an erotic novel that sold like hotcakes. She admitted to Breeanne that the suddenness of her success had taken her aback. She wanted to be a serious journalist, not a novelist.

Breeanne couldn't help feeling a stab of jealousy. Her own efforts at self-publishing had been abysmal, but then she reminded herself she'd gotten the job working for Rowdy and the other woman had lost out.

"I do apologize for being catty to you the day we met," Stephanie said. "That was tacky."

Breeanne hated not getting along with people, so she smiled, happy to let go of a grudge. "Apology accepted."

"I have no excuse for my bad behavior other than I was jealous," Stephanie admitted.

"Of me?" Breeanne pressed a palm against her chest. "Whatever for?"

"Of the way Rowdy looks at you. Like you're so delicious he could eat you up with a long-handled spoon and lick his lips afterward to make sure he sucked up every drop." The expression on the redhead's face said she couldn't fathom why that was the case. "You're so lucky to have him as your boyfriend."

Oh yeah, Breeanne had forgotten about that boyfriend thing. "He's not my boyfriend. He just told you guys that because he was feeling overwhelmed."

Stephanie waggled a finger. "You're not fooling me. I saw how he kissed you. Besides, Rowdy Blanton has never been overwhelmed a day in his life. That man is a force of nature."

True enough. Breeanne stuck her hands deep in the pockets of her skirt.

"Be proud you landed him, sugar," Stephanie said. "But don't get your hopes up. He's not the marrying kind."

Breeanne was well aware of that.

"So . . ." Stephanie lifted her shoulders to her ears, and then let them drop in a cutesy shrug. "There's a two-bedroom for rent over on Peach Street. We could go take a look at it if you want."

Did she? It had been a week since she'd taken out the ad, and so far no one else had applied. She could always ask Suki to room with her, of course, but she wanted to do this on her own, without any family support. That was sort of the whole idea of moving out.

The zipline adventure put things into perspective. Why not take a chance? It was past time to start her life in earnest. More importantly, she couldn't do that as long as she was living with her parents. Cut the apron strings. Strike out on her own. Leave the safety of the nest and fly. All the coming-of-age clichés her peers accomplished years ago.

What was the worst that could happen? If she and Stephanie didn't get along, one of them could always move out.

"I'm game if you are," Breeanne said.

"Let's do this," Stephanie said, and stuck out a palm.

Breeanne and Stephanie signed a six-month lease for the house on Peach Street. They would be able to move in on Saturday. First and last month's rent were due on signing. Breeanne didn't have enough in her bank account to cover the expense, but knowing she would soon have advance money from the book, she put it on her credit card, and planned to pay it off as soon as the check came in.

On Tuesday, she had a detailed telephone conversation with the book editor at Jackdaw, who suggested starting the book with Rowdy walking off the Gunslingers in protest over Price's firing, digress to Rowdy's childhood and formative years in baseball, and then conclude the book with the attack that ended his career. They set up delivery deadlines for the book. An outline and first chapter were due at the end of June.

On Wednesday, Jackdaw put out an official press release announcing that they'd acquitted the rights to Rowdy's autobiography. Since she was a ghostwriter, her name wasn't mentioned, but she didn't mind. She was doing it for the work and the money, not the glory.

They began the interview in earnest. As the editor suggested, Breeanne started by asking Rowdy about his relationship with Price Richards and the reasons he'd walked out on the Gunslingers. Rowdy's dislike for Dugan Potts was palpable. Every time the general manager's name was mentioned, a dark expression overtook his handsome face. He must really dislike the guy, since Rowdy was normally such an upbeat person.

When she pressed him for more details on his feelings regarding Potts, he would give her a long, unreadable look, as if trying to decide when to break some terrible news, and say, "We'll get to that in time."

Even though the look unsettled her, she let it go. There was plenty of other stuff to talk about until he was ready to confide in her.

Because Rowdy found it hard to sit still, she interviewed him in the gym while he worked off nervous energy, or they took Nolan Ryan for a walk around the property. Not wanting to miss a thing, Breeanne used a recorder to capture his every word, even as she also took notes.

On Thursday, she turned the conversation to his childhood, but every time she brought it up, he'd switch the subject, or make a joke, or give her a look that flustered her so completely she lost her train of thought. Finally, frustrated with the way he kept dodging her questions, she asked him point-blank how he felt when he learned of his father's devastating diagnosis.

"I'm hungry," he said. "You hungry? How about I make my famous spaghetti carbonara with caprese salad and garlic toast?"

"We're going to have to talk about this, Rowdy," she said gently.

"I know, but I can't think when I'm hungry. How are your knife skills?"

"What?"

"Can you mince, dice, slice?"

"I'm woefully lacking in the kitchen."

"C'mon," he said. "Give it a shot."

It wasn't that she didn't want to cook with him, but the thought of working side by side with him in the kitchen made her hormones do things they shouldn't be doing.

Feeling shy, she shook her head.

"Ah, Breezy, you gonna leave me hangin'?"

"I'd just be in the way."

He crooked a finger at her. "Let me be the judge of that."

She tried to think of a way out of it, but he took her hand and tugged her toward the kitchen.

"Rowdy . . ."

"Breeanne . . ." He grinned, and looked so disarmingly handsome that it took hold of her feminine parts and shook them. Hard.

"This isn't . . . I'm not . . ."

He canted his head and studied her. "What?"

"I tell you what," she bargained. "I'll help you cook if you'll stop avoiding my questions about your childhood."

He paused. "All right, but we cook first, talk later."

She bobbed her head, more to reassure herself that she could stand beside him in the confines of the kitchen, and not wig out with lust if they accidentally bumped elbows, than to convince him.

Rowdy set her to chopping the garlic and pancetta while he put the pasta on to boil, and then turned to make the sauce. She sliced a sidelong glance at him standing at the stove in faded jeans and a blue T-shirt, in a state-of-the-art masculine kitchen, with artful lighting that made all the chrome shine like diamonds. He looked like an Adonis.

"It's unfair," she muttered under her breath. "You're so damn perfect. How is a woman supposed to defend herself against such unstoppable charm?"

"Huh?" He swung his head around, clipped her gaze with his. A tuft of hair stuck up at the back of his head, but instead of detracting from his attractiveness, that recalcitrant cowlick made him all the more adorable.

She didn't stand a chance. She'd been a goner from the moment he first winked at her.

He smiled at her, and the way he was turned caused the track lighting over the stove to silver his blue eyes and highlight his long dark lashes. She could so fall in love with him.

Then she yanked her gaze away and went back to cutting precise cubes of pancetta. Every single woman in Texas—and a few married ones too—probably thought that whenever they looked at him, so it wasn't as if Breeanne was special. Not in that regard. Not when . . .

Oh to hell with it.

She shifted her eyes back to him and he was still staring at her, so she smiled like this was something usual, like it was okay, like they belonged together, and he grinned as if he was in on the joke. She wanted to laugh at herself, but it would hurt too damn much, so she just scooted out of the way when he reached around her for the olive oil.

Nolan Ryan joined them in the kitchen, sitting on the floor watching to see if anything got dropped. Breeanne couldn't resist sneaking the bloodhound bits of pancetta.

"I saw that," Rowdy teased.

"I just gave him a little."

"You'll spoil him."

"He deserves it."

"No wonder he's madly in love with you." Rowdy's eyes met hers.

Looking into those flame-blue irises roused scary desires. His scent, combined with the delicious fragrance of the food, smelled sweet. The shiny chrome appliances gleamed brighter than ever. Her mouth had already started watering for so much more than the pasta dish he plated. From start to finish, the entire meal took only twenty-five minutes to prepare.

Standing there in the kitchen, doing domestic things with Rowdy Blanton, made her want to laugh at the sheer romance of it all.

Calm down.

Everything she was feeling could be traced back to one source.

Sex.

Or the lack thereof. She'd never had sex. She wanted sex. And he was sex personified.

Whenever she was around him, she couldn't keep from thinking about sex. One look from this man and boom! She was thinking shockingly lusty thoughts. Like what would he do if she were to reach out and touch his zipper? Would he drop those plates piled high with spaghetti carbonara? Would he groan, lift her up on the kitchen countertop, and have his way with her?

Oh yum!

Fantasies were fine. She could dream about him all she wanted. But she couldn't cross that line no matter how much she wanted to do so. Because he had the power to move her in ways far beyond sex, and that was the truly scary part.

He said something, but she didn't hear what it was because she was busy imagining him naked.

"Breeanne?"

"Uh-huh?"

"Are you ready to eat?"

You bet she was, but not just for food. "Yes."

He carried the plates to the dining room table and they sat down across from each other. Thrown by the intimacy of the situation, she dug into her food, but avoided meeting his eyes.

"Oh my gosh." She moaned helplessly at the first bite. "This is so delicious."

"Told you." He puffed out his chest, full of pride. "Carbonara is my specialty."

"Forget baseball. You could be a professional chef."

"Nah," he said. "I cook to relax. If I had to cook for a living I wouldn't enjoy it anymore."

"If I were on death row"—she waved her fork—"I would request this as my last meal. Seriously."

He laughed at that, and she thrilled knowing she had made him laugh. "Why, thank you for the compliment, Breezy."

Breezy.

No matter how much she protested, she couldn't get him to stop calling her Breezy. So she'd given up and decided to roll with it. Now, whenever he called her by the special nickname, the "z" sound humming softly off his lips, sparking a secret buzzing sound that vibrated through the cells of her body, tickling her insides in a wholly erotic way.

"Did your mother teach you how to cook?" she asked.

"Nah. Mom is a miserable cook. It was Uncle Mick. He told me women love a man who can cook." He took off on a tale about his bachelor uncle and the man's multitudinous girlfriends.

"I really don't need to know about your uncle's sexual adventures," she said. "Although I can see how living with him impacted your view of the world. What I really want to hear about is how your family life changed after your father's diagnosis."

The smiled dropped off his face. "You're going to keep harping on this until I talk about it."

She lifted a shoulder to show she didn't mean to cause him pain, but that this was important for the book. "I'm trying to get under your skin. To see the world through your eyes so I can write authentically about you."

"You want to understand me?" His eyes narrowed.

She notched her chin to staunch the wobble in her knees. "I *have* to understand you to write about you."

"You can't understand me."

"Why is that, because you're the poor little misunderstood rich playboy? Boo-hoo." Okay so he'd pissed her off. Which was something new. She wasn't accustomed to losing her temper, but he had a knack for pushing her buttons.

His blue eyes flashed like cold steel. He was upset with her.

It was hard to sit still under the heat of his glare. Instinctively, she wanted to apologize, backtrack, smooth things over, but she had nothing to apologize for. She waited a heartbeat, then two, three, waiting for the impulse to pass before she spoke.

"No," he said. "You can't understand me because I don't understand myself."

In that moment he sounded so completely vulnerable that her frustration evaporated. "What do you mean?"

"Can't we find a way to tell my story without digging up the past?"

"No. Not really. The readers want to know who you are. In order to do that you've got to give them a glimpse into the events that made the man."

He pushed his plate way, his meal half eaten.

"I don't get it. If you didn't want to talk about the past, why did you agree to write your autobiography?" she asked.

"I'm writing the book because I want to tell the world about the truth about Dugan Potts."

"Which is?"

Rowdy's jaw jutted out. He looked so different from the teasing, fun-loving, adventuresome man she'd come to know. How much of that persona was real? Chill bumps raced up her arms as she realized she really didn't know him at all.

"You're right," he said. "This whole mess did start in my childhood."

"What mess?"

He looked haunted. "My life."

She gulped, not knowing what to say. She had not expected that interviewing him was going to be the most difficult part of the job.

"All right. You win," he said. "Tomorrow we'll pack a picnic lunch and go on a field trip."

"Where to?"

"The beginning. You want to know where I came from? You need to see it for yourself."

CHAPTER 11

A baseball game is simply a nervous breakdown
divided into nine innings.

—EARL WILSON

At ten a.m. on Friday morning, they stood in front of a run-down house on the seediest block in the seamiest neighborhood of Stardust. Breeanne felt strangely exposed in a high-necked powder blue tank top, white Bermuda shorts, and sandals, and wished she'd worn something more substantial.

Like body armor.

A shiver sliced through her belly. No wonder Rowdy had been reluctant to talk about his childhood.

"There it is." He folded his arms over his chest. "Home sweet home."

Breeanne stared at the dilapidated shack, windows boarded, roof sagging, porch caved in. A large red ant mound was centered in a front yard bald of grass, and busy insects formed a streaming trail from their bed to a doughnut box lying open in the gutter. In the side yard, a tire cracked with age hung suspended from a dead mimosa by a frayed yellow rope. Had Rowdy once played on that tire swing?

She turned on the digital voice recorder clipped to her waistband. "This is where you grew up?"

"It didn't look this bad back then." He picked up a rock, spun it with an underhanded pitch. The stone skipped over the bare patch of ground, hopped four times, then hit the droopy chain link fence with a solid *ping*. "At least I don't think it did."

A locomotive approaching the train crossing just beyond the house, blasted its horn. Breeanne covered her ears. After a while, the engine stopped honking, but it remained impossible to hold a conversation above the sound of the boxcars clacking across the rails.

Rowdy lifted his mouth in a sad half smile that said both nothing and everything. The sound of the train had been his childhood lullaby.

She looked into his face and felt the same zap of recognition she'd felt the first day on Irene Henderson's front lawn. As if a curtain had parted, and they could see straight into each other, deeper than anyone had ever looked at either of them before. He was not just a good-time Charlie jock. She was not just a mousy wallflower, bookseller, writer-wannabe. Labels. Those were simply labels that didn't begin to describe who they were or what they felt.

In his eyes she saw the reflection of everything he'd suffered. But more than that, she saw her own reflection, and knew that he could see the empathy of her own suffering in her eyes as clearly as she could see his. They passed it back and forth, this shared knowledge of each other. This simple but powerful understanding of who they were at their core.

He made her think of soulful kisses and tangled sheets and her bare legs wrapped around his naked back, and everything seemed obvious. It was a funny thing, hot desire. If it was one-sided it was a handicap. If it was a two-way street, it was a connection.

The connection was there, but she was leery of the inevitable ending. How many times had she shied from beginning because she was scared of the finale?

Then his smile changed, his mouth going down on one corner so it was only half of a smile—a sardonic, aren't-you-sorry-you-asked smile.

But no, no, she wasn't sorry. She felt privileged to be here.

Several minutes passed, marked by the exchange of glances and the long rumbling of the train. Finally, as the sound of the caboose raced away, she touched his forearm, and his smile brightened back to normal.

He winked.

The melancholy mood and their deeper bonding vanished as if she'd imagined it, his glib curtain dropping firmly back into place. The skin on this particular onion was not an easy peel, and if she wasn't careful, he was going to make her cry.

"Wanna see where we used to play?" he asked.

Did she? Images of dirty syringes and used condoms and ugly graffiti popped into her head. The poverty of his childhood piloted twin beads of sweat down her sides in a long, slow slide. She ironed her hands over her tank top, blotting up the moisture.

"You wanted me to open up. Here it is. Me opening up." He spread his arms wide. "You in?"

"Yes," she said, bracing herself for dark things she'd seen only on TV, generally over the top of a pillow propped on cringing knees so she could quickly hide her eyes. "Show me."

"Let's stop by the SUV first, and get the picnic basket."

"It's not lunchtime."

"It will be."

"Are we staying that long?"

"Now that we're here, yeah. Might as well make a day of it."

She surveyed the dreary surroundings, and any appetite she might have had vanished. Ugh. Was he trying to get back at her for dragging him out here in the first place?

But his tone was mild, his face soft. No resentment. How had he come out of this environment without a boulder on his shoulder?

"Not the ideal picnic spot," she said.

"Do you trust me?"

"If I didn't, I wouldn't be here."

He held out his palm. "Give up the recorder. All work and no play makes Breeanne a dull girl."

"I have a deadline."

"There's plenty of time."

"I might miss something."

"Yes, you'll miss the experience of being in the moment because you'll be taking notes and thinking too much. You think too much, Breezy."

He had a point. She did tend to overthink things.

"I'm your boss, right?" he said. "I declare you off the clock."

"What if you say something riveting?" she asked, her fingers curling around the recorder, reluctant to turn loose of the advantage. Why was it so hard for her to put the recorder into his upturned palm?

"I promise I won't." There it was again. That camera-ready smile he whipped out at will and flashed like a newly minted police officer flashing his badge. She liked the half smile better. It was more honest.

"You might without knowing it."

"Have I ever lied to you?"

"How would I know?"

"Solid point." Rowdy chuckled, the sound echoing strangely in the mirthless surroundings. When he lived here, he must have been the star of the neighborhood, brightening up the dreary blight.

"All right then." She let go of the recorder.

The smile turned into a lopsided, you're-a-good-sport grin that sent her lungs reeling, churning, stirring up air, but not really moving oxygen.

He sprinted to the Escalade on long, sexy legs wrapped in faded distressed Levi's and she thought, *I want.*

Simple as that. *I want.* Desired. Lusted. Craved *him.*

He came back with the picnic basket and a thick Santa Fe print blanket.

"This way," he said, surprising and delighting her by taking her hand and interlacing his fingers through hers. It felt nice.

Very nice.

Too nice.

He guided her around the back of the vacant house and over tracks still warm from the heat of the train.

She wrinkled her nose against the scent of oil and tar. "What's that odor?"

"Creosote."

"What's that?"

"A wood preservative railroad ties are soaked in."

"Stinky."

Rowdy inhaled deeply. "I like the smell."

"Are you kidding me?"

"I know it sounds strange, but growing up here we didn't have air-conditioning."

"In Texas? That must have been brutal in the summer."

"Actually, you get kinda used to it. But one year it was over a hundred degrees for three weeks straight, even at night. We kids would lie awake sweating in our underwear, no covers on, windows and doors thrown open, ceiling fans running full tilt. The smell of creosote got into everything—our hair, our clothes, our skin, our food."

"You'd think that would make you *hate* the smell."

Still holding on to her hand, he paused and leaned his head back and took another deep breath. "Yep, smells like home."

The man knew how to make lemonade from lemon seeds. She'd give him that. Breeanne squeezed his hand.

"Don't feel sorry for me," he said. "This is just where I came from, not who I am."

It was the most profound thing she'd ever heard him say. Sadness balled up in her throat and she wished like hell she could wave a magic wand and make his childhood pain disappear.

While you're waving it, why not wave the wand for yourself too? While she'd been well loved, her childhood hadn't been a walk in the park.

He shook his head, laughed, and chucked her playfully under the chin. "Don't look so serious, Breezy. I turned out okay."

"It could have . . . You could . . . Things could have gone down such a different path," she said.

"But they didn't." He led her over the last train track, the blanket-covered picnic basket swinging from his other arm. Ahead of them lay a pine forest lining the railway. As they approached, sunshine filtered through the branches, casting his face in dappled light.

"Where *are* we going?"

He dropped her hand, turned, and started walking backward into the pines, crooking a come-with-me finger. Birds twittered overhead. A brown squirrel scolded them from a tree limb. The damp ground, littered with pine needles, felt spongy beneath her feet.

Her writer's imagination went wild, and she pictured this place in the dark filled with the sharp call of whippoorwills and the shivery scream of screech owls. So easy to believe in those East Texas swamp stories of ghosts and goblins and things that went bump in the forest at night.

But the sun was high in the sky. Broad daylight.

She paused.

Rowdy drew farther into the copse of trees, almost disappearing from her view. "Breezy," he coaxed her in a provocative singsong. "Come along with me."

Lured by his Pied Piper voice, she followed.

The path narrowed and the deeper they went, the thicker the trees grew, squeezing too close, strangling each other for sunlight. While she'd grown up in the piney woods, she'd spent so much time in bed recuperating from surgeries, and her parents had been cautious and protective. She had not played in the woods much. And definitely not unsupervised.

"You used to play here?" she asked.

"When me and my friends weren't in a vacant lot playing baseball."

She pushed aside a bushy frond that sprang back to slap against her calf. "Why do I feel like Little Red Riding Hood?" she joked nervously.

"Are you saying I'm the Big Bad Wolf?" His teeth flashed white.

"It's spooky in here."

"But in a good way."

"Depends on what you mean by good," she mumbled.

"This," he said, parting tree branches in front of him. Sunlight shone on the other side, and he led her into a clearing where a blue pond, the same color as his eyes, shimmered.

An oasis.

A treasured gem buried in the center of a pine thicket. Rabbits and squirrels scampered in the undergrowth. Mockingbirds called. A carpet of colorful wildflowers spread over the ground. The odor of creosote was replaced with the sweet perfume of prairie verbena, scarlet paintbrush, pink buttercups, and lazy daisies. The train noises, the dilapidated shacks were a world away.

Magical. A fairy tale.

"Rowdy." She breathed. "It's beautiful."

"Told you." He settled the picnic basket down, and spread the blanket on the ground.

"Night and day from where we were," she marveled.

"Refuge. A surprising gift from Mother Nature to the people stuck living by the train tracks."

"Nature doesn't care if you're rich or poor," she said.

"As long as man doesn't come along, put a fence around it, and charge admission."

"We're not trespassing?"

"Public land."

He reached his arms behind him, fisted two handfuls of T-shirt, and in one relaxed move, peeled the shirt over his head. There he stood, cock-of-the-walk, the nearly noonday sun of late May flaring a hot glow over his sublimely naked torso, low-slung jeans hugging his lean hips.

"Um . . ." Breeanne gulped. "What are you doing?"

He didn't answer. Just flung her that born-to-sin grin. His thumb flicked loose his belt buckle, and he yanked the belt through the loops of his jeans. It hissed a seductive slithering sound, leather whipping against denim. He toed off his boots, peeled off his socks. Stood the boots, with the socks tucked inside them, near the blanket.

"Rowdy?" Her voice came out shaky.

He winked, slow and easy. Unsnapped his jeans.

Oh Lord! A thousand wicked thoughts of what she'd like to do to and with this man flooded her brain.

"What's happening?" she squeaked.

He looked utterly amused at her shock. Was she that big of a prude? "What do you think is happenin'?"

She noticed he dropped the "g" from "ing" verbs when he was being intentionally provocative. The potent charm of the Southern masculine drawl. Her mouth was so dry she couldn't even lick her lips, much less spit out any more words.

"Why, sweetheart, did you think I brought you here to seduce you? That's so cute. But you gotta get your mind out of the gutter. I'm hot and sweaty and the water's clear and cool. That's all."

Swimming. Oh. She felt a bit let down.

"You set the ground rules for this relationship, and I'm abidin' by them."

Her eyes were glued to his exquisite body. She'd seen him nearly naked before but she hadn't been so stoked by wild thoughts or so completely alone with him. Warwick was always lurking in the background. But now, it was just the two of them.

"I don't want to lose you before we ever really get this book started," he said.

All she heard was *I don't want to lose you.* Everything else he said was white noise.

"You're welcome to join me."

Her lungs burst into flames. She tried to breathe, but the five-alarm fire inside her burned up every lick of oxygen. It was all she could do not to rush over, tug down his zipper, strip the pants from his body, and touch every masculine inch of him.

"Last one in is a rotten egg." He turned his back to her, shucked off his jeans, and dove, buck-naked, into the pond.

The sexiest butt on the planet had just flashed her, and she wanted to pinch it to feel those rock-hard muscles. Which was most likely his intention. The tease!

He broke the surface, treading water, crooking that beguiling finger at her again. "C'mon in. The water's perfect."

"Wh-wh . . ."

"Speechless, huh? From the look on your face, I'm guessin' you've never been skinny-dippin'."

"No . . . no . . . nor am I about to start," she sputtered, scandalized, mortified, dissatisfied, and oh-so-tempted to join him.

"Aw, you gonna leave me hangin' here all alone?" He mocked up a faux-sad face, shook his head, and sent water flying off his wet, dark hair in all directions.

"You got yourself into this . . ." She cinched her arms over her chest, mainly so he couldn't see how her nipples were turning into marbles underneath her camisole.

"Live a little," he coaxed, smooth as the devil. "You know you want to."

Slowly, she shook her head, but she smiled. Why did she smile?

"It's liberatin'. Nothing between your skin and the water." He was messing with her. Assuming she didn't have the stones to take him up on his offer.

"I can get that any time I want in the bathtub."

"It's not the same. This is nature. Free and easy."

"Too free and easy." Gosh, she sounded like an old maid.

"You don't know what you're missin'." He sounded like he felt sorry for her that she'd never had the experience of swimming naked in a pond.

He was right about that. She'd missed out on so much in life.

"Tell you what," he said. "I'll make it easier for you. I'll turn my back, and you tell me when you're in the water."

Did she dare? "How do I know you won't turn back around before I'm ready?"

"I give you my word."

"For what that's worth," she muttered, but her irreverent fingers plucked at the hem of her tank top.

"Here I go." He raised his arms in a gesture of surrender as if a robber had a gun pressed to his back, and he turned around.

"Um . . ." The sensible part of her brain was frantically trying to put on the brakes. "How deep is the water? I can't swim."

"Woman, have you been living under a rock for twenty-five years?"

"Something like that," she whispered.

"I'm on my feet," he said. The water hit him in the middle of his muscled back. "It's not much more than four feet deep. You're safe. I would never let anything happen to you."

His heartfelt promise cinched it. She tugged the hem of her tank top up to her rib cage. Was she really doing this? A thrill chased over her, both scary and exciting.

"You have to get completely naked," he called. "No leaving your underwear on, that's cheating."

"Keep running your mouth," she said, "and you'll talk me right out of it."

"You're comin' in?" he asked, hope in his voice.

"Only if you hush up."

"I'm not saying another word."

Cautiously, she peeked over her shoulder, making sure they were completely alone, except for woodland creatures, before she stripped off her tank top.

So far so good.

She kicked off her loafers, took off her shorts, stood there in her panties and camisole, the wind brushing softly against her legs, the soft grass tickling her bare feet.

"Breeanne? You still there?"

"I thought you were going to be quiet."

"Sorry, forgot. My arms are getting tired."

"You can put them down. No one said you had to put your arms up." She took off her glasses, set them on top of the picnic basket. She was one step closer to bare-naked. *Hang in there, courage.*

"I'm keeping them up so you don't think I'm doing anything suspicious with my hands."

"Well, I wasn't imagining you might have been until you brought it up. Now I can't stop imagining it."

"Are you horrified?"

"I'm having second thoughts." She stripped off her camisole, felt gloriously slutty. "You should have kept your mouth shut."

"Aw, Breezy, don't back out. I take it back. Forget I said anything." He shifted as if to turn around.

She squeaked, scrambled for her clothes, held them up in front of her naked chest.

But he didn't turn around.

She let out a breath. Dropped her clothes.

The sun warmed her chest, put the scars under a spotlight. The older scars silvered with time, the latest one faded light pink at the seams. What was she thinking? He was going to see her scars. She wasn't ready for him to see her scars. She should stop this nonsense and get dressed immediately.

She shivered uncontrollably despite the sun's warmth.

Chicken. You claim you want adventure, but when one falls into your lap, you're ready to run.

Fair enough, but she wasn't ready to handle being naked in a pond with Rowdy Blanton. Not by a long shot.

When would she be ready? When she was twenty-six? Thirty-six? Fifty-six? Never?

Fine. Okay. She would do this. Let him see the scars. Let him see how she'd suffered. Let him see the real her.

What if he found her repulsive?

So what? It wasn't as if she ever had a real shot with him anyway. He was gorgeous, rich, famous, sexy, accomplished, and she was none of those things.

But there was no reason she could not make this memory, and she would forever own bragging rights to skinny-dipping with Rowdy Blanton.

That decided the matter. She stripped off her panties, and waded in.

CHAPTER 12

Players like rules. If they didn't have any rules,
they wouldn't have anything to break.

—LEE WALLS

"I'm in the water," Breeanne said. "You can turn around now."

To keep from scaring her with any sudden moves, Rowdy slowly lowered his arms and turned to face her.

Breeanne stood three feet behind him, the water lapping the tops of her shoulders, a sly smile on her face. He couldn't take his eyes off her.

"What do you think of skinny-dippin'?" he asked.

She closed her eyes for a moment, as if fully absorbing the experience. Or was it because he made her uncomfortable?

Feeling oddly nervous, he prodded, "Well?"

"Hmm. So interesting."

"First impressions?"

"The mud under my feet is kind of squishy. You're right, you don't get that in a bathtub."

He could tell by the way she smiled and swayed that she was curling her toes in the mud, and loving the experience. Christ, why did he have such an overwhelming urge to show her the world?

She giggled and sank lower until the water lapped

at her chin. The ends of her wavy hair soaked up the water, turning from dark blond to light brown. He imagined that those damp strands trailing across his face, and briefly closed his eyes against the idea of her straddling him the way she had when they'd fallen off the zipline platform, this time both of them naked and wet. He had to stop this. He was only making things harder on himself.

"If someone saw us they wouldn't know we were totally naked in here, would they?" she asked.

"Not from looking at us, but the clothes on the bank? Dead giveaway."

"Oh dear!" Her eyes rounded and she put a palm to her mouth. "Should I have hidden our clothes?"

"I'm pretty sure we're totally alone."

"What if kids come by?"

"It's almost noon. Kids are still in school until the first week in June."

"But it is the Friday before Memorial Day, and this neighborhood looks like the sort where kids play hooky. I bet you played hooky when you were a kid."

"Everyone plays hooky."

"I never did."

"Well, *you* didn't. But most people do. Ordinary people play hooky at least once or twice when they're growing up. Your mom never wrote you a note saying you were sick when you weren't so you could stay home for a play day?"

"I wanted to go to school. I hated being sick." She said it strongly, the expression in her eyes fierce. "Faking an illness to get out of school is irresponsible."

He raised his arms again. "I give. Clearly, my experiences were out of the norm, and not the other way around."

"Rowdy," she gasped, and the color drained from her face and her chin went twitchy.

"What is it?"

"Keep your hands and feet to yourself."

She looked so upset that warning buzzers fired off in his brain, loud as firehouse alarms. "What? I didn't touch you."

Her skin turned ghostly. "You didn't just rub your foot against my leg?"

"No."

"*Something* brushed up against my leg. If it wasn't you . . ." She looked like she was about to turn and sprint to the shore, and while he wouldn't be the least bit opposed to the sight of that, he hated that something in the water had freaked her out.

"Easy does it," he soothed. "It's probably just a fish or pond weeds or tree branch."

"Or a water moccasin?" Her voice cracked as it scaled three octaves.

"It's not a water moccasin," he said.

"How do you know?"

"It's okay. My friends and I swam here hundreds of times. We never saw a water moccasin. Water snakes, sure, but not moccasins."

"So there *are* snakes in here." Her voice warbled.

"Not poisonous snakes." At least not that he knew of, but he wasn't going to add that part. She was freaked out enough.

"Omigod, omigod."

"Don't panic." He pressed his palms downward. "It's okay."

"Don't laugh at me."

"I'm not laughing."

"You're smiling."

Hell, he was smiling to keep her calm. "I'm just trying to reassure you."

"Well don't."

He scrubbed a palm over his mouth. "Smile gone."

"I'm losing it."

"It's okay, it's all right. Take a deep breath."

Her shoulders hitched upward, but she couldn't seem to suck in any air.

"Exhale first," he coached. "Then inhale."

She expelled a loud breath, and then inhaled deeply.

"Good girl."

"I'm getting out of here. Please, turn around again."

Even though he didn't want to turn his back on her, he did it anyway. "Don't run," he cautioned. "You could—"

A yelp cut him off short, followed immediately by a loud splash.

Bile and dread spiked cleats up his throat. Rowdy spun toward her, but Breeanne was nowhere in sight.

She'd gone under.

The pond wasn't deep, but she couldn't swim, and in her panic she might forget that the water wasn't over her head. And what caused her to cry out?

What if she *had* been bitten by a water moccasin? Or a sinkhole had formed since the last time he'd been in the pond and she'd fallen in? Or what if she'd gotten tangled in barbwire someone had thrown into the pond and it pulled her under, or—

Screw the worst-case scenarios.

He lunged, diving into the water where she'd been standing just a minute before. His leg crashed into hers. He grabbed her. She floundered, fighting him. Terrified. She was terrified. The poor kid.

Rowdy scooped her in his arms, hugging her

naked body to his chest, and broke the surface of the water.

She was gasping for air, chest heaving, arms thrashing.

He tightened his grip on her, pressed his mouth against her ear. "Shh," he whispered. "It's all right. It's okay. I've got you. Nothing bad can happen to you now."

Her arms slid around his neck. She was trembling like a lost kitten.

Clutching her tightly against him, he carried her to shore. He laid her on the blanket. She curled her knees to her chest, shivering more from fright than cold. He bent to tuck the edges of the blanket around her and that's when he saw the scars.

Looking at the angry lines of her ragged scars tore him to shreds. A hot, messy mixture of anger, fear, and pain flamed through his system.

Who had sliced her up like sushi?

A dozen possible scenarios popped into his head, each worse than the last.

Dammit no. Just no. No fair. This sweet woman did not deserve to have suffered like this. He wanted to lodge a formal complaint against the universe. Foul ball.

He didn't want to stir up her old pain, but he couldn't leave it alone. He had to have an answer.

"Breeanne," he said, putting every ounce of empathy he could wring from his body into the question. "What in God's name happened?"

Breeanne huddled on the blanket, feeling like a fool. "Whatever was in the water brushed against my leg again, and when I tried to run, I slipped in the mud, and fell in. It completely freaked me out when my head went under water, and I thought I was going to drown."

"I'm not talking about that," he said, his voice rough and husky.

Oh. She blinked. Saw his gaze transfixed on her breastbone, and she swallowed past her shame.

He meant the scars.

She pulled the blanket he'd draped over her shoulders more tightly around her, pinching the edges together in front of her chest, and closed her eyes. She drew up her legs, ducked her head, and rested her forehead on her knees.

He was squatting, beside her. One palm pressed to the middle of her spine as he rubbed reassuring circles over her back. "Are you okay?" he murmured.

Nut bunnies. He felt sorry for her. She hated it when people felt sorry for her. She put steel in a don't-you-dare-feel-sorry-for-me tone. "I'm fine."

Using the edge of the blanket, he rubbed her hair with an efficient briskness like he was trying to kindle a fire. The effort told her that he didn't know what else to say or do, so he was trying to make himself useful.

"Any warmer?" he asked when he finished, flopping the edges of the blanket over her head like a hoodie.

She raised her head. His wet dark hair was slicked back off his forehead, those devastating blue eyes hooked on her face that made him so insanely handsome. He was completely naked and she didn't dare look down, but even so, she was acutely aware of his hard-muscled body.

"I'm sorry I flipped out on you."

His casual smile said, *Hey, we all act like doobers once in a while.* "Nothing to be sorry for. I forgot how scary it is to go naked into a pond your first time, and

I never took into consideration that you didn't know how to swim. I shouldn't have pushed."

"It's fine. I wanted to go in."

He kept rubbing her head. It felt too intimate. Too darn good. She stiffened against his touch. Desperate to keep him from finding out how exquisitely awesome his touch made her feel.

"What's wrong?" he asked.

"Mmm, could you put on some clothes, please?" she said, doing her best to keep her eyes to herself.

"What? Oh yeah. Sorry." He stopped rubbing—thank heavens for that—and stood up.

She felt him step away, heard him pick up his clothes, followed by a masculine grunt as he went about wrestling his wet body into dry jeans.

Unable to resist, she peeked over at him, and got a delicious eyeful of well-muscled male bum that made her fingers itch to touch it. Whew-wee.

Stop staring.

But how could she when that amazing butt was there on fleshy fabulous display?

He got his jeans shimmied up and she heard the *zzz* of his zipper hissing closed, and she barely managed to whip her head around before he returned to crouch beside her once more, a bottle of water in his hand.

"The color is coming back into your face."

"I really am fine. You don't have to worry about me."

He didn't touch her, but he just kept sitting there.

Ack! What did he want from her?

"Have some water," he said, unscrewing the cap and passing the bottle to her.

Happy to have something to do besides stare at him, she reached a hand from the blanket, lifted the bottle to drink.

His eyes followed her movements, hung on her lips

as she took a sip. The wetness sliding down her throat made her realize just how thirsty she was. She downed half of it, and passed the bottle to him. His big hand folded around it, and he tilted back his head.

She stared at him in the same way he'd stared at her, watching his lips close over the rim, right where her mouth had just been. Her hormones triggered, shooting urgent let's-have-sex messages through every feminine cell in her body.

He swallowed, his Adam's apple rising and falling as he swallowed. Transfixed, she watched him polish off the water and crush the plastic bottle in his hand, his lips glistening with moisture.

Rowdy studied her as she studied him, his pupils darkening erotically, his gaze dropping back to her chest, now securely covered by the blanket, but his vision seemed X-ray and X-rated. He knew what she looked like naked.

"You don't have to tell me about the scars," he said softly. "It's none of my business."

"It's only fair," she said. "I badgered you to talk about your childhood."

He left his shoulders in a half shrug. "It's what I hired you to do."

"The scars aren't a secret or anything," she said. "Everyone knows."

"You've had a lot of surgeries," he guessed.

"I've had ten surgeries in all. For a congenital heart condition, but I'm finally done." She smiled. "Got a clean bill of health. I'm off all my meds but one, and my doctor thinks I can soon wean off that one too."

He sank down beside her, bent his legs, and dropped his hands to his knees. "You've been through a lot."

She waved in the direction of the house he'd grown up in. "So have you."

"It's not the same."

"It is." She pushed back the corner of the blanket that he'd flopped over her head so that she could see him better from her peripheral vision. "Kind of. With your dad, you saw lingering illness firsthand. You know the toll it takes on a family."

His face clouded with memories, but she'd already figured out he wasn't the kind of guy who could hold on to that kind of pain for long. She saw it in the way he needed to keep moving whenever she brought up a tough topic, how he strived to be upbeat and focused on the best things in life rather than getting caught up in dwelling on the negative. He was an eternal optimist, and while she admired that trait it could translate into an inability to see life as it really was instead of what he wanted it to be.

Rowdy shook his head and grinned away whatever dark thought had momentarily intruded on his mind, but the smile was a little less genuine this time. "But you're all better."

"Yep." She kept her voice as cheery as his. She was learning from him.

"How serious was your heart condition?"

"I almost died several times."

"No kidding?" His face went slack.

"In fact," she said, not sure why she was telling him this, "the last time was the week before I first met you."

He looked confused. "You mean just before Irene's estate sale?"

"No." She laughed. "The very first time we met."

"We met before?"

"We have. Thirteen years ago. I was twelve, and you came to the Dallas Children's Hospital during your debut year with the Mariners."

"Really?" His old smile was back, supercharged and so full of energy it liquefied her bones.

"I had the hugest crush on you," she admitted. "I still have the autographed baseball you gave me."

"Breezy, that's um . . . wow." He ran a hand through his damp hair, managing to look both boyish and sheepish despite his absurdly potent masculinity. "You had a crush on me, huh?"

"I thought you walked on water." She rolled her eyes. "There's nothing more ridiculous than a preteen girl in the throes of her first celebrity crush."

"Ah," he said, his cheeks pinking. Was he blushing? Over her crushing on him? "I'm really flattered."

"Hey, I was just a sickly little kid whose head was easily turned by a handsome face and an autographed baseball." Even though she was fully covered by the blanket, she was acutely aware that she was still naked underneath it. And now here she'd gone and stripped her soul bare for him too. She might as well hand him a bow and arrow and tell him to sling away.

He still looked stunned by her confession. Nut bunnies. She'd gone and made things weird.

"Don't worry, it's not like I'm madly in love with you or anything," she said. "I'm not that silly seventh grade kid anymore."

"But you're still a fan, right?" If any woman ever held him at gunpoint, he could disarm her just by looking at her like that.

"Seriously?" she said. "You're Stardust's hometown hero. I'll always be an überfan."

"Well, shucks, Miss Carlyle, you've embarrassed me."

"I didn't mean to make you uncomfortable."

"You didn't," he assured her.

"This feels—"

"Fated," he said.

"Fated?" What did he mean by that? She thought about the softness of the cheetah-print scarf, the odd saying on the box, Suki's contention the quote was talking about soul mates. Knocked off guard, she struggled to mask her nervousness by watching butterflies flit among the flowers, but no matter how hard she tried, she couldn't escape the heat of his intent stare.

"Our working relationship," he added quickly. "Like we were meant to work together on this project."

Duh. Of course he meant their working relationship. How stupid of her to think he meant anything else.

Lord, he had such gorgeous lips, angular and darkly pink. She wanted to lick them, taste them, feeling them pressed hard against hers.

"Could you just turn around so I can get dressed? I'm feeling a little overexposed."

"My apologies. I forgot you were undressed." He retrieved her clothes and her glasses, and handed them to her.

"Thanks." She slipped on her glasses and twirled a finger in the air. "You know the drill."

He turned. She dressed.

"Okay," she said. "All done. I'm starving. How about you?"

They ate sandwiches while sitting on the damp blanket in the soft grass. The sun warmed their skin. The taste of roasted portobello mushrooms sandwiches with sun-dried tomatoes, melted mozzarella, and olive tapenade on rustic Italian bread enlivened their taste buds.

"Thank you for telling me about your illness," he murmured. "I better understand some things now."

"Um . . . what things?"

"Why you're such a late bloomer. Why you've never been skinny-dipping or played hooky or rode on a zipline. Why you're—"

"Still a virgin." Internally, she cringed. Had she really just said that?

"I was not going to say that. I was going to say why you're one tough cookie, surviving all you've survived."

A ribbon of yearning unfurled deep inside her, a big messy pile of it. Leaving her aching and lonely. Never mind that he was close enough to kiss. She wasn't going to kiss him, and he wasn't going to kiss her.

"What else was I going to do?" She shrugged like it was no big deal. "Die?"

He laughed. "Spunky to the core."

Unnerved by his compliments and the look in his eyes, she lowered her chin to her knees again, smelled the musky odor of pond water, and stared at the ground.

"You're thinking I feed all women a line of bull."

"Don't you?"

"Okay, yeah. I enjoy pleasing women, and if a compliment can make someone feel better—"

"Right," she said, both disappointed and vindicated. Ever since she took the job, she'd been lecturing herself about her dangerous feelings for him. "You were trying to make me feel better."

"That's not what I meant."

"No? What did you mean?"

"I've never brought a woman here before," he said, clearly trying to make her feel special. It was kind of him.

She slanted him a sidelong glance. "Not even when you were a teenager?"

"No," he said. "And you do have truly beautiful eyes."

"But the rest of me . . ." Her laugh came out harsher than she intended. "Not so much, huh."

"I didn't say that."

"You didn't have to. I know well enough that I'm plain."

"You're not plain." He sounded peeved. "You're just not flashy."

"I never learned how to attract male attention."

"Why not?"

"When you're sick for a long time, you forget how to be normal. Or in my case, since I was born this way, I didn't learn how to be normal in the first place, and it's easier for me to hide behind books, and my glasses."

"What are you so afraid of, Breeanne?" he whispered.

You. The way you make me feel. The things I want to do with you and to you.

"I spent years living in a cocoon of one kind or another—hospitals, pain, the bosom of my family, Stardust. Now I'm paralyzed by life's options."

"Just pick a path and go down it."

"But what if it's the wrong path?"

"Make a U-turn. Nothing is irrevocable, except for kids. Don't have children unless you're one-hundred-percent sure you want them."

"That's not necessarily true," she said. "You *can* skip out on kids. People do it all the time."

"Not responsible people. Not honorable people."

"How can we ever know what's in someone's heart? Running out on their kid might be the kindest thing some people could do."

"You're too forgiving. Sorry, but I can't get on

board that thought train." Rowdy stretched out on the blanket, propped up on one elbow, stared down at her. "Why do you think it's okay for parents to abandon their kids?"

"I didn't mean it like that."

"How did you mean it?"

The sun cast a halo over his head. Breeanne stared into those hypnotic blue eyes. Her heart swelled against her chest, grew bigger and tighter, pushing into her rib cage until she could scarcely breathe.

The wind blew a strand of hair across her face. Gently, he brushed it away, smiled at her as if she was a surprise gift he'd found on his doorstep and wanted to take his time opening.

Something warm and grateful crept through her veins and the words rolled out of her of their own free will, even though it wasn't something she talked about often. "I'm adopted. All my sisters and I are."

"No kidding?"

"I was adopted first. Although I'm not chronologically the oldest, I've been with Mom and Dad the longest."

He did not take his eyes off her. His attention flattered. Other than her father, she'd not had a man's undivided attention before. She soaked it up. *Watch your step. He's a heartbreaker.* Even knowing that, she didn't stop talking. Opening up. Letting him in. Showing him every inch of her vulnerability. She closed her eyes, felt the heat of his gaze on her face. "My birth mother abandoned me in the hospital when she found out about my heart condition."

He interlaced his hand with hers, squeezed hard. "What a stupid mistake she made."

Still keeping her eyes closed, she shook her head. It was easier to talk when she couldn't see the sympathy in his eyes. "No. Leaving me was the best thing she ever did. She was sixteen, a runaway. No one knew who my biological father was."

He stroked her palm with his thumb, reassuring and tender.

"My adoptive mother volunteered to rock babies in the neonatal ICU. She and Dad couldn't have children of their own. She says the second she laid eyes on me that she fell in love." Breeanne opened her eyes. "But I don't see how that's possible. I've seen the pictures. I was six weeks premature and I looked like a scrawny, naked baby bird."

"She saw past the superficial, to the beautiful baby inside," he said.

The lump in her throat threatened to choke her. He knew how to make women feel good. It was part of his charisma, but she couldn't mistake that charm for true caring.

Unable to bear the tenderness in his eyes, she sat up, dropped his hand.

"Mom and Dad brought me home. Took shifts tending to a sick infant with special needs. Many times, I was knocking on the Grim Reaper's door. The community helped out. People took up donations to help cover my medical expenses. They threw bake sales and held car washes. My parents' love and Stardust saved me."

She stopped, let out a deep breath that sounded like a sigh, and finally risked looking at him.

His gaze did not leave her face, and he took her hand again. "That explains why you try so hard to make other people happy."

"There's nothing wrong with making people happy. It's a virtue."

"There is if you make yourself unhappy in the process."

"I *am* happy," she insisted. "Growing up, as long as I had a good book to read, I was happy. I couldn't run and play the way the other kids did, but books got me through."

"And your love of books turned into a love of writing."

"Yes. If something gets under my skin, I write about it, and when I'm done, I've purged myself of the feeling. I can let it go and move on. Things in my world stay safe and calm."

"Writing as a form of anger management, huh?"

"Emotional management. It's not just for anger. Let the words come out of the pen and it's less likely to come out of your mouth. You probably should have tried writing about your feelings over the Gunslingers cutting Price Richards instead of walking out and calling Dugan Potts a hamster on national TV."

He dropped her hand. Not suddenly like she'd offended him, but a subtle letting go, his fingers loosening, slowly slipping away. She'd brought up the thing he wanted to avoid. Stirred his pain. It was fine for him to stir her pain, but she couldn't agitate his?

"Did you ever try to find your birth mother?" he asked, deflecting her attention. His tone had changed. It inched higher, more distant. Like a helium balloon breaking away from a crying child, and floating toward the clouds.

He wasn't ready to talk about it. Okay. She let go.

"No. I have no interest in finding my birth mother. Why would I hurt Mom and Dad that way?"

"Surely they would understand. Every kid is curious about where they come from."

"Not me," she said. "The woman didn't want me. Why would I ever want to know her?"

"I don't know. To show her what a terrific person she abandoned."

"There's no need for me to gloat. I have loving parents, awesome sisters, lots of friends and neighbors. What else do I need?"

"You're something else, Breeanne Carlyle, you know that?" He bestowed compliments so easily, never guessing how much they affected her.

He didn't necessarily mean those nice things. He was a charmer. That was what he did. Charm. She knew that.

Yes, yes she did, but she'd fallen for it anyway. She had revealed all her secrets to him, while he'd held tight to his.

She had nothing left to give.

Except for her scarred-up heart.

CHAPTER 13

*The great thing about baseball is that
there's a crisis every day.*

—GABE PAUL

On the drive back to his place, Rowdy kept the conversation light, discussing their favorite foods, the last movies they'd seen, their favorite TV shows. They'd covered some heavy ground today, and she seemed as eager as he was to leave the secrets they shared back there in the woods.

But like it or not, things had changed between them. Irrevocably, he feared, and he wasn't sure whether those changes were good or bad. They'd grown closer for sure, but that brought a whole set of new problems, and he wasn't in the frame of mind to think about what that meant.

Day by day his life was getting more entangled with Breeanne's and he could hardly wrap his head around the strange new feelings that caused his entire body to light up whenever she was around. He could kick his own ass for suggesting skinny-dipping.

By the time they got back to his house, he didn't know how he was going to make it through the next several months. When he held the front door open for her, all he wanted to do was slide his fingers through that hair, grown curly from her dunking in the pond. He caught a whiff of her scent and instantly felt himself grow taut with urgency. He wanted to kiss her. Kiss her until her eyes burned bright with passion. He wanted to taste that sweet mouth again, feel her tongue with his, inhale her into his veins.

Bothered by how severely he wanted to snatch her into his arms, understanding how the last thing he needed in his life was to get involved with his virginal ghostwriter, he hung back. Gulped. Twice.

She stopped at the end of the foyer, turned back to look at him still standing in the doorway. "What's wrong?"

Nothing. Everything. Instead of answering, he caught up with her. "I'm thirsty," he said. "Do you want something to drink?"

"That would be nice."

They entered the kitchen. Breeanne went for the bar stool. He headed for the refrigerator.

The doorbell rang.

Warwick would probably get it, if he was in the house, but Rowdy was still feeling out of balance, and answering the door seemed like the reprieve from their surging chemistry.

"I'll get that," he said, and jerked his thumb in the direction of the door.

But before he could move, the front door opened, and a familiar voice hollered, "Where the hell is my big brother? Is his lazy ass still in bed?"

Zach? His heart gave a jubilant hop. Rowdy hadn't seen his kid brother since he was in the hospital. But his joy was immediately replaced with an ominous thought. What was his little brother doing here? He was supposed to be in North Carolina pitching for the Mudcats. Oh crap, had Zach gotten cut?

"Is that your brother?" Breeanne asked.

"Sounds like it."

Zach rounded the corner and strolled into the kitchen. Nolan Ryan got up to greet him. His younger brother tussled mildly with the dog for a minute, and then straightened, grinning like a loon.

"Hey, there old man." Exuberantly, Zach wrapped Rowdy in a bear hug and lifted him off his feet.

"Kid, put me down, you'll ruin your back."

Zach put him down, and then struck a pugilistic pose, feigning boxing punches that Rowdy couldn't resist returning. He loved his kid brother something fierce.

"Don't fight!" Breeanne exclaimed.

Zach straightened and cast a glance in her direction. "Who is she and why does she think we're fighting?"

"Zach, meet my ghostwriter, Breeanne Carlyle. She grew up with all sisters. Breeanne, this knucklehead is my little bro."

"Sisters don't throw punches at each other?" Zach teased.

"Not generally and certainly not for fun," Breeanne said.

Zach tried to get off a roundhouse kick, but Rowdy caught his foot, knocking him off balance. Zach hopped away, and came back with another flurry of punches that Rowdy deflected.

Rowdy knocked the Mudcats baseball cap off Zach's head and ruffled his hair just to irritate him. It was damn good to see him, and the kid looked happy. Not at all like someone who'd just been cut.

Finally, Zach settled down and he shot Breeanne another glance. "Ghostwriter, huh?" He poked Rowdy in the ribs. "That means you have to listen to this old man's glory day stories. You have my sympathies."

Breeanne smiled. "It's not so bad."

"What the hell are you doing here, buddy?" Rowdy asked, putting Zach in a headlock.

"You're not happy to see me?" Zach squirmed away, picked up his cap, and adjusted it on his head at a cocky angle.

"I'm happy to see you, just curious why you're not in North Carolina."

" 'Cause . . ." Zach dusted his hands together, made a drumroll noise. "I'm going to The Show!"

"What?" Rowdy blinked. The kid had talent, and a strong fastball, and he was performing well this season, but not good enough to move straight to the bigs.

"Yep, you heard right. And get this, *your* agent signed me."

His agent, Barry Goldfine, had signed Zach, and not told him? Bad form.

Rowdy fought off jealousy. He was happy for his brother. Truly. But something didn't feel right about this.

"Yep, uh-huh. That's right. I'm takin' the place of the pitcher that Potts's just cut. The pitcher who took your place on the mound." Zach tossed his cap on the floor, stomped it with glee. "In your face, bro. In your face!"

After Zach dropped the bomb that the Gunslingers had called him up, Rowdy suggested Breeanne go home, telling her they'd make a fresh start of it on Tuesday after the long Memorial Day weekend.

This was good, she told herself, extra time to pack for the move to the house on Peach Street with Stephanie that weekend. But she couldn't stop worrying about Rowdy, and how the news of his brother's success would affect him. He was very good at hiding his feelings, but there was much more to the man than met the eye. What she'd learned today had only brought that fact home.

Absentmindedly, she rubbed her breastbone with her knuckles, felt the ridges of her scars, and wondered how this latest development was going to influence the book.

But it wasn't until she walked in the back door into her parents' kitchen that she remembered about the party.

Since Memorial Day was one of the busiest days at the store, her parents had closed Timeless Treasures early to host a backyard get-together for friends and neighbors to kick off the big weekend. Tonight it was a crawfish boil.

Dad manned the kettle over a propane cooker, his trusty stirring paddle at the ready along with a big jar of Cajun seasoning. Mom was in the kitchen putting the finishing touches on a chocolate pie. Jodi set the picnic tables with newspaper instead of a tablecloth, paper towels in festive holders, and strategically placed small metal buckets. Kasha put on Zydeco music and she was stringing Japanese lanterns through the redbud trees. In charge of the drink station, Suki iced beer and sodas in a galvanized bucket, and put out iced tea and lemonade on a folding table that also held crudités, chips, dips and other nibbles.

Her parents loved parties, and threw at least one a month.

When Breeanne was a kid she loved the flow of people who brought extra color and excitement into her drab world. Many times, she'd been forced to watch the goings-on from her bedroom window as she recuperated. As a moody teen, she'd often felt on the fringes. Not a real part of the gregarious Carlyle clan, and she'd sneak off to her bedroom to read in peace. Now she usually enjoyed being in the thick of things. Happy to just be included. Today she felt guilty for having forgotten all about the party.

"There you are!" her mother called out. "I thought you'd forgotten about the party."

Breeanne crossed the kitchen to drop a kiss on the cheek of the blond-haired nurturer who'd rescued her. "Did you need me for something?"

"Could you make the whipped cream for the pie?"

"Sure," Breeanne said, depositing her notebook computer and purse on the hutch, and rolling up her sleeves to wash her hands at the sink.

"You know this is more than just our Memorial Day weekend party. This is your going away party. I still can't believe you're moving out tomorrow," Mom said. "We're going to miss you so much."

Breeanne suppressed a sigh. "Peach Street isn't in Outer Mongolia, Mom. Just ten blocks away."

"It might as well be," said her mother, her voice heavy with woe, and passed her a dish towel to dry her hands.

She had to tromp down hard on guilt to stop from apologizing for moving out. Before making her way over to the refrigerator, she sneaked a quick peek out the screen door to see if anyone else might be coming inside to let her off the hook.

No such luck.

Guests had started drifting into the backyard. The kooky but lovable next-door neighbor, Trudy Wells, was helping Suki put ice in paper cups and set them out. Dad's best friend, Mr. Tice, who ran the lumberyard and lived next door, was doling out cooking advice. He hollered, "Don't be stingy with the Zatarain's, Dan," and then chuckled at his rhyme.

"You're at Rowdy's house all day, and working on the book in the evenings. When will we ever get to see you?" Mom went on.

"You're seeing me now."

"I'm being whiny, aren't I?" Her mother gave a rueful laugh. "It's hard watching your little ones leave the nest. You'll see one day."

She stepped over to give her mother a quick hug. "It's going to be okay."

"I know, I know. Just call me sentimental." Her mother patted her shoulder. "Your hair is damp. What happened?"

Not wanting to answer, but not wanting to lie either, she leaned over to pluck the spoon out of the chocolate pie filling and stick it in her mouth. "Mmm."

"I'm so going to miss these moments." Her mother opened the silverware drawer and took out a clean spoon.

"Don't worry, I'll come over to eat chocolate pie anytime."

"If that's the case, I'll put it on the nightly menu."

"Overkill."

"Three times a week?" her mother asked hopefully.

"Sunday dinner," Breeanne offered.

"Twice a week? You can bring anyone you want. Rowdy included."

"I can commit to Sunday dinner," Breeanne said, proud of herself for holding firm.

"Sunday dinner it is." Her mother nodded like she'd won a round on a game show. "How *are* things going with Rowdy, by the way?"

"Fine." She didn't look up in case the day's adventure showed on her face.

"He's not tried anything funny with you?"

"He's been a perfect gentleman."

"Well, that's disappointing."

"Mom!"

"What?" Her mother shrugged. "I'm ready for grandchildren."

"Rowdy's not the least bit interested me in that way."

"That's not what I've heard."

Breeanne took the whipping cream from the fridge and bumped the door closed with her hip. "What have you heard? And from whom?"

"Suki told me about the cheetah scarf. How it feels soft to Rowdy too."

"What a blabbermouth," Breeanne grumbled, and got out the hand mixer.

"It's a sign."

Breeanne stabbed the beaters into the mixer, jerked her head up, and studied her mother. "When did you get superstitious?"

"I've always believed in signs," Mom said. "I was volunteering in the NICU on the night shift on the same day you were born. You were only fourteen hours old. I wasn't even supposed to be there that night, but it was a full moon and crazy busy. The nurses called me in and asked if I could comfort babies. I'd no more gotten gowned up when one of the nurses directed me to you. She told me that your birth mother had left the hospital against medical advice as soon as they told her that you had a heart defect and that you hadn't slept a wink since you were born, and little wonder. You had half a dozen tubes and wires hanging off you, and Band-Aids were stuck all over your tiny body where they'd turned you into a pincushion drawing blood. I reached inside your incubator and stroked your little arm and you looked up at me, and fell right to sleep. And I instantly fell in love. I didn't know how at the time, but I just *knew* you were going to be mine someday."

Breeanne had heard the fanciful story hundreds of times, but she always thought her mother added that last part just to make her feel better for having been abandoned by her birth mother.

"Don't scoff at signs, Breeanne," Mom said.

"It's just a scarf."

Her mother's eyes met hers. "You know it's more than that."

Okay, the way the scarf had come into her life *had* been unusual, but a scrap of material didn't have the power to divine one's life partner.

"You've had a crush on Rowdy since you were twelve."

"So have a million other women."

"How do you feel about him now?" her mother asked.

Breeanne sighed. "To be honest, the more I get to know him, the more I like him."

"And that's bad?"

"C'mon, Mom. He's Rowdy Blanton, and I'm—" She swept a hand at herself. "Me."

"Don't sell yourself short. You have amazing qualities."

"Yeah, like you've ever heard a guy say, 'Look at the amazing qualities on her.'"

"If it's meant to be, you'll feel it." Her mother leaned over to press her palm to Breeanne's heart. "Right here."

She scooted away and turned the mixer on high to prevent further conversation on the topic, but her mind wouldn't leave it alone. She was back at the pond, being cradled against Rowdy's chest as he carried her from the water. In that moment, she'd felt utterly safe. Protected. Cared for. It was a dangerous feeling for so many reasons, but she couldn't dispel it.

Suddenly, the mixer stopped. She looked up confused, saw her mother standing there with the plug in her hand. "What is it?"

"I called your name three times," Mom said.

"You did?"

"You were a thousand miles away. What has you so lost in thought?"

"Sorry," she apologized. "What did you want?"

"To tell that you've whipped the cream so hard you've churned it into butter."

Breeanne looked down in the bowl and sure enough, instead of fluffy white peaks, the cream clumped yellow.

"It's all right," Mom soothed. "I'll send Suki to the store for Cool Whip."

"It's my mess," she said. "I'll go."

"All right, but walk, don't drive. You've got your head in the clouds today and we don't need any accidents."

While Breeanne was busy whipping the cream into butter, Rowdy hung up the phone from talking to his agent. His agent had confirmed the timeline that proved Rowdy's suspicions. The Gunslingers manager had called Zach *after* Jackdaw's official press release on Wednesday morning announcing they were publishing his autobiography.

"I know you don't like Potts," Zach said, "but he's not holding any grudges. He came down to meet me and said to be sure and tell you that he says hey."

Rowdy gnashed his teeth. That sonofabitch Potts was goading him through Zach. He shoved a hand through his hair. The kid had no idea he'd just stepped into a bear trap.

"You can't do this, Zach."

Zach's mouth dropped open. "Are you nuts? No one refuses The Show."

Rowdy wrapped a hand around his brother's forearm. "It's not a legitimate offer. It's a trap."

Zach jerked back, leveled offended eyes at him. "What are you talking about?"

"Potts picked you up to assure that I would keep quiet. He heard about my autobiography and now he's afraid I'm gonna spill the beans."

"Spill the beans about what?"

"For one thing, that was no jealous husband that busted up my pitching arm. Potts hired a guy to do it." Rowdy went on to explain his suspicions about the general manager in detail.

"Yeah?" Zach scowled. "You got proof?"

"I can identify the tattoo on the guy's arm."

"Did you go to the police?"

"Yes."

"What did they say?"

"It's not enough proof."

"There you have it."

"Zach, I *know* it's true." He pumped his fist twice against his chest. "I might not be able to prove it in a court of law, but Potts hired the guy to bust me up."

"What have you been smokin', man? You're out of your head."

"Kid, you're not ready for The Show and deep in your heart, you know it. Stop and think for a minute."

Zach knotted a fist, and shook it in his face. "You're jealous. That's what this is about. You're a washed up has-been who doesn't want to see his little brother take his place."

Acid burned his throat. He hated saying this, hated hurting Zach, hated realizing his suspicions about Potts were true. "I wish that's all it was."

"Fuck you, man." Zach looked like he was about to cry. It killed Rowdy's soul to tell him this. "Fuck you."

"Please be careful."

"I don't believe this." Zach's face reddened, his body shaking with fury. "You're a paranoid lunatic. The rumors are right. You do have a vendetta against Potts. What is your problem?"

"Mark my word, Potts is setting you up in order to get to me. There are things you don't know. Guard your back."

"Guard your face," Zach yelled, hauled off and punched Rowdy in the mouth.

Rowdy staggered back, saw stars, tasted blood, lost his balance, ended up on his ass. Whacked his head against the wall, his bell completely rung.

Nolan Ryan came over to lick Rowdy's busted lip, and whimpered.

He shook his head. By the time his vision cleared, Zach had stormed out, slamming the front door behind him, and Warwick was standing in the living room with his arms folded over his massive chest.

"That's been coming for a long time," Warwick said. "Need ice?"

"Naw." Rowdy swiped his palm across his bloodied mouth, levered himself to his feet. "I just hope Zach didn't use his pitching arm. Then again, maybe I do. If he ruined his pitching arm, it would take him off Potts's chessboard."

CHAPTER 14

Hitting is timing. Pitching is upsetting timing.

—WARREN SPAHN

If the cars parked up along the street and the sound of laughter and Zydeco music hadn't been a dead give-away, the smell of crawfish surely was. The Carlyles were throwing a party.

And there was nothing Rowdy loved more than a party. Too bad he was here as the bearer of bad news.

He'd spent the better part of an hour trying to think of a way around this, but there was only one solution. He had to call off the autobiography. Too bad Bree-anne was going to be another casualty in his war with Potts. Dammit, this wasn't going to be easy.

Maybe he should come back later.

He paused on the front porch, hand raised to knock, a box of autographed baseballs tucked under his arm. He'd brought them to smooth things over, a peace offering of sorts to soften the blow. Christ, he hated delivering bad news, especially to someone as nice as Breeanne.

Might as well get it over with. He could stall all he wanted, but the problem wasn't going away. Potts had him by the short hairs.

Just one more reason to despise the Gunslingers

general manager, Potts was causing him to hurt Breeanne.

Rowdy set his teeth and his shoulders, and bounced
the brass knocker against the door. He waited. No
one answered. He knocked again. Nothing. He spied
a doorbell, rang that. Nada.

Clearly, they were all in the backyard, and no one
heard him at the front door.

Go. Don't ruin the party.

It was so tempting to just run. He hated pain. Hated
experiencing it. Hated causing it even more. But firing
Breeanne was the lesser evil, although he couldn't tell
her that.

Tacking up a smile, he took a deep breath and
forced himself to head around the side of the house
toward the open backyard gate.

The sky was the sleepy orange-purple of encroach-
ing dusk, the temperature balmy, the light wind just
enough to keep bugs at bay. Honeysuckle in full
bloom grew over the privacy fence, sugaring the air.
The hum of pleasant conversation vibrated through
his bones.

He poked his head around the side of the house,
pausing to take in the scene, but he didn't get very
far. Right away, an older woman with beet red spiky
hair and numerous colorful tattoos spied him and
screeched, "Rowdy Blanton!"

In seconds, he was surrounded, a dozen people jab-
bering at once, all telling him how impressive he was.
Normally, he would have dove right into the attention
and wallowed around, but he was here to crush Breeanne's dreams. No glory in that. He glanced around,
searching for her in the crowd.

A man in his fifties, holding a wooden canoe paddle
and wearing a red rubber apron, came toward him,

hand extended. "Rowdy Blanton in my backyard? Pinch me like a crawfish and call me done. I'm in heaven."

Rowdy shifted the box of balls to his other arm and shook the man's hand. "Glad to meet you . . ."

"Dan, Dan Carlyle."

"You're Breeanne's father."

"That I am." Dan straightened, squared his shoulders, and stepped into Rowdy's personal space, slung the paddle over his shoulder like a baseball bat. "I trust you're treating my girl right."

"Yes sir. Pleased to meet a fellow ballplayer, sir," Rowdy said, strengthening his grip and ignoring the part about treating Breeanne right. Much as it pained him, he was here to do Breeanne wrong.

Dan Carlyle looked flattered and flustered. "You know I used to play ball?"

"Breeanne told me about your family, and her aunt Polly. I read all about you in her book."

"Oh yes, right. Breeanne's book. We are so proud of her. Thank you for giving her a chance."

Rowdy gulped, his mission growing more difficult by the minute.

"C'mon in, c'mon in." Dan ushered Rowdy deeper into the yard. Over his shoulder, he called out, "Suki, fetch our hometown hero a cold beer."

He allowed the small crowd to settle him at a picnic table, but all the while, he kept searching for Breeanne. He'd first gone to Timeless Treasures to look for her and found the place was closed for the day. A shopkeeper in the clothing boutique next door to the antique store had told him where the Carlyles lived.

He was about to ask where she was, but people were eyeing the box of baseballs, so he passed them out. There weren't enough to go around, but he issued rain check promises to everyone who'd missed out. After that people asked him to sign other things—a paper towel, beer bottle labels, body parts.

A blond older woman came out of the house and introduced herself as Maggie Carlyle. Breeanne's parents were friendly, gregarious, and welcoming—his kind of folk.

A cute girl with Asian features and an asymmetrical haircut put a beer in his hand. "Hi, I'm Suki, the younger sister."

"And I'm Jodi, the oldest." An auburn-haired, freckle-faced Meg-Ryan-in-her-romantic-comedy-days look-alike handed him a sturdy paper plate.

"Kasha," said a husky-voiced brunette, her thick, waist-length hair floating around her. Kasha was darker than her sisters, her skin creamy caramel, cheekbones high. A young Rae Dawn Chong with straight hair. She went barefoot, and wore a long, flowy dress. Images of recycling, organic vegetables, Volkswagens, and Seattle popped into his head. "I'm the sister in the middle between Jodi and Breeanne."

Dan, and another man about Dan's age, dumped the contents of a kettle onto the picnic tables covered with newspaper—bright red crawfish, corn on the cob halves, new potatoes, pearl onions, and smoked sausage.

People vied for food and conversation equally, everyone talking at once.

"Eat, eat," Maggie urged, using tongs to pile his plate with food.

"Where's Breeanne?" he asked, but Maggie had turned to answer someone else's question, and apparently she hadn't heard him. He stood, a paper plate loaded with food in one hand, a beer in the other, not knowing what to do.

That's when Breeanne came through the backyard gate with a plastic bag in her hand.

Golden twilight filtered through the mimosa trees, spreading shadows over the lawn like a Hallmark greeting card. Dying sunshine glinted off a dangly silver hook in her ear. He set down the plate and beer, and stared at her without breathing.

Through the dreamy dusk, she came toward him, moving gracefully, the dwindling sunlight darkening, shifting, shrinking around her. He stood motionless, struck by her softness.

She strolled toward the back door, a faraway expression on her face, swinging the sack in her hand in time to a melody that only she could hear. A honeysuckle blossom was caught in her hair, yellow-white and sweetly pleasing. She wore a blue sundress dotted with pink flowers that hugged her nicely at the waist, and pink flip-flops on her feet.

The cheetah scarf was tied at her neck. The print didn't match the outfit, but it didn't matter. At the sight of the scarf, he felt a surge of something hot and unexpected low in his belly. Something desperate.

Her hips swayed delicately as she climbed the back steps, and she paused when she reached the screen door, stopped, turned. Their eyes met.

She offered him a tiny smile, and instantly his heart swelled. He smiled back, hoping he looked more self-confident than he felt.

He moved toward her.

Everyone else stopped talking, and except for the lively Zydeco music, the backyard went silent. Without turning his head, he knew every eye was on him. That was okay. He was accustomed to the limelight.

He'd slipped off without Warwick. He should have learned his lesson about that on New Year's Eve, but he hadn't wanted his bodyguard hovering while he talked to Breeanne. What he hadn't counted on was her entire family and neighborhood doing exactly that.

He started up the porch steps after her.

Breeanne turned around, stepped into the kitchen.

"Go get her, Rowdy," someone hollered. It sounded like the cheeky older woman with the spiky hair and tattoos.

That brought a round of laughter and more urgings to go after her. It made him feel a little panicky. How were they going to view him after he fired her?

A stunningly beautiful calico sitting in the window narrowed her eyes at him, and her whiskers twitched as if to say, *Watch your step, buddy.*

He moved to the screen door, peered in at Breeanne. Suddenly, his heart was chugging the way it did when a heavy hitter took the plate in a tie game with the bases loaded. He raised a palm. "Hi."

She hugged herself tighter. "Hi."

"Can I come in?"

"Can you?"

"I'd like to come in."

"Please yourself." She shrugged like she didn't care, the casual gesture belying the tension in her voice.

The screen door hinges squeaked and he was inside. He paused a moment to turn back the audience. "Y'all can go on back to eating."

He waited a minute for the conversation outside to resume. Breanne didn't speak. Didn't move. She was good at staying still.

"What happened to your mouth?"

He raised a hand to his busted lip. "Zach."

"Sibling rivalry?"

"Something along those lines."

She took a deep breath, but didn't say anything else, just stood there sizing him up.

"Are you going to come get something to eat?" he asked.

"In a minute," she said. "After I put whipped cream on the chocolate pie." She took a tub of Cool Whip from the plastic bag and set it on the counter.

"Need any help?"

She turned to face him. "Why are you here?"

Gosh, how he wished he could take her hand and lead her back out to the party, tell her he'd come here to see her because he missed her something fierce, which was true, but it wasn't the real reason he was here. When had he started counting the minutes until they could be together again?

Forget that. As soon as he told her what he'd come there to say, it was all over. No more book. No more Breeanne. Dammit, he wished there was another way.

"I came to see you." He took another step toward her, the floorboards of the old Victorian creaking beneath his feet.

"What for?" The pulse at the hollow of her throat jumped visibly. She was nervous.

Hell, so was he. Today they'd seen each other naked. Things had shifted between them, but he was about to shift them again.

She moistened her lips.

His gaze hooked on that sweet, strawberry-colored mouth. Christ, how he wanted to kiss her. Wanted it so badly he knotted his hands into fists to keep from doing just that.

"I wanted to make sure you were okay," he said. "You know, after this morning in the pond."

A pink stain the same color as the flowers on her

dress sprang to her cheeks. "You came all the way into town to ask me that?"

"No," he admitted.

"What's up?" She canted her head, seeing straight through him. She had an uncanny ability to get to the meat of things.

"This isn't a good time," he said. "Your family is—"

Breeanne sank her hands onto her hips. She wasn't going to let him wriggle off the hook. "Out with it."

He stepped closer, trying to figure out how to phrase the sentence to soften the blow. She stood her ground, but the ends of the scarf trembled. She was shaking. Was she scared or excited? Maybe both? He was, for sure.

It was never his intention to touch her, but he couldn't seem to help himself. Rowdy reached out and ran a finger over the cheetah scarf, soft as a cloud. The scarf made him think of the day she'd gotten beaned on the head with the baseball and he'd got a provocative glimpse at her cheetah panties.

She was pretty. How in the hell had he ever believed her plain? He caught a whiff of her sexy scent—shampoo and cream and flowers.

Her lips parted, as if she was going to speak, but she didn't say anything. They both drew in deep, simultaneous gulps of air. He could kiss her now. They would no longer be working together. No more rules, nothing to hold him back. Maybe she wanted him to kiss her. Did she want him to kiss her? He wanted to kiss her.

Not smart. Not smart. Not smart. Especially when he was about to fire her.

His eyes captured hers. She was barely breathing.

"Well?" she said.

Resist, resist.

But he could not. He'd been resisting since the first

time he'd kissed her, aching to taste those luscious lips again. To find out if lightning would strike twice.

"Rowdy," she whispered, her green eyes clouded murky, beseechingly. She pursed her lips, licked them so that they glistened wetly. She wanted to kiss him as much as he wanted to be kissed.

The air fairly crackled with sexual tension. They could have been anywhere and nowhere. Nothing existed but the two of them.

She took a step toward him.

Rowdy let loose with a helpless groan and drew her into his arms. The feel of her skin against his, her warm breath fanning over his chin, and he was done for.

His head pounded, blood pushing tightly through his veins. This was sweet, naïve Breeanne Carlyle in his arms, not some random groupie who had shown up at the locker room door, and she was looking up at him with complete trust. He owed her the respect she deserved.

Ah shit, ah hell, ah no, no. How could this feel so right, but be so wrong?

She was everything he'd never known he wanted. Everything he shouldn't have. He was taking advantage of her, of the moment. If anyone else tried to do this to her, he'd beat the crap out of them.

Her eyelashes lowered, a sultry shade of acquiescent, her body melting soft in his arms. The emotion between them was so solid he could slice it like a prime rib roast, meaty and raw.

God, he wanted her more than he ever thought possible.

What was wrong with him? Why couldn't he stop fantasizing about her? Stupid. Stupid. She wasn't some party girl out for nothing but a good time, and he couldn't treat her as if she were, no matter how desperately he wanted to imprint her with his mouth. Take her. Claim her. Make her his woman.

Honestly, he treasured her. Admired her. She was easy to be with, cheery and smart.

"You've got a weird look in your eyes," she said, and then stopped talking as he leaned in closer, and hovered there.

Those gorgeous green eyes widened to half dollars and her teeth parted and she whispered, "Rowdy," and then he just went ahead threw her a crazy screwball pitch of a kiss, tenderly, easily, savoring every second of their bond—the way she tasted, the map of her lips, pliable and honeyed—and he heard her sharp intake of air and felt somehow baptized, fresh and new, his sins absolved. He didn't care that the kiss made his busted lip hurt. Her mouth was a sweet balm. Her arms tangled around his neck, pulling his head down lower, and then she was kissing him back, putting every bit of heart she possessed into it, leaving only one thought in his head, *Magic*, and he forgot that he'd come here to shatter her dreams, and cupped her cheek against his palm, and surrendered everything to her.

No other woman had ever made him feel this way. So helplessly out of control. No woman had ever stirred his hunger to this degree that wiped every rational thought from his brain. How had he gone an entire lifetime without this, without her?

After a generous time with the kitchen clock ticking off the seconds in long, jerky *tick, tick, tick*s, he separated his lips from hers and gazed down into her face. Her eyes were half closed and a creamy smile pulled the corner of her lips up into a moony crescent.

"What did you want to tell me," she asked in a dreamy whisper, and he said, "I don't remember," and kissed her again, deeper this time, chuckling when her delicate hand fisted the back of his shirt, and then someone cleared their throat, loud enough to make them jump apart.

Suki slammed through the back door. "Ignore me. I'm not here. They sent me after the pie."

"Bad timing," Breeanne mumbled, sounding sleepy. "I haven't topped the pie with the Cool Whip yet."

"I'll do it. I'm rescuing the pie before you drool all over it," Suki said, waving her hands like laundry flapping on a clothesline. "Shoo."

"Come with me." Breeanne took Rowdy's hand and dragged him into the living room.

"Treat my sister right," Suki called after them. "Or I'll bust your nose to match that lip. She's fragile as a hothouse orchid."

"I can take care of myself," Breeanne hollered over her shoulder. "I'm a damn sunflower, not an orchid."

"Hurt her, Blanton, and my entire family will hunt you down and kill you," Suki said cheerfully, ignoring Breeanne's angry declaration.

"Your family loves you very much." Rowdy wrapped his arm around her waist.

"Tell me about it." Breeanne rolled her eyes and yanked up her spine. He noticed a toughening around her edges, her mouth zipping into a straight line, replacing the usual accommodating smile. "Now, where were we before my sister so rudely interrupted?"

Yeah, about that. Hell, why had he kissed her? It only made things worse. He dropped his arm, stepped back, chuffed in a lungful of air, threaded his fingers through his hair, avoided looking directly into those green eyes damp with the desire he'd stirred up in them.

"I'm afraid I've got some unfortunate news," he said.

She expelled her breath through pursed lips, a slow hissing sound like a tire going flat. "I knew it."

"How?"

"I could feel it on you."

"How?"

"I don't know. I just can."

"I'm sorry," he apologized.

"Don't drag it out. Just tell me."

He saw courage in her eyes, for sure more courage than he felt. She might look frail, and her family might consider her a breakable orchid, but the woman was much stronger than anyone realized. His decision would be a blow, but she'd survived ten open-heart surgeries, she would survive this too. But he hated being the cause of her pain.

"I'm afraid I've changed my mind."

She frowned. "About what?"

Just say it. "I'm quitting the book."

"What?" She blinked the way he did when he was on the mound and the batter hit a homer off a pitch he thought was a strikeout.

Rowdy winced. "I'm not going to write the book. I'm canceling the contract, paying back the advance. I'm calling my agent first thing after the holiday, but I wanted to tell you first. It's over, Breeanne."

CHAPTER 15

Every strike brings me closer to the next home run.

—BABE RUTH

His words hit her hard as a slap, coming out of no-where, a sharp clip to the jaw. She thought he'd come here to enjoy the party, and instead, he'd just kicked her world in.

Ouch.

She raised a palm to her mouth. First he kissed her and now he smashed her dreams as easily as that.

"I know this comes as a blow."

He looked so twisted up about it that her initial inclination was to tell him it was okay, that while she was disappointed, she understood. Make things easy on him. Be accommodating. Smooth the waters. But she'd come too far to go back and simply say what she thought he wanted and needed to hear. She was tired of sweeping aside her own feelings to make others feel better.

Anger blistered a hot path up her neck. "You can't do that," she said.

He shook his head as if he'd misheard her, and even patted a hand against his ear. "What?"

"This is my dream. The only thing I've wanted

is to be a successful writer and you've taken it away from me."

He rubbed a hand over the nape of his neck. "It's nothing personal."

"Not personal? I made plans. I rented a house and put the payment on my credit card. I made commitments to a roommate. I—"

"You jumped the gun." He looked guilty for saying the words, but he said them nonetheless, as if it was her fault he was quitting the book. "You spent money you didn't have."

Oh no, he didn't just say that! The man needed a good, swift kick in the ego.

"You, you . . ." She couldn't think of the right word.

"Bounder," he said. "I know."

"This isn't fair."

"I know."

"You led me on."

"I know," he said.

There was sorrow in his voice, she heard it, but now that she was wound up, she couldn't seem to stop.

"Why are you doing this to me?"

"It's not got anything to do with you, Breeanne. It's my own issue. I wish you the best of luck with your writing career," he said, and then he turned and headed for the front door, like the discussion was over.

Breeanne stood there watching him saunter away as if he hadn't just annihilated all her hopes and dreams.

The front door snapped shut.

No!

Her skin blotched. She clenched and unclenched her hands repeatedly. Her neck tightened, and she let out a roar so angry it scared her. "No!"

She bulleted after him, stumbled across the front

porch veranda and down the steps, watched him climbing into his Escalade parked beneath a streetlamp.

Full of fury, she ground her teeth and sprinted across the lawn. She didn't know what had happened to change his mind about writing the book, but she damn well deserved an explanation. He owed her that much.

"Stop right there, Rowdy Blanton," she yelled.

Neighbors out in their yards turned to stare.

He paused, one leg inside the vehicle, the other still on the pavement.

"No," she said, toeing off with him. The air was rich with his manly scent but she refused to let that distract her. "You do not get to quit."

"Excuse me?" He put added emphasis on the "cuse" syllable, his tone dark and moody.

"You made promises. To me. To your agent. To Jackdaw Press. A responsible person does not behave this way."

"Something unavoidable has come up."

She shook her finger under his nose. "Unacceptable. No excuses. It's time for you to learn that your behavior has consequences. You make commitments, you live up to them."

"Oh yeah?" An amused expression lit his eyes, and his amusement made her even madder.

"I was right the first time I met you. You *are* a bounder and a cad and a—"

"Butthead."

"Yes, that too."

"Next time I piss off a woman, remind me to pick one with a smaller vocabulary."

"You made me hope." She knotted her fist, shook it at him. "You made me dream, damn you."

"I'm not responsible for your hopes and dreams,

Breeanne." His voice was mild, but his eyes turned fiery.

"No, but you are responsible for keeping *your* word." Her chest moved like bellows, air wheezing because she was so angry. "What happened? You're not a coward. Or at least I didn't think you were. What has you running scared?"

"You."

"Me."

"Look at yourself." He twisted the side mirror around so she could see her reflection.

Her jaw was set, her brow furrowed into a don't-mess-with-me scowl, her chest thrust out, and her body language aggressive. She looked determined, forceful, and strong.

For once, she liked the way she looked. "I'm sorry, but I am not going to let you leave without an explanation. You owe me that much."

His eyelids lowered halfway indolently, but she could feel the intensity rolling off him like summer heat. "There are circumstances you know nothing about."

She sank her hands on her lips. "So tell me about these circumstances. Let me decide if it's a bullshit excuse or not."

His body stiffened. "I don't owe you an explanation."

"Yes, you do. You reeled me in on this deal and now you're cutting bait and throwing me back? Postpone the book if you have to, but you are *not* quitting." Battling him took every drop of energy she had in her.

"God, I love it when people tell me what to do," he said, his tone dripping sarcasm.

"I'm serious." The adrenaline rush of anger was draining away, leaving her organs quivering.

"I can see that." He was grinning now. Mocking her?

She widened her stance. "May I ask you a question?"

"Do I have a choice?"

"Just tell me why you're quitting."

He shrugged.

"Is it because of Zach? Everything was fine until Zach showed up."

He lifted his shoulder in a half shrug, as if he didn't care, but the fire in his eyes told her he cared. He cared a lot. He just didn't want her to know it.

"You're jealous of your little brother."

He neither confirmed nor denied her accusation.

"I can't believe you're acting so petty. I thought you were a bigger person than that," she said.

"Watch it, Breezy." His tone was casual, but underneath, she heard the warning buzz as deadly as a rattlesnake's rattle. "You don't have any idea what you're talking about."

"Then tell me about it. Help me to understand why you're acting like a jerk."

"Look," he said. "You're right. It's wrong of me to pull the rug out from under you. I did make you a promise by hiring you. I'll cover the advance money that Jackdaw was going to pay to you. You won't be left high and dry. It's a win-win. You get the money, and I get to quit the book. No harm, no foul."

"No."

"No? What do you mean, no?"

She scowled. "I'm not the kind of person who would take money for work that I don't do. If you want to quit the book, then quit it, but I won't allow you to ease your conscience by paying me money I did not earn."

He stood staring at her for so long that she thought she was going to explode from the tension.

Finally, he ran a hand over his mouth, narrowed his eyes in a glare as hard as her own. "Okay, have it your way, Breezy. We'll write the damn book."

"Remember the corner of Rock and Hard Place isn't a destination, but rather a long journey to the grave," Warwick philosophized to Rowdy as they sat in lawn chairs on the back patio late that same night, drinking a beer and gazing up at the stars. Nolan Ryan lay in the grass between them, gnawing on a chew toy.

"Shut up."

"Hey, don't take it out on me because your girlfriend got to your soft spot. She's tougher than she looks."

"Obviously, I didn't fully understand that until this afternoon."

"There's none so blind as those who will not see."

"Babe Ruth?" Rowdy asked.

Warwick let out a hoot of laughter. "The Bible."

"I *do* have to read more."

"Wouldn't hurt."

"Breeanne would love it," he mused. "She's a book girl."

"You really like her."

"Yeah," he said, his voice coming out husky as he thought about how cute she had looked chasing him down the street to bawl him out. "I couldn't just burn her."

"This issue between you and Potts has been building for years. Breeanne just happened to get caught in the crossfire."

"Zach too," he said glumly.

"Zach too," Warwick echoed.

A shooting star streaked across the sky, and damn

if he didn't make a wish. Not a solidly formed, I-want-something kind of wish, but more of a one-word mantra repeated three times. *Breeanne. Breeanne. Breeanne.*

Breeanne and her cheetah print, sweet but sassy. The appeal totally unexpected, but far more real than anything he'd ever experienced with any other woman. He'd never counted on running across someone like her. Not in a zillion years.

"It would be so much easier if I could just cold-cock Potts the way Zach did me."

"I'd buy popcorn for that bout." Warwick reached into the ice chest and took out two beers, held one out to Rowdy.

Rowdy put up a palm, shook his head. "The kid worries me. He reacts before he thinks."

"Reminds me someone else I knew when he was twenty-five."

"Me?"

Warwick shrugged, dropped the beer Rowdy refused back into the cooler. "You're a passionate guy. Heart rules your head. No judgment. Just sayin'."

True enough. Otherwise, he would have been phoning Heath Rankin, instead of trying to figure out how to make this book thing work with Breeanne.

"So what am I going to do now? If I expose Potts, he's going to take it out on Zach. But it will kill my soul to let him get away with what he's done to people."

"Damn your pesky sense of fair play."

"I'm serious."

"Me too."

"What do I do?"

"Don't write anything about Potts."

"C'mon, Breeanne isn't going to let me get away with that. Jackdaw either, for that matter."

"Then tell the world what a wonderful human being Potts is."

"I'd rather take one of Babe Ruth's line drives to the face. No shit."

"That would hurt."

Rowdy groaned and closed his eyes. "I'm so screwed."

"Don't have to be that way."

He opened one eye, peeked at Warwick. "Meaning?"

"Since your sense of fair play won't let you renege on the book, you could always get Breeanne to quit."

The suggestion intrigued him. If he got Breeanne to quit, then he wouldn't have to be the bad guy. "How would I do that?"

"I dunno." Warwick lifted shoulders so big the movement shifted the muggy air. "Make her uncomfortable."

"How do you mean?"

"You could always focus on your sexploits. Talk up a blue streak about the women you've bedded. Give her nitty-gritty details. She embarrasses easy. That would probably send her packing."

"But also she has a ferocious stubborn streak. She gave me a big dose of it this evening." Rowdy fingered his tender lip.

"Alternately, you could try talking sense into Zach. Get him to understand that Potts is gunning for him and he has to be careful."

"Would you believe it if you were in his shoes?"

"No." Warwick set his beer on the patio table, slapped hammy hands on his knees, and stood up. "Sorry. That's all I got."

"I'm more likely to get traction with Breeanne."

"Guess there's your answer."

"What if it doesn't work? What if she doesn't quit?"

"Then prepare to pucker up and publicly kiss Potts's ass."

"Remind me again why I keep you around?"

"Because I keep it real, baby."

Real. Yeah. The reality was that he was stuck writing the book with Breeanne, and he couldn't see his way out of it. Warwick was right. In order to keep Zach safe, his only real choice was to focus on his sexual adventures, and keep the topic off the Gunslingers general manager.

Potts had him over a barrel. The sonofabitch had won again.

Breeanne spent a restless night, her mind occupied with thoughts of her move and with what had happened between her and Rowdy. Should she back out of the deal with Stephanie in case Rowdy flaked out on her again? But no, that wouldn't be fair to her roommate. Besides, she needed to move out. The time had come for her to stand on her own two feet.

While she was proud of herself for standing up to him, she worried that maybe it wasn't the smartest thing she could have done. Did she really want to write a book with a reluctant man? It had been hard enough getting him to talk about his past when he was fully into the project. Now, was every day going to be a battle?

What had really happened that caused him to backtrack?

She'd accused him of being jealous of his younger brother, but what if his reasons had nothing to do with his brother and everything to do with skinny-dipping in the pond with her?

All her old self-doubts came gnawing to the surface, relentlessly nibbling at her self-confidence.

But if that was the case, if he was somehow disappointed with her after what happened today, why had he kissed her in her family's kitchen, with the entire neighborhood peeping in through the screen door at them?

And damn her, she'd liked it.

Liked being kissed by him. Liked that he'd done it in front of people. Liked that he wasn't ashamed of claiming.

Then he'd gone and ruined it all by firing her.

Talk about mixed messages. No wonder she couldn't sleep.

Finally, she slept for a few restless hours, got up, had breakfast with her family—Dad made his famous pecan waffles for the occasion—and she took a few boxes over to the house on Peach Street. She and Stephanie had planned on painting the walls before fully moving their things.

Stephanie got to the house not long after Breeanne arrived and they drove together in Stephanie's red Mustang convertible to a big-box home improvement store in Tyler to pick out the paint and supplies. They looked at paint swatches and simultaneously, they fell in love with a satiny color called Magic Mist that was a blush of lavender mixed with a whisper of dove gray.

"It's romantic without being too obvious," Stephanie declared.

"And perfectly matches the couch my parents are giving us from the antique store," Breeanne said.

"Great minds think alike." Stephanie held up a palm for a high five.

Breeanne surprised herself by asking Stephanie if she'd mind going clothes shopping with her. Since she'd gained a little weight, she needed a new wardrobe. But that was an excuse, wasn't it? She wanted the stylish woman's opinion on clothing so she could look sexier for Rowdy. She'd do anything to keep him from quitting the book.

Well, maybe not *anything* . . .

They had a great morning shopping and giggling together. They grabbed lunch at an Italian bistro and then went back to the house to paint and hang curtains well into the night.

For the remainder of the Memorial Day weekend, with help from family and friends, they moved into the house. It wasn't until Breeanne was curled up in bed at night that she felt a little homesick, and missed Callie. Mom had said Breeanne could bring the calico to the new house as long as she brought Callie over to Timeless Treasures each morning. The calico was a fixture at the antique store and the customers loved her. But Stephanie turned out to be allergic to cats, so that ended that. To make up for it, Stephanie graciously gave Breeanne the master bedroom.

Tuesday morning, Breeanne awoke to the smell of bacon and eggs. She threw on a bathrobe and padded into the kitchen to find Stephanie standing at the stove with a spatula in her hand, fully dressed, a cheetah-print scarf tied at her neck. The table was set for two, complete with glasses of freshly poured orange juice.

"Good morning!" Stephanie chirped. "I thought I'd make breakfast."

"That's really sweet of you. Can I help?"

"No, no. Sit down. Have some juice."

"I have a scarf just like that one," Breeanne said.

Stephanie carried a Teflon pan over to the table and spooned scrambled eggs onto the two plates. "I know. It's yours."

"What?"

Stephanie's polished smile was smooth and even.

She put a French-manicured hand to the scarf at her neck. "I borrowed it. I hope you don't mind. You're so easy to get along with that I knew you wouldn't mind. But it perfectly matches my skirt." She swept a hand at her orangey-brown pencil skirt that did indeed match the spots on the scarf. "I have an interview with the *Longview News-Journal* at ten."

The scarf did look good on Stephanie. Much better than it looked on Breeanne.

"Isn't it scratchy?" Breeanne said, a bit irritated by Stephanie's high-handedness, and yes, there was a niggle of jealousy too.

"Now that you mention it, the material is rough, but it's so pretty I can overlook that. Thanks for letting me borrow it."

Breeanne opened her mouth to ask her not to wear it, but the words stuck to the roof of her mouth, clinging like peanut butter. Stephanie had been so nice to make breakfast. Maybe this was how it was with roommates? Share and share alike? What was proper roommate etiquette? She had no idea.

"It's okay, right?" Stephanie blinked, wide-eyed, managing to look both Bambi-defenseless and adorable.

"Um . . ."

Stephanie embraced Breeanne, giving her a quick, cool hug. "You are the best roommate ever! Feel free to borrow my clothes any time you want."

Yeah, right. Breeanne was a size zero, and Stephanie was a voluptuous size eight.

"Cross your fingers that I ace the interview." Stephanie crossed her fingers.

Feeling like a doofus, Breeanne smiled, crossed the fingers of both hands. and held them up for Stephanie to see. "Good luck."

"Rooming with you makes me feel so calm and peaceful. You're so easy to get along with." Stephanie giggled. "I feel as if I've found a soft place to land."

"Don't mention it," Breeanne said, and lifted a bite of eggs to her mouth, but she had no appetite.

CHAPTER 16

*Baseball is the only field of endeavor where
a man can succeed three times out of ten
and be considered a good performer.*

—TED WILLIAMS

Rowdy lounged on the patio chaise and pushed his sunglasses down on his nose for a better look at Breeanne, who was standing beside the infinity pool clutching her laptop computer to her chest, and his stupid old heart melted.

Today, she wore shorter shorts than she'd ever worn, daring red ones with cuffs that hit her mid-thigh, and he couldn't help hoping she'd worn them for him. Never mind that her legs were pale. He loved her coloring, and those adorable coltish legs.

He whistled at her.

She blushed and lowered her computer to cover her bare knees.

Maybe he shouldn't have done that. Then again, since he was trying to get her to quit the book, maybe he should be doing more whistling, and ogling, and . . .

Be careful. If he did too much of that other stuff, he'd be the one crying uncle.

Nolan Ryan loped over, and she set her laptop down on the patio table so she could lean over to pet him.

Rowdy took full advantage of the movement, studying the fine curve of her rump and salivating.

The last time he'd seen her, she'd looked like a Tasmanian she-devil out for blood. Her hair curled wild and frizzy from their day at the pond, her green eyes flashing fire, her chest heaving with angry breaths. And damn if he hadn't been super turned on by her fierce determination. He loved the hot fire that raged inside such a demure package and he couldn't help wondering what she would be like in bed once she got over her initial nervousness.

Ah shit, was he in serious trouble here?

The urge to grab her by the wrist and tug her down on top of him had Rowdy sitting up straight and leaning forward. But his chest tightened and his throat closed up at the same time that she thankfully, regrettably moved out of grabbing distance and sat down at the patio table, Nolan Ryan sinking down on her feet.

How was she going to be with him today? Shy or fierce? Prim or relaxed? How should he react? Pretend Friday never happened? Apologize again? Tease her? Keep his distance? Was she still mad at him for trying to fire her? Or had she already forgiven him?

Christ, he'd never second-guessed himself so much in his life.

Feeling like he was losing his grip, he pushed his sunglasses back up on the bridge of his nose to hide his eyes, and leaned back against the lounger as if he couldn't be bothered to get up.

"Good morning," she said with a big smile.

Apparently, all was forgiven. Relief poured through him. He was at the mercy of that smile.

"Hey," he said, his voice coming out so husky he had to clear his throat.

"Do you want to work out here?"

"Is the sunlight going to bother you on the laptop?"

"I can record you and transcribe later," she said, pulling a voice recorder from her purse and setting it on the patio table.

"I'm comfortable here if you are," he said, bracing the backs of his hands in his interlaced palms, hoping to look much more relaxed than he felt.

"Works for me," she said, sitting straight as a razor in her chair. "I heard through the grapevine that an anonymous donor gave money to have a community center, including a Little League field, built near a school in your old neighborhood. Did you have anything to do with that?"

Darn it. He'd wanted to keep that quiet. He wasn't looking for accolades. After visiting his old neighborhood on Friday, and seeing it again through fresh eyes, he'd met with the town's movers and shakers over the weekend, with stipulations on how the money would be used and under the condition that he was to remain anonymous. He couldn't believe it was already being broadcast through the local grapevine. He'd forgotten how quickly gossip moved through a small town.

Hell, half the town was probably already taking bets on when he and Breeanne would hook up, especially after he went to her family's crawfish boil. Why hadn't he left when no one answered the door? He should have left.

"It was you, wasn't it?"

He shrugged.

"Guilty conscience because you got out?"

"You're assuming I was the donor."

"That's a lot of money."

"I can afford it."

"Don't you need to be saving your money? It's not going to be rolling in like it used to."

She made a good point, but he'd been thinking of the kids that would benefit in a community center in that rough neighborhood and not of his own future. He had enough. He would be all right.

"Someday you'll want to get married," she went on, "and have kids. They'll need a legacy."

"You're assuming a lot," he said. "Like some woman would have me."

She snorted. "They'd line up for miles."

He grinned. "You never know. I'm not all that easy to live with."

"You've never lived with a woman before?"

"Other than my mother and sisters? No."

Was it his imagination or did she look pleased by this tidbit?

"But you want kids, right? I mean most people do."

He shrugged. "I don't think that far ahead, Breezy. I figure, take care of the kids who need it today and worry about the fictitious kids when and if they appear."

"Aha!" She held up a finger. "It was you."

"Busted."

Her face softened. "That was really sweet of you."

"Don't go putting me up on a pedestal, sweetheart. I'll just fall off and disappoint you."

"You could never disappoint me," she said so adamantly that he knew disappointing her was inevitable. That damn pedestal was way too high.

"You can't tell anyone I gave the money."

"Mum's the word, but people will guess."

He raised a casual shoulder. "Let 'em speculate. We're not going to confirm it."

The sun beat on his bare chest, sending a rivulet of sweat sliding down his breastbone. He tugged on his T-shirt, got up, and moved to the sheltering umbrella of the patio table. Purposefully, he pulled out the chair beside Breeanne instead of across from her.

Her gaze flashed up to his, and she pulled her bottom lip up between her teeth, her nipples hardening underneath her shirt and her eyes taking on a sultry cast. He turned her on.

Then again, she turned him on just as thoroughly.

She must have seen where his gaze went because she folded her arms over her breasts. "Ahem," she said. "Shall we get down to work?"

"Take it away, Breezy." He flapped a hand.

"I thought we could talk about Dugan Potts today and the animosity between the two of you."

"Let's not."

"We're going to have to talk about him sometime. Why not get it out of the way?"

"I'm not in the mood," he said simply.

"Oh." She canted her head, looked at him like an inquisitive wren. "What do you want to talk about?"

He leaned in closer, his knee almost brushing hers. The familiar pink flush crawled up her neck, but she swallowed hard, fought it off. "Let's talk about sex."

"Sex?" she whispered.

"Sex," he confirmed.

"What about sex?"

"You know." He kept leaning closer, until his face was mere inches from hers. "The women I've known. The places I've made love."

She squirmed. "Mmm, isn't that a bit graphic?"

"Hey." He shrugged again even though his muscles were so tense his shoulders ached when he lifted them. "This is a tell-all. And sex sells."

"Yes, but so do secrets, and I have a feeling you're hiding a doozy about you and Dugan Potts."

Boy, the woman had a one-track mind. What was

he going to have to do to derail her? Kiss her again? The thought was quite appealing.

"What's the matter, Breezy?" he asked. "You scared you're going to get aroused?"

She pressed her palms flat against the tabletop. "Not at all."

"Then you won't mind if I tell you about my thirtieth birthday when my team surprised me with a gigantic birthday cake in the locker room after the game."

She licked her lips. "How big of a cake was it?"

"Big enough for a buxom blonde to fit inside of it."

"Oh," she said. "*That* kind of cake."

"Yeah." He was so close now all he would have to do in order to kiss her was rock his head forward an inch. "That kind of cake."

Breeanne fumbled for the recorder, and switched it on. "Rowdy Blanton. Interview Number Seven." She leaned away from him. "So on your thirtieth birthday, the team got you a stripper in a cake. What was she wearing?"

"I dunno, I don't remember."

"But this was a once-in-a-lifetime event," she said. "How can you not know what she was wearing?"

"It was a G-string thing with pasties."

"I see. Is that how you like for your women to dress in the bedroom?"

"She was a stripper, Breezy, not one of my *women*."

"So you don't like for your women to wear G-strings and pasties?"

"Is this for the book? Because the question seems a bit far afield."

She reached over and hit the pause button on the recorder, and in a conspiratorial voice murmured, "Actually, this question is for my edification."

He narrowed his eyes, and studied her for so long that she dropped her gaze. "What do you mean?"

"I've been thinking about sex . . ."

"Oh you have?" he couldn't resist teasing.

"Yes. Being with you has shown me that I've been missing out on a lot and I just want to understand what guys like so that my first time will go as smoothly as possible."

"You got a particular fella in mind?" The thought of Breeanne having sex with someone other than him made Rowdy want to smack a ball so hard with a bat that it would fly over Stardust Lake.

"No, no. Just general information."

He blotted sweat from his forehead with the tail of his T-shirt.

"I'm inexperienced. I want to understand men and what they want. You've had a lot of sexual adventures, I figured I could learn a lot from you."

"You can't use my life as your sexual playbook."

"Why not?"

"Well for one thing, every man is different. For another, it would get you into a lot of trouble."

"I'm ready for a little trouble."

"Oh no, Breezy, trust me, you are *not*. That would be like turning a toddler loose in Times Square."

"I've never been to Times Square. I've not been anywhere. Except to hospitals. I've been to plenty of those."

"Why don't you tell me about that?" he asked.

She watched him and a sultry expression came over her face and he felt his body stiffen again. Damn it. Every time he was around her, he got an erection.

The scent of his sweat churned the air between. Her nose twitched and her gaze slid slowly down his chest. He forced himself to breathe slow and deep.

"About the birthday cake girl," she prompted.

He didn't want to talk about this anymore. *Shut up, Blanton, and tell her what she wants to hear.* If he didn't talk about sex, he was going to have to talk about Potts and his suspension and he couldn't risk going there. Not as long as Zach was part of the Gunslingers organization. His goal was to get her to quit the book.

"Forget the birthday cake woman. Nothing happened with her."

"Oh." She sounded disappointed. Nolan Ryan got up to get a drink of water from his dish by the back door. She shifted in her chair, crossing her legs at the knee. "Okay. Moving on. What was your grandest seduction of all time?"

He gazed down the hill to the valley below, but all he could see were shapely legs the color of fresh cream.

"Rowdy?" she prompted. "Are you all right?"

"Fine." His tone was as clipped as a GI's haircut. He heard her click on the recorder again, but he didn't look over, just kept his gaze trained on the lake, trying his best to tame his erection.

"You've had hundreds of exciting experiences. Readers want to live vicariously through you. Don't hold back. Share your secrets."

He stroked his jaw with his thumb and forefinger, and cut her a glance from his peripheral vision. She rested a hand beside his, she wanted to touch him, but then she snapped her hand back and tucked it underneath the pit of her other arm.

"Are you still with me?" she asked, her voice tremulous.

"Why don't we take a break?" he said. "Want some lemonade? I'll make us some lemonade."

"Are you embarrassed? Is that it? I won't judge you if that's what you're afraid of."

He scratched the back of his neck. She was so innocent. He didn't want to sully her with stories of his wild ways.

"I'm a writer," she said. "I need details, lots and lots of sensory details. I need to know what you saw and touched and smelled and tasted and heard and thought and felt. I need emotion."

"You gotta give me a minute," he said, stalling, unsure of how to handle this. "My memory isn't what it used to be."

She rested her elbows on the table, propped her chin in her upturned palms. "How many women *have* you been with?"

Not as many as the tabloids attributed to him, but enough that he didn't want to tell her, afraid she would think less of him. "It's tacky to get specific about numbers."

"What was your grandest seduction?" she pressed.

"I once flew a woman to Paris in a private jet," he said, unable to think of how to stall her. He didn't want her bringing up Potts again.

"Aw, just like an episode of *The Bachelor*."

He turned to face her. "Don't pretend you wouldn't like being whisked off to France in a private jet."

"You're right. That was sour grapes. I'm jealous. What was her name?"

He tapped his chin, trapped between his playboy reputation and his fear that she would find him sleazy. Should he come clean or pretend he didn't remember? Habit and fear of letting her get too close won out.

"Um . . . Lucy . . . no, Lacy . . . no," he said. "That's not right."

She gave him that look. The one that said, *You're better than this.*

No. No, he wasn't. But when he was around her, he wished that he were a better man. He wanted her to admire, and respect him.

"You flew this woman to Paris in a private jet and you don't remember her name?"

"It was a long time ago."

"How long?"

"I dunno. Nine, ten years?"

"If a guy flew me to Paris I'd remember his name for the rest of my life."

He felt like a total scoundrel. What was it she'd called him? A bounder? She was right. He was one.

"Laila." He snapped his fingers. "Her name was Laila. Laila Navinski. She wore a yellow sundress the day we strolled to the Champs-Élysées. The dress had blue polka dots on it, a really short hem, and had those skinny little straps . . ." He motioned toward his shoulders with both hands.

"Spaghetti straps."

"Yeah, spaghetti straps, and she smelled like magnolias. Her perfume reminded me of East Texas." He stared off in space for a moment. "I think that's why I liked her. She smelled familiar."

"Ooh, keep going." Squinting against the sun's glare, she started pecking at the keyboard.

He studied her profile. She had a nice profile, even with the dark glasses perched on the end of her cute little nose.

"This is good," she said. "Great stuff. Perfect. Exactly the kind of details your readers are looking for. What happened with you and Laila?"

"Nothing. We came home. I went back to Seattle,

where I was playing with the Mariners at the time, and she went back to wherever it was she was from."

She raised her head. "That's it?"

"What did you expect? I've already told you I don't do long-term relationships."

"You didn't see Laila after that?"

He shook his head. "No. Not that I recall."

She made a noise, half irritation, half exasperation. "That's just plain sad."

"What do you mean?"

"Don't you ever want more?"

"What more is there?" He shrugged, but his gut pitched and rolled the way it had when he'd gone deep-sea fishing. "We had a terrific time."

"You liked her, she liked you. She smelled like East Texas and you went to Paris together. The relationship should have gone somewhere. Why didn't it go somewhere, Rowdy?"

Why, because he'd been waiting to feel something monumental, something that he hadn't felt until now. With Breeanne. But he wasn't ready to think about that, much less tell her. He had enough on his plate worrying about what Potts might do to Zach. He needed to have his head in the game.

"It's hard being the girlfriend of a professional base-ball player," he said, giving her the pat excuse. "We're on the road all the time. Laila wanted somebody who would stay home and work in the garden with her."

"Do you think Laila found what she was looking for?"

"Why are you so worried about Laila?"

"She sounds nice. You treated her crappy. She de-served happily-ever-after."

"I didn't treat her crappy. For crying out loud I flew the woman to Paris. I gave her the trip of her life."

"And you only remembered her ten years later when I forced you to remember her. Poor Laila. Didn't she deserve more than that from you?"

"I was twenty-four. My career was just getting started."

"Then why did you lead her on by taking her to Paris?"

"Believe me, Laila was a big girl. She knew how to take care of herself."

"I bet you broke her heart."

"I didn't."

"You might have."

"I *didn't*."

"How can you be so sure?"

"Look, why do you care? If I had hooked up with Laila I wouldn't be here with you now, would I?"

"But you're not *with* me, are you? You're not with anyone unless you count Warwick. You're alone, out of a job, your career is over, your brother has taken your place on the mound, and I'm nothing more an annoying ghostwriter who is forcing you to examine your life."

"Yeah," he said. "You are."

He snapped his jaw shut. Pressed into a hard line. He got up and stalked inside the house feeling like a total shitheel.

Chapter 17

I let the other guys handle the talking. I love playing.

—Andy Pettitte

She'd pushed too far.

Breeanne tucked her computer under her arm, and ran after him. "Rowdy, I'm sorry."

He didn't look back. Disappeared into the house.

She found him in his office rummaging through his desk. She closed the door behind her. He didn't look at her. Her stomach slunk into her throat.

"Did you hear me? I said I'm sorry."

Frowning, he dug deeper into the drawer.

"I pushed you to talk," she said, "and when you opened up, I got judgmental. That wasn't fair and I have no right to judge. Who am I to judge anyone? I'm just a spinster virgin. What do I know?"

He pulled out a stack of baseball cards, closed the drawer, sat and shuffled through them as if they were a Hoyle deck.

Sinking into the chair opposite his desk, she watched him. What was he looking for?

Rowdy found the card he was searching for, tossed it across the desk. It landed upside down in her lap.

She turned it over. "Joe Renner. Who's he?"

"Read the card."

"Shortstop for the Florida Marlins from 2005 to 2008." Glanced back up at him. "And?"

"Have you ever heard that old Simon and Garfunkel song 'Cecilia'?"

"I think so. Is it the one about a guy who is making love to his girlfriend one afternoon and he gets up to go to the bathroom and when he comes back she's with another guy?"

"That's the one."

"So . . . Laila and Joe Renner?"

"In Paris."

Sympathy for him pushed at the seams of her heart, in a way that she found alarming, and she rubbed her chest with the heel of her palm, shook her head. "No, Rowdy, no."

"Two in the morning Laila gets a craving for quiche from an all-night restaurant on rue St. Dominique where we'd gone earlier in the week. It was halfway across town, but I went because it made her happy."

"Aw, dammit. I am so sorry I pried."

"I came back to the hotel. I had just stepped off the elevator, carrying quiche Lorraine, whistling 'King of the Road,' because life was good and I was in Paris with a pretty girl."

Breeanne tensed, gripped the arms of the chair, and leaned forward, dreading to hear what he was going to say next.

"And there in the middle of the night, our hotel room door opens and out saunters Joe Renner with a shit-eating grin on his face as he zipped up his pants."

She longed to plug her ears, but she had started this. She had to see it through.

"Renner takes one look at me and lights off for the stairs, running faster than he ever ran bases." Rowdy paused. "That enough detail for you, Breezy?"

"That bitch!" Breeanne smacked the desk with her fist, sending the pencil holder jumping.

"Simmer down, sweetheart, it was almost ten years ago." He chuckled. "Laila was playing by the rules I set up. No strings. No commitments. No emotional attachment. Keeping things light and easy. How could I blame her for playing by my rules?"

"The woman lacked decorum. She sent you on a fool's mission so she could cuckold you."

"Cuckold?"

"Traditionally, the term refers to the husband of a flagrant adulteress. I used it in this case because she was damn brazen with her cheating. Why didn't she just suggest a threesome?"

"You've got strange ideas about me, Breezy. Just because I like to have fun and enjoy spending time with women, doesn't mean that I'm up for anything. I might not be into long-term commitments, but when I'm with a woman, I'm with her and only her. She, and she alone, is my focus." His hot gaze sizzled. "Got it?"

"Got it." Her hands were trembling. "Still . . . for Laila to go all 'Cecilia' on you? Uncool. Totally uncool."

He shrugged it away as if he were rinsing soap off his back in the shower. "I should have known something was up. Laila liked taking risks and having sex in places where there was a chance of getting caught."

The idea of making love outdoors thrilled her. Then again, the idea of making love anywhere thrilled her. "Name places where you guys had adventuresome sex."

"We did it in the ladies' restroom at the Louvre. You can put that part in the book, but do me a favor and leave out the Joe Renner thing."

"Whatever you say. But Laila deserves to have her dirty laundry aired."

"To tell the truth, it would probably make her day."

"Let's not do her any favors." Breeanne straightened. "Beside, you have too much class to stoop to her level."

"No one has ever accused me of that."

"Well, you do. And you showed a Herculean self-control for not punching Renner in the face."

"I might have punched him." Rowdy's laugh was dry and humorless. "If I could have caught him."

"Wait a minute. How was it that Joe Renner just *happened* to be in Paris at the same time you guys were?"

"He wasn't. She made a booty call and he hopped on a plane."

"Oh my God! Does the woman have no shame?"

"I count my blessings that it happened before social media was big. Today, she would have been all over Facebook bragging about her doubleheader."

"I'm so sorry I ragged on you about mistreating her when she was the one who broke *your* heart."

"Nah." He waved a dismissive hand. "Just bruised the hell out of my ego."

"If you would be upfront with me, I wouldn't go jumping to conclusions."

"It's fun to watch you get froggy." He winked, but the wink didn't have his usual perk in it.

She picked up the Joe Renner card. "If Laila didn't break your heart, then why did you keep this?"

"I didn't. I bought a stash of baseball cards for the kids I'm coaching."

"You coach Little League?"

"I sponsor a three-day baseball clinic at a summer camp for underprivileged kids. I wish I could coach Little League, but I'm too well-known."

"Why didn't you tell me?"

"I just did. It's not something I usually share because I don't want people to think I'm using what I do for the kids as a pedestal to hoist myself up on."

"That's fine, but I'm your ghostwriter, you can't keep secrets from me. You have to tell me everything."

"Are you sure you want to know? There are a lot of skeletons in this closet."

"I can handle it."

"You say that now . . ."

Breeanne tapped the face of Joe Renner's card. "This card honestly doesn't mean anything to you?"

"Nothing."

"Do you mind if I have it?"

"It's all yours." Rowdy cocked his head. "But why do you want it?"

"To take out my anger on your behalf." She held the card in both hands and ripped Joe Renner's smiling face right off his body. Then she ripped the pieces in two. And then ripped those up, until nothing was left of Joe Renner except for tiny bits of glossy paper.

Rowdy's pupils widened, and amusement pleated his lips. "Remind me never to get on your bad side."

Consumed by the sexual tension that had plagued them all day, and Rowdy's heartfelt confession about Laila and Joe Renner, Breeanne barely slept that night.

Thoughts of the day turned into a review of everything that had happened from the moment she'd gotten beaned with his baseball. The events of the past month circled in her head, as she reviewed them again and again. One memory would land, she'd examine it, and then it would fly away and another memory would swoop in. She'd worry over the one for a time, doze, and then another memory would nudge her awake.

That went on until dawn, an endless merry-go-round of mental photos, both remembered and embellished.

In her mind's eye she could see Rowdy, a boy of eight or nine, sitting on the saggy porch of the run-down old house, tossing a baseball into the air, playing catch with himself while listening to the Texas Rangers on the radio.

She could smell the pungent creosote. Could taste the tar in the air. Could hear the sound of the mournful train whistle, and the endless clacking of the railroad cars upon the tracks.

Then they were in the forest of pines, dark and spooky and cavelike in its thickness, and crossing that woodsy threshold into the clearing and the beautiful oasis waiting for them there. Because she'd dared to step outside her comfort zone, she'd found a sparkling gem. The special place that Rowdy had never taken another woman.

How glorious it had been, naked in nature. The sun kissing every inch of her bare body, and filling her with life-giving energy. Rowdy with his arms in the air, turning his back to her while the sound of his teasing laughter bounced off the trees. The mysterious water, where unknown things lurked, lapping at her breasts.

She poked the scary moment when she believed a snake had brushed against her leg. She cringed at how she'd panicked, slipped and fell. But her spirits soared remembering what it had felt like as Rowdy's arms went around her, his deep voice promising that as long as he had her, she was safe.

She couldn't forget the look in his eyes when he saw her scars for the first time. How he'd been concerned and caring, but not repulsed. She savored again the flavor of his mouth when he'd kissed her in her parents' kitchen. How he'd fired her and then immediately re-hired her when she called him on the carpet.

Each thought, each memory, each feeling brought her to the same place. She wanted him.

Yes, he was a charmer.

Yes, she was stepping off an emotional cliff.

Yes, she was not going to end up with him. Not for the long haul.

None of that mattered. She wanted him. More than that, she wanted to live a little. She wanted to get on the dance floor of life, and shake her booty. She wanted experiences. Hungered for them. Craved them. Yearned for them.

She wanted to have sex, and she wanted to have it with Rowdy Blanton. It should be an easy enough goal to obtain. He'd been with scores of women. He was the one she wanted to give her virginity to. If she was going to lose it, she wanted to lose it big. She wanted someone who could not only show her the ropes, but give her the ride of a lifetime.

And she had a plan.

Question was, was she brave enough to go through it?

While the sun peeked over the horizon that second day of June, she got dressed, gathered up her purse, her car keys, and her courage, and went to ask her younger sister how to seduce a man.

After talking to Suki, Breeanne came away with a plan to seduce Rowdy and tame the sexual tension that was making working together so difficult, but she had no idea how or where she was going to pull it off. She couldn't just fling herself into his arms and holler, *Do me*, although it was tempting.

"You wore the scarf," Rowdy said when he opened the door to her that morning, and her knees almost buckled when he reached out to stroke the scarf at her neck.

"My good luck charm. I thought it might help me focus on the work today. We're so far behind."

"*Our* good luck charm," he corrected. "If it hadn't been for the scarf I would never have hired you."

"Oh?" she said.

"Yeah. Once you told me that only we could feel the softness of it, I knew we were on the same wavelength."

Her heart fluttered hopefully at the same time doubt clutched her. She wanted sex with him, she'd convinced herself she could have sex with him and be okay with nothing more than a physical relationship, but when he said romantic things like that she wanted to run away. If she seduced him, ultimately she was in for a world of hurt. Was the momentary pleasure worth the pain?

He led the way into his den, and while he wasn't looking, she whipped off the scarf and tucked it into her purse.

Inside the den, the TV was turned to a sports talk show on ESPN and they were talking about how well the Gunslingers were doing. As Breeanne sank into the plush leather armchair, Rowdy leaned his blue-jeaned butt against the majestic mahogany desk. The mother-of-pearl snaps at the cuff of his Western-style shirt caught the light from the deer-antler chandelier hogging the ceiling.

She settled the notebook computer on her lap and powered it up.

On the ESPN talk show the commentators were speculating about Zach.

"You know," said one commentator. "You have to wonder why the Gunslingers called Zach Blanton up. He's got promise, but is he really big league material?"

The camera flashed to a second commentator who said, "It makes me wonder if Potts picked up the younger Blanton just to get a dig in at his older brother."

Breeanne shifted her gaze from the TV to Rowdy. A shadow of beard dusted his tightly clenched jaw. He folded his arms over his chest, and scowled.

"Seems like a bad decision to me," said a third commentator. "Letting a personal vendetta get in the way of a strong pitching roster."

"Makes you wonder what really happened between Dugan Potts and Rowdy Blanton," the first commentator added.

Rowdy picked up the remote control from the desk, flicked off the TV, and strode across the hand-scraped oak hardwood flooring in custom-made cowboy boots. With each step he took, Breeanne's heart beat faster. He dropped onto the black and white cowhide couch next to her chair, slouched against the cushions, propped his feet on the rustic coffee table, and cradled the back of his head in his interlaced palms. In spite of his relaxed posture, his muscles were tensed.

"Have you heard from Zach since your run-in?" Breeanne asked.

Rowdy lifted a hand to his lip that was almost healed. "He won't take my calls or answer my texts."

"You wounded his pride."

"I know." Rowdy rubbed his temple, winced.

"Tension headache?"

He grunted. "Yeah."

Was he knotted up over conflict with his brother? She got to her feet. "Would you like some aspirin?"

"Sit. I already took aspirin. It didn't cut it. Those weeks I spent on painkillers after my attack raised my tolerance."

She eased back into the chair. Rowdy was usually so laid back. She hadn't ever seen him this tense. "Is there anything I can do?"

"I'll be fine. Let's get to work."

"You know, because I had so much pain after my surgeries, the doctor recommended alternative therapies in conjunction with medication. I find acupressure and reflexology techniques can be helpful for pain management."

He squinted at her, grimaced.

"Light sensitive?"

He barely nodded.

She got up, switched off the chandelier, and pulled the blinds. "Better?"

"Thanks." His face was the color of chalk.

"You look miserable. Do you get headaches a lot?"

"Not since I was a kid worried about how I was going to take care of Mom, my sisters, and Zach."

She imagined him as a child burdened with headaches from growing up in that rough neighborhood with an ailing father, and her heart wrenched. "Would you like for me to massage the acupressure point for you?"

"Hell, I'm ready to try anything. The damn headache started in the middle of the night and it feels like Santa's elves are building a workshop inside my skull."

"I think I can make it better."

"What do I need to do?"

She set her computer on the coffee table and got up. "Take off your boots, and lie down on the couch."

He moved to the couch she'd just vacated, and leaned over to take off his boots, but he winced and slumped back against the cushion. "Give me a minute. Bending over makes the pounding worse."

She went over to him. "Stretch out."

Closing his eyes, he rested his head on the armrest, his long body taking up the remainder of the couch. The man was always in motion. This was the first time since she'd known him that he'd been so still.

She took off his boots and socks and settled them on the floor, surprised at how intimate doing so seemed. As if they were a couple. Her pulse sped up the way it always did when she was close to him. Would this feeling ever go away?

Stop thinking this way. You're not a couple.

She lifted up his legs, sat down on the couch beside him, his legs across her lap, and began rubbing the big toe of his right foot.

"This is supposed to help my headache?"

"I know it's hard for a smooth talker like you, but be quiet for a minute." She looked everywhere except at his sexy feet. There was something far too intimate about this.

He was quiet for all of ten seconds. "That feels good. You could do this for a living."

"Shh." She moved to the other foot, and kneaded that big toe.

He didn't last ten seconds that time. "Gosh, Breezy, no one's taken care of me like this since . . . Well, I don't believe anyone has ever taken care of me like this."

"I don't believe that for a minute."

"It's true. My mom was so busy taking care of my dad and holding down a job and raising four kids, essentially on her own, that I sort of slipped through the cracks. Not that I'm whining. Mom did her best."

"None of your girlfriends ever took care of you?"

"I don't date the kind of women who are into nurturing, if you know what I mean."

She did. He preferred party girls who weren't looking for anything more than a good time. "What about when you were recovering from your injuries? Who took care of you then?"

"Okay, Warwick does look after me, but he's not as pretty as you are." He raised his head, winked.

"Your headache is better?"

"It's completely gone. You're a miracle worker."

"Not a miracle worker." She smiled, praying it did not give away how much touching him unraveled her. "Just forced to find various ways to deal with pain."

"Hey," Rowdy said, sitting up and reaching for his boots. "Bet you never guessed that the suffering you went through would end up bringing pleasure to others."

He was right about that. All those times she lay in a hospital bed, battling to keep from dying, it never once entered her head that she'd be rubbing away pain for a major league baseball star.

"You know," he said. "I think I'm going to Dallas this weekend. The Gunslingers are home, and maybe if I show up in person Zach will talk to me."

"It couldn't hurt," she said, a self-serving thought popping into her head. If Rowdy went out of town for a day, it would be the perfect time to go through with the seduction Suki had helped her plan. "When would you be back?"

"I'd go over on Friday evening, see if I could make contact with Zach. Maybe see some old friends. I'd be home by Saturday evening. Warwick is going to be out of town this weekend and I couldn't leave Nolan Ryan alone for longer than that.

"Hey," she said, marveling at the opportunity he'd just dropped into her lap. "If you want, I can feed and walk Nolan Ryan while you're gone."

CHAPTER 18

Being with a woman all night never hurt no
professional baseball player. It's staying up all night
looking for a woman that does him in.

—CASEY STENGEL

The scene was set.

A bottle of sparkling wine chilled in a silver bucket on the bedside table. Two wine glasses, a tray of chocolate-covered strawberries, and a box of condoms sat beside it. And she had a seductive playlist loaded in the mp3 player, LL Cool J currently crooned "Doin' It." Two scented candles—one vanilla, one cinnamon—flickered and danced on the dresser on the other side of the oversized, totally masculine bedroom. A black and gray comforter topped the king-sized bed and on the wooden spindles of the headboard, she'd tied the cheetah scarf.

She took off her glasses and studied herself in the full-length mirror mounted on the closet door, both shocked and pleased by the vixen she spied there decked out in Victoria's Secret. Suki had done her makeup for her and while her sister had been heavy-handed with the eyeliner and mascara, Breeanne couldn't believe the transformation, with the paint and spackle she could actually pass for pretty. Suki had been after her for years to use more makeup and she wished she'd listened.

What would Rowdy think when he saw her?

Chill bumps raced up her arms and she couldn't stop imagining the slow grin that would slide across his face. Soon she would be one hundred percent a woman. But she was ready to go and there was no one to do it with.

Her gaze shifted to the clock. Seven-fifteen.

That was the only fly in the ointment of her grand seduction. Rowdy had said he'd be home on Saturday evening, but he hadn't been specific as to the exact time. She'd finished arranging everything at six-thirty and now she felt at loose ends.

She paced the bedroom, hummed along to Sade singing "By Your Side." Was the song too romantic? She didn't want Rowdy getting the wrong idea and thinking that she expected anything more from him than just sex, because she didn't. Well, that was a lie. She did. But she knew better than to wish for that. She'd take what she could get. Sex was plenty. It would be enough.

Oh God, was she making a huge mistake? Should she bag up all this stuff and get out of here while she could?

Snap out of it.

Running away wasn't going to get her anywhere. She craved excitement, adventure, and a life like every other single woman her age.

Should she text him? Ask when he was coming home, but then he might ask why she wanted to know. She needed something to calm her down. Walk Nolan Ryan again? Get dressed and get sweaty? The wrong kind of sweaty. Then she would have to shower and risk ruining her makeup and what if Rowdy came home when she was in the middle of it?

What she really needed was something to chill her out.

Her gaze fell on the wine bucket. Surely, he wouldn't mind if she opened it without him. She was probably supposed to be letting it breathe anyway, but she didn't know the first thing about wine. Truthfully, she hardly drank. She had a sip or two of champagne for New Year's and celebrations, but her old heart medications hadn't mixed with alcohol and she hadn't had a chance to experiment since going off them.

A couple of sips of wine might be the ticket to calm her jangled nerves.

This was her first time opening a bottle of bubbly and she wasn't sure how to go about it. In movies champagne corks were always going wild and shooting around the room, ricocheting off stuff. The last thing she wanted was to put her own eye out.

Forget the wine. Let Rowdy handle it when he gets here.

She couldn't remember a single old movie where the woman opened a bottle of her own seduction champagne or sparkling wine.

Right. She perched on the edge of the bed. Watched the number on the digital clock flip. Seven thirty-five. Seven thirty-six.

She shivered again, this time from cold. She'd tried to turn the temperature up a tad, but he had one of those complicated modern thermostats she couldn't figure out, downside of growing up, and working, in old buildings.

Wine might warm you up.

She picked up the bottle of Prosecco. The guy at the liquor store had said with a leer, "Good wine to get jiggy wid it," when she'd asked his recommendation for what wine best paired with a romantic evening, leaving her to wonder if she did indeed want to get "jiggy wid it," whatever he meant by that.

"You know how to open that?" he had asked, ringing her up.

"Yes," she'd lied.

Caterpillar eyebrows climbed up his short forehead an uh-sure-you-do expression.

As she was walking out the door, he hollered, "Don't put your eye out with that."

She wished Rowdy would get her so they could get "jiggy wid it" together. She picked up the wine, ice water sluicing off it, to drop on her bare toes. She shivered again. Things were starting to unravel.

Soldier on.

Breeanne studied the bottle. Opening it seemed pretty clear-cut, but she didn't want to make a mistake, so she Googled "how to open a bottle of champagne."

Google took her to an article on WikiHow, and yes, uncorking champagne—aka sparkling wine when it wasn't from Champagne, France—was as straightforward as it looked. But the article did come with the dire warning: *Don't put your eye out.* Causing her to wonder exactly how many people had put out an eye with a champagne cork?

Gingerly, she followed the directions in the Web site article, and was rewarded with a soft, gentle pop. The cork landed elegantly in the middle of the comforter. Would you look at that? She was no longer a virgin at opening champagne bottles. Hopefully, her next virginity-busting move would be equally as satisfying.

Except it was eight o'clock and Rowdy still wasn't home.

What if he'd changed his mind and decided to stay in Dallas? What if he and Zach had made contact and were bonding with a night on the town? What if he'd hooked up with a woman?

What if, what if, what if.

To keep from wigging out completely, she poured a glass of the Prosecco, and took a sip. The bubbles tickled her nose. The lightly, sweet, fruity taste reminded her of the Moonglow pears that grew on the backyard trees at Timeless Treasures.

Idly, Breeanne picked up a chocolate-covered strawberry. By eight-thirty, she'd eaten three chocolate-covered strawberries, drank the glass of Prosecco, and poured another. "I Threw a Seduction and Nobody Came," she said to her reflection in the mirror. "That'll be the name of my autobiography."

Not that anyone would publish her autobiography because she hadn't done a damn thing with her life except not die.

"Ha," she said, and raised the glass of sparkling wine to her reflection. "Take that, birth mom. I didn't die. *Pppttt.*"

She hiccupped, pasted a palm against her mouth. "Oops."

Narrowing her eyes, she glared at her reflection. "What's that? I need to get past not dying and start living? Well, I gave it a shot and you see how this is turning out." She flung her arm wide and wine sloshed from her glass, splattered the rug.

Oh crap. At least it wasn't red wine.

Headlights cut across the window, the sound of a vehicle engine motoring up the drive.

Rowdy! He was here! He was here!

What to do? What to do?

Okay, okay, she could handle this. She wrung her hands and her pulse took off like she was running the Kentucky Derby in high heels. She downed the remaining Prosecco, parked the glass beside the ice bucket, rearranged the remaining strawberries so they didn't look so sparse, dove onto the bed, and struck what she hoped was a sexy, come-hither pose.

That's when she glanced down and saw a big blob of chocolate had fallen off the strawberry, fallen the middle of her bustier and started melting.

Seriously? You gotta be freakin' kidding me!

Rowdy couldn't wait to get home, see Nolan Ryan, and slide into his own bed.

In Dallas, he'd called Zach repeatedly and kept getting his voice mail. He called the three guys on the team who were still talking to him, a lot of them were still mad that he'd staged the walkout, and one of them told him where Zach was living. He'd driven to the condo and spent the night in his car, but his brother had never shown up. On Saturday, he'd hooked up with old friends who told him tales of Zach's wild partying behavior. The friends insisted on taking him to dinner, but the entire time he kept sneaking glances at his watch, anxious to get back to Stardust.

When had he become such a homebody? Before he was sidelined, on the nights he wasn't working, he was either out on the town or throwing parties. Now, that lifestyle held the shine of an old boot.

Instead, he wanted to hang out with Breeanne and talk baseball for hours and cook her spaghetti carbonara.

And that scared him. A lot. He didn't know who this new Rowdy was. Or what world he fit in.

He pulled into the driveway and spied Breeanne's Sentra. A helpless smile spread across his face. She was here checking on Nolan Ryan.

He hurried into the house, eager to see her and tell her what had transpired in Dallas, but the house was dark and quiet. Nolan Ryan greeted him at the door. He flicked on the light, and squatted to hug his dog.

And heard the distant sound of music drifting down from upstairs. Curious as to what Breeanne was up to, he followed the music to his bedroom.

The door was open a crack.

He smelled vanilla and cinnamon, identified the song. "Between the Sheets" by the Isley Brothers. A strange feeling grabbed hold of him. One part anticipation, one part dread, one part . . . What *was* that other part?

He toed the door open wider.

Candles flickered shadows on the wall, illuminating Breeanne in a soft glow as she lay stretched out across his bed, elbow bent, propped up her left side, palm cradling her cheek. A bottle of sparkling wine was open with two glasses sitting beside it. One of the glasses had a quarter inch of wine in the bottom.

Her sexily tousled hair tumbled about her shoulders. Her slim right arm rested down the curve of her hip. She would look as adorable as a basket of calico kittens if it were not for what she was wearing.

A tight black bustier tucked her in and pushed her up, amplified her meager cleavage. A tiny triangle of cheetah panties invited him to stare at the sweet V of her thighs. A lace cheetah garter belt held up black fishnet stockings, and call-girl-high cheetah peep-toe stilettos clad her feet.

Holy Frederick's of Hollywood.

Someone must have given her makeup techniques because she'd taken off her glasses and mastered the smoky-eyed look of a French cabaret singer. "La Vie en Rose" replaced the Isley Brothers on the playlist.

The sight of her shiny red lips filled his mouth with the taste of candied apple and sent molten steel shooting straight to his dick.

Va-va-va-voom-vamp-vixen.

She flicked out the tip of her pink wet tongue and slowly licked her lips.

His pulse slammed in his windpipe. His chest ached. His legs quivered. The room shrank. Walls closed in. Ceiling dropped. Floor lifted.

Aw shit, aw damn, aw hell.

"I need you," she whispered.

His head buzzed. The hairs on his arms stood up. His nerve endings burned electric, pitching hot tingles up and down his body. It was all he could do not to crawl right up on that bed with her and do what both Breeanne and nature were begging him to do.

Don't!

She was a virgin, and while she might not believe it, he was the last thing she needed.

"What you need," he drawled, calling on every ounce of willpower he possessed, "is a cold shower."

A flash of uncertainty crossed her face, but her smile hardened in place and she patted the quilt beside her. "Let's get dirty first, then we can take one together."

"As invitin' as that offer is, I'm afraid I'm gonna have to decline."

Her bottom lip trembled slightly, that plucky smile losing its starch. "You're not attracted to me?"

Rowdy stepped over to the dresser, picked up the baseball sitting there. The first baseball he'd ever thrown in a major league game tossed it into the air, snagged it, tossed it again, higher this time, stepped forward, and caught it behind his back.

"I know I'm not all that pretty, but I thought this

getup would help." She sat up, swept a hand at her outfit while at the same time grabbing for one of the king-sized pillows to hold in front of her.

"Are you nuts? You're gorgeous." He kept tossing the ball, catching it, concentrating hard to keep from saying, "Screw it all," and sweeping her into his arms.

"I am?"

"Not in an obvious way, but dammit, Breezy, from the moment I saw you across Irene Henderson's lawn, I wanted you."

Her throat moved as she gulped. She was hugging the pillow, knees to her chest, and unwittingly giving him a luscious view of the section of sweet flesh where her upper thigh melded into her butt cheek.

"Really?" she whispered.

"Hell's bells, woman, can't you see what you do to me?" He glanced down.

Her gaze tracked below his waist, and underneath the overdone makeup, he could see her blush.

"I can't stop thinking about you. The smell of you is all over my house," he said. "Every time I turn a corner I get a whiff of springtime, fresh and green, mixed with the scent of old books. A sweet, woodsy library smell that makes me want to read. I go around the house sniffing things you've touched."

"You do?"

"When we're working, I steal sideways glances to keep from outright ogling and when you're not around . . ."

Her lips parted, and in a husky, Marilyn Monroe whisper, she said, "What?"

He shrugged, and looked down again at the bulge straining his zipper.

"Oh," she said, her eyes widening. "*Oh.* You—"

"Yeah." He nodded. "I do."

"Well." Her shoulders straightened. "Now you don't have to go it alone. I'm right here in front of you."

"I can see that." He raked his gaze over her. She dropped the pillow to her lap and her breasts were moving up and down in that tight little bustier every time she breathed. "But this ain't happenin'."

She fixed her eyes on his. "Why not?"

He held her stare, tossed the baseball from palm to palm now instead of up and down. Smacking it against his skin. Back and forth, harder, faster, building an escalating rhythm. "You're my ghostwriter. You know too much about me."

"Ah, you're afraid I'll spill your deep, dark secrets."

She didn't know his deep dark secrets, but he wasn't going to bring that up. "I don't do long-term. Not romantically. Not deeply. Not for the long haul, and you're a long-haul kind of woman."

She slipped her legs off the bed, stood up. The pillow fell to the floor. He tried not to stare. Failed.

"You're assuming," she said. "And that makes an ass out of you and me."

"Look, if I take your virginity you'll imprint with me like a baby duck. I can't have you following me around all starry-eyed and moony."

"That's pretty egotistical of you. Thinking you're so irresistible that I'd lose my head over sleeping with you."

"Hey, it's happened before."

"It must be such a burden carrying around the weight of your ego."

"I just don't want you to get hurt."

"Because you care so much about me?"

"I like you. You're fun to be with."

"So what's the problem?" She came toward him, acting bold, but he saw that her hand was trembling.

"Your first time should be with someone you're in love with."

"Were you in love with the woman who took your virginity?" She took another step.

He couldn't stop tossing the damn baseball. *Smack. Smack. Smack.* "No."

"Then why do you think I have to be?"

"It's different. You're a woman."

"The old double standard, huh?"

"Women *are* different. Sex means something to women."

"And it doesn't mean anything to men?"

"Sex means sex. Love is love. You can have sex without love and love without sex."

"And you don't think I understand that?"

"I don't know if a virgin can separate the two."

"Why don't you let this virgin decide for herself?" She was toe to toe with him now and almost eye to eye in those stilettos.

"You deserve better. I don't want to use you."

She rolled her eyes. "If you start singing 'Baby, Don't Get Hooked on Me,' I'm seriously going to belt you."

"I'm not much of a singer."

"Good thing." She touched his arm.

He dropped the ball. It hit the floor with a thump and rolled under the bed.

They stared into each other's eyes, breathed the same air so charged with sexual tension it smelled like ozone.

She plastered her palm against his chest.

He was struck by her bravery, and that was the only thing that kept him from walking away.

"I don't want love from you," she said.

He gulped. Twice. "You're sure?"

"I want action and excitement. I want to know what

I've been missing, and from all the stories you've been telling me, I know you're the man for the job."

"You're sure?"

"You're repeating yourself."

"I know."

"I want my first time to be wild and crazy and uninhibited. When you're in love, you're too busy worrying about the other person. I don't want to have to worry about what you want or feel or think. I just want you to make me feel good." She slipped her arms around his neck, leaned in close. "Got it?"

When had his sweet kitten turned into a tiger? Her plan sounded perfect. Right up his alley. Why did it feel so wrong?

"I want you to teach me how to have mind-blowing sex. There's only so much you can learn from a book. I'm ready for a hands-on—and I do mean hands-on—tutor."

He shook his head. "I'm no teacher."

"But you *are* a good lover." She pressed her lips to his, wriggled her hot little body against him.

She smelled of chocolate-covered strawberries and wine. Ah, she was tipsy. That explained why she was so ballsy. Not that he minded. Normally, he would approve of a woman who asked for what she needed, but not her. Not now.

Her eyes held a bright sheen and she was wobbly on those heels that made her legs look like those of a runway model. He ached to taste those tipsy lips, taste the wine on her tongue. He groaned. Even the strongest man had his breaking point, and Rowdy did not usually deny himself pleasures of the flesh. But if he kissed her now, he was done for.

Gently, he unhooked her arms from around his neck. "Look," he said, desperately searching for something to throw her off. "You might enjoy yourself, but what about me? Novices aren't much fun."

Her breathing stilled. The uncertainty returned to her eyes and he felt like a shitheel.

"But . . . but . . . I want you."

"The Rolling Stones said it best. You can't always get what you want, sweetheart."

Her eyebrows dipped into a frown and her body stiffened. "Dammit, it's not fair." She swatted his shoulder. "I've been waiting twenty-five years to have sex and I'm alone in a big fancy house with a sizzling hot major league baseball pitcher with a playboy reputation. I'm dressed in sexy cheetah print, your favorite, and I'm not interested in a long-term relationship and I still can't get laid? What's wrong with me?"

"There's nothing wrong with you."

"Then do me!"

"Breeanne, I can't."

"Bullshit." She dropped to the floor, tears smearing the smoky-eyed makeup she'd spent so much time on.

It killed him to see her so torn up. "Are you okay?"

She folded her arms over her chest, and started up at him with raccoon eyes. "Admit the truth. You don't want *me*. I'm too skinny, and scarred and I'm not pretty enough for you. That's it, isn't it?"

He reached down a hand to help her to her feet. "Bullshit. You're perfect."

"You don't have to lie. I know what I look like."

"You wanna know the real truth?" he growled.

Gingerly, she placed her palm in his hand and allowed him to tug her up, her stare distrustful. "Yes."

"Your passion scares the hell out of me."

CHAPTER 19

Things could be worse. Suppose your errors
were counted and published every day,
like those of a baseball player.

—AUTHOR UNKNOWN

"It does?" That brightened her for a moment.

"Scares the pants right off of me."

"Oh goody. I'll help you get out of them." She reached up for his waistband.

He hopped back.

"If the biggest womanizer in the world won't have sex with me, who will?" she wailed. "Who will?"

"First of all, I'm not the biggest womanizer in the world."

"Yes you are. I'm your autobiographer. I should know."

"I might have overexaggerated my number a tiny bit." He measured off an inch with his thumb and forefinger.

"How much?"

"Sixty percent."

He could see her doing the math in her head. "That's still a lot," she said.

"I've had a good time, okay. But I'm not a heart-breaker. I don't go around breaking hearts."

"Aha!" she said, raising an index finger. "Caught you in a bald-faced lie."

"What?"

"You said sex means something to women. If sex means something to women, then you were breaking those women's hearts. Ergo you're a liar."

"Ergo?"

"It's a word, look it up."

"The women I've been with know it's just fun. I make that clear up front. Just like I have with you."

"That's all I want. Fun. A good time. Why does everyone get to have fun except me?"

"You wanna have fun?"

"Yes! That's what I've been saying all along. Do me!" She started undoing the stays of her bustier, but her fingers got tangled in the laces and she hiccupped.

"How long were you waiting for me?"

"Dunno. An hour? Maybe longer."

"And how much wine did you have?"

"I'm not the least bit drunk if that's what you're insin . . . insin . . ." She hiccupped again, slapped a palm over her mouth.

"You're tipsy. You wouldn't be doing this if you weren't at least a little tipsy."

"Like you know me so well."

"I've spent as much time with you as you have with me."

"Yes, but you're always doing all the talking." She was inching her back up the wall, her boobs jiggling beneath the loose ribbons of those stays.

He couldn't stop staring. He wanted her so damn badly. His body was harder than it had ever been, and yes, that was counting his super horny teenage years.

"You're driving me crazy, you know that?" she said. "Absolutely batshit crazy."

Rowdy gulped. She was driving *him* batshit crazy. Why did he want her so damn much, and why was he so fascinated by her tits? They were no bigger than peaches, but they were round and high and firm and he found himself craving peach cobbler something fierce.

She folded her arms over her chest. "You think I'm too small."

"Says who?"

"You told me about all those big-breasted women who waited for you outside the locker room."

"Don't worry about it, Breezy. More than a mouthful is a waste anyway."

"I bet one of these would fit in your mouth with room to spare." She unfolded her arms, gave him a good look.

He tilted his head, eyed those sweet gems. Oh man, it was hotter than a Swedish sauna in here. "There would be no room to spare."

"We could try it and see."

"Sweetheart, you've had too much to drink to try anything."

"One measly little glass." She hiccupped a third time. "Okay, maybe two."

"Let's get you to bed." He peeled back the covers.

"Finally! Now we're talking." She rushed over.

"We're getting *you* to bed. I'm not coming with you."

"It's the scars, isn't it? That's the turn-off. Not only are my boobs tiny, they look like railroad tracks from all the surgeries."

"It's not the scars. Besides, I grew up by the railroad tracks. They're home. I like railroad tracks, remember?"

She held her arms wide. "So come home."

God, how he wanted to just let it happen. He wanted

to rip that flimsy getup off her body and explore every inch of her with his tongue.

"Please," she whimpered.

He couldn't do it. Couldn't be the one to take her virginity when she was in this condition, but he could show her a good time, as long as things didn't go too far.

Rowdy took her hands and drew her to the bed. Her heart was thumping so hard he could see the pulse at her throat fluttering. She was a heart patient. He couldn't forget that. Too much excitement could give her a cardiac arrest.

"What now?" she whispered.

Yeah, Blanton, what now?

"Have you asked your doctor if it's okay for you to have sex?"

"You sound like a Viagra commercial." She lowered her voice. "Before engaging in sexual activity consult your doctor . . ."

"Stop laughing. I don't want to be responsible for killing you."

"You won't kill me. I'm fine. But if you did kill me with your powerful sexual prowess . . ." She smiled, sighed, and wriggled against him. "What a way to go."

He shouldn't have, but he hung on to her, loving the feel of her body so close to his. Then she pulled his head down and kissed him.

It was as if someone flicked a lighter in a roomful of propane. Whoosh!

Every nerve ending in his body went up in flames.

She smelled like springtime, and new beginnings— crisp linen sheets, magnolia blossoms, a fresh coat of paint. She tasted of chocolate milk, strawberries, and Prosecco. She was dawn slipping through bedroom blinds—new, but old-fashioned, a sweet original. She made him feel things—secret longing, and remembered dreams that he'd let slip through his fingers, of being young and eager and passionate and wanting something so badly he feared dying of need.

Hoisting her off her feet, he settled her onto the bed.

She looked up from the pillow, those raccoon eyes devastating him. "Is it happening now? Is tonight the night?"

"You've been listening to too many Rod Stewart songs, Breezy." He climbed onto the bed, straddling her waist, his knees on either side of the mattress.

"But are we going to make—er, have sex?" Her voice went high.

"Nervous?"

"Excited."

"Scared?"

"Anticipatory."

"Frightened?"

"Eager."

He stroked her cheek with his index finger and she shuddered. "Terrified," he whispered.

"You say potato, I say pat-tot-to."

"Do you?"

"What?"

"Say pat-tot-to."

"Nobody says pat-tot-to."

"Somebody must have said it once. There's a song about it."

"Why are we talking instead of doing it?" she asked.

"I'm trying to prove to you that you're not ready for this."

"I am ready." She hardened her stubborn little chin.

"Let's do a little experiment and see."

She gulped and her wide eyes doubled in size.

"What kind of experiment? Sex toys? Vibrators? Nipple clamps? Ball gags?"

"Ball gags? Good Lord, woman, you need to stay off the Internet."

"Have you ever tried it? Could be fun. If it's something you have not tried before maybe we could do that. We could be ball gag virgins together."

"You have no idea what you're talking about, do you?"

"Nope, but don't let that stop you from getting creative. I'm open."

"Let's just stick to the basics."

"For now," she said.

"For now," he echoed.

He slid his hand on the ribbons and lace, his fingertips grazing the scars beneath. She cringed a little, drawing her shoulders inward.

"Don't be ashamed of those scars," he said. "You're a survivor."

"They're ugly."

"They're beautiful badges of honor. Be proud. You fought hard to earn them."

"You believe that?"

"You don't?"

"When I look in the mirror all I see is . . ."

"What?" he murmured.

"Damage."

"You need to get a new mirror, sweetheart, because all I see is strength and courage."

"Really?" She inhaled.

His fingers trailed lower, past the road bumps of scars to where her skin turned smooth and creamy at her belly button. He scooted his knees toward the foot of the mattress, and at the same time he slid his other hand underneath her buttocks, holding her in place.

"Where are you going?" she asked.

"Shh." He dipped his head and planted kisses at the warm spot between her navel and the apex of her thighs.

He savored the taste of her, mildly guilty that he was letting things get this far. She was vulnerable and tipsy to boot. He should know better, but damn, she tasted so good and he hadn't been with a woman since before New Year's Eve.

"Rowdy?" Her voice came out thin and high.

"Are you ready to stop?"

"Can you kiss me a little?"

Hell man, what are you thinking? She's a rookie and you go straight for the sweet spot?

"Please?" she whimpered.

This was his chance to pull a hamstring and take himself out of the game. He wasn't the guy to awaken her sexuality. He knew it as well as he knew his own name, but her arms were around his neck and she was tugging him up to her and, well . . . hell . . . he was only a man.

He scooted up again, bracing his weight on his elbows. She was such a tiny thing that he feared crushing her. He peered down into her makeup-smeared face. She looked so comical that he almost laughed, but managed to bite back the sound, scared that she would think he was laughing at her, and not because he found her cuter than a speckled fawn.

She smiled at him, a generous smile, wide and welcoming. What a beautiful mouth she had, plump and pink and juicy. Gorgeous.

Lowering his head, he claimed her mouth.

She let out a happy sigh and wriggled against him.

He debated whether to keep this kiss safe and innocent despite the fact she was in his bed and scantily clad, or scare her off with a real kiss—hot, hard, and demanding.

But the bold little thing took the decision out of his hands. She softened her jaw, parted her lips, and darted her tongue past his teeth.

Okay, Breezy, you asked for it, you got it.

He inhaled her, sucking her into his mouth like the greedy bastard he was. Her honeyed taste nourished him. He enjoyed her lips, so willing and yielding, he forgot about why this was a bad idea. Forgot about her stubbornness and prim ways, because she wasn't prim or stubborn now.

Her eager, inexperienced excitement made him remember what it was like to feel fresh and new. Kissing her made him feel clean, as if his soul had been washed to a sparkling shine.

His hands weren't idle. Gently, he kneaded her butt, while his other palm slipped beneath the string-thin waistband of that teensy scrap of cheetah print masquerading as panties.

She gasped, giggled, and damn if her tongue didn't do a crazy tango right there inside his mouth.

He pulled back so he could see her, cradled her head between his palms. "Where did you learn *that* move?"

"I read about it in a book."

"Seriously? There are books about kissing?"

"Rowdy," she said as if his head was as dense as marble. "There are books about *everything*."

"What would I do without you to set me straight?"

She giggled again and pulled his head back down to finish where they'd left off. In no time she was letting loose with a series of soft moans that dismantled him.

She arched her back and he helped, cupping her butt with both hands and pulling her upward until she was pressed flush against his crotch.

If he wasn't still wearing jeans . . .

She wrapped her slender legs around his waist, forcing him down on top of her. He broke into a full body sweat. Things were getting way out of hand.

"Breeanne, we gotta slow down." He rocked back, but she hung on and he took her with him. Somehow he ended up on his butt between her spread legs and his legs were around her waist. Her arms were locked around his neck and they were eye to eye and breathing hard.

"That's just it, Rowdy, I want to speed things up."

"Trust me on this. If we speed things up, you aren't going to have a lick of fun."

"But I'm already having fun."

"Sweetheart, this is nothing."

Her eyes widened. "It gets better than this?"

"We haven't scuffed the ball. It's fresh out of the box." He disentangled her arm from around his neck, slid off the bed. "Where are your clothes?"

"Over there." She waved in a general direction.

He craned his neck looking for her things. "We need to get you dressed and I'll drive you home." He opened the nightstand and found her clothes folded and stacked on the second shelf. He held out her pullover top. "Arm through here."

"I don't want to go home." She drew back from him, her big green eyes pleading. "Don't make me go home."

"No matter what you might think, the truth is, you're not ready for me, Breeanne. I don't know if you'll ever be."

"I know." She sank down to the floor again. "I'm

pathetic. A virgin drunk on one and a half small glasses of sparkling wine."

"Not pathetic. Special."

"Yeah. I've been told that before." She curled her upper lip.

"That's not how I meant it," he softened his voice, cushioning her with his tone, and crouched in front of her.

"Doesn't matter. Ends up the same. I don't get to have fun or sex because I'm *special*." She met his eyes, and bounced to her feet so fast that he stumbled backward getting up.

Rowdy put a hand to the wall to regain his balance. "Whoa. Slow down. If you're making me dizzy, you've gotta be making yourself dizzy."

"You know what?" She tossed her head like a spirited filly. "I'll go somewhere nobody knows me. Somewhere I'm not special. I'll go to a nightclub and pick up a random guy and—"

Alarm blistered his brain. "What? No!"

"I got it in my head that you would be the perfect person to deflower me because you don't do relationships." She bobbed her chin back and forth with exaggerated movements. "And all I wanted was to have sex and stop being a virgin . . ."

"Stop doing that, you look like a bobble head."

She bobbed her head that much harder. "But it doesn't have to be you. Any man will do. Well, not *any* man. Not someone old enough to be my grandpa, or anyone with poor hygiene, or—"

"Stop!" he commanded. "Stop talking."

She narrowed her eyes. "Or what?"

"Or I'll have to throw you over my lap and spank you for such wrongheaded thinking."

"A spanking? Oh goody." She clapped her hands. "At last, we're getting somewhere."

"You want a spanking?" His voice lowered along with his eyelids, and he moved toward her like he was intending on obliging.

Breeanne was starting to regret starting this conversation, but she'd asked for his attention and she'd gotten it. She was backing down now. She raised her chin. "How would I know? I've never had one."

He held up his big palm. "Looks like it would just fit that bottom of yours."

"Um . . ." She covered her fanny with both hands and backed up against the wall to protect her assets. Mistake. Now there was nowhere to run.

"You *have* been naughty. Ambushing me with chocolate-covered strawberries and a bustier." He took another step closer, within touching distance.

"I didn't know that was a corporal offense."

"Oh yes." He nodded. "Breaking and entering."

"You gave me access. No lawyer would take your case."

He swiveled his head from side to side. "You see any lawyers around here?"

"Um, no."

"That's right. What we've got here is a case of pioneer justice."

"The punishment should fit the crime," she said. "I throw myself on the mercy of the kangaroo court. Remember, I'm special."

"You sure are. And we give special punishment to special people."

There was no space between them now. The tips of his cowboy boots were butted up against the toes of her stilettos. She had no idea how to walk in the damn things, by the way, much less run. She'd bought them on Suki's advice, strictly for bedroom foreplay.

"You do?"

They were both staring down at their feet and simultaneously they moved again, their eyes meeting once more.

"Uh-huh." Rowdy slapped one big palm on the wall to her right, and then the other palm on the wall to her left, hemming her in.

"More than a spanking?"

"Worse than a spanking." He growled and lowered his head.

"Wh . . ." Her lips stuck because she'd been pressing them together so hard. She cleared her throat. "What's worse than a spanking?"

"Do you honestly want to know?"

"Yes. No. What's happening?"

"Sweetheart, you are in over your head."

"What's worse than a spanking?" she whispered, both thrilled and terrified to know the answer.

"You're about to find out. Just remember you brought this on yourself." His hands dropped from the wall to her waist. The next thing she knew, he'd picked her up, tucked her into the crook of his arm, and strode toward the bed.

"I think I prefer the spanking," she said, tilting her head to look up at him. "At least I know what that punishment entails."

"Since when do perpetrators get to pick their punishment?" His voice was softly menacing. Instantly, Breeanne's insides liquefied, and she was wet all over— with perspiration, desire, and feminine hormones. Her body was ready, and she wanted him more than she'd ever wanted *anything* in her life.

He sat down on the bed, pulled her across his lap, her butt in the air. He placed one big hand on the middle of her back, holding her down. She couldn't see his hands from her upside-down position, but she felt his left hand move upward. Was he really going to paddle her?

"Because I'm a lenient judge, I'm going to give you a choice. For the last time, do you want a spanking or the other punishment?"

"How can I make an informed choice?" she quipped, when all she wanted to do was strip off his clothes and straddle him like a wild mustang.

But he was in full control. She might have planned this seduction, but he'd taken over. This was the Rowdy Blanton Show, and she was simply along for the ride. He intrigued her, and she trusted him implicitly. And while she ached to find out what he had in store for her, she was nervous about the unknown.

Blood pounded through her body. Her head was dizzy—from wine, from innuendo, from having her pelvis pressed against Rowdy's crotch.

"Time's up." He made a noise like the *Jeopardy!* buzzer when someone got an answer wrong. "She'll take option number two, Alex for three hundred strokes."

"Strokes of what?" Breeanne gasped, but before the words were out of her mouth, Rowdy flipped her on her back in the middle of the bed, whipped the cheetah scarf around her wrists, and tied her to the wagon wheel headboard as if he were a rodeo steer roper instead of a baseball player.

She looked up at her hands, the cheetah scarf soft, but snug. She was hot and turned on and scared he was suddenly going to remember who he was and that he could have any woman he wanted.

He reached for her panties.

"Don't, don't, don't . . ."

He pulled her teeny thong panties down over her legs and tossed the scrap of material over his shoulder. "Too late. You had your chance."

"No." She kicked her legs, but weakly. "I've been drinking. I'm tipsy. Drunk. I didn't know what I was doing . . . I . . . I . . ."

He grinned wickedly and spread her legs apart, climbed up onto the mattress on his knees, slid his hands underneath her butt, scooped her up until she was resting on his forearms. "Your antics earned yourself a tongue-lashing, sweetheart."

She gave a hiss of delighted alarm as he lowered his head. The heady excitement of their love play crested into a bombardment of sensation that spread through the pathways of her body like hot oil.

His tongue went to places she had not dreamed were possible, his mouth overwhelming her. Everywhere he touched, heat burned. Her nipples beaded hard and she arched her hips up, writhing against his relentless tongue, tugging on the scarf that held her anchored to his bed.

He was over her, around her, licking and stroking. A stagger of riveting enjoyment imprisoned her, locking her to the mattress. She stretched down both hands to twine her fingers through his thick hair, fully absorbed in the crazy upheaval of sensation his mouth wrought.

Hot rolls of pleasure crashed over her and her breath left her body. Her mind followed her breath, and she floated to the ceiling as if watching what he was doing to her at the same time she felt it through every cell, every pore, every nerve, every physical pathway possible.

The pressure and heat in her pelvis grew to an unbearable level. She didn't think she could stand one second more. She whimpered and begged. "Don't stop, don't stop, don't stop . . ."

But he wasn't the one who stopped.

Her body stiffened, quivered, and a hot bolt of exquisite loosening flooded her in wave after wave of sweet ebbing release. She gasped, went completely still. Closed her eyes, sucked in her lost breath. "Wh-what was *that*?"

"Unless I miss my guess, Breezy," he said, a satisfied smirk in his voice. "I'd say you just had yourself an orgasm."

CHAPTER 20

Life will always throw you curves,
just keep fouling them off . . . the right pitch will come,
but when it does, be prepared to run the bases.

—RICK MAKSIAN

Rowdy spent a restless night in the guest bedroom. He lay with her cuddled in his arms until she fell asleep, but unable to trust himself not to take things further than she was ready to handle, he abandoned her in his bed.

It could be said that he was hiding out from her, and there was truth to it. While making love to her with his mouth had been fun, the light of day was sobering. He couldn't believe how responsive she'd been. A few flicks of his tongue had sent her sprinting around the bases for her first home run. He couldn't remember any woman he'd been with who had come so quickly. It gratified his ego, but worried his mind.

Breeanne was ripe for the picking, and if he didn't fulfill her needs for her, he feared she'd get someone else to step up to the plate. She'd said as much when she made that crack about going down to the local bar.

Just thinking about that scenario made his blood churn.

He flopped over in bed, the rich scent of her femi-

ninity rising up from his chest, and making him have
an erection. Dammit. He was as hard up as she was. It
had been six months since he'd had sex, and if she kept
throwing herself at him, he didn't know how much
longer he'd be able to hold out.

His plan to make her quit the book had well and
truly backfired, because now, no matter what happened, he couldn't quit her.

What in the hell was he going to do?

The headache knifed her right between the eyes. Breeanne groaned against the sunlight flooding in through
the half-opened blinds and pulled the pillow over her
head. Whose big idea was it to make daytime so damn
bright? She burrowed deeper under the covers, determined to go back to sleep, when it hit her.

She wasn't at home.

Where was she? She pulled away the pillow. Sat up.
Groaned. Cradled her head. Looked around. Remembered.

She was in Rowdy's bedroom. Alone. She'd slept
here alone, despite her intentions to the contrary.
Where had he slept?

Memories of last night bombarded her. Drinking
too much wine, her failed seduction, Rowdy's refusal
to have sex with her and then the surprising turn-
around where he'd done delightful things to her with
his mouth.

Then he'd untied her, kissed her forehead, told her
to go to sleep, and walked away. Leaving her sated,
curious, frustrated, and eager for more.

Big question. What did he think of the whole thing?
Was he amused? Smug? Pitying? Indifferent? If she had
been dizzy on wine and the intoxicating effects of his

mouth, she would have driven home not knowing if she'd succeeded or been defeated. Did this mean they were going to have a sexual relationship? Or had he been trying to show her that she couldn't handle a casual fling with him?

Color her confused.

She couldn't face him. Not yet. Not until she had time to regroup, assess, and put this into perspective. If that was even possible. Either way, she had to get out of here.

She slipped from the bed, still in her bustier smeared with melted chocolate. She searched for her clothes and shoes, found them—thank you, God—thrown off on the other side of the room. She couldn't remember how they'd gotten over there. Instead of putting on the stilettos, she carried them in one hand and cracked open the bedroom door.

Canting her head, she paused, listening for the sounds of someone stirring, heard nothing, and eased out into the hallway.

Coast clear. Go.

The floorboard groaned beneath her feet. She paused, cringed. Shh. Please, please, please don't let Rowdy catch her sneaking out.

This would be her first walk of shame. It felt kind of thrilling. Too bad it couldn't have been an official walk of shame where she could strut the loss of her virginity.

But it was a start, right?

Or not. What if this was all she got from him?

Her bottom lip trembled, and she blinked hard, surprised by the inexplicable urge to bawl. Out. She had to get out of here. Her mind and her feelings were a ball of badly tangled yarn.

Tiptoeing down the stairs, she caught the scent of

frying bacon. Her mouth watered and her stomach growled. Ages since she'd eaten. Someone was in there cooking breakfast.

Nut bunnies.

She had to slip past the kitchen on her way to the front door. What if it was Rowdy? What if he was cooking her breakfast? How awkward would that be?

Face it. Everything between you is going to be awkward from now on.

She had no idea where she stood, and they still had months of working together ahead of them. She should have thought about that before she started this. But how was she to know? She was a virgin, for crying out loud.

Still.

But she had had her first orgasm. That was something to cheer about. Yay.

Except she didn't feel cheery, in fact, she felt frustrated.

Not ready to face him.

Wait, she could slip out the back way. She stopped, changed directions, but dog tags jangled against a collar buckle, and there was Nolan Ryan. He plopped down on her feet, stared up at her with soulful eyes.

"At least someone around here wants me," she muttered under her breath, and leaned over to pet him.

"Might as well stay for breakfast," Warwick called from the kitchen.

Busted. Double nut bunnies.

Warwick whistled and Nolan Ryan got up to lead the way into the kitchen.

For once, the bodyguard wasn't wearing his sunshades. He had on a black Tom Waits T-shirt stretched over biceps the size of a honey ham, black jeans, and cowboy boots.

"Sit." He motioned at the bar stool with a spatula. "You need to eat."

She might be working on overcoming people-pleasing tendencies, but when a man the size of Warwick told you to do something, it was a good idea to comply. She edged over to the bar, hitched her butt up on the edge of a stool. The movement intensified the pounding in her head and she massaged her brow with two fingers. No more Prosecco for her. Ever.

Warwick put a glass of water and a bottle of aspirins in front of her.

"Thanks." She palmed three tablets.

"How do you like your eggs?"

"Don't go to any trouble for me—"

"Eggs," he commanded. "How do you like them?"

"Over easy."

He put a nonstick skillet on the stove, clicked the gas burner, and dropped a dollop of butter into the pan.

Breeanne tugged at the hem of her shirt, attempting to pull out the wrinkles. Didn't work. But it was better than sitting there watching Warwick cook her breakfast.

"Is he up yet?" she asked to break the silence. "I wanted to be out of here before he wakes up. Nothing against your cooking, but—"

"Relax. He's not here."

"Oh." She should be relieved. Instead, she felt disappointed. "Where'd he go?"

"Don't know, but he told me to feed you." He cracked an egg, slid it into the melted butter, and tossed the shell over his shoulder without looking. It dropped neatly into the trash can behind him.

"Did Rowdy tell you—" She couldn't bring herself to say it.

"Don't worry about it. You're not the first woman

to ambush him in his bed." He dusted the egg with salt and pepper.

Jealous burned like hot coals in her belly. What had she expected? She had no illusions about the life he led. "Do women chase him wherever he goes?"

"He's got a live-in bodyguard, doesn't he?" Warwick fished bacon slices off the griddle, arranged them on a paper towel to absorb the grease. "He's got a way with the ladies. They flock to him. Always have. Always will. The woman he settles down with, if he ever settles down, will need to know what she's up against."

She cringed, lifted her shoulders to her ears. She was no different from the other women who chased after him. Well, except he'd refused to have sex with *her*. "How long have you known him?"

"Most of my life. We grew up in the same neighborhood. Our buddy Price Richards did too. We were the Three Musketeers. What one did, we all did. Although Rowdy had tons of other friends and people followed him everywhere. He was the Pied Piper of Stardust. There was always one kid or another trying to be D'Artagnan, but the three of us were tight. No one else ever made the cut."

"I didn't realize that Rowdy's friendship with Price reached back that far."

"I'm a couple of years older than Rowdy and Price, but the three of us were in the same grade. My birthday is in September, so I started school a year later than everyone else, and then I got held back a year in second grade when I had the measles. I towered over the rest of the kids, but no one screwed with me."

"I imagine not." She leaned forward, rested her elbows on the bar, and propped her chin in her palm. "Rowdy didn't mention that he'd known you in grade school. In fact, he skims over his childhood as if it's a time he barely remembers. What was he like as a kid?"

Warwick raised his head, pierced her with black eyes. "You interviewing me for the book now?"

She gulped. "No, just curious. I won't use anything you tell me in the book."

He flipped the egg and she was certain they'd reached the end of the conversation, Warwick being the strong silent type and all, but he surprised her by answering the question. "Rowdy was the class clown. A prankster. He loved making people laugh. Still does."

She nodded. "I see that."

"As a kid, his pockets were always bulging with interesting things he found—rocks in unusual shapes and colors, bugs, flower buds, twine, pieces of colored glass, tree frogs. You never knew what was going to come of that kid's pockets. He called 'em his treasures."

In her mind's eye she imagined Rowdy as a seven-year-old, gap-toothed and grinning, pulling endless items from his pockets, and she fell in love with that sweet boy.

"Neither of our families had much money." Warwick fed wheat bread into the toaster. "We didn't get toys except on our birthdays and Christmas, and even then it wasn't much. But as long as we had a baseball we were happy. We didn't need a bat. Broom handles worked in a pinch."

"Rowdy took me to see the house he grew up in."

Warwick gave a grunt. "The neighborhood is a pit, huh? But we didn't know we were poor." His tone was light as if he, Price, and Rowdy weren't strong sprouts that had sprung from cement cracks.

"How could you not know?"

"When you've got baseball, and good friends to play it with, that makes you feel rich enough." With an expert wrist, Warwick flipped the egg onto a plate, added two strips of bacon and buttered toast points, and set the plate in front of her.

"Thank you." Breeanne tucked into the food. "What happened to your friendship when Rowdy got shipped off to Houston to live with his uncle?"

"Price and I grew closer, but we never forgot Rowdy. The minute he came home it was if he'd never been away."

"He was lucky to have you."

Warwick met her eyes. His expression was so intense that she couldn't hold it. "I was lucky to have *him*. Wherever Rowdy is, good times follow, and I needed those good times. He's got a talent for side-stepping pain, and replacing it with fun."

"How did you two get to be friends?"

"Rowdy found an old baseball in the ditch. The schoolyard bully demanded Rowdy give it to him. Rowdy tried to make friends, but the bully was in a punching mood. Back in those days, Rowdy was about as skinny as you are, but he wasn't scared. He was taking a pretty good whipping when I came upon the fight and made short work of the bully. Rowdy was lying on the ground, one eye swelling shut, lip busted, and says through the blood, 'Do you play baseball?' and that was that."

"And you've been his bodyguard ever since?"

"The path was windier than that. Lots of road between then and now."

"Price and Rowdy went into professional baseball. Did you try that career path?"

"The option wasn't open to me." His lips clamped shut and she could tell from the expression on his face that she was not going to get anything more out of him in that direction.

"I'm afraid I made a fool of myself last night," she confessed.

Warwick started loading the dishwasher and didn't meet her gaze. "I wouldn't worry about it too much. Rowdy's used to women flinging themselves at him. I imagine he's forgotten about it already."

If Warwick was trying to make her feel better, it was not working. The pounding in her head worsened. She'd told Rowdy that she could separate sex from her emotions, and while she'd done a pretty good job of convincing herself, the feelings knotted up inside her gut told her it was a lie.

Good thing they hadn't had sex. Hadn't slept in the same bed together.

Otherwise, no matter how much she swore she wouldn't go there, she would start picturing the two of them together. Spooning together after sex, their legs intertwined, gazing deeply into each other's eyes. Breakfast in bed. Taking long, hot showers together, steaming up the mirrors. Going for long drives in the country. Holding hands. She would read her favorite books aloud to him, and he would teach her how to pitch a screwball.

Who was she kidding? She was already doing it—dreaming dreams, having hopes, making wishes. Believing in the silly prophecy on a silly hope chest, banking on the fact that their similar experience with the cheetah scarf's softness meant something when it didn't.

How she burned for him!

He was funny and charming and full of life. Like a prism, he dazzled the girl who'd spent her childhood in hospital beds or on the couch, watching the world go by. He was the color she'd always lacked. He was a glorious peacock and she a dull, drab peahen. He possessed the physical stamina she would never have. He was a man who was so far beyond her reach she had no business whispering to herself, *I want him*.

Oh God help her. They hadn't had sex and she was already in love with him.

She put a hand to her stomach. Warwick had gone to all this trouble to make breakfast for her, but if she took another bite, she would throw up.

What was she going to do? She couldn't back out of the book deal. She had credit card bills and she had asserted her independence to her family. How could she turn back now? She was the one who'd forced him into following through on the contract when he wanted to quit.

She *had* to stay.

Reality smacked into her like a wrecking ball—hard and relentless, laying waste to the fib she'd convinced herself was true. She could *not* separate love from sex. After last night, after the beautiful thing he'd done to and for her, there was no way out of this.

She *was* going to end up with a broken heart.

On Monday morning, queasy about having to face Rowdy again, Breeanne arrived at his house. Part of her wanted to call in sick, or consider quitting the book. But she'd signed a contract. Made a promise. Things might be awkward, but they'd get past it.

That was her hope anyway.

Warwick opened the door. "He's in the pool."

Oh great. He was half naked again. As if this wasn't hard enough when he was fully clothed. Bracing herself, she went into the backyard.

He was swimming away from her toward the far end of the pool. He hadn't seen her yet. It wasn't too late to run.

She closed her eyes against the red-hot memory, embarrassment burning her from the inside out. She'd been foolish to think she could handle a cosmic baseball star and his devastating smile, a man who trailed broken hearts in his wake. She was simply the latest casualty.

"Good morning, Breezy." His cool voice soothed, balm on the sunburn of her shame.

Her eyes flew open.

He sauntered toward her, water trickling down his flat abdomen, toweling his hair, and grinning like he knew a big secret. He did. He knew how to make her come.

Her cheeks flamed. She needed more of that balm.

"Have a seat," he invited, and nodded at the umbrella-covered patio table. For the first time she noticed the table had been set with breakfast for two—orange juice and mini-quiches and fresh fruit.

She'd had a bowl of cereal earlier, but he'd gone to so much trouble, she zippered her lips.

He draped his towel over the seat of the patio chair, and waved her down beside him.

It was hard to breathe sitting so close to so much bare masculine skin. Not knowing what else to do, she settled her laptop on the table and sat down. Nolan Ryan, who'd been lying in the sun, got up and came over to sit between them.

"Try the spinach." He slid his cell phone from the middle of the table over to the side, and pushed the tray of quiches toward her. "They're the best."

She accepted one, nibbled on it, bits of flaky crust falling to crumbs on the table. She tried not to fidget, but it was impossible while he was looking at her with that unruffled, carefree gaze.

"Mmm." She couldn't taste a thing, not while he was watching her like she was a canary, and he was a hungry tomcat.

Nolan Ryan looked baleful.

"Not good for you." Rowdy shook his head.

Nolan Ryan trained his woe-is-me-eyes on Breeanne.

"Don't go begging to her. She's not falling for it either, buddy."

Nolan Ryan turned his head back to Rowdy, stared at him without blinking.

"Okay, but just half of one." He broke one of the cheese quiches into two pieces and slipped it to the bloodhound.

He leaned back in the chair, letting his arms dangle, and studied her for a long moment. Unable to hold his gaze, she reached for a strawberry, but that made her remember the chocolate-covered strawberries, and she left it on her plate uneaten.

Finally, he said, "Give me your phone."

"What? Why?"

"I'm going to program my phone number into it."

"I've already got it programmed in," she said.

"No, you have the number of my public phone."

"You have more than one phone?"

"Yes. Only a few people have access to my private phone." He nodded at the cell on the table between them. "My mom, my sisters, Zach, Warwick, Price . . . and now you."

Her heart fluttered erratically. "Are you sure? It sounds like your special number is reserved for special people?"

He lowered his eyelids, and his voice, but kept his gaze trained on her. "I thought we'd already determined you're pretty special to me, Breezy. Do you want my private number?"

Omigosh. What did this mean? Hoping he didn't see that her hand was trembling, she pulled her cell phone from her purse and passed it to him, watched while his shaggy dark head of hair bent to program his number into her phone. This was one time when special felt good.

He handed her the phone, smiled.

"How many women besides family members have you given this number to over the years?" she asked.

"What don't you get about being special, Breezy? You're the only one."

"I promise not to use this unless I absolutely have to." She clutched her cell phone, still warm from his hand, to her chest.

"Use it anytime you want," he invited.

Wow. This was really happening. She had access to Rowdy Blanton's private phone number. That twelve-year-old kid he'd come to visit in the hospital would have been pinching herself black and blue. Oh, who was she kidding? It was all she could do not to pinch herself right now.

"I've been thinking about Saturday night," he said, casually tossing the topic on the table like it was perfectly normal breakfast conversation.

If he was going to be straightforward and broach the subject boldly, there was no point playing coy. What she wanted to say was *I have no memory of Saturday night*. "So have I."

At the same time he said, "If you want to do this, I'm game," she said, "Let's pretend it did not happen."

They both said, "What?"

"You're in?" she asked.

"You're out?" he said.

Their eyes met, they laughed at the same time. Her laughter was jittery, his easy.

Breeanne pressed her knees together, tucked her feet underneath her chair away from him. "Why did you change your mind?"

"I got to thinking," he said. "You've been so long without one of life's finest pleasures, who am I to deny you?"

"Well, thank you so much, Mr. Ego. But don't feel obligated to do me any favors." She started to get up, but she wasn't mad. If he was doing this to ease her embarrassment over Saturday night, it was working.

He reached out and touched the hand she'd placed on the table. "That sounded douchy. I didn't mean that way."

She stared at his hand, his touch was already melting her like the chocolate she kept dropping on herself. But she was already a goner. Had been since Saturday night. "How did you mean it?"

He pushed back the chair, went down on his knees in front of her, held her hand as if he were about to propose.

What was he doing? A flutter of something scary yet wondrous flapped its wings inside her chest.

"Breeanne Carlyle, will you do me the honor of allowing me to be your humble coach in the ways of lovemaking?" It was so like him to make a joke of it.

Before she could stop it, the thing in her chest pushed a giggle out of her. Oh great, now she sounded fourteen. She opened her mouth to reply, but he held up a quelling palm.

"But wait," he said, in the comically dramatic tone of an infomercial huckster. "Before you give me an answer, there are ground rules."

Curious, she leaned forward. He still had hold of

her hand, and the look on his face was surprisingly earnest for the silly conversation. "Sell it, Casanova."

"I am the coach, and you are the rookie. You don't start pitching your first night in the bigs."

"Meaning?"

"Rookie Rules for Great Sex. We do this my way, the slow way. No bedroom ambushes. I'm in charge."

"Do I get to voice an opinion?"

"You can voice it, but I have final veto."

"That gives you all the power."

"No it doesn't. You can always walk away. No harm, no foul. Now that you understand the terms of the agreement, you may give me your answer."

"Seriously, do women usually fall for this shtick?"

"I don't know," he said. "You're the first one I've tried it on. Is it working?"

"I have to admit it's a generous offer, but . . ." she said coolly as if her inner Snoopy wasn't gleefully dancing. She was going to have sex with Rowdy Blanton. *Woo-hoo*. But it wouldn't hurt him to sweat over her answer.

He cocked his head, closed one eye, as if it would blunt the sting of her rejection.

"Well?"

She said nothing for a long moment, letting him fret.

He got antsy. Shifted his weight back and forth, clenching and unclenching his fists.

Once Breeanne accepted that she was heading for heartbreak no matter what she did, heading down the risky path was easier. She wanted this. The adventure of a lifetime.

Smiling, she let him off the hook. "Did you really have any doubts?"

CHAPTER 21

*Baseball is a game where a curve is an optical illusion,
a screwball can be a pitch or a person,
stealing is legal and you can spit anywhere you like
except in the umpire's eye or on the ball.*

—JIM MURRAY

According to Coach Blanton, the Rookie Rules for Great Sex were deceptively simple. Do nothing for three weeks but kiss. Hands below the shoulders were considered fouls, and resulted in an immediate time-out.

Breeanne protested. It was impossible to keep such rules.

"Think of it this way, sweetheart." Rowdy kissed her forehead. "You've missed out on a lot of kissing."

"What comes after three weeks?" she asked eagerly. "After all the kissing?"

"Two weeks of second base."

"What exactly *is* second base?"

"Wait and see."

"And after that?"

"A week of third base."

"Didn't we get to third base the other night?"

"We got tagged out and had to start over. Besides, *I* got to third base, you didn't, and this is all about you. You're the rookie."

"Yes, Coach," she said, and snuggled against him, heating over the memory of their night together. Damn, would she ever stop blushing over sexy thoughts?

"Now is your time to play catch-up for lost time."

The man could kiss! She quickly discovered there was a whole world of kisses, and they wasted no time mapping the territory.

Instead of a means to an end, kissing became a destination unto itself.

They kissed while they were working, pausing between sentences and paragraphs to smooch. She'd read what she wrote out loud and he would clarify or suggest changes. They'd celebrate another page written with more kisses.

They kissed until their lips chapped. Sharing one breath, drinking from the cool pool of each other. They kissed copiously, ravenous. They kissed rollickingly playful. They kissed flagrantly bold.

They kissed as if they'd invented it—in the kitchen, in the living room, on his desk, in the gym, at the lake on blankets in the sun. They kissed furtively, sneaking quick sips when they were in town. Ducking behind the canned goods aisle at the HEB, in the Escalade while in the Dairy Queen drive-through lane, in the back row of the picture show where they went to see an action-adventure flick they couldn't remember the name of afterward.

Each kiss was different. Adding layer upon layer to the foundation of that first kiss, that first day when he kissed her in front of those other women and claimed she was his girlfriend.

Was she his girlfriend now for real? It was a question she was afraid to ask. A boat she hated to rock in case the answer was no. She didn't know what this was, but she was determined to enjoy every second of it.

By the end of June, she'd finished writing and editing the outline and first chapter of Rowdy's autobiography and sent it off to the editor at Jackdaw Press. Rowdy's kisses had worked them both up into a fevered pitch and they eagerly proceeded to second base.

Which she discovered, in addition to the kissing, extended to anything above the hipbone, and that included bare skin. She couldn't get enough of touching his muscled chest and abdomen.

Touching him led her outside herself, and when they explored each other's scars, tracking tongues and fingertips over ridges, puckers, and flattened spots of healed cuts, she felt connected to him in a way she'd not felt with another human being. They rejoiced in the feel of each other. Touching his bare skin gave her a different grasp on life, a new perspective. He made the world more tantalizing, richer than it had ever been before. Until she touched him, it was as if she'd lived in a sensory desert, and had now stepped into a lush forest full of exotic surprises.

Rowdy started giving her thoughtful little gifts—a cheetah-print book light, a coupon for a free dipped cone, a box of her favorite herbal tea, a small soap figurine of a bunny eating a peanut.

"Where on earth did you find this?" She laughed.

"I carved it," he confessed.

"Seriously? Where did you learn how to do that?"

"In rehab. My physical therapist had me start whittling soap to help me regain fine motor skills." He wriggled the fingers of his left hand like he was going to tickle her.

She giggled and stepped out of reach.

Life was romantic and sweet and fun. Being with him was the easiest thing in the world and she tried hard not to think about the future. Right now was future enough.

He taught her how to make spaghetti carbonara, putting her at the stove in front of him, encircling her waist with his hands while he whispered instructions into her ear. He'd just taken her hand and was helping her stir the onions as they caramelized when his private cell phone, which was sitting on the bar, dinged that he'd gotten a text.

"Do you need to check that?"

"Concentrate," he said. "We need more butter."

She sliced another chunk of butter from the stick beside the stove and dropped it into the skillet with the onions.

His phone dinged again.

"Don't you want to get that? It's got to be family or your best friends."

"Keep stirring. I have an app that will read it to me." He buried his nose in her hair, kissed the nape of her neck. She wriggled gleefully.

At that moment, a robotic female voice started reading the message. "Bro, they're starting me on the Fourth of July against San Diego. You're the only one who understands what this means. I hope you'll come. Got two tickets waiting for you and a guest at will-call."

"Looks like Zach is finally ready to make up," she said. "Why don't you call him back?"

"After cooking lessons."

"This will wait. Zach is more important. Call him."

Rowdy moved away, going for the phone. The space behind her was now empty, leaving her feeling lonely. The man had such presence. He'd ruined her for anyone else. Was she addicted to him? Oh gosh, she had it bad.

He picked up the phone, but didn't dial. "Breeanne."

She raised her head to see him standing in the sunlight cutting through the window, his gorgeous dark hair curling in all directions like crazed ocean waves. "Yes?"

"Do you want to come with me?"

Yes! She'd never been to a professional baseball game. "I was so scared you weren't going to ask."

"So that's a yes?"

"Absolutely," she said, and it was only then that it fully sank in that Zach was pitching on the Fourth of July.

That afternoon when she left Rowdy's place, Breeanne stopped by Timeless Treasures to let her family know she wasn't going to be the family's big annual Fourth of July blowout.

The Fourth of July was her family's favorite holidays, bigger even than Christmas, because it was the date they'd flown to Korea to bring Suki home. Their friends and neighbors had taken up a collection so she, Jodi, and Kasha could go as well, although Breeanne had only been three at the time and didn't remember going.

Mom was behind the counter, checking out the last customer of the day. Dad was carrying a Tiffany lamp out to the car for an elderly lady. Suki spotted her from the balcony, and came running downstairs to greet her.

"You've gained weight," Suki said as she hugged her. "Looking good. Rowdy agrees with you."

"Thanks." She'd told Suki about the seduction that went awry, but she hadn't told her about their Rookie Rules arrangement.

Suki hugged her again. "I have so missed you. When are you coming back? It's so boring up there. People keep asking me stuff like 'What was John Irving's first book?' I mean who knows—

"*Setting Free the Bears.*"

Suki rolled her eyes. "Who cares?"

"Book lovers. You are running a bookstore. That's your customer base."

"See there? That's the problem. I'm *not* a book lover. I mean they're okay, but I don't have a passion for them. Now if we were talking jewelry or clothes . . ." Suki turned to their mother. "Mom, can we turn the bookstore into a boutique?"

"No," their mother said without looking up. "Breeanne will be back when she finishes writing her book. Suck it up, Suki."

The customer laughed. "I love the way you and your children interact, Maggie. It's one of the things that keep me coming in. How is the book coming, Breeanne?"

"Great. Busy, busy, busy."

"That's right, we hardly see her anymore." Mom shot Breeanne a chiding look that said, *You've been neglecting your family, young lady.*

Her chest tightened. She glanced away, curled her fingers into her palms. Breaking the news that she was not going to be at their Fourth of July celebration wasn't going to be easy.

"Honey," Mom said after the customer left the store. "Could you fix your delicious seven-layer dip for Saturday? Brent Taylor is on leave from the army and he's coming to the party. He specifically asked about you, and your dip."

"Mom's playing matchmaker," Suki whispered to her behind her palm, as if Breeanne couldn't figure that out, as if Mom couldn't hear her. "She's worried Rowdy is having a negative influence."

"Beverly Crownover saw you two at the picture show," her mother said. "She said you were kissing in the back row."

"Good going!" Suki grinned.

"You and Rowdy what?" Dad asked, coming up behind them.

Oh no. Telling Mom was one thing, Dad was another solar system altogether.

"I want all the dets later," Suki whispered in her ear. "You just made minding the bookstore worth it."

"Breeanne?" Her father came around to join their mother at the counter and add his disapproving look. "What's going on?"

Backing down would be so easy. But that was the problem, wasn't it? Because her life had been filled with so much struggle and pain, she had learned to take the easy way out when it was an option. She couldn't avoid surgeries and hospital stays, but she could avoid disturbing her parents. Taking the quiet road, the soft road, the easy road had kept her stagnant. If she ever hoped to flower and grow, she had to make noise, drive over a few of life's potholes, make mistakes.

Loving Rowdy might turn out be the dumbest thing she'd ever done, but she would learn from it. She would change. And once the pain of losing him had passed— because she would eventually lose him, of that she had little doubt—she would flourish in her newfound sexuality.

No pain, no gain. If she hadn't endured that pain of surgery, her heart would not have survived. But because she'd gone through it, she was healed.

"Breeanne," Mom said. "Is there something you need to tell us?"

Looking into her parents' troubled faces stirred up guilt—guilt that she'd moved out, guilt that she'd abandoned the bookstore, guilt that she felt so trapped by the love of the family that had sacrificed so much for her.

A family she had not been born into, but rather a family that had chosen her and loved her unconditionally when her birth mother had abandoned her, a family that had stuck by her through health crisis after health crisis that drained their money, time, and energy.

And now that she was healed, she was walking away from them. What an ungrateful child. They had never said such a thing to her. They didn't have to. Her conscience shouldered all the blame.

Shame overcame her. As a child she'd loved fairy tales, and her favorite was Sleeping Beauty. Waiting for the kiss of a handsome prince to bring her to life. What the fairy tale had not addressed was what happened to Sleeping Beauty after her awakening? Happily-ever-after might work in fairy tales, but in reality waking up from a sleepwalking life caused upheaval.

And there was nothing fun about upheaval.

Secretly, she always feared that if she spoke her mind, didn't go along with the agenda, or made waves, her parents would decide they'd made a mistake and send her back to the hospital. Abandoning her the same way her birth mother had because she was too much trouble.

In a flash of a second, all the feelings she'd suppressed since infancy rushed over her—anger, fear, hurt, shame, and despair. They battered her, first one emotion and then the other, until she fell all the way through them and came out the other end, empty and peaceful.

She looked at her parents' worried faces, smiled softly, and said, "Mom, I can't bring the seven-dip because I won't be at the Fourth of July celebration. Suki can make it for Brent."

Everyone spoke at once. Her father said, "Of course you're coming to the party. It's not a party without you."

Mom put a hand to her forehead as if she'd suddenly acquired a splitting headache. "What are you doing for the holiday? Surely, you're not working. You've already been pushing yourself too hard. We don't see enough of you as it is."

"Hey," Suki protested. "Can you see me with GI Joe? I'm not going be Mom's matchmaking stand-in. You've *got* to come."

For a moment, the vestige of the old Breeanne kicked up a fuss. She loved them. How could she hurt them? *Back down. Smooth the waters. Assure them it was only a joke. Ha. Ha. You'll be there.*

She held up a palm, to quiet both the old Breeanne and her family. "I will be at the Dallas Gunslingers game with Rowdy on the Fourth. I hope you understand. This has nothing to do with you. It's not my intention to hurt your feelings."

"Honey, you're with that man five days a week, eight hours a day," her mother said. "Can't you go to the game on another day?"

"Pass me the phone, Maggie. I'll call Rowdy and get this straightened out." Her father held out his hand. "I'm sure he'll understand. We Carlyles have a Fourth of July tradition to uphold. Instead of going to the game, you can bring Rowdy to our party."

She could explain about Zach being the starting pitcher, and try to convince them to get on board with her decision, but that would still be trying to smooth ruffled feathers, placate them because she had decided to please herself for once.

"Family, I love you so much. But I want to be with Rowdy. I want to go to the baseball game with him and I'm going."

Everyone's jaw dropped open.

"And yes, Mom, Beverly Crownover was right. I was kissing Rowdy in the back row at the movies. I'm young and single and responsible only for myself. I can kiss anyone I want."

If a stranger had come walking into the store that moment and seen her family's shocked, reddened faces, they might have assumed Breeanne had just slapped them all.

Everyone fell silent. Cemetery silent. As if at any moment a backhoe would appear and start digging someone's grave silent.

"Well?" Breeanne settled her hands on her hips, bracing herself for the fallout. "Anyone have anything to say?"

"What do you know?" Suki grinned like she was awarding Breeanne with a medal. "You finally grew a pair."

"Honey," her mother said. "Are you sure this is what you want?"

Her father blinked. "You're dating Blanton?"

"Yes," she said. "I'm dating Rowdy. I know he's a good-time Charlie. I know he's not the kind to ever settle down. I know he's out of my league. I know it's going to end badly. I know he's going to drop-kick my heart. But this is what I want and I'm going to do it anyway. You let my sisters make their own mistakes, it's time you let me do the same."

Her parents looked at each other. Her mother whispered to her father, "I told you so."

"You never know," Suki said. "Have hope. You might just be the one who makes settling down worth it. There is that scarf, after all. It's gotta mean something."

"No, Suki. For once, I'm not living in the fantasy world of happily-ever-after. I know the truth. I accept the consequences."

Her father scratched the back of his neck. Shifted his weight. Looked at a loss. "All right, Breeanne, as long as you understand what you're getting into."

"Really?" Asserting her independence had been that easy, and that impossibly hard. But she'd done it. Made it through. Overcame her deeply ingrained fear that if she spoke her mind, her parents would no longer feel the same way about her. She let out a deep exhale. Smiled gratefully. "I do love you so much."

"And we love you." Dad hugged her.

Her mother nodded. "Much as we'd love to keep you our baby forever, apparently we've been stunting your growth. Go ahead." She shooed her. "Spread your wings, and fly. We'll always be right here cheering you on."

CHAPTER 22

Us ballplayers do things backward.
First we play, then we retire and go to work.

—CHARLIE GEHRINGER

It was a typical Fourth of July in Texas, hot and muggy.

Thankfully, it was an evening game. They arrived at the stadium at six-thirty for the seven o'clock start. The air smelled of hot dogs, peanuts, popcorn, and beer. Kids carried giant foam fingers and waved miniature flags emblazoned with the Gunslingers logo. Mothers carried diaper bags and pushed strollers. Fathers hoisted little ones on their shoulders. Teenagers horsed around, wrestling, fake punching, and goosing one another.

She wore a white ruffled sleeveless blouse, with the cheetah scarf knotted at her neck, and a pair of brown shorts much shorter than she ever dared wear. Rowdy rewarded her with frequent appreciative glances at her legs. She might not be a beauty, but she did have good legs.

Rowdy leaned over and nuzzled her neck. When she turned into him, he kissed her, hard, and she cupped his cheek with her palm and kissed him back, tumbling into the same fiery, dazzling surge she dropped into every time he kissed her, so glad to be touching

him, to have his hand hitched through her hair, to be
with this man who made her feel as soft and sensual
as the cheetah scarf at her throat. When he finally
broke the kiss, she stayed close to him, not ready to
separate.

Rowdy grinned like a god, and she relaxed, knowing the day was going to be perfect. How could it not
be when they were together on her favorite holiday,
and next week started their first day of third base. She
shivered just thinking about it.

"Excited?"

"Uh-huh." *You have no idea.*

Spirits were high, the Gunslingers had been on a
winning streak, and they stood in the will-call line listening to pennant race buzz.

"Gunslingers are going all the way this year," said
one college jock in line behind them to his buddy. "Feel
it in my bones. This is our time in the sun."

"Way too early in the season for speculation,"
Rowdy murmured to Breeanne. He wore sunglasses
and a baseball cap pulled down low, and he'd shaved
his scruff of beard in hopes of avoiding recognition.

She loved his clean-shaven look, and couldn't get
enough of running her palm along his smooth jawline.

"Heard the manager is starting Zach Blanton. I
don't see the wisdom in that. Zach ain't got the pitchin'
arm his brother did," replied the jock's buddy.

"We sure lost something special when Rowdy got
busted up by that jealous husband," the jock replied.
"Too damn bad the dumb sonofabitch couldn't keep it
in his pants."

Rowdy tensed beside her, hunched his shoulders,
put a hand to her back, and leaned in closer.

"Ignore them," she whispered. "They don't know
what they're talking about."

He moved her in front of him, wrapped his arms around her shoulders. She smiled as she felt his arousal nudge her bottom. A thrill of excitement that she had swiftly grown to anticipate pushed through her.

"Rowdy?" a feminine voice called through the crowd. "Rowdy Blanton, is that you?"

He ducked his head to her shoulder. "Oh no. We should have brought Warwick after all, but I wanted an evening alone with you."

A young, beautiful woman in another ticket line was waving like a crazed game show contestant. "Yoo-hoo. Don't you hide from me. I can see you there. Rowdy. It's Christy. Christy Jones. We sat next to each other at a banquet last June."

People were turning around, craning their necks, striving for a better look.

"You've been recognized." Breeanne tried not to sound dry, hot, and prickly, but she didn't think she pulled it off.

"Dammit. I was afraid this was going to happen. I apologize in advance," he said.

"For what?"

A long squeal erupted from another female. "It is! Oh. My. God. It's Rowdy Blanton!"

A stampede of clattering heels, a cloud of feminine perfume, as a throng of gorgeous women surrounded them. Rowdy tried to hold on to Breeanne's hand, but the pawing females separated them.

Breeanne was nothing but flotsam in the wake of his magnificent ship. Her earlier exuberance vaporized. She couldn't enjoy an evening out being reminded how she couldn't measure up to the hundreds of women who wanted him so desperately. Her stomach sank, and she wished she was at her parents' Fourth of July party instead of watching this feeding frenzy.

She felt a hand clamp around her wrist—a strong masculine hand, towing her back toward him like fisherman reeling in a skiff gone adrift from the dock. Rowdy pulled her up against his side, draped his arm over her shoulder, and held her close.

Terrific. Now she was close enough to see fawning fan girls drool on him.

"Who's this?" asked the girl named Christy, tilting her Barbie doll platinum blond head and blinking big eyes so green she had to be wearing colored contacts. No eyes were that color in nature. "Your little sister?"

He puffed his chest out proudly. "This is my girlfriend."

The words sounded so sweet to her ears, but he'd called her his girlfriend before, using her as a shield to ward off predatory women. Breeanne notched up her chin. If it helped him to use her that way, she'd accept it. But she refused to let herself fall for the yearning that burrowed deep in her belly, a yearning that wanted to be his for real.

"Her?" Christy sounded incredulous.

The women shot each other bamboozled, what-could-he-possibly-see-in-this-schlump looks.

Breeanne reached up, patted Rowdy's chest, and said smugly to the gathered women, "I give exceptional blow jobs."

"Burn!" The jock behind them heehawed like a donkey. He held a palm up to Breeanne. "Give me skin, sista."

She hopped up to slap his big palm.

That reduced the tension. Rowdy tucked his sunglasses in his pocket, signed autographs, and chatted with his fans for twenty minutes. The entire time, he kept his arm locked around her, holding her close.

As if she belonged there.

A girl could get mighty used to this, and therein the seductive danger. *Enjoy the moment for what it is. Just don't start believing it's going to last.*

The crowd thinned out as people strolled into the stadium. Rowdy broke up the fanfare by angling his head toward the ticket counter. "We've got to pick up our tickets. I want to see my little brother making his starting debut," he said to them.

The fans good-naturedly waved him toward the will-call window, and walked into the stadium, shaking their heads and marveling. No one else was in line now.

Rowdy went up to the window. "Will-call tickets waiting for me. Rowdy Blanton."

The ticket taker got off her stool, held up a finger. "If you could just hold on a minute, sir . . ." She disappeared from view.

"Looks like she wasn't impressed with you," Breeanne said.

"Happens every once in a while." He winked.

"Are you getting nervous about seeing Zach pitch?"

"Yeah," he admitted. "I'm scared he's not up to the challenge."

"I've reviewed his stats from the Mudcats. Why did Dugan Potts call him up?" It was something Breeanne had been wondering for a while, but hadn't brought up because Zach's transition to the Gunslingers was a sore topic with Rowdy.

Rowdy gave a nonchalant one-shoulder shrug, as if he didn't care enough to lift both shoulders, but she saw distance come into his eyes and knew he was no longer in the moment with her, but kicking around a painful memory.

She changed the subject, stood on tiptoes to peer into the ticket cage. "I wonder what the holdup is. Where did that ticket taker go?"

"Rowdy Blanton?" a stern voice said from behind them.

They turned to see two beefy security guards, who looked as if they might be twins, standing there, hands poised over the stun guns clipped to their belts.

Rowdy broke out the patented grin. "Hey, fellas, what's up? Want an autograph?"

"We're going to have to ask you to leave the premise," the slightly taller of the two said, his gaze noncommittal, but his twitchy hand ready for action.

"I'm here to see my brother throw his first starting pitch in the bigs, boys."

"No, you're not," said the second guard.

Puzzled, Breeanne looked from Rowdy's beaming face to the scowling guards standing shoulder to shoulder, blocking the way to the entrance. What was going on here?

"Um, Rowdy." She plucked at the sleeve of his shirt. "I have a feeling you're still persona non grata around here. Let's go."

Simultaneously, the security guards widened their stance and undid the snap on their stun gun holsters. If these two weren't twins, then they'd tandem-practiced their intimidation techniques.

"Are you guys twins?" Rowdy asked, his grin just getting wider and wider. "You look a lot alike. Who is the oldest?"

"He is." The slightly taller one inclined his head toward his brother, and seemed unhappy about it.

"You guys know how it is. I know you know how it is. Your brother gets on your last nerve, but still, he's your brother. You're proud of him when he does good. You take his ego down a peg when he gets too cocky." Rowdy's voice was smooth and easy. "That's what brothers are for."

The game had already started, the announcer's voice boomed over the PA system. "Pitching for the Dallas Gunslingers is Zach Blanton making his big league starting debut."

"When your bro is sick, you take him to the hospital."

"Fucking A," said the older twin.

"And if he tells you that he left tickets for you at the will-call booth on the day he makes his big league starting debut, well, you wanna be there. Am I right?" Rowdy nodded as if trying to get them to agree.

Like magic, the twins bobbed their heads in unison.

"What's your name?" Rowdy asked the taller one.

"We're not here to get chummy. We're here to escort you to your vehicle and make sure you leave the grounds."

"Right. I got that. You made yourself clear, but there's no reason we can't be friendly about this. C'mon, you know my name, it's only fair that I know yours."

"Abel," said the smaller one.

"Please tell me you're not Cain," Rowdy said to the other one.

"I'm Alec."

"This is Breeanne." Rowdy slung his arm around her again. "My girl."

The words "my girl" set off a fizzy firestorm in her stomach, and she didn't want to let him down. Breeanne raised a hand, not sure what to do. "Hi."

"Look," Rowdy went on. "We drove over two hours to get here. I know you've been given orders to keep me out of the stadium and I completely respect your position."

"Good," Alec said. "It makes things easier."

"I'm not asking to take a seat or anything, but if

you could just let us get a peek at the field. Let me watch Zach throw out one pitch, I'd appreciate it. You can stay with us the entire time, and escort us right out afterward. C'mon, where's the harm? I'll sign an autograph for you."

The brothers looked at each other, considering it.

"Just one pitch?" Abel asked.

Alec shook an Eeyore head. "We have our orders."

"But he's right." Abel lifted his shoulders. "How many times does a guy get to see his brother's starting debut pitch on the mound in the major leagues? You'd do everything you could to be there if it was me and I'd do the same for you."

Alec scratched his chin, considering.

Rowdy was going to succeed. He was going to charm them into letting him into the stadium. The man was something else.

From behind the security guards came the sound of someone applauding in a slow, sarcastic way. "Gotta hand it to you, Blanton, you're slicker than snot."

Sheepishly, the twins separated, one moving left, the other moving right, revealing a squat silver-haired man with an unlit cigar clamped in the corner of his mouth, walking toward them, smacking his palms together harder and harder the closer he got. He had eyes like a Boston terrier, chubby hamster cheeks, a potbelly hanging over his belt, and low-slung, bowlegged gait.

Breeanne recognized him from TV. It was Dugan Potts, the Gunslingers general manager.

Rowdy tensed beside her, his arm going heavy around her waist.

"But then I know how you are, so I came down here myself to make sure these two idiots did their job." Potts glared at the twins like they were something he'd flushed down the toilet bowl.

It might just have been her imagination, but Abel's knees looked like they were shaking, and Alec's Adam's apple convulsed. These big guys were scared of the diminutive general manager.

"We were just escorting him off the property, sir." Alec stood marine-stiff and she half expected him to salute.

Potts ignored the security guards, and fixed Rowdy with a stare so malevolent it sent an arctic chill straight through Breeanne. "I heard you were writing a book."

Rowdy said nothing. Gone was the wit and charm he'd pulled out for the security guards.

Potts waddled closer, but not within striking distance of Rowdy. "I'll have to preorder my copy. Check if you got your facts straight."

"Don't bother. You're not mentioned in the book." Rowdy smiled sweet but when he spoke his voice held a warning burr.

What? Of course Potts was mentioned in the book. It would be a pivotal part of the climax of his autobiography.

"No?" The cigar seemed permanently stuck to his lower lip. When Potts talked the cigar bobbed, as if it was saying yes, yes, yes.

"Not once."

"I find that strange. A book about your life and you don't mention me? My feelings are hurt." Potts gave a nicotine-stained, bulldog-in-a-spiked-collar smile.

"I saw you on television," Rowdy said as lightly as if they were best buddies having drinks at a bar, but he leaned forward aggressively. Loomed over Potts. His hands clenched into fists, back flat, arms welding stiffly to his sides. His entire body was a hard, straight line. As if he was a sheer mountain face about to fling a crushing boulder down onto the general manager.

"Yeah?" Potts's hands went to his hips and his chin jutted up, eyes hard and dark, as if just daring Rowdy to make a physical threat against him.

"You were with a guy who looked exactly like the man who attacked me. Right down to the snake tattoo on his right forearm. Imagine that."

"No kidding?" Potts grunted, shifted the cigar to the other side of his mouth. "You know what they say, everybody's got a look-alike."

They eye-wrestled each other. Neither one blinked.

Breeanne pressed her palms together, brought her fingertips to her lips, thought, *Mongoose and cobra.*

"Why did you pick up Zach?" Rowdy's voice turned steely enough to cut Irish oats.

"Why do you think?"

The humid air twisted with tension. The men stayed locked in their stare-down. Abel and Alec kept glancing at each other and shrugging. Something was going on here that no one except Rowdy and Potts knew anything about.

"I just want you to know," Rowdy said, "that you're not in the book."

Why did he keep saying that? She was going to have to corner Rowdy about this. They couldn't finish the book without including Rowdy's suspension from the Gunslingers. When and why had he decided to leave Potts out of the book? He disliked the guy, and clearly, the guy disliked him right back.

The veins at Potts's temple bulged, and he laid on the sarcasm like butter. "Thanks a lot for leaving me out."

Rowdy raised a fist. "Hands off Zach."

Breeanne pasted a palm to her mouth, smothering her gasp. Was he going to deck the general manager?

"Or what?" Potts sneered, but his fingers were

twitchy, tapping along his belly like he was playing piano keys.

"You know what."

"You threatening me?"

"About as much as you're threatening me."

Potts pointed a militant finger in the direction of the exit. "Get off my property." To Abel and Alec, he snapped, "Do your job, dammit."

Immediately, each man clamped one of Rowdy's arms, spun him around, and marched him to the parking lot. He didn't try to charm or cajole or resist.

Breeanne hurried after them.

"Young lady," Potts called.

She stopped, turned back around, put a hand to her chest. "Me?"

"Yes, you. Heads-up. Don't believe a damn thing that character says. He's a liar and a cheat."

"I haven't found that to be true."

"You don't know everything there is to know about him."

That was true enough, but she was not about to betray Rowdy. "And I don't know everything about you either."

"Fine." Potts waved a dismissive hand. "Go ahead and trust the sneaky sonofabitch, but you can't claim you weren't warned."

CHAPTER 23

I don't know why people like the home run so much. A home run is over as soon as it starts . . . The triple is the most exciting play of the game. A triple is like meeting a woman who excites you, spending the evening talking and getting more excited, then taking her home. It drags on and on. You're never sure how it's going to turn out.

—GEORGE FOSTER

"What happened back there?" Breeanne asked as the Escalade sped toward Stardust.

Half an hour into their two-hour drive back to Stardust, and those were the first words either of them had spoken. The radio was on, and they were listening to the play-by-play of the game. Zach was pitching decent for his starting debut in The Show. But then, for no discernible reason, Zach was pulled from the game.

Rowdy white-knuckled the SUV through Dallas traffic, his shoulders stiff, his eyes intent on the road, his body language yelling, *Don't tread on me.* She had not ever seen him this angry, and she'd been afraid to broach the topic until he had time to take a deep breath, and calm down.

There was a beat inside the car, like the pulse of a contracting heart. As if she were the top part of the heart, the atrium, responsible for setting the pace and regulating the blood flow into the bottom part of the heart.

And he was the ventricle. The strong pump responsible for flooding the body with oxygenated blood.

She rubbed two fingers down her breastbone, felt the ridge of scars, and the reassuring throb of her own heart. She had to set the pace, control the rhythm. She would not push. She would wait until he was ready.

A heartbeat passed. Another. And then another.

Finally, he said, "Dugan Potts happened."

"You're not talking about just tonight, are you?"

He clenched his jaw, turning his profile hard.

A skip of her pulse, an erratic beat. *Breathe.*

"Were you serious when you told him you weren't going to mention him in your book?" she asked.

"Yes."

"Why?"

"I have my reasons."

"And you're not going to share them with me?"

He swallowed so hard he made a strangled sound as if he was choking on poisonous words.

"Your publisher is going to be upset about this," she said. "We're starting the book with your suspension."

"We can write about the suspension without mentioning Potts by name."

"How?"

"We'll just say general management suspended me for insubordination and I freely admit I was insubordinate."

"You called Potts a hamster on television. Fans want to know what provoked it. They will feel cheated if you don't go into details."

"Fans don't own my soul."

His jaw snapped back into place so hard it sounded

like the snapping turtle she found in the backyard when she was a child. The thing had come at her with its mouth open, moving startlingly fast for a creature with a plodding reputation. She'd fallen back on her palms, scrambling away from it like a crab. Grabbed for anything she could use to protect herself, found a stick and thrust it at the turtle. The thing cracked the stick cleanly into two pieces. Her shrieks had brought Dad running. He scooped her into his arms and carried her into the house.

Whatever was eating on Rowdy was buried deep. Could she dig it out of him? For years, he'd been using charm, and constant activity, and physical pleasures as a shield. All the hours she'd spent with him over the last few weeks told her that his lifestyle, values and beliefs, goals and ambitions, all related back to things he would not talk about.

She curled her hands into fists to keep herself from touching him, from pushing. But she had to push. If the atrium didn't do its job, then the heart pump would fail. Set the pace. Guide the rhythm. It was up to her.

"You owe Jackdaw the manuscript you promised them," she murmured.

"Too bad. If they don't want the book we turn in, I'll pay the advance back. Get out of the contract."

"What happens to me? I will have to give back my portion of the advance too."

"Don't worry," he said. "I'll cover your part of the advance just like I promised when I tried to quit."

"I don't get it. There's something else going on here. Something you're not telling me. Something you've not told anyone. Something you've been holding on to for a long time."

He slung his head around, pinned her to the seat

with a hard-edged stare. For a moment, he looked like a complete stranger.

She drew back, instinctively angling her body closer to the door.

How well did she know this man? She believed that because she'd gotten him to open up about his past lovers, and he'd given her tidbits about his childhood, she knew him. During their budding romance she believed she'd bonded with him, but had she really? And that silly scarf had made her believe they shared a connection, but it was all silliness, wasn't it? How well could two people really know each other? Especially two people who'd been together less than two months.

Deep down, she feared she didn't know him at all.

The SUV bulleted into the night. Rowdy kept his focus trained on the highway. Breeanne didn't say anything for a long time, giving him space to open up on his own. But finally, she couldn't take the silence any longer.

"Is it true?" she asked, taking a different approach.

"Is what true?"

"That the man who attacked you is connected to Potts?"

"Yes."

She gripped the shoulder harness of her seat belt with both hands. "You're saying that Potts hired someone to attack you?"

"He did."

Blood pounded through Breeanne's ears. There was a sharp tearing away of her mind from her brain, blood, and bones—cells and nerve endings burned into cinders, her heart bumped, and the hollow air of her lungs hissed out of her throat, over her lips, and spilled into the Escalade.

Her body numbed, her mind floated free—a helium

balloon detaching from its tether—as she struggled to process what he'd just told her. Potts was capable of orchestrating a beating so severe that it had ended Rowdy's career?

Abhorrent.

She floated in the separateness for a moment. It was safer here, in this weird suspended animation where people's employers did not arrange to have them beaten up, but the buffer was an unsustainable haven.

Eventually, she dropped back into her body, blinked. The sun had slipped over the horizon, and darkness filled the sky.

She kicked off her shoes, tucked her feet up underneath her in the seat, folded her arms over herself, shivered. Despite all her parents had done to shelter her, raising her in a sweet place like Stardust, loving her with everything they had in them, the world was not a safe place. She'd forgotten that.

Feeling lost, she raised a hand to the downy scarf. When had it become her touchstone? It was the thing that now brought her back to herself when she felt lost. She had a strange thought that as the threads of the surgeon's suture had sewn her physical heart together, this scarf had sewn her emotional heart to Rowdy's. It was a fanciful thought at best, but the notion felt so true, cosmic and inescapable.

Suddenly, every part of her body that had gone numb before came tingling back to life—her toes stinging, ears ringing, heart burning at the center of her chest.

"Do you have proof?" she whispered.

"Nothing other than my word."

"That's why you agreed to write your autobiography in the first place. To tell the world who Dugan Potts really is."

His fingers tightened on the steering wheel. "Yeah."

"Do you mind if I record this? Just in case you change your mind about not putting it in the book."

"I don't know if that's such a good idea."

"Just for my reference. In case you do. Change your mind."

He nodded tersely.

She slipped the recorder from her purse, clipped to the left side of her waistband, and switched it on. "Rowdy Blanton. Interview Number Twenty-six."

He slid a glance over at her. She could find nothing in his eyes of the carefree Rowdy she knew so well, but she was no longer unsettled by this new face he showed her. In fact, it calmed her. He trusted her enough to let her see all sides of him.

"That's why Potts picked up Zach, isn't it? To have something he could hold over your head, and to keep you from mentioning him in your book. He knew you weren't scared of litigation, so he grabbed for the only bargaining chip on the table. Your brother. That's why you tried to quit the book. Why every time I bring up Potts you shift the topic to your fun-loving lifestyle."

Rowdy pulled a palm down his face. "I've changed my mind, Breeanne. Please turn the recorder off."

She wanted to protest, but the seriousness in his voice kept her from arguing. "All right," she said and switched off the recorder.

"To answer your question, yes," he said.

"Wow. Potts is incredibly Machiavellian."

"You don't know the half of it." His voice came out hard and rough.

"You have Potts running scared, so he hit you where you were vulnerable. Family."

"He's got a knack for knowing where to kick."

"So why did Potts hire someone to beat you up? If

he hadn't done that, you wouldn't have agreed to write the book, right?"

"He did it to get back at me because I wouldn't play ball."

Confused, Breeanne kneaded her forehead. This was going to take some doing to wrap her head around. "With what?"

"I don't want to talk about this right now." Rowdy clamped his jaw shut.

Just when they were getting somewhere, he clammed up on her. Breeanne leaned her head back against the seat, allowed several minutes to go by before she dug in again.

"Why did Potts *really* let Price Richards go? While Price's stats had slipped, he was still a strong second baseman. Most everyone in baseball was wondering the same thing. It was certainly no reason to let him go, especially for the player they substituted in his place."

They passed the sign telling them the exit to Stardust lay ahead. They were almost home.

"You want something to eat?" Rowdy asked. "I'm hungry."

"I could eat." She had to tiptoe lightly here, or he was going to turn off completely and she feared she'd never coax him into speaking of it again.

"We'll stop at the drive-through at the turnoff."

"Okay."

A couple of minutes later, he took the exit ramp and pulled into line at a burger joint. He stopped at the order speaker, studying the posted menu for a long time, the glow from the sign casting his face in an eerie orange light.

Without turning to look at her, he said, "Price's contract was up for renegotiation."

"And he wanted too much money?"

"No," Rowdy said. "Being out of contract made Price a sitting duck."

Intrigued, she angled toward him. "What do you mean?"

"What do you want to eat?" he asked.

"One of the small hamburgers will do."

"Fries?"

"I'll share fries with you," she said, "but I don't want an order of my own."

"What do you want to drink?" He leaned.

She wanted to grab him by the shoulders, pull him back in the car, and yell, *I don't give a damn about food. I want to know what happened that's got you so screwed up.*

"Ice water."

He placed the order, sat back against the seat, and drove up to the window, on automatic pilot. He looked like she'd felt when he told her Potts hired someone to attack him—disconnected, disjointed, disturbed.

They turned north toward Stardust, but instead of taking the street that would lead to his house, he drove the road that curled around Stardust Lake.

Five minutes later, he pulled to a picnic area beside the water. The sun had set and fireworks exploded on the other side of the lake at the marina, lighting up the sky with holiday celebration.

The SUV engine ticked as it cooled down. They sat on the cement picnic table, watching Roman candles explode, eating burgers, and not saying a word. The food was already starting to get cold, but she didn't much notice.

They put their hands into the French fries container at the same time, and their fingers brushed. They stopped and looked up into each other's eyes.

"What I am about to tell you next is strictly off the record. This part is for your ears only. It's never to be made public. Not for the book. Not for anything."

His ominous tone of voice lifted the hair on her arms. This was a big step, for him, for their relationship. He was about to tell her unsavory stuff. She could see it by the look in his eyes.

He was going to trust her.

The air left her body. She nodded and double checked to make sure the recorder was turned off. "All right."

A ghostly mist rolled over the water, punctuated by pops and flashes from the fireworks. Frogs croaked and crickets chirped.

He got up, walked over to the Escalade, rested his butt against the grille, crossed his legs at the ankles, and folded his arms, biceps bulging at the seams of his short-sleeved shirt. In the shadows, he looked more cowboy than baseball player, his angular jaw cleanly honed and defined in the moonlight. She half expected him to dip his head and light a cigarette like the Marlboro Man.

She approached him, walking on eggshells, afraid that if she made a quick move, or said the wrong thing, he would change his mind about talking to her and shut down.

"Rowdy?" her voice came out small in the wide expanse of darkness and stars.

He reached for her, drew her into the circle of his arms. Held her close. Kissed the top of her head.

More fireworks lit the night sky and she wished the circumstances could have been as they usually were with him, light and fun, but this was serious business and she was getting near the nitty-gritty of what made Rowdy Blanton tick. So close to pulling back the veil and seeing the raw man who hid behind that bright smile.

She wrapped her arms around his waist, pressed her head to his chest, thrilled to the beat of his heart as strong as a lion, and savored being with him. Happy to be here. No expectations.

He swayed with her in his arms, a quiet dance in time to the exploding rockets. She drank in his scent. Enjoying every nuanced smell—the cotton of his shirt, the spice of his cologne, the masculine fragrance that was all his own. Womb Wrecker, she'd named it when they'd fallen off the zipline platform together. But his aroma deserved a far more potent name than that. World Wrecker was more apt.

One of his hands slid to the small of her back, and he lightly caressed her there until her body grew warm and supple. What was he up to? If he didn't stop that she'd forget all about this confession. Which was probably his goal.

Hauling in a deep breath, she took a step back from his distracting hand. "We have a conversation to finish."

He gave a short laugh, a dear effervescent sound that lifted her spirits and her hopes. "I should have known I couldn't derail you with full body contact."

"Oh, you derailed me all right," she said. "All I can think about is tomorrow when we get to the third base of the Rookie Rules."

"It's all I've been able to think about all month. You have no idea how hard it's been for me to hold back. I want you so much, Breezy, that I can't stand it."

"How have you managed to hold on to your control?" she whispered, turned on and fascinated by this big, complicated man.

"Lots and lots of cold showers."

"You haven't been tempted to call one of your old girlfriends or take advantage of a groupie, or—"

"No!" he said so forcefully that she startled. He snaked out his hand to pull her up against him again. "You're the only one I want, Breeanne Carlyle. You got that?"

She tipped her head back to get a good look at his face, and saw the reflection of the fireworks spectacular in his eyes, just as the finale illuminated the sky behind her. There was no better place to watch fireworks than in his eyes. The air filled with a flurry of whistles, pops, and snaps that reverberated through her body, ringing with joy. *He wants only me! Rowdy Blanton wants only me!*

His blistering mouth overtook hers. She absorbed his body heat, moaned softly with arousal, and she enjoyed the kiss for as long as she dared before breaking it off.

"You're trying to sidetrack me again," she whispered raggedly, saying it because if she didn't they were going to end up making love right there in the grass.

"You're a determined little thing." He groaned and let go of her. "As annoying as that is right now, it's one of the things I admire most about you."

"I'm spoiling the moment, aren't I?" She ducked her head.

"It's okay, Breezy." He tipped up her chin, forcing her to meet his gaze. "We're going to have a lot more moments like this."

"Really?"

"Well," he said, suddenly looking so uncertain it caused her stomach to slide and dip like a breaking fastball. "I hope so. Maybe you won't think so after I tell you what I did."

The shameful expression on his face drove a cold

shudder down the backs of her legs. What on earth had he done? She stroked her palm over his forearm, letting him know she wasn't the kind of woman who took off on a guy just because he'd made a few mistakes. "Tell me."

He chuffed out a breath, spiked fingers up the back of his neck, glanced out over the water, a faraway look in his eyes. "Have you noticed how much the Gunslingers have improved since Potts took over?"

She nodded against the tightening of her chest. "Before Potts came on board, the Gunslingers rank near the bottom of the league, but that's not unusual for a young expansion team."

"Exactly, and in three years he's taken them to pennant contenders."

"That is a spectacular achievement."

"It's because it's all smoke and mirrors," Rowdy said. "He's cheating."

CHAPTER 24

Baseball is like a poker game.
Nobody wants to quit when they're losing;
nobody wants you to quit when you're ahead.

—JACKIE ROBINSON

Breeanne squeezed Rowdy's arm. "What do you mean? Cheating how?"

"How do you think?"

Was he talking about performance enhancing drugs? Had Rowdy taken them too? Was that why he couldn't look her in the eye? "Doping?"

He barely nodded, his chin turned to granite, his eyes hooded.

"How is he getting away with it?" she asked. "I thought the league was super diligent about drug testing."

"Lance Armstrong methodology," he said. "Where there's a will, there's a way."

"How does he keep something like that quiet?"

"He's got a lot of people in his pocket, unscrupulous doctors, players and staff members who will do anything to win. People who flat-out take bribes to alter laboratory documentation. Or people he has a hold over."

"You're talking about blackmail?"

"Yes."

"I can't believe he's able to pull off something of this magnitude, and have the arrogance to think he won't get caught."

"He's making people money and he's getting results so no one is looking too closely. Lance Armstrong got away with cheating for a lot of years, and Potts has learned from Armstrong's mistakes. He's sneaky. The man's a master at gaming the system."

"That's despicable. Doping is ruining baseball!"

"Not to mention the players."

Breeanne put a palm to her forehead. "My mind is boggled."

"Imagine how I felt when I found out about it."

She stepped back, put a hand to her stomach. "It sickens me."

As soon as she said it, she regretted it. What if Rowdy had been involved in the doping? What if that's what he wanted to tell her, and she'd just made a value judgment?

"See why I have issues with the way the Gunslingers are being run?"

"Absolutely, but how do you know all this?" She was about to ask him why he hadn't gone to the authorities with the information, but bit her tongue. If he were involved with the doping, he wouldn't want to incriminate himself.

"From Price. The players involved are caught in Potts's web. They're either making too much money off the scam, and in too deep, or they have too much to lose by exposing him."

"The blackmail issue."

"Yeah. He'll find a way to put you between a rock and a hard place."

"Like he's done to you with Zach. He'll do something to harm Zach and his career if you don't stay silent."

"You got it."

"Was Price in too deep, or was Potts holding something over his head?" she asked.

"Price and I didn't know what was going on at first. We just wanted to play baseball, and when we found ourselves on a winning team together, so close to home, we thought we'd landed in a honey pot. Little did we know we'd landed into the honey pot from hell."

Breeanne laughed. Not because it was funny, but simply to lighten the tension that stretched her muscles taut.

Rowdy smiled, his teeth flashing white in the night. "Yeah, it's a case of you have to laugh to keep from crying."

"And Price?" she prompted. "What caused Potts to cut him?"

"Potts approached Price because he'd been in a slump. Offered him a way to boost his performance. Price told him to shove it nine ways to Sunday and that's when Potts cut him."

"And that's the real reason you walked out."

"Yeah." He pressed his lips together in a thin line.

"Why didn't Price go to the authorities and report Potts?"

"Because he threatened him. Price has a wife and three kids. He couldn't afford to take the hit, buck the system."

"What did he have on Price? Do you know? Can you say?"

Bleak eyes landed her on, searched her face, an explorer looking for something he wasn't expecting to find. It was an expression she'd never expected to see on this laid-back man. "The same thing he had on me."

"This is what you don't want recorded."

"Yeah."

A frigid chill seeped into her bones. What it would take to warn her again? "Did Potts ever ask you to use banned substances?" she ventured.

"No. I was a top performer without them. Plus he knew I pride myself on having a strong sense of fair play, and I wouldn't go along with his scheme. But Price . . ." He shook his head. "Since Price's game was slipping, and he had a family to support, he was the logical choice for Potts to try and corrupt. And I suppose he was counting on that if he reeled Price in, I'd follow."

"Ah, I see the big picture. You couldn't go to the media with this information because it was second-hand, and you couldn't reveal the source of the information or you'd put Price's secret at risk."

He nodded laboriously, as if it hurt to move his head. He got quiet for a minute, his eyes went distant as if lost in the past, or regretting the present. Regretting what he had to tell her? Worried that his confession would end them? Would it?

Breeanne made a fist. Pressed it to her mouth. He didn't say anything else, so she forged ahead. "With no other real option, you walked out in protest over Price's getting let go instead."

"It was the only play I had. I was hoping I could force him into reinstating Price."

"But it didn't get you anywhere, did it?"

"Where it got me was busted up." His award-winning smile was bright, but there were no teeth in it. His right arm went to his left shoulder. Gingerly, he fingered the seam of his shoulder joint.

"You weren't falling into line. He couldn't have a loose cannon roaming around that he couldn't control."

"I've been called high-spirited more than once." He held his palms up at his sides, shoulder-width high. "Usually by my mother."

"This thing Potts had on you and Price, are you ever going to tell me what it is?" She tilted her head, offered him what she hoped was a trustworthy smile.

"Give me a kiss first," he said. "After you find out my deep dark secrets, you might not want to ever kiss me again."

What on earth had he done?

She took a deep breath to quell the fear gelling in the pit of her stomach, added arrowroot to her knees, hoisted up a faded smile.

They stared at each other. The only sounds were the chirrup of insects, the shriek of tree frogs, and the slap of fish tails against the water. The wind kicked up, sending the pine trees swaying overhead, blurring the star canopy in the sky.

She went up on tiptoes and raised her head for his kiss, loving him anyway, whatever his secret might be. Not caring what he'd done, or who he'd been in a previous life. She loved the man who was standing in front of her now.

He lowered his head, captured her mouth with the sweetest of kisses. She wrapped her arms around his neck, pulled him down to deepen their joining, but he gently reached around and unlatched her hands from his neck. "No more for now. I have to tell you before I lose my courage."

She dropped her hands to her sides, felt her fingertips brush her bare thighs, and wished she'd worn more coverage. She wasn't used to being so exposed. "You're scaring me. What did you do? It can't be as bad as you're making it out to be." Her voice quivered. "You didn't kill anyone, did you?"

He laughed. "It's not as bad as all that."

"Then just tell me." The extended lead-up was causing her to imagine all manner of awful things.

He let out a shaky breath, leaned back against the Escalade again. "I've told you how sick my father was for years. How broke we were."

She nodded. She'd seen where he was from. Understood that desperation might have driven him to do socially unacceptable things. She braced herself for what he had to tell her, planting her feet solid in the grass strewn with pine needles.

"I was sixteen when Mom called me home from Houston. And like you said, I'd got into trouble down there because Uncle Mick let me get away with everything. Hell, he even bought me a beer on occasion." Rowdy shook his head. "I'm not gonna lie. I was a cocky kid."

She rubbed her upper arms, watched his face as he spoke.

"My dad didn't have long to live. A week max, so Mom brought us home in time to say good-bye." Rowdy paused, stared out across the lake. "But I . . . I . . ." The remainder of his thought unstitched into the empty space between them.

She pressed her palm against his, interlaced their fingers.

He squeezed her hand, swallowed, and finished the sentence. "I wasn't prepared."

"I can't imagine what that must have been like watching your father die."

"And I can't imagine what it was like for you, a little kid having those major surgeries."

She lifted a shoulder in a water-off-a-duck's-back gesture. "What doesn't kill us makes us stronger."

"That's what they say."

"Unless it kills us," she said. "*Then* it doesn't make us stronger."

He laughed, and it made her happy to bring an honest smile to his face, especially in this tough moment. "I go into my dad's bedroom. It's dark, and smells bad. He can barely move his hand, but he motions me into the chair beside him."

"You don't have to go into detail."

"I need you to understand my choices. I'm not making excuses, just putting it in context."

"I'm listening."

"I sat down beside my dad, and for an instant his face cleared and his eyes were bright, like he'd been waiting for me to come home so he could give me this speech."

A breeze blew across the water, sending a chill through Breeanne even though the air was warm.

Rowdy moistened his lips. "He told me how much he loved my mother and us kids."

"That's so sweet, and so sad." She traced an index finger over his cheek, and his muscles tensed beneath her touch. He shook his head and she dropped her hand, feeling chastised for touching him, even though he knotted their joined hands into a mutual fist.

"Dad motioned me to closer. I edged over. He grabbed me by the neck of my shirt, and pulled my head down to his face. He was so thin, and his skin is stretched tight over bones so that he already looks more like a skeleton than my dad. I'm scared shitless. I'm at the stupid age where I'm thinking crazy things. Pod people kidnapped my real dad and replaced him with this replica, stupid crap like that."

He paused a moment to watch her face. She was careful to control her response, kept her expression neutral. She didn't want to make a mistake. "Dad told me, 'Son, don't tie yourself down. Life is full of adventure and I missed out on all of it. I got married too young, had too many kids. Don't make the same mistake I did. Be like your uncle Mick. Do what you love. Play baseball. Make love to as many women as you can. Drive fast cars. Go out there and grab life by the throat. Live for me.'"

"Wow," Breeanne said.

Behind them, something made a big splash in the water. The smell of spent fireworks still lingered in the air.

Rowdy lowered his voice. "My parents were high school sweethearts and Mom got pregnant in her junior year. They both dropped out of school, got jobs. Their whole life was about nothing more than struggle, and raising kids. Dad never got to enjoy a damn thing in his life. It wasn't fair, Breezy. It damn well wasn't fair."

Here was the link into Rowdy's psyche she'd been searching for. The thing he'd been hiding from her. The reason he was so afraid to get serious about relationships. He was afraid of ending up trapped and in pain.

"Everyone has regrets, Rowdy. It's a shame your father chose to express his doubts so vividly, at such a dramatic time to a confused teen. It marked you," she whispered.

"Yeah," he admitted, and rubbed a palm down his face. "Any time I got the slightest urge to take a relationship beyond that initial thrill, I'd break things off."

"You won't end up like your father, Rowdy. You've got enough money to last you a lifetime. You've had your share of fun. Marriage and kids wouldn't wreck your life."

"I'm finally starting to realize that." He peered

deeply into her eyes and her heart gave a berserk thump. "Tell you the truth I should have been in therapy. My whole family should have, but we were on that ugly ridge of the income level, a hair over the poverty line. We didn't qualify for freebies, but neither could we afford the luxury of mental health care."

"Still," she said. "You've managed to not only survive, but thrive. Look at where you came from and all you've accomplished. Baseball saved you. Be proud of yourself."

"I can't," he said. "Because it's all based on a lie."

His dark secret. They were finally getting to it. Cold clung to her bones.

"After my dad died, I was so desperate to get out of my neighborhood, to get out of Stardust, and do something big with my life. I was already a pretty damn good ballplayer. Playing ball is all I did. And being a lefty gave me an edge. But it wasn't enough. I had to make *certain* I got out of here."

She wondered where this was headed, but she wasn't going to guess or press. It was his story. He was in charge of telling it his way.

"Price and Warwick . . ." His voice cracked. "They felt the same desperation. They wanted out as badly as I did. My situation was bad, but at least my parents loved me. Neither Price or Warwick had that."

She wrapped her arms around him again, put her ear against his chest once more, and held him to let him know his secret didn't scare her.

He squeezed her tightly. After a long time he finally went on. "In our neighborhood, getting your hands on illegal substances wasn't all that hard. A baseball scout was coming to town."

Silence dripped like spilled milk oozing off a breakfast table.

"I took steroids. I did drugs." Sandbags of regret weighted his voice and he loosened his arms from around her.

Breeanne stepped back so she could see his face, settled her hands to her hips, knocking the recorder off her waistband. She'd forgotten it was there. The recorder clattered to the ground. She picked it up, checked to make sure it was turned off, and stuck it into the back pocket of her shorts.

"Sorry about that," she apologized. "Go on."

"I took drugs to boost my performance. Warwick and Price did too. We rolled the dice, took a chance the way only stupid teenagers can. It worked. We impressed the scout and suddenly, everything we dreamed was coming true . . ." His eyes were tortured. "Because we cheated."

"You don't know it was because of the steroids. You could just have easily impressed the scout without the drugs," she said.

"I'll never know. It's tainted." He swept a hand at the Escalade, a symbol of his success. "All of it."

"But that was the only time you took performance enhancing drugs, right?"

"I never touched them," he said. "Price and I got away with the doping. Back then the drug testing was random, not mandatory. But Warwick, because he was so big, and older than the other kids, he got tapped for testing. His baseball career was over before it ever started. He ended up going into the marines, while Price and I skipped off to the Mariners farm team."

"It's why you hired Warwick as your bodyguard. You feel guilty."

"He's loyal to a fault. Never ratted out Price and me. We had our careers because of him. I owe him more than I can ever repay."

"Okay." She pressed both palms downward. "Let me get this straight. Potts found out that you and Price used steroids to jumpstart your baseball careers and that was how he planned on getting you to go along with *his* doping scheme?"

"Yes."

"He thought because you'd done it once, you were corruptible."

"Yeah." Rowdy folded his lips inward. "When we refused to play ball, Potts threatened to doctor our clean lab results to look dirty."

"The reverse of what he was doing with dirty players."

"You got it. He said, 'You cross me, Blanton, and I'll make sure your pee will light up like a Christmas tree. When people find out you used steroids in high school, it won't be an isolated incident. It'll be a pattern.' How could I fight that?"

"He had you in a straitjacket."

"Not completely. I had one move. Walk out of the Gunslingers in protest over Price's being let go."

"Which got you suspended."

"But that ended up backfiring on him because the suspension caused more media attention than my walking out."

"So he hired someone to get rid of you permanently."

"Not completely, I'm still here, but that's why he acquired Zach. To stop me from uncovering his cesspool in my autobiography."

"There's something I can't figure out. If no one ever knew you and Price took steroids, how did Potts find out?"

Rowdy shook his head. "I don't know. He's got uncanny ways of digging up dirt."

"I wish you'd trusted me enough to tell me this sooner," she whispered.

"I didn't want to know the bad things I'd done," he said. "You're so pure and—"

"Not that pure," she said. "And I've always tried not to judge people. It's easy to draw conclusions about people's behavior but until you've walked a mile in their shoes you have no way of knowing what they've been through."

"Ah, Breezy," he said huskily, "I don't deserve you."

"Rowdy," she said. "You deserve all the happiness in the world."

Was that a mist of tears glimmering in his eyes? He blinked and it was gone, but he took her in his arms and lifted her off her feet.

She wrapped her legs around his waist, rested her chin on his shoulder, whispered in his ear everything she felt in her heart. "To hell with third base, take me home, slugger, and make love to me with all you've got."

CHAPTER 25

This is a game to be savored, not gulped.
There's time to discuss everything
between pitches or between innings.

—BILL VEECK

The minute they were inside his house, Rowdy dropped his keys on the foyer table, held out his arms, and said, "C'mere."

Breeanne hopped into Rowdy's arms as if she'd been doing it her entire life, and would continue to do so for the next seventy years or so. It was that easy.

He held her close, and nuzzled her neck.

She locked her legs around his waist, hanging on for all she was worth. A level five tornado couldn't have sucked her loose from his embrace. Her breasts were smashed flat against his chest, and she could feel the strong, steady pounding of his heart.

He plucked at the scarf around her neck—the incredible softness of the scarf that only the two of them could detect—loosening the knot, sliding it around the nape of her neck where it flowed like water, before letting it fall off his fingertips and drift to the ground.

A sigh popped from her lips, dreamy and poetic.

He slipped her glasses off her face, settled them

onto the table with his keys. He kissed her neck, while one hand slipped up her shirt to stroke the small of her back. "Sweetheart, are you sure you want to do this?"

"I've never been more certain of anything in my life."

"I don't want to lead you on. I can't promise to tell you what you want to hear. My life's a mess. I'm a mess—"

"Shh." She pressed a finger to his lips. "I know that. I don't care. I just want to live in the moment, to be happy right this minute. For today, tonight, I can be happy with you. We can be happy together now. Nothing further required."

"I could—"

She pretended to button up his lip. "I don't want to hear another word about it. All your secrets are safe with me."

He tilted his head back, looked up at her, his eyes gleaming with sexual hunger.

For her. This glorious, flawed man wanted her. It was enough. Tonight, he was all hers and she was going to enjoy every second without worrying about tomorrow.

"After this, will we still be friends?" he asked.

She smiled at him, her heart wobbly with a bittersweet joy. "We will *always* be friends."

His eyes darkened and the muscles at his mouth tightened and he looked as if he wanted to believe that as much as she did. As if he wanted not only friendship but a whole lot more.

A flicker of hope caught fire. He was changing, and so was she. Could they find a way to each other?

Don't, Breeanne. Don't sugarcoat reality. He's vulnerable now because he told you his secrets. It doesn't mean he sees this as a permanent thing.

And yet she had all this hope, and nowhere to place it except on him.

"Let's make this a night for the record books," he said, and carried her upstairs to his bedroom.

When they got through the door, she dropped her legs and slid down the length of his hard body. He gazed deeply into her eyes, tilted her jaw up with three fingers, and lowered his head.

The pressure of his warm, moist mouth kindled a blistering heat that ravaged her nerve endings, and it felt as if every quivering cell in her body had been preparing for *this* moment, with *this* man. How she loved him!

His lips were firm, but gentle, and she parted her teeth, and let him in.

He slipped the tip of his tongue between lips, slow and easy, sending her pulse into a heady gallop. She went up on tiptoes to thread her fingers through his silky hair, tugging his head lower, and meeting his tongue with her own.

The hem of her blouse rode up, the cool of his air-conditioned bedroom sent goose bumps over her skin. Or maybe it had nothing to do with the air-conditioning, and everything to do with the man teasing her with hot kisses.

Tonight's the night. And the Rod Stewart song of the same name played inside her head.

Everything *was* going to be all right. No matter what happened. She'd chosen the right partner to have her first sexual experience with. Of that, she had no doubt. It was not a hastily made choice. She was one-hundred-percent committed.

His tongue slid in deeper, and she reached up to cradle either side of his face between her palms. His heavy beard, already growing stubble again, was scratchy against her skin. She pressed her body as close to his as she could get, eliminating any last bit of space separating them.

She savored every detail, every breath—his taste, his heat, his touch. Her hands roamed to his shoulders, her fingertips dug into the rippled muscles there. They could have been in the middle of a six-lane freeway and she wouldn't have noticed traffic whizzing past. They might as well have been on the moon.

Her head spun. She'd been so engrossed in cataloging every sensory detail that she'd forgotten to breathe. Gasping, she broke their connection, whimpering because she'd been forced to do so.

He inhaled simultaneously with her, chuckled. "I forgot to breathe too."

"Old hand like you?" she teased. "I thought breathing while you kiss was second nature."

He growled low in his throat and nibbled the outside of her ear.

She gasped again.

"Exhale," he murmured.

"I can't." She squeaked, her lungs seizing up, holding on to the stale air. "Not as long as you're doing *that*."

"You don't like having your ear nibbled?"

"No. I love it so much that I can't breathe."

He pulled back. "Now there's a dilemma. Loving something so much that it's bad for you."

Oh, she already knew that. Breanne let out a desperate exhale.

"How about this?" He migrated from the top of her ear to the lobe.

"Rowdy." She panted.

"What is it, Breezy?"

"I'm ready for the good part."

"Patience," he said. "Relax and enjoy the journey."

"I'm going to rip your clothes right off your body if you don't stop that."

He nibbled some more.

"Oh, so that's how you want to play it?" She grabbed the hem of his Western shirt and pulled her hands in opposite direction. The snaps popped open as easy as shelling peas.

"Whoa." He laughed.

His glorious, naked chest was in front of her, just waiting to be touched. She ran her palms along his sculpted pecs. Trembled.

He shrugged out of the shirt, letting it float to the ground. Snatching her wrist, he tugged her to the denim love seat beside the huge bay window. He sank onto the plush cushion, pulled her into his lap so that she was straddling him. He'd slouched and they were almost eye to eye, and her crotch was level to his. His rigid erection strained against his blue jeans, poking against the thin cotton material of her shorts.

He was so big. Was this going to hurt? She hadn't considered that.

"See what you do to me?" His voice came out heavy, and husky.

She dipped her head to hide her pleased smile. *She*, mousy Breeanne Carlyle who'd never had a boyfriend, had caused Rowdy B's ginormous boner.

"You're gloating."

She wriggled her hips. "A little."

He got harder. "Now that's just mean."

"Relax and enjoy the journey." She tossed his words back at him.

"You can be a smartass. Anyone ever tell you that?"

No. Because this sassy side had cropped up since she'd met him. She ground her hips against his.

He groaned.

"Is this what they call a lap dance?" she asked, keeping up the bump and grind.

"If you play with fire, sweetheart, you're gonna get burned," he warned.

"Promises, pro—" She didn't get the rest of the word out of her mouth.

He grabbed the bottom of her blouse with both hands. Whipped it, along with her camisole, over her head as slick as if he were an accomplished magician performing the classic yank-the-tablecloth-out-from-under-a-perfectly-set-table-without-ruining-the-meal parlor trick.

She supposed he *was* a magician of sorts. Making women's clothes disappear like that.

"God," he said. "I love when you wear camisoles instead of a bra."

"It's about the only benefit of being the president of the Itty Bitty Titty Committee. I can go braless."

He snorted. "Stop selling yourself short. These beauties might not be huge, but they are perfect. And those delicious pink nipples are just begging me to come play with them."

His hands spanned her waist, and he pushed her down against his crotch, holding her firmly in place. Her breath shot out in hot little pants. She could not take her eyes off him. What was he going to do next?

Rowdy leaned forward.

Breeanne tensed.

Still keeping his hands around her waist, he lowered his head and took one of her pert nipples, which sat up hard and high, into his mouth.

A strangled cry escaped her lips.

She plunged her fingers into his hair, held on to him as securely as he was holding on to her. Drawing her knees up, she rocked forward into him. He opened his mouth wide around her breast, sucked her inside him.

Her body was doing strange things, growing moist and hot, writhing and squirming as if it belonged to someone else. A heavy pressure weighed her pelvis, aching and urgent. The throbbing between her legs was almost unbearable.

He left one achy breast and went for the other, the cool air touching where his hot mouth had been.

She shivered, violently sweet.

His left hand trailed from her waist, and slipped between her legs. His knuckles raked along the tender skin of her inner thigh. He drew his knees up on the edge of the love seat, creating a place for her to rest her back as he repositioned her for easier access. She took off her shorts and settled back into place.

The wandering hand traveled from her inner thigh to her outer leg, sliding up into the leg of her panties, his thumb expertly snagging the waistband from the inside, and as he turned his hand, the panties rolled down as far as they could while she was still straddling him. The waistband stretched across her butt.

She drew her knees up, making sure her feet were firmly planted into the cushion on either side of him. She rested her arms on his shoulder and stood up, balancing there while he slid her panties to her knees.

She raised her left leg and he stretched the panties to capacity. They would never fit the same again, and she smiled at that. He managed to slide the panties over her heel, and they dropped to her right ankle. But she didn't bother kicking them off.

Whimpering, she sank back down as fast as she could. *Game on*. She wanted more. *Now*.

Breeanne attacked his jeans with unbridled glee,

fumbling for the button closure, finally getting it undone. Ah. She struck gold. A patch of masculine skin dusted with dark brown hair.

"You're not wearing any underwear!" she exclaimed, delighted.

"Commando all the way, sweetheart. Don't you remember from the day at the pond?"

"I was trying not to look." She covered her face with her hands. Giggled. She felt as if she'd chugged ten glasses of Prosecco in a row—fizzy, effervescent, love drunk.

"Feast your eyes now. I'm all yours."

She clapped her hands, and beamed so bright she could pass for a lantern. "Goody."

Her bare crotch rubbed against the denim, sent hot electrical pulses throbbing through her groin. They were both breathing so hard they sounded like phone sex workers. She'd gotten the button undone, but there was still the matter of the zipper strained so tight by his erection that her fingers kept slipping on the tongue of the metal.

She wrestled with it. "I can't get it down, dammit."

"I got it, I got it," he said, brushing her hands away so he could attack the uncooperative zipper.

"Hurry, hurry." She pounded her fists against her knees.

"Dammit, I can't get it open either."

"Scissors. Where do you keep the scissors? I'll cut those jeans off you."

"I got it." He jerked the zipper down.

She leaned over and pressed her lips to his exposed flesh, felt his erection grow harder still. How was that possible?

Soon, very soon, that thing was going to be inside her. Whoa!

She felt as if she'd unwittingly been standing on a trapdoor and someone had just pulled a secret lever that sent her tumbling down a dark unknowable rabbit hole.

Well, you got yourself into this fix. Hang on for the ride. You're about to enter a whole new world.

Thrill mixed with terror shot through her. Rowdy Blanton was going to be inside *her.* He'd been with scores of beautiful women. How on earth had she ever believed she could satisfy a man like him?

She gulped, a guppy sucking air. Her legs turned to rubber. A wave of heat rushed over her, followed by an equally strong rush of cold. Her ears rang. Her vision tunneled, and she saw Rowdy disappear into dark stone catacombs. Her brain looped back on itself.

You're not prepared. You can't handle this. You're in over your head.

"Want to back out?" he asked, brushing her hair from her forehead. "There's still time."

"No!"

"Good," he said vehemently, and kissed her hard. Pulled back, assessing to see if she meant it.

Their eyes met.

He smiled that Rowdy smile she'd come to cherish, and her fears blended into the masculine wallpaper, leaving her with nothing but love for him. She loved him. It was going to be okay. He didn't have to love her back. That was okay too. She loved him, and he couldn't stop her. She would love him every day of her life.

"We're going to hit this out of the ballpark." His eyes made promises. Big promises.

"Yes." She bobbed her head, agreement filling every corner of her heart, mind, and body. "We are."

He framed her face in his hands, and kissed her

more sweetly, more gently than he'd ever kissed her before.

She melted into a gooey chocolate puddle.

His fingers curled around her arm, solid and encouraging. He waltzed her to the bed and stretched her out on the mattress. He stepped back and looked down at her as if she was the Mona Lisa and he, Leonardo da Vinci.

Special.

She felt special in a good way, a great way, the best way of all—cherished, treasured, cared for. It might not be love on his part, but he sure knew how to make her feel it. The man had a gift. No denying.

He kissed her forehead.

She kissed his neck.

He gave her another smile, this one less cocky, more endearing. "How have you imagined this moment unfolding?"

She ducked her head, peeked at him from underneath her lashes. She'd spent all summer dreaming of this moment. "I'm a writer. I have a creative imagination. I've pictured this hundreds of different ways."

"Which is your favorite?"

"We're going to reenact my fantasy?"

"You've waited this long, sweetheart, you should have it exactly the way you want it."

"My fantasy involves the cheetah scarf."

"Ah," he said. "No wonder you wore it tonight. Where did it get off to?"

"It's in the foyer."

He set her in the middle of the bed, kissed her cheek. "I'll be right back."

She watched him move, his supreme buttocks flexing, and her heart went with him. What a sight. What a view. What a man.

The moment was so aching sweet. This was her first sexual experience, and she was miserably, gloriously in love.

Melancholy pierced her heart, but she shook it off. No. She wasn't going to let herself get sentimental. Nor was she going to back out. If he never loved her the way she loved him, it was going to be okay. It was truly better to have loved and lost than never to have loved at all. Her heart would survive this, and would be richer for having known him.

She went up on her knees in the middle of the bed, angling her head to quickly check herself out in the mirror. Her hair lay every which way, and her lips were slightly swollen from the kissing.

And there was no missing those scars, slicing right down the middle of her chest, visceral evidence of her pain. Okay, so she wasn't a beauty queen, but Rowdy didn't seem to mind. In fact, he seemed to think she was gorgeous.

She shifted her weight from knee to knee, wondering if she should go brush her hair or her teeth or both. Should she get under the covers? It felt weird being naked in full view.

Before she could decide, he came back into the room, completely naked too, carrying the cheetah scarf and a box of Magnum condoms.

For the first time, she got a good look at him. She'd known he was big. But an erection safely tucked away inside his pants was a whole other story when it was right out there in the open, on proud display. Omigod, he was beyond magnificent.

No wonder the women were gaga for him.

Her mouth went dry and her pulse revved like a sports car engine. She pulled her bottom lip up between her teeth, shook out her hands.

His gaze hooked on her neck where her pulse fluttered at the hollow of her throat. "Are you certain your heart is healthy enough for sexual activity? Did you check with your cardiologist to be on the safe side?"

She laughed at his earnestness. "My doctor has given me a clean bill of health. I'm good to go."

"But if you've never had sex, how can you be sure?"

"Look at it this way, think of all the fuel it would add to the flame of your ladies' man reputation if you killed me with your . . ." She trailed off, dropped her gaze to his erection.

"You can say the word, Breeanne. Go ahead. Give it a try. I know how much you like words," he teased.

"What did other women call it?"

"Everyone finds their own way." He chuckled, and the sound was music. "You could be straightforward and say penis. But it lacks flair, and you go in for gentler words. You could say cock, but it's a bold choice. You need more sheet miles for that."

"Sheet miles." She giggled.

A sheepish shrug humped his shoulders. "There's always dick. Which falls somewhere between penis and cock. Those are the three biggies. There's dong, but that's got a sixth grade ring to it. Or you could go redneck and call it a pecker."

"Now you're just poking fun at me."

"Never," he said. "But poker *is* an option."

"Oh, the possibilities."

"There's prick, but that tends to be more of an insult. A woman might use that if she was dissatisfied." He wrinkled his nose, shook his head. "Let's toss that one. You're going to be satisfied. One-hundred-percent guaranteed."

"Big boast," she teased.

"Nope. Honest truth, not ego. I won't stop till you get what *you* need. So what's it gonna be?"

She mentally thumbed through her own vocabulary, searching for a word that wouldn't make her blush. "Hmm. How about Johnson? It's a name. Sounds substantial, and upstanding."

"Johnson?" Amusement yanked up the corners of his eyes like invisible strings. "That's what you're going with?"

"For the time being, yes. What do you call Mr. Johnson?"

"How do you know I call him anything?" His eyes twinkled, full of mischief.

How she loved this side of him. "Don't all men nickname their . . . um . . . you know?"

"Not all men do anything."

"You're right. Hyperbole. So you don't have a name for it . . . him?"

"Sorry to disappoint you," he said. "But the closest thing I've come to naming my"—his devilish eyes met hers—"Johnson . . . is Little Rowdy, but feel free to try names at random, and we'll see what sticks."

"Little?" She put a palm to her mouth. "Now that's a misnomer."

"Sweetheart, you are priceless. One in a million." He leaned over to kiss the corner of her mouth, a sideways kiss that was as unique as he was. He crawled up onto the mattress with her.

They were face-to-face, both of them on their knees in the middle of the bed. He had the cheetah scarf wrapped around one hand, a condom clutched in the other. None of her fantasy scenarios went quite like this. It felt a little confrontational, sort of gunfight at the OK Corral–ish, except that he was the only one with a gun in the fight.

"Gun?" She said what popped into her head.

"Huh?"

"Another name for Mr. Johnson. Pistol's good. What do think of pistol?"

"Naw, he's a lover not a fighter." His eyes held hers and she forgot to breathe again. She did that a lot when she was around him. Should she have talked to her cardiologist before embarking on this adventure?

He dropped the scarf onto his erection, flexed his muscle so that the scarf bobbed and fluttered.

Laughing, she reached for the scarf, but he snatched it away from her, wrapped it around his hand.

What was he intending on doing with it?

He scooted closer. She sat back on her heels, looked up at him.

His left hand, the one with the cheetah scarf wrapped around it, traveled up the nape of her neck, his fingers spread, sliding through her hair. He pulled her nearer and they kissed deeply, quickly finding the rhythm they'd lost in conversation.

Finally, he pulled away. "Let's take our time. We have the whole rest of the weekend. Let's make it last."

"Yes." She nodded eagerly. "Could we make love until the sun comes up?"

"We'll see."

"See about what?"

"We'll have to keep an eye on your stamina, and if we plan on lasting until dawn, we *have* to pace ourselves."

"Tell me what to do, and I'll do it."

"Close your eyes," he said.

She didn't question him. Simply obeyed. He was the master lover, and she the love slave. He was the sultan, and she his willing concubine. He rubbed Aladdin's lamp and she was the genie. His wish was her command.

"Aladdin's lamp," she said.

"What?"

"Another name for Mr. Johnson. Because when you rub it, magic comes out."

"You gotta stop making me laugh, Breezy. If we never start making love, we won't be able to keep at it until dawn."

"I thought Aladdin's lamp was clever."

"Too clever for your own good. Close your eyes."

Slowly, she lowered her eyelids. Felt the silky scarf touch her face. His fingers tied a knot in the material behind her head, making a blindfold of it.

"But I want to see you," she protested.

"First," he said, "you feel."

She gulped. What did he mean by that?

He took her hand in his, and guided her to Not-So-Little Rowdy. Her fingers grazed flesh that was at once brick firm and velvety soft. She had no idea a penis could feel so plush, and yet at the same time so hard.

"You . . ." she whispered, her fingers breaking free from his hand to go exploring on their own. "You."

"Me," he whispered back, his warm mouth against her ear again.

The shape of him intrigued her. More contrasts—straight but rounded, smooth yet ridged.

He was right. Her sense of touch was far more acute with the blindfold on.

She slipped her hand down to cup the heavy sacs beneath his shaft.

"Easy there, sweetheart." His deep voice vibrated through her. "The boys are sensitive. They appreciate a light touch."

She explored him for the longest. Taking her time. Making him groan. She loved it.

"If you want to last until dawn, you're going to have to stop touching me now." He manacled her wrist, and she let go.

She reached for the blindfold.

"No," he said. "Leave it on for now."

It felt weird to touch him, taste him, hear him, and smell him, but be unable to see him.

His lips touched her bare breasts, and she let out a cry. How sweet, the hot suction of his mouth. While his mouth played with her nipples, his hand slid down her belly. Her body went rigid, anticipating. Slowly, he stroked over her hip, the warmth of his caress crept under her skin, burned a fever through her.

Tenderly, he touched the warm, moist spot between her thighs and she came undone. His mouth was hot on her shoulder, her collarbone, her breasts, her belly. Everywhere. He was everywhere.

"Ooh, ooh."

"You like that, huh?" Pride tinged his rich, deep voice. Using his finger, he played her as if her body was a finely crafted instrument, and he was a virtuoso.

He was all hands, and lips, and tongue, and teeth. He smelled of earth, and sky—solid, infinite, abundant. His strong masculine fingers combed through the tuft of hair at the apex of her thighs.

"Are you disappointed that I don't wax there?"

"I didn't expect you to."

"A lot of women my age do."

"You're not them," he said. "And I like you just the way you are."

His kiss silenced her, and she drank from his lips, quenched and nourished. He tortured her with his caress, investigating her with his fingers. Touching her in places that made her cry out with sheer joy.

She arched her back, pushed into his hand. He murmured happy noises. She parted her thighs, eager for his exploration. Her body was slick, hot, ready for the finger he slipped gently inside her. He moved his hand rhythmically, taking her back to the delicious place where his mouth had taken her before.

Behind the scarf, colors popped on the backs of her eyelids. She could smell them. Red was the fragrance of bricks and cinnamon—spicy, dusty, fertile scent. Green smelled of limeade, the pond water they'd skinny-dipped in. Yellow gave off the aroma of butter, and sun, beachy and hot. The more he touched, the more colors exploded, the more scents she smelled. Pink bubblegum. Blue smelled of backyard pools. Brown smelled of creosote. Black stoked the fragrance of patent leather.

His fingers drove her to the top of the mountain, and once she got there, she looked into the abyss, and discovered there was only one way down—over the mountain and into the void. She let go. Let him take command.

She hung suspended on the peak. A roller-coaster ride stopped in the middle of a segment—dangling, waiting, frustrated that she was going to lose the sensation before she crested.

And then . . .

Chaos—neon neurons firing over pathways, electrical impulses sparking up nerve centers, chemical signals racing headlong to oblivion. Any, and all, primal desires clamoring for connection.

She fell, fast and long. A thin keen broke from her lips, and she was gone.

CHAPTER 26

When you're in a slump, it's almost as if you
look out at the field and it's one big glove.

—VANCE LAW

Rowdy made waffles at dawn, and they ate breakfast in bed, dribbling syrup on each other in interesting places and licking it off.

"These are delicious," she declared, waving her fork around as sunlight peeked in through the partially open blinds. "I'm glad I picked a lover who can cook. No runs to IHOP at six in the morning."

"You're delicious," he said, dipping his pinky in the syrup on his plate, dabbling it behind her ear, and proceeding to kiss it off. "Mmm."

"That's not me! That's the maple syrup."

He laughed. "You're so much fun."

"So are you."

He chucked her under the chin. "Are we going to spend the day in bed together?"

"I've been holding my breath."

He took the plates away, stacked them on the bedside table, and dragged her down under the covers. He swept his mouth along her naked bare belly, delighted to her laughter, a sweet-pitched sound of glee. He was light-headed, dizzy with the taste of her on his tongue, and dazzled that he was her first lover. He'd never been with a virgin before. It was as novel for him as it was for her. With Breeanne, he felt fresh and new again. His first time on the mound as a professional pitcher, he felt the same, felt . . .

Invincible.

He reached for another condom, flipped her over onto all fours.

"Ooh, doggy style. Fun!"

Her innocent enthusiasm was catching, and he had to think of baseball scores so he could keep things slow and gentle. While things were still new for her, she needed it this way. Later, he would teach her just how pleasurable her body could be.

For hours, they dozed, and made love. Talked, and made loved. Ate, and made love.

They took a bath together in the claw-foot bathtub and then took their time drying each other off. Breeanne bemoaned the fact that she hadn't polished her nails for him. He found a bottle of red nail polish someone had left behind and coaxed her into letting him paint her toes. Kneeling on the bathroom floor while she propped her foot on the side of the claw and slowly dragging polish over her nails was one of the most erotic things he'd ever done in his life.

Mischievous Breeanne insisted on painting his toenails to match hers. And he went along with it because it made her so happy. Giggling, she lined her feet up beside his and took a picture on her smart phone, and when she said, "This is so going on Facebook," he didn't protest.

Obligingly, she then removed the polish from his nails, and he noticed she didn't ask why he had women's nail polish at his house. He was glad of that. He didn't want to talk about the other women he'd been with.

Not with her.

Not for today.

Not ever.

In fact, he had an immediate impulse to grab up a trashcan and run through the house throwing away everything that belonged to other women.

He carried her back to bed, curled his body around hers, pulled her up snug against him, and rested his nose in her hair, her delicate scent turning him inside out. He liked this. Liked being with her.

They cuddled, spooning together. Sometime in the early evening, he woke from a nap to see her lying with her hands stacked beneath her cheek, staring at him. He smiled and reached for her, but she didn't smile back and resisted when he tried to draw her closer.

"What is it?" he asked. What had he done to displease her? A strand of hair had fallen across her cheek, and when he moved to brush it away, he was alarmed to find his hand was shaking. "Breeanne?"

She sat, the sheet falling away from her, revealing her lovely breast marked by scars. He wanted to press his lips to those scars, kiss away her pain, but she pulled the sheet up to her neck and leveled him a look so mournful he was instantly sick to his stomach.

"What is it?" Had she thought about what he'd told her last night and decided she simply couldn't be with a cheater?

"Rowdy," she said after a long moment when he stopped breathing. "I've got something I need to tell you, but I'm afraid it might scare you away."

If any other woman had said something like that, he'd already have one leg in his pants, hopping out the door. But Breeanne was different. He couldn't imagine anything she could possibly say that would scare him off.

He plumped his pillow against the headboard and sat up beside her. He took her hand in his. She was trembling too. Now *that* did scare him. "What wrong, sweetheart?"

"It's about the cheetah scarf."

"What about it?"

"You know how only you and I can feel that it's soft?"

"Yeah." He ran his thumb over her knuckles. Her skin was as soft as the scarf.

"There's more to it than that."

"I'm not sure I understand what you mean, but okay."

"I don't want you to think that I believe this story, or anything, but seeing as how this is Stardust, it's going to get out sooner or later. And I'd rather it come from me."

He didn't know what to think. "What story?"

She told him how she'd come to find the scarf in an old hope chest. About the odd old woman she'd bought the chest from. About the prophecy written on the chest. About the wish she'd made for her writing career and how it had come true. Then she told him about the prophecy that was carved into the box that the scarf had come in.

" 'One soft touch identifies the other, and they are at last made whole,' " she quoted. "My sisters think it means that if two people feel the same thing they're soul mates, but that's silly. Right?"

Her voice went up on a hopeful note, as if the last thing she wanted was for him to confirm that the quote was indeed silly.

He didn't look at her, just tightened his grip on her hand and kept rubbing her knuckles, a storm of emotions whizzing through him. If any other woman on the face of the earth had told him this strange story about a soul mate–detecting scarf, he would have been long gone. But this was Breeanne and that made all the difference.

"It's weird though, isn't it, that the scarf is cheetah and cheetah is your favorite animal print. It seems almost—" She broke off.

Finally, he glanced over at her. She tilted her head so that her hair fell into her eyes and she could study him from underneath a camouflage of fringe. God, she was cute as hell.

"Fated," he finished for her, thinking of the day he'd first caught sight of her and those cheetah panties.

Her cheeks pinked. "It's not only superstitious, but pretty nuts to believe that."

"You don't think we're fated, Breezy?" he whispered, leaning in toward her, surprised by how panicky he felt at the thought that maybe confessing his secret shame to her had changed the way she looked at him.

Her eyes widened as if he'd asked a trick question and he suddenly realized he didn't want her to answer that in case the answer was no.

That's when he knew that he truly wanted more. And he'd been wanting it for a long time, but admitting it felt too much like walking off a cliff.

Until now.

Until Breeanne.

His father had loved his mother, and he had loved his children, but as he lay dying, he regretted getting married and having four kids so young. He never had the time or money or health to enjoy life. Rowdy had clutched that lesson to his heart, and held on tight. He'd strived to emulate his uncle Mick, who was still single at fifty.

But it didn't have to be an either/or extreme. He could have a balanced life. He had money. He wasn't a kid anymore. He could have a substantial future beyond baseball. He could be a real part of a community. Volunteer. Coach Little League. He had had his day in the sun and that was all right. He had played in the major leagues for over a decade. How many people could say that? He had a legacy, but what good was it if he had no one to share it with? It wasn't until he met Breeanne that he fully understood how empty his life had become. He'd dated free-spirited women who didn't want strings attached any more than he did. Women like Laila.

An old childhood fear had kept him believing that if he stopped moving, stopped having fun, stopped long enough to let himself feel anything deeper than physical pleasure, he'd end up like his father. Trapped in a life he didn't want to be in, and couldn't get out of.

It seemed obvious now. Why hadn't he seen it before? Warwick tried to tell him, but he simply hadn't listened.

Breeanne.

She was the one who'd gotten through to him. His last good hope. A lifeline. How stupid would he be not to grab hold before he ended up like his uncle Mick, a bloated, middle-aged party boy trying hard to prove he wasn't lonely.

Around Breeanne, he felt good in a different kind of way. A way that didn't leave him hungover, or with buyer's remorse for a hotshot toy he'd blown money on, or sheepishly sneaking out of a woman's apartment in the middle of the afternoon.

He didn't know what he'd done right to deserve this sunshine that had fallen into his life, but he wanted more. He wanted more from life.

He wanted her.
Not just for now.
Not for a week.
Not for a month.
Not for a year.
But for a lifetime.

Monday morning, Breeanne took her second walk of shame. She'd had breakfast with Rowdy, and he'd told her to take the day off. He intended on phoning Zach and explaining why they hadn't been able to watch him pitch on Saturday night.

On the way home, a tire on her Sentra blew out.

She could have called Triple A and waited in the car in the muggy July heat for over an hour. Or she could have phoned her father, but she didn't want to explain her situation to Dad. Or she could have called Rowdy to the rescue.

But she didn't need rescuing.

Her house lay two blocks away. She could call Triple A from there in the comfort of home and not have to bother anyone. That meant she had to stroll Stardust as people rushed off to work.

Fine. She wasn't ashamed. Head held high, shoulders back, wearing the same wrinkled brown shorts and white ruffled blouse she'd worn to the ballpark on Saturday, purse slung over her shoulder as she strutted down Main Street. Waving at everyone she passed.

Kasha was coming out of DeLite bakery, balancing her usual blueberry bran muffin and a cup of coffee in one hand, while opening her car door with the other. Their gazes met and her sister's eyes bloomed open like morning glories, while her mouth fell like a broken elevator, and her coffee cup and muffin splattered to the ground.

In the past, Breeanne might have rushed over, apologizing for causing Kasha to spill her breakfast, but today, she simply called, "Good morning," and continued on her way.

Did she look different? She certainly felt stronger, braver, prettier, sexier, and happier and . . . well . . . just about every kind of "er" there was.

Tossing her mussed, freshly-rolled-out-of-Rowdy-Blanton's-bed head, she walked through the front door of her house. Stephanie sat at the kitchen table eating a bowl of Honey Nut Cheerios.

"Well, well, look what the cat dragged in. Sit, tell me all about your weekend." Stephanie smiled like Sylvester the Puddy Tat with a mouthful of Tweety Bird.

Breeanne set her purse on the table, fished out her cell phone and keys. "I've got a flat. Need to call Triple A first."

"Okay." Stephanie wriggled her fingers.

Breeanne went to shower and change clothes, and then she popped back into the kitchen, but Stephanie had already gone. After she got the flat fixed she planned on getting down to work, spending the day transcribing the conversation she and Rowdy had on the drive home. Not knowing how much of the interview was on the recording, she dug in her purse for the recorder.

But it wasn't there.

Had she put the recorder back in her purse? Or was it still on the table in Rowdy's foyer? She was so love addled, she couldn't remember. She rubbed her forehead. What she did remember was the big kiss Rowdy laid on her before she left the house that morning, bending her over backward as if they'd danced the tango, kissing her so hard and deep that her head buzzed muzzy.

She rubbed her forehead. Think. It could have fallen out in the Sentra. She'd check when she went back to meet Triple A.

She shouldered her purse, headed out the door, only to be ambushed by Kasha, Jodi, and Suki on her front porch.

Suki grabbed her left arm, Jodi her right. They strong-armed her back inside and sat her down at the table.

Jodi folded her arms over her chest, stared at her like a prison guard prepared to frisk an inmate for contraband. "Where have you been?"

"What are you guys doing here? Don't you have lives?"

Once upon a time, she would have placated her sisters, smoothed their ruffled feathers. Then again, once upon a time, she wouldn't have spent two wild nights with a gorgeous playboy baseball pitcher.

"Ham's watching the B&B," Jodi said, referring to her handyman. "This is an emergency."

"I don't have to open the bookstore until ten." Suki plunked down beside her.

"I called in late," Kasha said. "I had to go home and change out of my coffee-stained clothes because a certain Miss Thang decided she was going to strut the walk of shame in the same clothes she was wearing on Saturday evening. You owe me breakfast, by the way."

"Cereal in the pantry." Breeanne flapped her hand.

"I would have paid to see that." Suki leaned in to whisper to her, "When these two are gone, I want dets."

"I can't believe you were so incautious. Mom and Dad are going to hear about this."

"And realize that . . . gasp . . . I'm having sex at twenty-five. I'm not that sickly little kid anymore. I'm happy, healthy, and trying to live a normal life. Don't I get to do that?"

Jodi looked woeful. "Rowdy's going to crush your heart."

"I know that," Breeanne said quietly, and folded her hands on top of the table.

Her three sisters exchanged surprised glances.

"You're not dreaming of happily-ever-after with him?" Jodi sat on the other side of her.

"Just because I read fairy tales doesn't mean I think they're real, but that also doesn't mean I can't enjoy the fantasy," she said.

"And that's what you're doing with Rowdy?" Kasha sat down at the end of the table with her cereal bowl.

"Yes. I know he's a good-time Charlie. I don't care. I wanted to be with him and I accept the fact that I'm in love with him and I'm going to lose him."

"You're in love with him? Aw damn." Suki snapped her fingers. "Rookie mistake."

Breeanne lifted her head, stared at her sisters one by one. "Are you telling me that you all didn't fall hard for the first guy you slept with?"

"We came here to stage an intervention for you, not talk about *our* sex lives." Jodi stood up. She was touchy on the topic of love since she'd been stood up at the altar six months ago.

Breeanne got to her feet as well. "I don't need your intervention, but I do thank you for your concern. It's good to know I have sisters I can count on. I've got to go now. Triple A is coming to fix my tire."

"Not without a hug," Jodi said.

"As long as you're passing out hugs." Suki threw her arms around Breeanne and Jodi. "I'm in."

"Kasha." Jodi motioned her over. "You too."

"We know we love each other, why do we have to do the group hug thing?" Kasha grumbled, but she joined the circle.

"Okay." Breeanne dusted her palms. "Together. That's enough sap for one day, but I truly do love you guys."

"Just let us know when you need the Häagen-Dazs and Kleenex," Suki said, "and we'll be here."

"Go to work." Breeanne shooed them.

As they walked out the door, she heard Jodi whisper to Kasha, "I do believe that whatever happens she's going to be just fine."

"I think you're right," Kasha whispered back. "She's walking into the relationship with her eyes wide open, whatever mistakes she makes are her own."

The door clicked closed behind them. Thinking about her sisters' confidence in her, Breeanne smiled. Finally, they were starting to realize that she *could* take care of herself.

Now if she could only convince herself of that.

CHAPTER 27

It never ceases to amaze me how many
of baseball's wounds are self-inflicted.

—BILL VEECK

Zach wasn't answering his calls again. Damn
Potts for screwing up his relationship with his little
brother. No doubt his brother believed that he hadn't
shown because he was jealous, and that killed Rowdy's
soul.

He picked up the phone to call Breeanne, but put
it down again. Just imagining the sound of her voice
cheered him. He smiled. She'd been on his mind all
day long, but she told him she needed to reconnect
with her family, and he respected that. Her family was
a close-knit bunch, and they worried about her. He
didn't want them believing that he was standing in the
way of her seeing them.

If things went the way he wanted them to . . . well
. . . it was a little too soon for that. But he hoped he'd
be seeing a lot more of the Carlyles in the future.

He tried several more times to call Zach, but got nowhere. To burn off worry, he worked out in the gym.
But he couldn't stop worrying about Zach. Restless,
he quit the gym after thirty minutes and took Nolan

Ryan for a walk instead. Warwick had gone to town to pick up supplies, and he was at loose ends in his own company.

To keep from worrying over Zach, he thought of Breeanne and wondered how she was doing. He resisted the urge to call her for as long as he could, but finally unwilling to go to sleep without hearing her voice, he phoned her just before he went to bed. It was almost midnight and her cell phone went to voice mail. His little meadowlark was probably already sound asleep.

"My bedroom smells of you," he said, hoping she could hear the smile in his voice, and he almost added, "I love you." But he stopped himself. Not because he didn't want to tell her. Hell, he wanted to shout it from the top of his zipline tower to the entire town of Stardust. No, he wanted to do this right. In person, over a romantic dinner he cooked for her.

All night long he dreamed of Breeanne and his plans for their future.

He was dead asleep when Warwick came barreling into his room on Tuesday morning, ripping the covers off him.

"Wake up," Warwick commanded. "Now."

Rowdy jerked upright. "What is it? What's going on?"

Warwick found the remote, switched on the big-screen TV on the wall opposite his bed.

"What are you doing?" Rowdy yawned. "What time is it?"

"Eight o'clock in New York."

"News flash, this isn't New York."

Warwick flipped through the channels, stopped when he found what he was searching for.

"GOZIP TV?" Rowdy groused. "Are you kidding me?"

"Shut up. Watch."

"That stuff is pure bullshit. GOZIP is known for taking things out of context and—" Rowdy rubbed his eyes. "Is it Zach? Tell me? What's happened?"

"Watch," Warwick growled.

Rowdy got out of bed. Grabbed his T-shirt from off the floor, wrestled it on.

"Where did this recording come from?" the TV personality asked the reporter.

"The source prefers to remain anonymous, but the recording has been authenticated. That is Rowdy Blanton's voice," the reporter confirmed.

He stared at the TV, not fully comprehending what was going on until the announcer asked the reporter to play it again.

In our neighborhood, getting your hands
on illegal substances wasn't all that hard.
A baseball scout was coming to town,
and I took steroids. I did drugs.

Rowdy heard his voice spin out across the airwaves, and the cute little fantasy world with Breeanne he'd stupidly convinced himself was real, caved in.

Two minutes later, the phone rang. It was Rowdy's agent, Barry Goldfine, who told him it was wise to lawyer up over the GOZIP thing. While he was on talking to Barry, Heath Rankin buzzed through wanting to know how and why details that belonged in the autobiography had gotten leaked to a TV tabloid. Rowdy didn't have an answer for him, but he had a horrible suspicion.

He'd no more than hung up when Zach called.

"Rowdy?" His brother's frightened voice trembled.

"What is it, Zach? What's wrong?"

"I'm in trouble deep, bro."

Rowdy squeezed the phone, if he could have grabbed his brother through the airwaves and pulled him into the safety of the room with him, he would. He'd been waiting for a call like this since Potts picked Zach up. The kid had no idea of the level of hurt he was in for.

"What happened?" Rowdy asked. Nolan Ryan sensed his distress, came over and leaned against him. He bent to scratch the dog's ears, calming himself down.

"When you didn't come watch me pitch on Saturday, I was feelin' kinda sorry for myself."

"I was there, buddy, outside the stadium. Potts wouldn't let me in."

"Oh." Zach sounded tearful.

"Tell me what happened."

"I went to blow off steam after the game and I met a couple of pretty girls. I don't know what happened. I guess I drank more than I thought. One minute I was partyin' and the next minute it was mornin'." Zach's voice cracked.

"Do you think you might have been roofied?"

There was a long silence. "Hell, dude, could be. I woke up in a bed with two men dressed in women's clothing. I *know* I didn't have sex with them. I was out cold. But . . ."

He could hear sniffling. "Whatever you did. Tell me. I can't help you if you don't tell me everything."

"I did drugs. I don't remember doing drugs, but they were all over the apartment—cocaine, marijuana, steroids. My place looked like a pharmacy."

"Let me guess." A cold anger peeled up the back of his neck, and he could feel it growing up his brain stem, a gathering storm of fury. "Dugan Potts called and told you to come in for random drug testing."

"Shit, man, how'd you know?"

"That's how Dugan Potts works. He sent those trannies to get you doped up. I promise you there's pictures out there showing off your wild night. Check social media."

"What? No way."

"Potts is behind this. He wants you down, and he wants you vulnerable. He wants to own you."

"What for? I pitched good. I pitched damn good."

"And he had the field manager pull you from the game."

"I know. I was pissed."

"He likes to mess with people's heads, and he likes having things he can blackmail you with. Plus he's using you to get back at me. You are a weapon in the chess game he plays with me."

"That sounds cocky."

He could hear the kid puffing up over the phone, getting that sullen sixth grader look on his face. "Don't get testy, Zach. I wish it wasn't true. But it is."

"Okay. All right. I'm listenin'. What should I do?"

"First call your field manager say you're sick, and you can't come give the specimen today." He could feel the anger building in his head like a pressure system generating a storm. He was a laid-back guy, but enough was enough. Potts had gone too far this time, putting Zach in the vise.

Come after my brother, you sonofabitch, and you're gonna pay for it.

"Then what?" Zach asked.

"You leave that to me, little brother. Just leave that part to me."

Breeanne heard about it on the radio and she drove as fast as she could to get to Rowdy's house, but it looked like she'd picked the exact wrong moment to walk through the door.

Rowdy set his cell phone on the foyer table, turned, and gave her a look that said if she were a witch at the stake in puritan times he'd be the first one to light the match.

Nausea scaled the walls of her stomach, but she breathed in to keep from running. He had no idea how hard it was for her to face him. To stand here and bear his justified anger without trying to sweet-talk, smooth it over, or make things better.

No excuses, she had to absorb his anger, tolerate the pain. She was the cause of it. If a samurai had run her through with a steel sword, it would have been a mere tickle compared to the butchery in his eyes.

"Rowdy, I—" Anxious dread moved through her, numbing her limbs, tingling her hands, and toes.

He held up a silencing hand. "I've got to give it to you. You're good. Coming up here, looking for a job, but then refusin' to take it, playin' coy, and when you had your hooks in me, I was easy pickings. And here I thought Laila was cruel. She ain't got nothin' on you, sweetheart."

"No," she whispered. "No. That's not—" She bit off the words. It didn't matter what she'd intended. Her carelessness had caused this.

"You were playing me all along." Bruises filled his

laughter, wet and hurt, like fleshy summer peaches picked too late and shipped too far.

"No." She barely breathed.

His nostrils flared, bellows feeding his anger. "Using your virginity as a tool to get me to lower my guard."

"You don't believe that." She made her voice small, hoping it hid the wall of tears threatening to fall. "If you believe that, then nothing we shared this weekend was real."

His chin quivered, and he jammed his hands in his pockets. "All I know is that I trusted you. I opened up to you. I let you in and you kicked me in the teeth. No wait. You're a stickler for the right words, aren't you? Let's use them. It feels like you kicked my testicles into my groin."

She promised herself she wouldn't try to defend her mistakes, but she couldn't have him believing that she's done this intentionally. She pressed her palms together. *Please, please let him believe her.*

"It wasn't me, Rowdy. I didn't leak the story. It was my roommate, Stephanie. I thought I lost the recorder, but obviously she stole it. It's the only explanation."

"You were responsible for safekeeping my information. You should have told me you lost the recorder, so I could at least have been prepared for this. Instead, I get blindsided because I was dumb enough to trust you."

She infused her eyes with apology and regret, hoping he could see how truly sorry she was that her incompetence had caused his private secrets to get splashed all over the media. "Rowdy, I am—"

"No." He punched the air with an index finger in front of her face. "You don't get to pull the big-eyed, helpless waif card."

Helpless waif? It was either that or calculating

bitch. Her remorse shifted into bone-deep hurt, but she didn't own the luxury of self-pity.

"You promised me that the story was off the record." His voice was so cold it could have field-frozen peas, and his eyes, those laughing blue eyes, looked dead.

Burned to the marrow of her bones by his dry-ice emptiness, Breeanne shivered. "I turned off the recorder, but somehow it must have gotten turned back on when we were kissing. I never would have intentionally put you in this position."

"It doesn't matter what your roommate did. Your carelessness caused this."

His words were true, every one of them. His life was in shambles because of her. His reputation shot, his brother's career in jeopardy. She deserved everything he was pitching out and more.

"Both my agent and my publisher warned me not to go with an unproven writer, but I didn't listen. I had to have things my way. Prove I was still in control when everything else in my life was falling apart." His eyes were so bleak.

"I am so very sorry." Anguish squeezed her heart to pulp.

"I thought we had something here. For a time, I believed it was possible to find someone I could build a life with." He ran a hand over his nose, blinked hard. "How stupid was that?"

His suffering cut Breeanne to her soul. *She* had caused his pain. She was the instrument of his wound. She reached out a hand, whispered his name. "Rowdy . . ."

He turned away, turned his back. "You should go."

On stilted legs, she moved in jerky, mechanical steps. Her eyes watered, burned. Her shoulders curled inward, pulled together. The tears were running down her cheeks now, streams, buckets. She couldn't stop them no matter how hard she tried.

She knew when she went into this relationship that she was going to end up with a broken heart. What she never guessed was that she would be the cause of it.

CHAPTER 28

Baseball is reassuring. It makes me feel
as if the world is not going to blow up.

—SHARON OLDS

When Breeanne returned to the house, Stephanie was there, directing two lunkhead bodybuilder types on how to load her things into a U-Haul.

"You're back." Stephanie gave her a Miss Georgia Peach smile. "I—"

Breeanne marched right up to her. "You thought you'd move out while I wasn't home."

"Well, clearly our arrangement wasn't working out, and—"

"Oh don't pretend." Breeanne surprised herself by getting right up into the woman's face. She bundled up all the anger, pain, and disappointment she felt at herself and directed it at the smug redhead. "You intentionally played me for a sucker. You convinced me to move in with you. You snooped through my things. You were planning all along on scooping Rowdy's autobiography out from under me."

"I never—"

"Zip it," Breeanne commanded. "When you found my recorder, you stole it, and when you listened to it, realized what you had. You could sell to tabloid TV and make a tidy sum."

"Yeah." Stephanie jerked a haughty shoulder forward. "So what? You can't do anything about it."

"I'm going to press charges. Theft is theft. I know you'll find a way to wiggle out of it. People like you always do. But it will inconvenience you for a while and cost you money."

"I . . . I didn't steal it." Stephanie shoved her nose in the air, shook her head, and sent her a lofty glance. "I borrowed it."

"If you borrowed the recorder, then where is it?"

Stephanie snapped her jaw closed, glared. "GOZIP has it."

"Hmm, I know you have a degree in journalism from the University of North Texas and I don't, but let's review the definition of theft. Theft is the taking of another's property without that person's permission or consent."

"We said share and share alike, remember?"

"No, you said it. I never agreed."

Stephanie pushed her lips out in a pout, folded her arms over her chest. "If I get it back, will you not press charges?"

"*If* you get it back. Either way, when I write Rowdy's story, your little stunt will be in. Everyone will know exactly what kind of person you are." She wasn't about to tell Stephanie that she wouldn't be finishing Rowdy's autobiography. Let her sweat it out.

"You . . . you . . ." The color drained from her face, and her brow pleated. "You can't do that."

"Watch me."

"I'll sue you for libel."

"You can't sue me," she said. "Not when it's true."

"Well." Stephanie twisted off, nose in the air, made

a twirling motion with her index finger. "Let's get out of here, boys."

A scattering of applause broke out.

Startled, Breeanne looked up to see her family standing there, all of them—Mom, Dad, Kasha, Jodi, Suki. She knew without asking that they'd heard what happened, and had showed up to give her moral support.

"Now that was an amazing dressing-down," Kasha said.

Breeanne's face flushed. She was proud to have stood up to Stephanie and glad that her family had been here to see her personal growth, but she was far too upset about the pain she'd caused Rowdy to take any pleasure from her accomplishment.

"Honey," her mother said, wrapping her in her arms. "You were magnificent, but are you ready to move back home?"

"No Mom." She met her mother's eyes, and then shifted her gaze to her father. "Dad. It is time for me to have my own place."

Her mother's forehead pleated in concern. "Will you come back to work at the bookstore?"

"For a while," she said. "Until my writing career gets going."

Every member of her family gave her a hug and told her it would be all right.

Yes, eventually she would get past this. She would train herself not to think about Rowdy every time she heard the crack of a baseball bat, or the "Star-Spangled Banner." And in, oh, forty or fifty years, she probably wouldn't remember which of her lovers it was that made the best spaghetti carbonara in the world. And who knew? One day, she might even eat dipped cones again without bawling her eyes out.

Her family went ahead of her. Breeanne took three faltering steps, blood rushed into her ears, her head spun, her knees collapsed, and she fell to the ground crying, utterly broken.

Her family rushed back to comfort her, fearful she was physically hurt, but when they saw the damage was entirely emotional and she waved them away, they respectfully left her to her grief.

Rowdy drove to Dallas to confront Potts, but he couldn't stop thinking about how harsh he'd been on Breeanne. She happened to walk into the house at exactly the wrong moment. His fury and frustration with Potts spiked at an all-time high. His worry over Zach eating an ulcer into his stomach, his own touchy humiliation that the world knew he'd taken steroids in high school. The most shameful thing an athlete could be accused of, and now, thanks to Potts, Zach was traveling the same road.

He kept seeing Breeanne's green eyes shadowed, her body shaking, her skin pale. She'd flinched as if he'd struck her, hunching over, drawing in, the light draining from her face.

Turn around. Go back. Tell her you forgive her. Beg her to forgive you.

The next exit ramp loomed. He headed toward it. His cell phone rang. It was Price.

He took the ramp, pulled onto the shoulder of the road. Price had heard about what happened. He wanted to come forward and tell about his experiences with Potts. In fact, he also informed Rowdy that he'd already called a lot of the other guys on the team and told them what had happened.

In the middle of the conversation another call came

through. It was a player Potts had blackmailed. He wanted to come clean about his past and expose Potts.

By the time he got to Dallas, he'd gotten a dozen calls. People were tired of the bully, tired of keeping secrets. They were ready to talk.

Caught up in the biggest scandal in baseball in recent history, Rowdy was stuck in Dallas for several days, doing damage control for Zach's reputation and helping clean up social media sites, meeting with the other players to come up with a game plan for exposing Potts. Leading the charge to talk to the baseball commissioner, the media, lawyers. Barry flew in. Heath Rankin. Everyone wanted to talk to him.

But through it all, he couldn't stop thinking about the shabby way he'd treated Breeanne and he couldn't wait to get back to Stardust, so he could apologize.

The best thing about being back at the bookstore, besides the books and the customers, was having Callie around every day. Breeanne had sorely missed her cat.

Potts and the Gunslingers scandal was all the media could talk about. Rowdy came out of it the poster boy for doing the right thing. Every time she saw him on TV, her heart stumbled.

A week had passed, and the bulk of her grief had ebbed, but the pain of losing him didn't hurt any less today than it had the day before. When was it supposed to get better?

On Friday, when she was moving a bookshelf, she found the hope chest her mother had put away. She took one look at the thing, and fresh tears sprang to her eyes.

She sank to the floor beside it, traced her finger over the words.

Be careful where wishes are cast, for reckless dreams dared dreamed in the heat of passion will surely come to pass.

Breeanne dropped her head to her knees, and let the sobs come. Tiptoeing footsteps surrounded her. She looked up to see her sisters hovering.

"Want me to make a voodoo doll of Rowdy so you can stick pins in it?" Suki asked.

Kasha bumped Suki with her hip. "Shh."

"I mean it," Suki said. "I'll do it. Anyone messes with one Carlyle woman, they mess with us all."

Her three sisters nodded in solidarity.

Breeanne accepted the tissue Jodi handed her, dabbed her eyes and blew her nose, got to her feet. "You don't get it, Suki. I don't want to hurt him. I love him. I don't ever want to see him in pain."

"But he hurt you. I wanna punch him in his handsome face for that." Suki knotted a fist.

"She doesn't get it," Jodi whispered, squeezed Breeanne's hand. "She's never been in love."

Breeanne closed her eyes. "I'm okay, you guys. Really. I'll be all right. Things are as they should be. The universe has realigned. I'm back at the bookstore. Life will rock on as it did before. No harm, no foul balls."

Except *everything* had changed. Including her, and she no longer knew where she fit in the world.

On Saturday afternoon, she sat at the counter reading when she heard the stairs creak. She didn't look up. Bookstore customers browsed leisurely. If they were looking for something special, they would come ask for it.

The footsteps grew closer.

She turned the page of the book she was reading, a book that had nothing whatsoever to do with either baseball or happy endings. She was done with both of those, at least until her heart mended.

And it would mend. This wasn't the first time her heart had been ripped apart and stitched back together. Except it was the first time it had been ripped apart by love.

A man cleared his throat. "I need a book."

At the sound of Rowdy's voice, Breeanne froze, her eyes glued to the page. "A book about what?" she whispered.

"Do you have any books on how to apologize? A smart woman once told me there's a book for everything. I came to see if that was true."

She bit her bottom lip as joy filled her sagging heart, and floated it right up to her throat. She lifted her head, peeked over the rims of her glasses.

He stood before her, holding a bouquet of red roses in one hand, her cheetah scarf in the other. "I've never unbroken up with a woman before. I'm not sure how this goes. Are the flowers too obvious?"

"They *are* a cliché. But pretty."

"You left this at my house." He held up the scarf. "I brought this with me in case you told me to get bent, and told me that you never wanted to see me again and threw the flowers in my face."

"I would never treat such lovely flowers so thoughtlessly."

A look crossed his face as if he'd been kicked in the gut. "Of course you wouldn't treat flowers the way I treated you because you're too kind."

Callie lay on the bookcase just above his head, her tail switching back and forth.

Uh-oh, she recognized the signs. The calico was about to pounce.

"Um, Rowdy—"

"Yes, Breezy?" A hopeful smile edged the corners of his mouth upward.

Callie's tail went swish, swish, swish, swish, swish.

Uh-oh. She stood up. "You better leave."

His smile fell to the floor like a heavy boxer had knocked it there. "I know. I'm sorry. I deserve that. I—"

"I mean it, go now, before—"

But it was too late.

Callie dropped from the bookcase like a Serengeti lion falling on an unsuspecting wildebeest. "Rr-rowww!"

"Yow!" Rowdy grabbed for his head. The roses, and the scarf, tumbled to the ground. "What's happening? What's going on?"

Lightning-quick, Callie sprinted down his back, ran across the store, and scaled the bookcase behind the counter.

Rowdy was swatting at his head as if the cat was still perched there. The calico sat up prettily, wrapped her tail around herself, and gazed at him with regal disdain, as if to say, *Take that for pulverizing my mistress's heart, you big dope.*

He straightened, looked around warily, trying to figure out what had happened.

Breeanne tried not to laugh. Being the victim of one of Callie's sneak attacks was disconcerting, but she couldn't help herself. Seeing Mr. Macho Ballplayer brought to his knees, humbled by one cool cat, well . . . it was kind of funny.

"Rowdy," she said with a flourish of her hand. "Meet Callie. She's a Hurricane Sandy survivor with PTSD flashbacks and has a tendency to go on the offensive."

He rubbed his head, eyed Callie.

The calico lifted her nose in the air, looked away from him.

"I think she hates me."

"Jumping on you doesn't mean Callie dislikes you. She's an equal opportunity attack cat. If she's in a mood, anyone is fair game. You were in the wrong place at the wrong time."

"Like you were," he said, bending over to pick up the roses and her scarf. "When I found out the story had been leaked. You were there, and I was angry—"

"Your anger was justified. I let you down."

"I could never stay mad at you, Breezy. I was never mad at you in the first place. I was hurt, and for a minute I believed you'd set me up. But I know you would never intentionally hurt someone you love."

"You were perfectly within your right to say what you did. I was in the wrong. I was responsible for keeping your secret safe, and I didn't do my job."

"Your roommate took advantage of you to make a profit. She was the one I should have called on the carpet."

"Oh, don't worry. I handled that."

"Did you?"

"You should have seen her," Suki called from downstairs. "She kicked ass."

Breeanne went to the balcony railing. "Mind your own business, Suki."

"Oh yeah, now that Mr. Handsome's back, you don't need my shoulder to cry on."

"Buzz off."

"Later." Suki raised a hand and scooted out of the back of the store.

Breeanne turned back to Rowdy.

"I've been watching you on TV. You did a pretty good job of taking Potts down. Kudos." She gave him thumbs-up. She was trying not to get excited about him showing up, but she couldn't help it. She *was* excited. He looked so good. Better than ever.

"I would have called, but I felt the apology should be face-to-face. It was a whirlwind in Dallas. I'm still not finished with all the testifying."

"I imagine it's going to take a while to clean up the damage."

"Turns out, my secret getting spilled was the best thing that could have happened. Once I was exposed and took the first hit, it was amazing how other people came clean. I guess deep down, we're all longing for forgiveness." His voice was wistful.

"Even the Stephanies and Pottses of the world."

"I imagine so."

"Anyway, back to my apology . . ." He pulled her into his arms and she did not resist.

She looked up into his eyes, and found home.

"What I said was unkind. I feel terrible about it. I intend on spending the rest of my days making it up to you."

"Wh-wh-what do you mean?" she whispered.

"Jackdaw wants an inside story on the Gunslingers scandal and your name came up."

"I haven't finished writing the first book."

"We better get back to work then."

"Just like before?"

"Well, things might be a little different this time."

"How's that?"

"The owner of the Gunslingers offered me a coaching job," he said.

She sucked in a deep breath. Put her palm to her mouth. "Are you going to take it?"

"Well . . ." he drawled, and leveled her his best come-hither look. "That all depends."

"On what?"

"He's trying to ask you to marry him, doofus," Suki hollered.

In unison, she and Rowdy leaned over the balcony. "Mind your own business, Suki."

"Hmph," Suki said. "I'm so underappreciated."

"Well, now that your sister let the cat out of the bag . . ." Rowdy went down on one knee.

Her breath caught and her poor old pieced-together heart filled with so much love she didn't know if it could contain it.

"Breeanne Carlyle, would you do me the honor of marrying me?"

She was trembling all over, her body going from hot to cold and back again. "Rowdy, are you sure? I mean you could have any woman in the world. Beautiful women chase after you. I've seen it."

"Hey, you're the woman I want."

"But why me? I'm so ordinary."

"Why you? Other than you're the most loving, generous person I've ever met."

"Yes."

"Well, Breeanne, here's the deal. I'm a superstitious guy. I believe in hope chests that grant wishes, and cheetah scarves that feel scratchy to anyone who is not your soul mate."

She giggled.

"I believe in Nolan Ryan, and he only sits on the feet

of good people. I believe in Dairy Queen dipped cones, skinny-dipping in a magical pond, and I believe that my spaghetti carbonara is just this side of nirvana."

"It is." She nodded.

"I believe, like your family, that you should entertain often and invite the whole community. I believe in fair play, Dugan Potts's disgrace, and the American way of life. I believe that a good screwball is trickier to pull off than a knuckleball, and that baseball should be played for the love of the game and not the almighty dollar. I believe in Fourth of July fireworks, the 'Star-Spangled Banner,' the seventh inning stretch, and dot races."

"Aren't you getting a little far afield?"

"Hang on, I'm getting there. Breezy, I believe that I was meant for you and that you . . ." He stumbled a little, his voice going thick. ". . . were meant for me."

"Rowdy." She breathed.

"Breeanne, I love you. I've never said that to another woman that I wasn't related to. I love you. I love you. I love you."

"Really?" She could hardly believe it was true. "Because I love you. I love you so much, Rowdy Blanton."

He got up and swung her into his arms, and kissed her with every ounce of love he had in him. All the love he'd been saving up, just for her. Breeanne melted into him, like dipped cone chocolate.

"Be careful what you wish for," Suki called up the stairs. "Because you *will* get it."

"I guess we better not wish for you to go away then," Breeanne called back. "While you are a pain in the butt, we kind of like having you around."

"You never did answer the man, Breeanne," her mother spoke up. "After a speech like that, if you don't say yes, I will."

"Hey!" Dad protested.

"Your mother brings up a good point." Rowdy lifted an eyebrow. "What do you say? Will you marry me?"

"Yes, Rowdy Blanton, I'll marry you," she said, and pulled his head down for another long, soulful kiss that promised a lifetime of happiness.

EPILOGUE

*I consider myself the luckiest man
on the face of the earth.*

—LOU GEHRIG

The day after Rowdy proposed, Breanne carried the hope chest into the boxcar that served as the front desk at Boxcars and Breakfast.

Jodi looked up from the computer screen where she was working. "What's this?"

"All my dreams have come true," Breeanne said. "I no longer have any need for the hope chest. I thought you could use it."

"Are you saying I'm hopeless?" Jodi bristled.

"I'm saying it's time you moved on," Breeanne said staunchly. "Here's hope."

"I have moved on." Jodi folded her arms over her chest.

"You haven't had a date since Ryan left you at the altar."

Jodi's mouth dove down. "What am I supposed to do with it? There's no key to open the other locks."

"You'll figure it out," Breeanne said. "But be careful what you wish for because you *will* get it."

And then she winked and walked away.

A stroke of the cheetah scarf.

The erotically soft sensation punctuated Rowdy Blanton's life. Permeated everything. Seeped into his dreams.

From the fateful hope chest, to his fiancée's slender neck, to the silken tie now manacling his hand to his headboard, a stroke of the cheetah scarf spelled freedom. Freedom from the empty life he'd once mindlessly chased, searching for something he hadn't known where to find. Freedom from the sins he'd committed, absolved by forgiveness in her understanding eyes. Freedom from the loneliness that had dogged him from the wrong side of the tracks, until he'd found unconditional love in Breeanne's arms.

Freedom from pain.

How on earth had he ever once believed that loving one woman for the rest of his life would bring him suffering? Valentine's Day, their wedding day, couldn't get here fast enough. Six months into their engagement and he'd enjoyed more hot sex and romantic spontaneity than he'd experienced in thirty-three years as a single guy. Why hadn't anyone ever told him what he was missing?

Um, your married friends tried, remember. He'd just been too pigheaded to listen.

"Now," she said with a wicked grin. "To fully celebrate turning in the book."

"What do you have in mind?" he asked. He was naked in their bed, held happy prisoner by the cheetah scarf, totally exposed. Open. Vulnerable.

And he loved it.

Breeanne, wearing his baseball jersey and a pair of cheetah panties, was straddling his waist. "Guess."

"Role playing? You're the Gunslingers super-hot new female pitcher, and I'm your adoring groupie?"

She giggled that adorable sound that never failed to arouse Mr. Johnson. "Nope."

"You didn't buy ball gags, did you? Because I'm not sure I'm a fan of the idea—"

She shook her head, her wavy dark blond hair bobbing seductively around her shoulders, and reached for a paper bag on the other side of the bed.

"Don't tell me. You've dipped cone chocolate in there and you're going to lick it off my body."

"No, but I like the way you think."

"All right. I give up. What sexy adventure do you have planned for us tonight?"

She pulled a paperback from the bag. *Love's Throbbing Fury*, and he started grinning.

"What better way to celebrate finishing writing a book than by reading a book," she said.

"You'll make a reader of me yet."

"Oh, just wait," she said. "I'll have you running to the bookstore every Tuesday when the new releases come out."

She opened the book and started reading. " 'Her mouth wrapped around his stiff cock and he could barely breathe, much less think. Around and around she swirled. Up and down. A tantalizing, mind-blowing blend of expert maneuvers that had him wondering how she knew so well the secrets of his body.' "

Then Breeanne put down the book and proceeded to act out the paragraph she'd just read, leaving Rowdy gasping for air. He wanted to touch her, wanted to get her naked, wanted to feel her hot, damp skin flush against his, but he was tied to the headboard . . .

And she had other plans.

She read and then acted out each passage, blow by

blow, until he was crazed with lust for her. She increased the intensity of her strokes, pushing him closer, ever closer to the edge. He lost all ability to think, to even move from his staked position on the bed. He felt the orgasm building and building and building, hard, hot, and unstoppable.

He was lost. Gone. Adrift in ecstasy.

She reached up and untied him.

He grabbed her, pulled her to his chest, whispered, "Breezy, Breezy, Breezy."

She wriggled against him. Fierce. Tiny. Amazingly beautiful in his eyes. Dark blond hair. Bewitching green eyes. Bunny rabbit nose quivering. She sat up, stripped off his baseball jersey, flung it behind her. He spanned her waist, lifted her bottom to his face, and chewed the thin strap of her G-string panties in two.

His lover wrapped the softest material on earth around her hand, rubbed that sweet hand over the hardest part of his body, and with each caress she whispered, "One soft touch identifies the other."

A stroke of the cheetah scarf.

A sizzle of sex.

And at long last, Rowdy Blanton was made whole.

Find out how the next Carlyle sister
finds love in
New York Times best-selling author

LORI WILDE'S

second *Stardust, Texas* novel

RULES OF THE GAME

Coming June 2015 from Avon Books!

*G*ive in to your Impulses!

These unforgettable stories only take a second to buy and give you hours of reading pleasure!

Go to *www.AvonImpulse.com* and see what we have to offer.

Available wherever e-books are sold.

AVON IMPULSE